The author would like to acknowledge that this book was written on the traditional lands of the Darug and Gundungurra people of the Ngurra nation, and pay her respect to Elders both past, present and future.

Roll With It

Alex
Ravenscroft

Published by Alex Ravenscroft

ISBN 978-0-6452525-0-7

A catalogue record for this
book is available from the
National Library of Australia

Cover design and illustration by Emily Mulvey and Sky Chiverall

Printed and bound by IngramSpark

For every girl who ever gave up something she loved for a guy who wasn't worth it.

And for my ma. Look! I finally finished the bloody thing!

(PS Please don't read the sex scenes.)

CONTENT WARNING

**The following content warning contains
potential spoilers.**

Read at your own discretion.

This book contains discussions and/or depictions of and
allusions to domestic violence, homophobia, death of a
parent, traumatic injury and pregnancy loss, which some
readers may find distressing.

Reader discretion is advised.

PROLOGUE
CAMPBELLMEAD, 2000

Ainslie Wynter was only a tiny thing when she first set foot inside the Campbellmead Rollarena. Clinging to her mother's hand as she gazed upon the collection of roller skates that lined the shelves of the skate hire, she breathed in a smell she would remember for the rest of her life — thirty-year-old leather, and feet. It probably should've churned her stomach but instead was ripe with nostalgia. Even years later, whenever she caught a whiff of that pungent aroma, it still somehow managed to warm the cockles of her heart.

She peeked around a corner and caught a glimpse of the enormous rink. It was dark inside and far too loud for small ears. The beat of a nineties dance song thumped through the air, and a shiny silver ball hung from the ceiling, peppering colourful lights all over the smooth, blue floor.

The building was like a time capsule that someone had put on the corner of Queen Street and Briens Road back in 1973 and had failed to tend to ever since. Which, as it happens, was exactly what had occurred. Some walls were coated in chipped paint. Others were carpeted with garish, neon patterns. All of them were dotted with decades' worth of fossilised chewing gum. The snack bar, with its bright orange laminate benchtops, boasted slushies, popcorn, hot pies and sausage rolls. The ceiling was missing a few panels here and there — knocked out by a wayward hockey puck, no doubt.

Nestled away in a back corner of the building, a long-since abandoned parquet dance floor was now home to a few sad arcade machines, blinking and whirring away, hoping to lure in whoever might have some loose change in their pockets. The grandstand was closed for maintenance and had been for nearly a decade. A large red sign screamed Caution: Keep Out, and the structure itself looked as if it might collapse under a light breeze.

Of course, none of this was any concern to a five-year-old with an untapped competitive streak and an insatiable need to be instantly great at everything she tried. Ainslie was enchanted by the lights and sounds. Riveted by the people flying around the rink with grace and ease. She needed those wheels on her feet immediately.

"Have you ever skated before?"

Ainslie looked up to see a portly older man with grey whiskers and kind eyes peering over the carpeted counter.

She shook her head and tried to hide behind her mother.

The man smiled. "Let's get you all fixed up then, shall we?"

1

He produced a pair of tiny orange-and-black skates. They were floppy little things with scales of leather flaking off them. They looked as if they'd been beaten to death by Father Time. Their bright orange wheels were caked in a layer of dust, and the matching orange stopper at the front was worn down to a stub. The man pulled a tool out of his pocket and began tinkering away at the grimy wheels. When he was done, he sat the skates on the counter and rolled them back and forth. Or rather slid them back and forth.

"See?" he said. "I tightened them a little bit so they don't go rolling away from you."

Ainslie's little green eyes glistened with excitement as her mother took the skates and thanked the man before leading her into the rink.

With the skates strapped on, she marched with confidence across the carpet. Her knuckles whitened as she grasped her mother's hand, the only indication of her anxiety.

Her fantasy of flying around with the other skaters was quickly dashed when she stepped down onto the blue concrete floor and fell flat on her backside. The enchantment began to leave her eyes and was replaced with sheer determination.

Ainslie was relegated to the small warm-up area, which was set off to the side of the main rink. There, she spent the entire session waddling around as best she could, her tiny hands grasping at the cold, steel handrail, her feet refusing to cooperate with the rest of her body. By the time the music stopped and the lights came up, a disenchanted little Ainslie had decided that this whole roller skating thing? She sucked at it. She swallowed her disappointment as her mother unlaced her skates. And then she saw the most wonderful thing she had ever seen.

The uncoordinated masses of the general session had been replaced. Now the rink was filled with something else. Tall, strong, beautiful girls on white skates — and a couple of boys, too, but their skates were black. *Their* skates weren't grimy and orange, and they certainly didn't make that awful grinding sound Ainslie's did. The girls wore pretty dresses in all sorts of lovely colours, and they were gliding so effortlessly around the blue floor it looked as if they were floating on air. Then they began to twirl and spin and leap and dance. A boy even lifted one of the girls up over his head and spun her around as if she weighed nothing at all.

Ainslie stood beside the rink, mouth agape, her smelly orange skates in hand, mesmerised by what she saw.

Her mother called to her that it was time to leave, but she was transfixed.

"Ainslie Jade!" Mrs Wynter scurried over, finally realising what had enraptured her little girl.

"Mummy, can I do that?" Ainslie asked, pointing at a brunette girl who was spinning in the corner.

Mrs Wynter looked at the girl then back at her daughter, who had spent the better part of the last two hours either glued to a handrail or prostrate on the floor. "You want to do *that*?"

Ainslie nodded with so much enthusiasm her mother thought her head might fall off.

"It's called artistic roller skating."

The voice belonged to the man who'd helped with her skates. "It's kinda like figure skating on ice, but it's on wheels instead. That's my daughter, Alana." He pointed to the girl Ainslie was fixated on.

"You know," he said as he turned to Mrs Wynter, "we have a Learn to Skate program. Classes are held every Wednesday afternoon. Alana teaches Level 1. If you're interested, I can get you signed up today."

Mrs Wynter looked at Ainslie, who was expectantly bouncing up and down on the balls of her feet.

"Okay." She shrugged. "Sign us up, I suppose."

Ainslie let out a squeal of delight and began imitating the movements she saw the skaters performing on the rink. She made a promise to herself that afternoon that one day she would be the best roller skater in the whole world.

CHAPTER 1

Rosa Charis prided herself on being Australia's number one source for artistic roller skating news and gossip. Was there much demand for such a source outside her very niche target market? None whatsoever. Artistic roller skating was virtually unheard of in the Australian sporting landscape, probably because it wasn't football, cricket or swimming. Despite that, those who *were* involved were obsessed. Australian artistic roller skaters lived in quiet hope that one day everything would change and television stations would be knocking each other over for the rights to air the competitive season. However, until that pipedream came to fruition, artistic roller skaters got their information (and gossip, of course) from Rosa Charis.

She was a twenty-nine-year-old former freeskater who hadn't had the most illustrious career but who sure had a knack for media spin. After she had retired from competition and completed a Bachelor of Journalism, she saw a gap in the market that she took upon herself to fill. So, she started the podcast *Rolling with Rosa* and began networking with as many skating sources as she could. Her lifelong love for the sensational meant that her news was not always reliable, but it was always entertaining.

Rosa was quite the social butterfly, and during her skating career, she had been better known for her prolific troublemaking than for her achievements. In fact, she was *best* known for being the skater who ended up in a scandalous relationship with her much-older coach, Luke Browning, whom she had recently roped into being her reporting partner. Rosa recruiting Luke to co-host a podcast that focused on drama was ironic, considering he had been one of the greatest causes of drama in Australian skating history.

Of course, he'd sent heads spinning when it came to light that he was having an affair with Rosa. But that had been only the latest in his long list of scandals. The most notable was back in the eighties when he had abandoned his injured skating partner (and wife at the time) in her hour of need to skate singles and he became the first and only artistic roller skating world champion Australia has ever produced. He had been caught at that same World Championships with a young British skater shacked up in his hotel room. Nobody except Luke Browning, Australia's skating golden boy, would have been able to get away with something like that. But Luke had gotten away with a lot in his fifty-six years.

Even though most people were wary of Rosa's reporting methods, they never failed to tune in every time she released an episode. Whether they liked it or not, most people were just as thirsty for gossip as Rosa was. Of course, the subjects of her lampooning were usually less enthusiastic about tuning in than most.

One of her frequent targets was Ainslie Wynter, a twenty-four-year-old pairs skater from New South Wales. As far as Ainslie could remember, she'd never done anything to either Rosa or Luke to warrant the nearly constant barrage of unwanted publicity that she received, but it came nonetheless.

*   *   *

Ainslie Wynter was sitting on the floor at Gate 49 of Heathrow Airport awaiting her flight home and making use of the free wi-fi when she received the notification that a new episode of *Rolling with Rosa* had gone live. As usual, curiosity got the better of her, and she clicked the link.

"The Australian team is returning home from the 2019 Artistic World Championships as we speak," Rosa said.

"It was an incredibly strong team this year," Luke Browning added. "Fifteen skaters across almost all disciplines."

Ainslie screwed up her nose at the sound of his voice.

Rosa continued. "We had Dylan Porter, Sarah Grey, Laura McLachlan and Tania Wesley in freeskating, and we had Amelia Benson, Kylie Lewis and Lucy Huong in solo dance."

"We also had Amanda Dickinson and Marianne Ryan in figures," Luke said, "the dance team of Aliya Driver and Peter Hutchins, and two pairs teams — Ainslie Wynter and James Sunderland, and Tessa Strong and Antony Bryce."

Ainslie heard a noise come out of Rosa that meant the podcast co-host was about to say something stupid.

"Let's talk about Ainslie and James. They were a favourite going in, as usual. After their amazing performance at Nationals this year and their world ranking of fifth in 2018, all eyes were on them going into 2019 Worlds. They skated a personal best, and after the short program were ranked third, which is so amazing for Australian skaters!"

Ainslie's eyes widened. Praise from Rosa Charis? She wondered what was coming next.

"Disappointingly," Luke said, "they were knocked off the podium after the Spanish team De Leon and Romero produced an amazing long program, pulling them up from fifth to take the bronze."

Ainslie pulled a face. Disappointing was an understatement. Obviously, they were proud of fourth place, but they'd come so close to tasting bronze that Ainslie couldn't help but feel a little downtrodden.

"No Australian has come that close to a podium finish at Worlds since you in '85," Rosa said.

Ainslie rolled her eyes.

"They're definitely Australia's best hope for another world gold," Luke said. "They've been skating together almost their entire lives, and they just keep improving. They've been moving up the rankings every year since their Junior debut in 2012, and if you ask me, next year could be their year."

"Now." Rosa clapped her hands together, signifying that she was transitioning from news to gossip. "Ainslie and James, or 'Jameslie' as they are more affectionately known, are crowd favourites for a very *specific* reason. They have such good chemistry when they skate that it just … makes you wonder. Is something more going on behind the scenes? I mean, there's a reason people 'ship' them."

Rosa spoke in a singsong voice, and it sounded as if she was wearing a shit-eating grin. Ainslie would've liked to have slapped it clean off her face. Rosa's implications about Ainslie and James always made Ainslie incredibly uncomfortable. Mainly because those implications took a toll on her personal life.

"Well, yes," Luke said. "The true nature of their relationship is always a point of contention. But by all accounts, they're both spoken for."

"It's easy to see why people talk, though," Rosa said. "When you watch them skate together, they're just so … intimate and passionate. You've gotta love it."

Ainslie nearly gagged. She'd had enough bitter run-ins with Rosa to know all these compliments were hidden behind a very thin veil of passive aggression.

"Well, regardless," Luke said, "I'm excited to see what they bring next season."

"Whatcha doing?" James Sunderland slid down the wall and plonked himself on the floor beside Ainslie.

"The latest episode of *Rolling with Rosa* is up." She pulled out one earbud and handed it to James.

"Anything interesting?"

"The usual. Rosa going on about how *passionate* and *intimate* we are when we skate." Ainslie bumped her shoulder against his.

James folded his arms and screwed up his nose. "Gross."

*   *   *

When their flight finally touched down in Sydney, the New South Wales contingent of the Australian team was met by their welcoming committee, led by Lucy Huong's parents, who had organised a Welcome Home banner and were waving proudly. Standing with the Huongs was Tim Dawson, who was there to pick up his wife and the New South Wales team coach, Sandra Dawson. Beside them stood Rachel Percival and Aidan Corbin, there to pick up their significant others. Rachel was wearing a huge, bright grin and was holding a single balloon with Congratulations plastered across it, which she nearly let go when she spotted James emerging from customs. Aidan was standing slightly off to the side and was looking at his phone, doing everything he could to avoid having to speak to anyone. He only looked up when Rachel squealed and barrelled towards James, who scooped her up into a hug. Aidan was far more restrained when he greeted Ainslie. He pecked her on the lips and shoved his phone in his pocket.

"Welcome home," he said. "How was the flight?"

"Long," Ainslie replied, "and uneventful."

"So, you came fourth, huh?"

"Yep." Ainslie smiled proudly.

"Damn. That's too bad."

Ainslie frowned. It was only an offhand comment, and he probably hadn't meant for it to sound so disparaging, but it was the wrong answer. She glanced over at James to see if he'd heard the remark, and she caught him rolling his eyes.

James and Aidan weren't exactly cordial. Mostly because the only thing Aidan disliked more than skating was Ainslie spending copious amounts of time with someone who wasn't him. Although if you asked James, he'd say it was because Aidan was the most arrogant, condescending prick he'd ever met. That and the fact that Ainslie seemed to have undergone a personality transplant when she had started seeing him.

"That guy is such a dick, Ains," he'd told her when he'd met Aidan for the first time.

She'd turned red and glowered at him.

"No, he isn't. Don't say that."

"Hey, it's none of my business who you go out with." James had thrown his hands up in surrender. "But as your oldest friend, I gotta tell you, I think he's a dick."

Ainslie had argued that she'd appreciate it if, as her oldest friend, he actually made an effort to get along with her boyfriend. James had promised he'd try, but Aidan didn't make it easy. And her request had seemed a little hypocritical, considering that when James had met Rachel four years later, Ainslie hadn't exactly gone out of her way to befriend her. But that was mostly because the two were so different they didn't really have a whole lot to talk about.

Ainslie could tell that Rachel was quietly uncomfortable with James being surrounded by fit, lycra-clad girls on a daily basis, but at least she tried to be supportive. Which was more than could be said of Aidan.

The skaters said goodbye to their interstate teammates, who had to rush ahead to catch connecting flights. Rachel was going to head back to James's place, and Aidan had planned to take Ainslie out for brunch. She gave James an awkward side hug, the only kind of hug she felt comfortable giving him in front of Aidan.

"I'll see you later," she said, failing to suppress a yawn.

"See ya." He patted her on the back and whispered, "Chin up, Goose. Don't listen to him."

Ainslie didn't reply. She just smiled weakly and patted his back too before she collected her luggage and followed Aidan out of the terminal.

CHAPTER 2

There were many interesting things to know about James Sunderland. He could speak a little German, he could draw, and he could play the piano. Nothing too fancy — he had never formally performed or anything — but his father had played and had taught him on the old, slightly-out-of-tune piano that sat in their living room.

He was also a twin. He and his brother weren't identical, not that they had seemed to realise that growing up. Despite the fact that James was tall, lanky and blond and Jason, with his dark hair, was as stocky as he was short, when they were children, the two still switched places as if nobody would notice. James's endearing goofiness had continued all throughout his teenage years until the tragedy that struck his family forced him to grow up.

When the boys were eighteen, their father passed away in a freak accident that had left James with an overwhelming fear of head injuries. That certainly wasn't ideal for a pairs skater. But after years of therapy, he'd managed to get on top of it, and now he was one of the best pairs skaters in the world.

Despite all this, there were only two things about James Sunderland that most skating girls seemed to care about. First, he was good looking, with the sort of boyish charm that made girls want to take him home to meet their mother. And second, he was straight. The ratio of males to females in the Australian artistic scene was painfully lopsided, and as such, he'd spent the entirety of his formative years surrounded by a flock of girls who had all been vying for his attention. At the time, he thought he was just really good at making friends. Eventually, he figured it out. And he secretly loved it.

He'd known Lucy Huong and Ainslie since he was in Learn to Skate, and he'd been paired up with Ainslie when they were six years old. He always pretended not to notice the jealous glances that Ainslie would get from time to time, but he knew her well enough to know she would've loved the attention just as much as he had.

After nearly twenty years of friendship, James could safely say there was no-one he'd rather be paired up with. And it certainly didn't hurt that she was easy on the eyes.

*   *   *

"Was Ainslie happy with how you skated?" Rachel asked as they inched their way out of the airport car park.

"Yeah. Kinda bummed we missed out on bronze, but still happy."

Rachel fixed her eyes on the road and chewed her lower lip. There was a long silence, but James was too tired to read much into it.

"You don't think she's holding you back, do you?" Rachel asked hesitantly.

It took James a minute to register what she'd said.

"What?"

"Well," Rachel said slowly, "you're such an amazing skater. Do you ever think about going solo? Then you wouldn't have to be accountable to anyone or have to rely on anyone."

"Rach, I haven't skated solo since I was six. I don't *like* skating solo."

"I know." Rachel pouted. "But you're so good."

"I mean, technically, Ainslie's better than me."

"Well, maybe she could benefit from going solo too. You know Aidan isn't keen on you two skating together. Maybe some of that tension could be relieved if you both just … did your own thing."

"Where's this coming from?" James looked at her. "I thought you were cool with skating."

"I am." Rachel pursed her lips. "But sometimes it sucks that Ainslie gets to spend so much time with you and I get left out."

"You don't get left out."

"You're at the rink nearly every day! And when you're not at the rink, you're at the gym. You go away with her for skating comps all the time, plus Nationals and Worlds every year. *We've* never even gone away for a weekend because you're always too busy training!"

"I don't go on *holidays* with her, you know. We're elite athletes. We're basically business partners. It's more like *work* than a vacation."

"I know, and I *am* proud of what you've achieved, but …" Rachel sighed, and her voice dropped to nearly a whisper. "Aidan isn't the only one tired of sharing his partner with someone else."

James turned away and stared out the window, drumming his fingers on his leg.

"Well, what do you want to do?" he asked. "Do you want to go away somewhere? Over Christmas? Because you need to know, I'm not going to stop skating right now."

"I just want you to make time for me. You seem to have all the time in the world for skating — and for Ainslie. I just don't want to be an afterthought, okay?"

"Rach, you're not an afterthought." He reached across the console and squeezed her knee.

"Okay." She smiled. "Just please show me you mean it."

* * *

James lived in a nineteenth-century terrace house on a quiet backstreet in the inner-city suburb of Redfern. On the outside, it was baby blue and a little dilapidated, sitting like an eyesore between two beautiful, newly restored residences. On the inside, it looked as if a furniture store specialising in cheap flat packs had thrown up. But it was only a short drive to the rink, a hop, skip and a jump to Ainslie's place, and a couple of train stations away from the bar he worked in.

He shared the place with a revolving door of housemates who were more often than not students from the nearby university. Rachel had once hinted that she wouldn't be against moving in once one of the others eventually moved out, but James had only responded with an awkward chuckle and changed the subject. In truth, he wasn't sure about living with Rachel. Not yet, anyway. Especially if it meant sharing with strangers. And with Sydney's housing prices, there was no way that a full-time skater slash part-time bartender and a full-time university student were going to be able to afford a place of their own any time soon.

*   *   *

Rachel helped James unpack his things as he filled her in on Worlds. If she hadn't been there, he probably would've left the bag lying on the floor until it was time for the next trip. But Rachel was fastidious, and she immediately set to work sorting through his things while he did his best to assist, despite his jet lag having caught up to him.

When she'd finally finished fussing about, they curled up on his bed, and he began transferring his trip photos to his laptop. Rachel laughed at a photo of him pretending to fall into the Thames. She laughed even harder at a picture of him, Ainslie and Lucy all poorly edited into a novelty photo from The London Dungeon. James flipped through more photos until he reached one of himself and Ainslie at the top of the London Eye, the city sprawling out beneath them. Rachel let out a tiny huff.

"Look at that picture." She pouted. "You two *look* like a couple. We don't have any pictures that nice!"

James winced. Rachel was right — they did look like a couple. A dangerous thought shot through his mind like lightning. The thought that they actually looked like a very cute couple. He shook it away and flicked to the next photo, turning his attention back to the perfectly lovely girl by his side. But he couldn't help but let his mind slip every now and then to wondering what it would be like if she were Ainslie.

CHAPTER 3

Ainslie slumped into the passenger seat of Aidan's car. The fog of her exhaustion weighed heavily on her eyelids, and she was in absolutely no mood to be trifled with.

"Where do you want to go for brunch?" Aidan asked.

"Don't mind. Wherever you want."

She rested her head on her hand and glared at the passing traffic. Closing her eyes and letting the sun warm her face, she ignored the few moments of tense silence that passed between them.

"What's your problem?" Aidan asked eventually.

Ainslie didn't have the energy to engage in an argument, so she kept her eyes closed, hoping he might think she'd fallen asleep. Apparently, he saw right through that.

"You clearly have the shits with me. So, what's your problem?"

"I don't know." Her voice was thick with sass. "You *could've* sounded a bit happier with our result. Fourth in the world isn't exactly a small achievement."

"How many were in it?"

"Thirteen!" She finally lifted her head and shot him a look. "What, did you think there were only four?"

"I was just asking! Jesus!"

Ainslie's fatigue was exacerbating her irritability, but she wasn't about to let Aidan dull her shine.

"If we managed fourth this year, especially after coming third in the short," she said, "then there's definitely a chance we could be on the podium next year."

"So, you're going to keep skating next year then?" Aidan asked, eyes fixed on the road.

She looked at him sideways. "Yes?"

"I just thought maybe next year you'd want to start thinking about settling down."

She could tell by the tone of his voice that it was more than just a suggestion. She looked over at him as he drove, his jaw tight, his brow a little furrowed. Aidan was attractive in a conventional sense. He had thick, dark hair that was always styled with some sort of delicious-smelling product. He had clear, olive skin peppered with just the right amount of perfectly groomed facial hair. He had strong, sharp features and dark eyes, and he always carried himself with the kind of air that could make anybody, including Ainslie, feel two inches tall.

"Aidan, I'm not ready to retire yet." Ainslie tried her best to sound tough, but her voice wavered. "It's been our goal from the start to place at Worlds, and we came so close! We can't just stop now!"

"You keep saying 'we', Ainslie, but what about *us*?" Aidan snapped. "You're constantly at the rink. You and *James* practically live in each other's back pockets. I wish you had that kind of time for *me*. For all I know, you could be fucking around with *him* after practice."

The way Aidan always spoke about James, it was as though simply saying his name caused bile to form in the back of Aidan's throat. Ainslie chewed her lower lip and swallowed down the lump that had formed in the back of hers. She hated crying in front of him, but she wasn't sure she had the energy to fight it much longer.

"How can you say that to me?" She sounded weaker than she would've liked. "Am I not allowed to have other people in my life besides you?"

"As far as I know," Aidan said, spitting out the words in anger, "James is the only other person besides me with his hands all over you. All day, every day."

He'd hit a nerve.

"I'm not having this conversation again, Aidan. You knew my situation when you met me."

"Fine. Just think about what you really want, Ainslie. And think hard. Because I'm not going to wait around for you forever."

They always had the same argument after Worlds every year. And every year, Aidan's fuse got shorter. Surely it wouldn't be long before he blew completely.

"And I'm *certainly* not going to play second fiddle to a man in spandex." He scoffed.

Ainslie felt a pressure building between her ears, as if her head were being crushed in a vice.

"You know what?" She clenched her jaw. "Just take me home. I'm not hungry."

Aidan pursed his lips and changed his route.

They drove the rest of the way to Ainslie's apartment building in silence. When they arrived, Ainslie flung the door open, marched around to the boot and hauled out her luggage.

"Do you want me to call you later?" Aidan said out the window.

"I'll probably be sleeping."

"Fine." He shrugged. "I'll see you, then."

"Yeah, bye."

She closed the boot a little harder than necessary.

*　　*　　*

Ainslie lived in a twelfth-floor apartment in a building on Gadigal Avenue in Waterloo. Which was convenient because it happened to be a five-minute drive from the Randwick Rollerdome, the rink that their coach, Sandra, had built after the closure of the old Campbellmead Rollarena.

Ainslie had moved into the apartment with Lucy when they'd started university, and they had been joined a couple of years later by Jaz Bannister. Jaz's family had moved from Yorkshire, England, to Australia. She and her brother, Chris, had been an ice dancing team, but after only a few months in Sydney, Jaz had defected to artistic roller skating and Chris to inline hockey, much to their mother's chagrin. Jaz considered it payback on account of the fact that their mother had not only saddled them with the surname *Bannister* (which they'd both heard plenty of jokes about) but also named them after the British ice dancing icons Torvill and Dean. Yes, Jaz's legal name was Jayne, and there was no way in hell anyone would ever get away with calling her that to her face.

Ainslie stared at her reflection in her building's lift mirror. She looked rough. Her eyes were red and weary, and the tears she'd been fighting since the end of the car ride were getting ready to make an appearance. She had bags under her eyes, and the messy bun she'd tied her copper hair into more than twenty hours ago was making her scalp ache. Her skin was dry and blotchy, and she was definitely dehydrated. She sniffed the air. Her Australian uniform was beginning to smell a little ripe too.

She crammed her key into the door of the apartment and nearly jumped out of her skin when Jaz cried out "Welcome home!" before the door had even opened completely.

Jaz barrelled towards her, nearly knocking her over with a hug. "Bloody hell, I missed you!"

Jaz's golden-retriever personality was usually very endearing, but at that moment, Ainslie's jet lag was making it difficult for her to match Jaz's enthusiasm. Jaz always thrived in the presence of company. Ainslie didn't know how she'd coped while they had been away. She was just relieved that she hadn't burned the apartment down in that time.

"Hey, Jaz." Ainslie sighed. "I missed you too."

"What's wrong?" Jaz pulled back and held Ainslie by the shoulders. "You seem pretty narked off for someone who just became world number four. Also, weren't you meant to be going to brunch with —"

"Yes!" Ainslie rolled her eyes. "I was."

She wriggled out of Jaz's grip and dumped her bag on the floor by the linen cupboard.

"What happened?" Jaz asked tentatively.

"Wanna take a guess?" Ainslie slipped into the kitchen and switched on the kettle. "Same thing that always happens. The classic Aidan guilt trip. The whole 'you spend too much time skating and not enough time with me' routine. Saying I should retire and settle down, getting all pissy about James, suggesting we're messing around behind his back ..."

"Well, we've all thought that at one point or another." Jaz smirked.

Ainslie bristled. "Not the time."

"But you're not actually thinking of retiring yet, are you?" Jaz looked concerned.

Ainslie stomped over to the lounge and flopped down, a mug of tea in hand.

"No way. I can't retire *now*! With *fourth*? We have to skate *at least* another season, just to see if we can do it."

Jaz looked relieved. "I can't imagine you not skating. And I reckon if you retired, James would too. I can't see him skating by himself."

Ainslie sipped her tea and winced when she burned her tongue.

"I mean, I'm not stupid. I know I'll have to retire eventually."

Jaz dropped down on the lounge beside her and pouted. "Team Jameslie can't die yet!"

Ainslie laughed. Jaz had been the one to coin the portmanteau. It had caught on in the wider skating community, and Jaz was very proud of it.

"Don't worry, *nothing* is going to stop Team Jameslie in 2020. But I *do* know that if I want to have a normal life with Aidan, I'm going to have to seriously reassess for 2021."

"You know who you wouldn't have to quit skating to have a life with?" Jaz winked.

Ainslie rolled her eyes and let out a tired laugh. "Stop it!"

Jaz had always enjoyed ribbing her about James. Jaz was like a six-foot-tall seven-year-old, and if Ainslie and James were her toy dolls, she would spend hours sitting on her bedroom floor making them kiss. When she first met them, she had assumed they were a couple. When she'd found out they weren't, she couldn't understand why not. Ainslie got the impression Jaz was holding out hope that they might still get together one day. Most of the time, Ainslie would brush it off, maybe even play along for laughs, but after Aidan's comment in the car, she wasn't really in the mood for jokes of that particular nature.

Ainslie excused herself, collected her suitcase and trudged down the hall to her bedroom. She pulled the blinds down in a feeble attempt to make the room as dark as possible and flopped onto her bed, too tired to even have a shower. She felt as if she was lying on a cloud after twenty-four hours crammed onto an economy flight. In her pocket, her phone vibrated. One new text message from James.

You ok, goose?

She punched back a response.

Yeah, I'm fine. Just tired.

How was brunch?

Ainslie frowned.

Didn't go. Just went home. Gonna nap now.

You shouldn't sleep now. You know that. You should
stay up until tonight so you get back into routine :)

Ainslie smirked.

Mate piss off. I'm tired af :P

I know better than to argue with a cranky goose ;)
Good night/morning

Ainslie put her phone on the bedside table. James always managed to make her smile.

Aidan could learn a few things from him.

Lying in her room in the semi-darkness, the morning sun forcing its way through the gaps in the blinds, Ainslie began to overthink everything — something she often did when she was exhausted. She had to consider that perhaps this would have to be it for her. Maybe it was time she and James gave it one last shot. One more year to try for the podium finish and then hang up the skates for good.

She knew Aidan had a point. Her whole life revolved around skating, and she did seem to spend more time at the rink than she did with him. She couldn't have a normal life with Aidan if she kept competing. She couldn't get married and start a family if she never had any time to spend with them. She knew she couldn't skate forever but had always imagined that the day she'd retire would be a lot further in the future.

Pesky tears started pricking at her eyes again, and she blinked them back in frustration. There was no way she could make a decision that important on so little sleep. She closed her eyes, and before long, she was off. Dead to the world, having a peaceful, dreamless sleep at last.

CHAPTER 4

Ainslie needn't have worried about throwing out her sleeping pattern by having a nap at midday. She woke at seven the following morning, disoriented, famished and absolutely busting to go to the bathroom. Despite the marathon sleep, she still felt worse for wear. She caught a glimpse of herself in the mirror on her wardrobe door. The bags under her eyes had faded slightly, but her face felt like sandpaper, and there was a bird's nest on her head where a messy bun used to be.

The light on her phone was blinking away, and she drowsily reached for it. Squinting into the blinding blue light, she saw several texts from Aidan. The first was an apology and an invitation to dinner. The subsequent messages were him concerned about why she hadn't responded. She frowned and skipped to the next thread. James had sent a message at around 3 pm the day before.

Wanna grab coffee and talk about 2020? Assuming you haven't already fallen asleep lol

Ainslie punched back a reply.

Sorry. I'm not dead. Just slept all day and night haha. We can do coffee today if you like.

She dragged herself to the bathroom and finally had a shower. As the hot water melted her stiff muscles and relaxed her aching body, she began to feel herself slowly coming back to life. By the time she was done and had returned to her room, James had replied.

Glad ur not dead. The bean?

She typed back.

Where else?

She was just about to reply when her phone rang. Aidan. She grimaced and kicked herself for not responding to his text.

"You're alive," he said. "Glad to hear it."

His voice was a lot softer than it had been the last time they'd spoken.

"I slept all day and night, I was that tired," she said. "Sorry I didn't message you back."

"So, you saw my message then?"

"Yeah."

"I'm really sorry, Ainslie. I didn't mean to insinuate fourth place wasn't something to be proud of. I *am* proud of you. You know that, right?"

Ainslie smiled. "Yeah, I know."

"And I'm sorry for that crack about James. I know you've been mates forever, but it's hard. You're so gorgeous, I wouldn't be surprised if he'd thought about it. I know he has a girlfriend, but you're *so much* hotter than she is."

Ainslie cringed. She could hear the smirk on his face.

"Stop worrying about James. Seriously."

"I'll try. I'm flat out with work this week, but do you want to go out for dinner on Friday night? We'll go somewhere really nice."

"Sounds great."

"Great. Wear something sexy."

Ainslie chuckled. "You too."

"Love you."

"Love you."

She breathed a sigh of relief as she hung up. Maybe her relationship wasn't as doomed as she had thought. At least he hadn't mentioned retirement again.

*   *   *

Jaz and Lucy were already up when Ainslie walked into the living room. Lucy was sitting at the dining table, head propped up by her hands, eyes practically falling out of their sockets. Jaz was sitting in the chair beside her, bright-eyed and shovelling cereal into her mouth.

"You slept well." Jaz glanced at Ainslie. "I thought you'd died."

"I wish *I* would die," Lucy interjected dramatically, speaking into her coffee mug. "I fell asleep after I got back from my parents' place yesterday. Then I woke up at midnight and have been awake ever since."

Ainslie winced sympathetically.

"Where are you off to?" Jaz asked.

Ainslie hesitated, knowing exactly what her response would trigger. "Grabbing coffee with James."

Jaz hid a smirk behind her cereal bowl.

17

"We're just meeting to debrief and go over the 2020 game plan."
Jaz snorted at the word "debrief", and Ainslie gave her a side eye.

*　　*　　*

It was springtime in Sydney, and that particular morning was picture perfect. The sun in the cloudless sky had a little bite to it, but the heat was countered by the pleasantly cool breeze. As the warmth of the sun embraced her and the crisp air kissed her cheeks, Ainslie came alive. The city was humming with businesspeople bustling to work and students rushing to school. Ainslie enjoyed being able to ignore the rat-race. It was nice not to have to do anything or be anywhere for once. She always treasured the post-Worlds break, but it was also the time of year she found herself most inspired. If she was totally honest, the only place she wanted to be was at the rink learning new choreography and working on new skills. The Bean with James, simply talking about their next year together, would have to do for the time being.

The Bean was a quaint, industrial-style café on the corner of Ainslie's block. They roasted their own fair-trade, organic coffee beans and made a fantastic vegetarian open grill. It was a regular haunt for her and the girls whenever they needed a stronger pick-me-up than their off-brand coffee maker could provide. It was also the go-to meeting place for Ainslie and James whenever they wanted to catch up somewhere that wasn't one of their houses.

James was already standing out the front when she got there, shaking his head in mock shame.

"Someone dawdled today." He tutted.

"Shut up." She smirked, shoving him in the shoulder.

He threw himself back dramatically in response, and they went to order food and find a table on the balcony.

*　　*　　*

"You know," Ainslie said and sighed, tilting her head back and letting the sun warm her face, "even though I slept for twenty hours straight, I'm still absolutely buggered."

"Me too," James replied. "Rachel's been kinda clingy ever since I got home. I didn't get much sleep last night."

Ainslie snorted.

"Not like that, ya sicko." He laughed. "We were up all hours chatting."

"That's nice, though. At least you have someone who cares about what you do. Aidan didn't ask me anything other than, 'Oh, so you came fourth, huh? Too bad'." Her Aidan impression left a lot to be desired. "And clingy is the last word I'd use to describe him."

"Abrasive, arrogant, condescending, gronk …" James counted the words on his fingers.

Ainslie cocked her head, staring at him quizzically.

"What? I'm listing all the words I'd use to describe him before 'clingy'."

She kicked him under the table and tried not to laugh.

"'Gronk'? Really?" She smirked. "I haven't heard that one since primary school."

When their food finally arrived, Ainslie's mouth practically filled with saliva. She hadn't eaten a proper meal in days.

"Hey," she said between bites of avocado and poached eggs on toast, "what does Rachel think of skating?"

They'd spoken about it a few times in the past, and she knew Rachel was pretty supportive. Though she'd started to wonder if, like Aidan, time had changed her tune.

"Uh, she's okay." He scratched the back of his neck. "But she did mention yesterday that maybe I should consider doing singles. So, there's that."

Ainslie raised an eyebrow. "Is she trying to bust up Team Jameslie?"

James took a long sip of his coffee and then grinned. "God Themself couldn't bust up Team Jameslie."

"Maybe not, but Aidan sure is trying his best."

"He is?"

"Are you surprised?" Ainslie explained the conversation they'd had in Aidan's car.

James leaned forwards and folded his arms on the table. "You're not actually thinking of retiring, are you?"

Ainslie used her teaspoon to play with the froth in her cappuccino, doing all she could to avoid looking at him. "I mean, I'm going to have to eventually."

"Goose." James tried to pull her attention away from her coffee. "Talk to me. What's going on?"

The use of his nickname for her only made it harder. She took a deep breath and finally met his gaze.

"I told Aidan I wouldn't retire until I was ready. But I've been thinking about the future, and I just don't know how long I can keep going."

James's eyes narrowed as he processed this information. "What are you getting at?"

"Maybe this should be my last year." Tears threatened to spill for the second time in as many days. "Maybe we should have one last go in 2020, then wrap it up. Move on with our lives. Me with Aidan, you with Rachel. They need us."

"Is that what you really want? Tell me honestly that you want to retire after 2020, and that's fine. We can pack it in. But only if *you* want to. If you're only doing it to satisfy Aidan, then I really think you should reconsider."

"I don't know." Her voice wavered. "I really don't know. I want to get married eventually. I want to have kids one day. And I don't *think* I'm ready to retire just yet. But Aidan has needs …"

"Hey." James put a hand on her arm. "Your needs are important too, Ainslie. Don't go off sacrificing your own happiness for Aidan's. You're just as important as he is, and skating has been part of your life a lot longer than he has."

She slumped back in her chair.

"How did you manage it? How did you find someone who doesn't resent the greatest passion in your life?"

James let out a weak laugh and shrugged. "Just lucky, I guess."

Ainslie couldn't help but wonder if he'd intended to sound so noncommittal.

CHAPTER 5

When Ainslie was a child, her family had appeared to be the quintessential skating family. Her mother had handmade her costumes and ferried her to and from the rink. In the early days, her father had never missed a competition and was often a little *too* competitive. But behind closed doors, the Wynters hadn't been as picture perfect as they'd seemed.

Ainslie's father's enthusiasm for the sport had begun to wane as Ainslie got older and things became more expensive. He had been investing so much money into her career that if at any time she hadn't lived up to his expectations, things got ugly.

Dennis Wynter was short-fused and had a rampant drinking problem, so when things got ugly, they got *very* ugly. He had never hit her, but Ainslie always felt that he could if he really wanted to. Her mother was under his thumb and rarely, if ever, defended Ainslie when things went sour.

Her family situation had been all the more reason for Ainslie to get out of there and move in with Lucy (whose parents were the absolute antithesis of the Wynters and were more than willing to cover any gaps in the girls' rent).

Things only got worse when Ainslie dropped out of university after eighteen months to focus on her skating career. When her father found out, he had drunk-dialled her, screaming that she was wasting her life. He'd even threatened to come around to her apartment — which was an empty threat because he didn't *actually* know where she lived. After that, she blocked his number, and she hadn't spoken to him, or her mother, since. Ainslie took no issue with cutting them off — her friends were her real family, anyway.

Ainslie and Lucy's move to the city happened to coincide with the grand opening of the Randwick Rollerdome. Their coach, Sandra, who had always dreamed of owning a rink of her own, came into a sizeable inheritance and built the state-of-the-art rink in the Eastern Suburbs. Ainslie, Lucy, James and a few of Sandra's other skaters had followed her, and the Randwick Ravens Roller Skating Club was born.

*   *   *

It was during the brief time that Ainslie had actually attended university that she first met Aidan. Her only friends had been Lucy and James, and she was always so busy training that she didn't bother to go out of her way to make more. She was happy in her skating bubble.

But one Friday night, the week after Nationals that year, the stars aligned. A girl from one of her classes invited her to a house party. James had to work, and Lucy didn't do parties, so Ainslie was on her own. And she hadn't gone out on a weekend with anyone other than skating friends in years, so she decided to take a chance. But after arriving and realising she recognised only a few faces here and there, the regret began to sink in.

She stood awkwardly in a corner and people-watched, still a little tired from Nationals. And then she was approached by Aidan. He was tall and good looking, and as smooth and charming as anything. He was also older and seemingly wiser, which had made Ainslie feel extra flattered that he was showing an interest in her.

He was in his final weeks of studying law, and he boasted that he already had a position reserved for him at a firm for when he passed the Bar Exam. Ainslie was completely taken by him, and she let him chat her up for a while until she finally gave him her number. He was a sports enthusiast, and when she told him she was an athlete, he was thoroughly impressed.

How times had changed.

They saw each other casually a few more times, and it was obvious there was something there. But it was the first time he accompanied her to training that Ainslie saw (and subsequently ignored) a couple of red flags. For a start, Lucy didn't gel with him, and when Lucy didn't like somebody, it usually meant they were bad news. And when he met James, he changed completely. He'd puffed out his chest and looked down his nose at him, clearly wanting to assert dominance. James had just looked at him as if he was completely unstable, and it had been all downhill from there.

Later that day, as Aidan drove Ainslie home from training, he had piped up. "That guy you skate with sure is handsy."

Ainslie had been caught off guard.

"That blond guy. Hands all over you. If he were straight, I might feel threatened."

"James *is* straight."

"Seriously?"

"Yes …," Ainslie had said through gritted teeth. "And he isn't *handsy*. That's just how pairs skating works. You have to actually, you know, *touch* your partner."

"I know. But he seems kind of … overly friendly."

"Because we're *friends*!" She'd scoffed. "We've known each other since we were kids!"

That was their first argument and the first time Ainslie's new boyfriend — her first serious boyfriend — showed that he felt threatened by her skating partner. And it definitely hadn't been the last time, either.

* * *

By the time Friday night rolled around, Ainslie had spent enough time away from Aidan that she was eager for their date. She'd spent the entire week doing very little — a nap here, a stretch there — and she finally felt like herself again. She'd granted Aidan's wish and worn a very short, very tight black dress. She checked herself in the mirror and enjoyed the way the fabric clung to the slight curve of her hips. She let her mind wander to later in the evening when the dress would inevitably be peeled off, and she shivered.

Aidan picked her up around seven, looking as suave as he always did, wearing something that probably cost more than the girls' monthly rent. They climbed into his car and headed towards the city.

Ainslie had always adored Sydney at night. Even when she had lived out in the suburbs, she'd travel into the city almost every weekend, just to be among the hustle and bustle. But she had never experienced Sydney quite like she did when she was with Aidan. When she was with her friends, they'd frequent Luna Park or King Street Wharf, parking in a dank, underground car park somewhere before walking half a kilometre to their destination. When she was with Aidan, she'd see a whole new side of the city she had only ever imagined. And finding a parking space had become a thing of the past.

Aidan pulled up out the front of an upscale hotel and casually handed his keys to a valet, taking Ainslie on his arm and leading her along the Quay. The lights from the Harbour Bridge and the waterfront restaurants reflected off the gentle ripples and turned the water into a sky full of stars. A cacophony of conversation and music pumped through the night air from the Opera Bar, and the white sails of the Opera House stood to attention at Bennelong Point.

Ainslie relaxed into the feeling of his fingers laced between hers, and she breathed in the cool night air, allowing a smile to spread across her face. When things were as perfect as they were in that moment, she could almost forget the pressing retirement issue weighing on her mind.

They arrived at a stunning high-end restaurant that overlooked the water. Aidan checked his reservation, and the hostess led them up the glittering spiral stairs to the balcony, which had a spectacular view of the entire harbour and the million-dollar yachts that bobbed on top of it. She poured them each a glass of champagne and left them to peruse the menu. It didn't have prices on it, which only meant one thing. The place was *expensive*. As if that wasn't already obvious enough from the location.

"Aidan, this place is ridiculous," Ainslie whispered, side-eyeing him.

"Nothing is too good for you." He smiled. "I've been planning this night since before you went away, and I wanted it to be special. So don't be ridiculous and get a stupid salad. Get whatever you want."

Ainslie pursed her lips and went back to the menu. There actually weren't that many options for her. She didn't eat meat, so a *stupid* salad seemed like the only choice.

"So," Ainslie said after the waiter had taken their orders, "why is tonight supposed to be so special?"

Aidan took her hand across the table and drew circles on her palm with his thumb.

"Well, you were gone for two weeks. And work has had me flat out. I've missed you. Plus, I acted like such an arse when you got home. I just wanted to show you how sorry I am."

"You're forgiven." She smiled. "For now."

Aidan listened intently as Ainslie filled him in about Worlds. He was smiling and asking questions, and things felt normal again. Ainslie felt herself relax even more as the champagne and delectable scent of his aftershave swirled around her head.

He looked amazing, particularly in the candlelight. His eyes were so dangerous and dark, Ainslie could easily get lost in them. He was a charmer; it was one of the reasons he was such a successful solicitor. Of course, it didn't hurt that his father owned the firm he worked at, but Aidan was brilliant in his own right. He was only thirty, and he made more money than Ainslie could even fathom.

He owned a stunning apartment in Kirribilli on the north side of the Harbour. It looked out over the water, across to the Opera House. He'd once suggested that Ainslie move in with him, but something had held her back. She'd told him she didn't want to live with him until they were married, which was more of a convenient excuse than the truth.

After dinner, Aidan picked up the bill and slipped his arm around Ainslie's waist.

"Come on," he said, sliding his hand a little lower and giving her backside a squeeze. "I have an idea."

He drove across the Harbour Bridge towards North Sydney and pulled up at Balmoral Beach.

Ainslie smiled and looked over at him. "Feeling sentimental, are we?"

Aidan shrugged. "Maybe a little. I told you I missed you."

Their first date had ended up at Balmoral Beach. Or rather, in the backseat of his car along The Esplanade at Balmoral Beach. On a summer's day, the place bustled with sun-kissed locals, but by night, it was dark, peaceful, and all but abandoned.

Ainslie enjoyed the feeling of the sand, still warm from the day, swallowing her bare feet as they padded across the beach. The sea breeze was cool, and the stars were sprawling out to the horizon. The moon was close to being full and shone over the water, making it gleam. It was idyllic.

Aidan wrapped his arms around Ainslie's waist from behind and pulled her to his chest.

"I'll tell you what," he said, his lips brushing against her ear. "I'll give you a ten-second head start, and if I catch you, I get to take you down."

Ainslie giggled. The champagne and the moonlight were making her feel extra flirty. She wiggled out of his embrace and took off as fast as she could across the sand. Aidan rolled up his trousers and, moments later, was off after her. Ainslie glanced over her shoulder, laughing into the night air. She was fast, but Aidan's legs were a lot longer than hers. She slowed a little, allowing him to catch up completely. Before she knew it, he'd captured her and wrapped his arms around her waist. He flung her around in a circle as if she were weightless, and she let out a squeal of joy. They toppled to the ground, and he pinned her down.

"Gotcha." There was fire in his gaze as he claimed her lips with his.

He ran his hand up the length of her thigh, pushing the boundaries of the hem of her dress. He left behind a trail of goosebumps where his fingers roamed, and Ainslie shivered, kissing him back as if her life depended on it. She wrapped her arms around his neck in an attempt to pull him closer, the weight of his body on hers the only thing grounding her in reality.

She was just about to suggest they head back to the car when Aidan pulled away, sitting upright beside her. Ainslie furrowed her brow, sitting up and brushing the sand out of her now dishevelled hair.

"What's wrong?" She struggled to see his face through the darkness, but something had definitely shifted in his demeanour.

"Nothing. I just …"

Ainslie's heart beat a little faster, and she squinted at him, trying to work out what he was up to. Then he reached for his pocket, and everything came crashing down. The high-end restaurant with the million-dollar view, the expensive champagne, the sentimentality and the romantic moonlit romp. It all made sense now. The pounding of her heart started to reverberate in her head.

"Ainslie, the last five years have been amazing," Aidan said, one hand still in his pocket. "You know, I always thought I had everything. And when I met you, I finally did."

Ainslie watched as he drew a small, teal box out of his pocket. She was vaguely aware that he was still talking. He was saying something about how much he loved her and how he wanted to spend the rest of his life with her, but his words had started to bleed into each other. All Ainslie could hear was a ringing in her ears, and everything seemed a little hazy, as if she were watching the entire thing unfold from outside her body. Her brain finally kicked back into gear when the words "Will you marry me?" fell out of his mouth.

Time seemed to freeze. She had played this moment over and over in her head during the course of the last five years. She hadn't doubted for a second what she wanted in those fantasies. In her dreams, she always answered with a resounding "Yes". No hesitation, no fear. But now, finally faced with reality, she couldn't shake a nauseating feeling of uncertainty.

A million questions raced through her mind in the few seconds between Aidan asking the question and her finally verbalising a response.

Was she ready to be married? And did she want to spend the rest of her life with Aidan? Would she be happy? She'd have no choice but to retire from skating now.

Is that why he's proposing? No, not everything's about skating. What will James say? What am I doing thinking about James at a time like this?!

She felt as if she'd been silent for hours. The look of concern on Aidan's face told her he felt the same. She had to say something.

Aidan had always been good to her. All couples fought from time to time.

And she couldn't deny that a life with him would be financially comfortable. And he was gorgeous.

She brushed her doubts from her mind, dismissing them as just a natural part of being faced with having to make the most important decision of her life.

This is probably how everyone reacts to being proposed to.

A smirk played at the corner of her lips. "Well, are you gonna get on one knee or what?"

Aidan laughed, his body finally dropping its tension. He pushed himself out of the sand and rose to one knee.

"Ainslie Jade Wynter. Will you marry me?"

Ainslie clambered to her knees to meet him.

"Yes, I will." She threw her arms around his neck, and he wrapped her up in his embrace, squeezing her close to him.

When they parted, Aidan slipped the ring onto her finger, a satisfied grin on his face. He took her face between his hands, kissing her softly. Ainslie smiled against his lips, doing her best to focus on the moment and ignore the niggling feeling in the back of her mind that reminded her that everything was going to have to change now. Realistically, marriage was going to have to mean retirement. Not immediately, but soon. She'd always known her skating career had a use-by date. Would it really be so bad, giving up one life to start a new one? And Aidan could offer her a wonderful life. She watched her ring sparkle in the moonlight.

"Do you like it?" Aidan beamed.

"Like it?" She cupped his cheek and stared deeply into his dark eyes. "I love it."

Yes. I'm doing the right thing. She mentally repeated the words like a mantra.

She brushed her nose against his and kissed him once more.

"And I love you," she mumbled against his lips.

It was time Ainslie got her priorities in order. It was time to grow up, time to move on. Move on with Aidan. The thought was bittersweet, but she'd made up her mind.

Tomorrow, she would tell James and Sandra that 2020 was going to be not only *their* year but also their *last* year.

CHAPTER 6

When Ainslie walked into her apartment at nine o'clock the following morning, slightly hungover but still riding the post-engagement high, Jaz looked her up and down and gave her a knowing grin. Lucy just shook her head in mock disapproval.

"Really, Ainslie? Getting drunk the night before training goes back?"

"I see you and Aidan put aside your differences and made up," Jaz quipped, tongue in cheek.

Ainslie rolled her eyes. For a moment, she'd forgotten about the telltale diamond weighing down her left hand. A moment was all it took for Lucy to notice.

"What is that!" she said with a gasp, pointing an accusatory finger at Ainslie.

"Surprise," Ainslie said, the stupid grin from the night before returning to her face.

"You got engaged?!" Jaz said.

"Yes." Ainslie put a hand to her head. "And would you keep it down?"

"This is massive!" Jaz cried, not lowering her volume at all. "Have you told James yet?"

"No. I haven't told *anybody* yet."

"That's going to be an awkward conversation," Lucy said. "This is absolutely going to affect your skating together."

"Aidan's really gonna be pushing you to retire now." Jaz sounded deflated.

Ainslie waved a hand at her. "Aidan's not going to be *pushing* me to do anything."

Lucy and Jaz looked relieved, but it was short lived.

"However," Ainslie said, "I've been doing some soul-searching, and I think maybe this *should* be my final year competing."

"Are you serious?!" Jaz said in a whiny tone.

"It's time for me to grow up, Jaz. Yes, it's sad, but I need to be an adult. This skating thing was never going to last forever."

"*This skating thing* was part of your life long before Aidan ever came into the picture," Lucy said.

"I know," Ainslie said, pinching the bridge of her nose. "And I'll always have the memories. And I'll always have you guys, and James, and Sandra. But I can't have the happily ever after with Aidan and continue to compete. It's not practical, and it's not fair on him."

Jaz looked as if she might cry, which made Ainslie want to cry. And she knew telling James was going to be even more difficult.

*　　*　　*

Lucy had been right. Ainslie was seriously regretting having had so much to drink the night before. As she got ready for training, she tried to shake her headache with a strong, black coffee and some paracetamol. The night may have been a cause for celebration, but the repercussions of that celebration weren't going to make the conversation she had to have with James and Sandra any easier. She shot them a quick message in their group chat.

> Hey. Just wondering if we can have a talk at the rink before training this afternoon. Got some stuff on my mind re. The new season.

Sandra replied almost instantly, suggesting they meet at her office at four thirty. James just responded with a thumbs up emoji. Seconds later, another message from James came through, this one for Ainslie's eyes only.

> Hey Goose, what's going on?

Ainslie frowned and typed back.

> Can't say over text, just wait until this arvo. Don't worry. All g.

*　　*　　*

Ainslie's vague message tied James's stomach in knots, and no amount of "All g" could help him shake the feeling that something was wrong. He ran every outrageous scenario over in his head as he paced around his house like an expectant father, just wishing she'd call him and tell him what was going on.

He got to the rink a little before four thirty, as summoned, his legs unsteady underneath him as he climbed the stairs to Sandra's office. It felt like stepping onto the floor at Worlds, only he had no idea what to expect. When he arrived at Sandra's door, it was ajar. Ainslie was already there, looking at her phone with her back to him.

"You finally ready to get back into it, Goose?" He playfully jabbed her in the shoulder, and she nearly jumped out of the chair.

"Jesus, James," she said, gasping. "Are you trying to give me a heart attack?"

"I'm trying to lighten the mood," James said, frowning, "because frankly, you've had me worried all day."

She looked away. He furrowed his brow and sat in the chair beside her. Then he noticed it. He reached over and took her left hand.

"What's this then?" He already knew the answer.

She snatched her hand away. "You don't miss a trick, do you?"

"Wow." James's eyes widened. "That's massive."

Ainslie glanced at him, and he tried not to look too disappointed.

"Congratulations," he said, smiling lamely. "I'm happy for you. I really am."

"Thanks."

"But I have to ask," he said slowly. "Is this why you called this meeting? This is gonna change things, isn't it?"

Ainslie looked at her shoes. "Can we just wait for Sandra to arrive? I don't want to have to explain myself twice."

*　　*　　*

Sandra Dawson was a strict but fair woman in her late fifties. Her second husband was an ex-hockey world champion named Tim, and together, they had full custody of his young granddaughter, Rosie.

Sandra had once been part of a champion pairs team herself. She'd skated with her first husband in the eighties, but the end of their marriage had spelled the end of their partnership. She'd had an illustrious but tumultuous career, and she had every hardship she'd ever overcome etched on her face. She had short blonde hair, and she'd retained her svelte, athletic figure, assisted by her lack of biological children. Her skaters were her children, and despite her rarely wearing a smile, those like Ainslie and James, who'd been under her wing since they were children, knew the truth. She was a teddy bear.

"Welcome back, kids," she said upon entering her office. "Did you have a good break?"

"Yeah," the pair replied in a flat chorus.

Sandra raised an eyebrow and moved behind her desk.

"Anyway," she said and sat down, "what's going on with you, Ainslie?"

Ainslie took a deep breath and stole a peek at James. He dropped his head.

She put her left hand on the desk. "So, I got engaged last night."

Sandra's face lit up. "Congratulations! Oh, I'm so happy for you!"

"You won't be for long," James muttered, and Ainslie shot him a glare.

"I wanted to have this meeting because I've been doing some serious thinking and re-evaluating," Ainslie said. "And I realise that now I'm getting married, I'm gonna need to get some priorities in order."

James folded his arms and leaned back in his chair. "Just say it, Ains. We both know what you're getting at."

Ainslie glowered at him, but when she saw just how deflated he looked, her heart sank, and she softened.

"Basically, I've come to the difficult decision to make 2020 my last competitive year." Her voice came out small and strangled.

Sandra looked sombre but understanding. James looked as if he wanted to cry. Ainslie just wanted to vanish. She'd disappointed far too many people for one day.

"Ainslie," Sandra said, resting her elbows on the desk and leaning forwards, "we all get to a point in our lives when we need to move on. I'll be sad to lose you, but at the same time, I get it. And we'll always be here if you ever decide you want to come back."

James rolled his eyes and scoffed a little too loudly.

Sandra raised her eyebrows and turned to him. "Do you have something you'd like to share, James?"

James looked like a scolded child, but he didn't back down.

"Let's face it, Ains, you *won't* be coming back," he said bitterly. "You won't be *allowed* to."

Ainslie chewed the inside of her cheek.

"So, yeah," he said, "I think the whole thing fucking sucks. But what can you do?"

Sandra frowned at him as he held her gaze defiantly.

"Okay," Sandra said after a beat, slapping her hands against the desk. "Well, if this is gonna be your last year, let's make it a good one."

Ainslie stood up and left the office, James following her begrudgingly. Once they were out of Sandra's earshot, he grabbed her arm and turned her to face him.

"Hey," he said, trying not to sound as upset as he felt, "are you sure about this? Did you make this decision on your own or —"

Ainslie wrenched her arm away. "Yes, I did make this decision on my own. I'm not a child, you know."

"Only because a week ago, you didn't seem that keen on retirement."

"A week ago, I wasn't getting married. I'm sorry, James. I really am. But I have to do this."

"Why? Why do you *have* to do this? Retire completely. Why should you have to give up skating for him?"

"Because. I want to have a life with him!"

He could see her eyes becoming glassy, and he could feel his own tears starting to threaten.

"What, you can't have a life and skate?"

"No! You can't! You *know* that! How am I supposed to buy a house, or start a family, or have a career if I live at this rink?"

He knew he couldn't answer because he knew she was right.

"Everyone retires eventually, James," she added in a tiny voice.

His eyes searched hers, frantically looking for any indication she might change her mind. But he found nothing.

"I just think if Aidan really loved you," he said, "he'd take you and everything about you, just as you are."

As soon as the words were out, he regretted saying them. Not because he didn't think they were true, but because of how Ainslie's posture changed. She turned red and blinked up at him, a tear finally sliding down her cheek. She looked like he'd slapped her in the face.

"It's called *compromise*. It's what *adults* do." Her voice had grown cold. "Now please get out of my face, or I might just decide to retire early."

James didn't say another word. He just watched as Ainslie stalked downstairs ahead of him towards the change rooms. He kicked himself for lashing out. Never in nearly twenty years of friendship had he ever made Ainslie cry. He wanted to cry himself. He knew the fate of their friendship. Once she married Aidan and quit skating, everything would be different. He'd seen it happen before. She'd drift further and further away until she was gone for good.

*   *   *

By the time Ainslie got to the change room, her tears were flowing freely. She'd never fought with James like that before, and she didn't like it one bit. Sure, they'd bickered in the past, but mostly over stupid things that were forgotten minutes later. She'd never yelled at him before, and he'd certainly never reduced her to tears. But what made it worse was that he was right. She wasn't ready to retire. In fact, the idea was so painful she thought her heart was about to explode. And yes, she hated that Aidan couldn't accept one of the most important parts of who she was, but she didn't need James reminding her of that.

By the time she'd washed her face, changed into her training gear and hauled her skates out to the rink, her tears had subsided a little. James was already sitting on the grandstand, lacing up his skates. She stood beside him and put a hand on his shoulder.

"I'm sorry, James," she said softly. "I don't want our last season to be like this. I just ... I'm really gonna miss skating with you."

He sat upright and stared at her. She could see the disappointment in his eyes, but his face didn't soften like she'd hoped it would.

Instead, he just shrugged. "Then why stop?"

Ainslie fumed, throwing her skates on the grandstand. "I already told you! Are you really gonna make me say it again?"

He opened his mouth to reply but was stopped short by a looming shadow.

"Whatever it is, you better work it out before you step on my rink," Sandra said as she walked by. "I could hear you yelling from my office. Do you kids think I'm deaf just because I'm old? Now get your skates on and get moving."

CHAPTER 7

Normally, Ainslie and James would warm up together, but as soon as they stepped onto the rink, James flew off ahead. Ainslie rolled her eyes and warmed up alone. They were stretching against the barrier when Sandra joined them.

"Let's talk music," she said. "I'm still tossing around some ideas for the short program, but I'm pretty sure I've decided on the long. It'll be a challenge. You'll have some very big skates to fill."

Ainslie glanced at James, forgetting for a second that they were fighting. Sandra skated to the far corner of the rink, stepped off the skating surface and climbed into the music box. Moments later, the building that had previously resonated with nothing but tense silence filled with the first few quiet strains of a piece of music they both recognised immediately.

Maurice Ravel's "Bolero". The song that had been used for what was probably the most iconic ice dance performance in history.

Ainslie had always loved it. She'd seen it done a few times before, but none quite like the original couple's. It was a slow, hypnotic piece that built in intensity until it exploded in a climactic flourish. It had the kind of quality that told Ainslie this was going to be another intensely romantic program. She didn't mind that (after all, intense chemistry was what they were famous for), but in their current state of animosity, and considering how cold James had been towards her since they'd stepped onto the rink, she couldn't imagine they were going to have much success.

"Okay, first position." Sandra side-eyed them. "Try not to freeze each other."

The coach directed their two bodies as if they were a couple of mannequins, manipulating their limbs and heads and placing them in the perfect starting pose. James dug one toe stop into the ground as he held Ainslie to his side. She leaned into his body, with her free leg wrapped around his hip, his hand splayed against her thigh.

It wasn't unusual for them to be placed in such an intimate position, but as they stood there in such close proximity, Ainslie could feel the anger radiating off him. Sandra positioned Ainslie's left arm around the back of James's neck, her right hand on his chest. She instructed them to look at each other but with little success. Eventually, she threw her hands up in frustration.

"Listen!" she said through gritted teeth. "The pair of you need to snap out of it, or you can both take your skates off and go home! I want to see all this *rage* you two seem to be harbouring right now channelled into something I can actually use."

Ainslie fought to not roll her eyes as she turned her head to look at James. He was already looking at her. And it was a look that stirred something deep in the pit of her stomach. Apparently, it was exactly what Sandra was looking for because a smile crept onto her face, and she applauded.

"Yes, James! Just like that!"

Ainslie found it difficult to focus on creating her own expression because she was so baffled by his. He'd never looked at her like *that* before. They'd portrayed lovers many times, but there was a strange sense of veracity behind this particular gaze, and it gave Ainslie an unwelcome case of butterflies.

Even more infuriating was the fact that he didn't even flinch. He just stared into her eyes (although it felt as if he were staring directly into her soul), and for the tiniest, smallest fraction of a split second, she found herself overwhelmingly attracted to him. She tried to ignore the feeling as she did her best to mirror his expression, but it was next to impossible.

She'd never found it difficult to hold eye contact with James before, but in that moment, his eyes were so dangerously intriguing, she was scared that if she looked too long, she'd accidentally fall into them. All she knew was if that look was the result of James taking all his anger and channelling it into something Sandra could use, then he must have been fucking furious.

Ainslie must have looked as flustered as she felt because Sandra chuckled.

"You guys wanna get a room?"

Ainslie pulled herself away, and James finally broke the expression, looking very pleased with himself.

For the rest of the lesson, they only really spoke when they absolutely needed to. Sandra ignored them, pressing on as she continued choreographing. She added an opening transition, a throw triple Salchow and another short transition, and then set them to work on a new lift.

On any normal day, there was nothing Ainslie enjoyed more than doing overhead lifts. The feeling of weightlessness that came with being hoisted into the air was unparalleled. It was the closest thing she could get to flying, and it gave her an adrenaline rush like nothing else. When up there, her face might be fixed in a steely look of concentration, but inside, she would be glowing.

Lifts were an outwards expression of the trust between them — a way of showing the world just how special their bond was. Their relationship was a unique one, with a very specific kind of intimacy defined by unspoken communication and their apparent ability to read each other's mind.

They'd had their fair share of falls. Ainslie had tumbled down from great heights more times than she would care to remember. Most of the time, James caught her before she hit the ground. Other times, he'd pull her on top of him, protecting her from the impact by throwing his own body on the line. But no matter what, she always felt safe.

But that was on any *normal* day. *This* was the first day Ainslie had wondered if the idea of dropping her on her head had crossed James's mind.

In their new lift, she was going to be flipped up over his head and supported by one of his hands on her stomach. Then, she was supposed to grab her left foot and pull it to the back of her head, making a ring position, while he rotated.

Sandra explained that once they had nailed it, she would add another position, which would turn it into a combination lift. The plan was to finish the long program with it, make it a real climax. Ainslie could tell it was going to be spectacular eventually, but with the little bit of champagne still running through her system and the fact that they were both a bit rusty from their week off, it felt rough.

After several unsuccessful attempts, Ainslie began to wonder if she would even make it out of the rink in one piece. On their last try, she could feel that something was out of place as she ascended. She felt unstable as she was flipped up, and as James pushed her into the air, she was slightly off kilter. Nevertheless, he supported her with both hands, and she reached for her foot.

As he removed one hand, she felt herself go. For the split second that she was falling, she wondered if he would even bother to try to catch her. She squeezed her eyes shut, bracing herself for the impact, but instead felt two strong, familiar arms catch her and set her safely on her feet. She immediately felt awful for ever doubting him.

"Thanks," she said, a little shaken.

"No problem," he replied without so much as looking at her.

*   *   *

When their session was over, James wasted no time flinging his skates off and stalking moodily towards the change room. Ainslie raced to catch up with him, grabbing his arm and forcing him to look at her before he disappeared through the door.

"Hey," she snapped, "are you just gonna keep ignoring me and acting like a dick for the rest of the year? Or are you gonna at least *try* to make our last year a good one?"

"Ainslie," James said as he folded his arms and leaned against the doorframe, "I think you're forgetting just how long I've known you for. I think you're also forgetting how *well* I know you. You think you can be best friends with someone for nearly twenty years and not know when they're lying to you? When they're lying to themselves?"

She narrowed her eyes at him. "What are you talking about?"

"You told me you're happy with the decision you made, but I'm pretty convinced you're full of shit," he said bluntly. "I don't even care if you lie to me. I'll get over it. But I *do* care that you're lying to yourself. You said you wouldn't retire until you were ready and that you would only retire on your own terms. And unless I'm mistaken, if you look deep down in here" — he poked her in the chest and then gently flicked her nose when she dropped her head — "you'll find that you're not ready."

He turned to enter the change room, but Ainslie wasn't finished yet.

"Why don't you want me to be happy?!" she said, tears welling once again.

James turned to her and sighed sadly.

"Goose," he said in earnest, "there's nothing in the world that I want more than for you to be happy."

Then he slipped away.

*   *   *

Ainslie walked home alone. James had left the rink before she had a chance to talk to him again. As she walked, she swatted away more tears. She never imagined that fighting with him would hurt so badly.

When she walked into her apartment, she lowered her head, hoping to make a beeline for her room without Lucy or Jaz noticing she was crying.

"Ainslie!" Lucy cried, dropping her paperback into her lap. "What's wrong?"

"Nothing," Ainslie muttered.

"Did you and Aidan have another fight?" Jaz asked.

"No." Ainslie let out a sob. "Me and James did, though."

"James?" Lucy said. "You two never fight."

"Well, we do *now*!"

Ainslie briefed them on the argument, and Lucy shook her head disapprovingly.

"Maybe he's jealous," Jaz said.

Both Lucy and Ainslie shot her a look.

"Not like that." Jaz groaned. "Maybe he's jealous you'll be spending more time with Aidan and less time with him. You *are* best friends, after all."

Ainslie sighed.

"But you know," Jaz said, pumping her eyebrows up and down, "he could also be secretly in love with you."

Ainslie knew she was trying to lighten the mood, but it was the last thing she needed to hear. Especially considering how difficult she was finding it to shake the feeling she'd had earlier. That feeling of confusion as she stood there, her leg wrapped around him, his eyes boring into her.

Ainslie excused herself and retreated to the privacy of her bedroom. She lay on her bed and stared at the ceiling, a few stray tears still blurring her vision and turning the city lights into starbursts through the window.

Her mind was racing. She had known James would be disappointed, but she hadn't expected him to react quite as emotionally as he had. She allowed herself to entertain the notion that maybe Jaz had a point. Maybe there was some level of jealousy there. That may have explained that look. But she also knew he was a good actor.

She decided it was much more likely that he was just messing with her. She brushed the ridiculous idea out of her head, but that night, that ridiculous idea caught up with her, and she had an exceptionally unsettling dream.

She was training with James. Their new "Bolero" routine was complete, and they were skating it to perfection. And they were back to their normal selves. Their anger and frustration were gone, replaced by the usual passion and chemistry they were so renowned for. But there was something more. Every time they touched, there was a surge of electricity. Every time they caught each other's eye, there was fire there.

When the routine came to an end, Ainslie skated over to the barrier and grabbed her drink bottle. She went to take a sip, but before the bottle hit her lips, a pair of hands clutched her and spun her around. The bottle went flying out of her hand, and she found herself face to face with James. He was standing before her, staring down at her with the same heated look from earlier, his fingers digging into her hips.

He felt so real. He *looked* so real. She could even smell his deodorant. His blue eyes were unmistakable, and a loose lock of his sandy hair had fallen across them. She fought the urge to brush it away. God knows what would happen if she touched him back.

He didn't say anything. He just gripped her tightly and effortlessly lifted her up, as he so often did. He propped her up on top of the barrier and stepped between her thighs, taking her face roughly between his hands, his gaze burning into her. She opened her mouth to say something, but before she had the chance to speak, he'd captured her lips with his own, kissing her passionately and relentlessly, his tongue hot against hers.

And that was it. She was gone. She kissed him back, matching his intensity, wrapping her legs around him, pulling him closer, dragging her hands across the taut muscles of his back and up into his hair. His hands found their way to the hem of her top, and he pulled it over her head, tossing it aside. She felt his arousal pressing against her, and she moaned into his mouth.

Then she jolted awake.

Her heart was racing, and she felt as if she were on fire. She took a moment to try to slow her breathing, furious that her subconscious would be so cruel. That wasn't the first time James had made an appearance in one of her dreams, but it was certainly the first time he'd shown up in one to ravish her mid-training session. She could still feel the tingling sensation of his hands on her body and his lips on hers.

She rubbed her face and tried to make the feeling go away, but there was one thing she couldn't shake. She'd reciprocated. And it had been good. Very good. She wasn't sure she'd ever be able to look him in the eye again.

She closed her eyes and tried to think about anything else. Anything to take her mind off his body pressed against hers and how much she'd enjoyed it.

CHAPTER 8

Ainslie slicked her hair back into a high ponytail and ran a lint roller over her black work shirt, readying herself for her first shift since returning from London. She knew some of her friendlier co-workers were bound to mention the engagement ring on her hand, and quite frankly, she wasn't in the mood. She was too preoccupied with the remnants of last night's dream that were still lingering in the back of her mind. It was all she could think about on the short bus ride to the café where she worked, and the ghostly feeling of James's hands on her hips still lingered, even as she clocked on for her shift and took her place behind the coffee machine.

She focused all her attention on the endless list of coffee orders, which was a pleasant reprieve for a while. But eventually, she found herself thinking about just how many coffees she was going to have to make over the course of the next twelve months to pay for both a potential trip to Barcelona for Worlds *and* a wedding. The thought made her feel a little woozy.

She doubted she'd get much help from her parents, and she didn't really want any. She hadn't even told them about her engagement yet, and considering their history, she wasn't even sure she *wanted* them at her wedding. Of course, Aidan would be more than able to foot the bill, but Ainslie was far too proud to let him pay for everything.

She was in the middle of mentally calculating how many shifts she was going to need per week when a familiar voice wrenched her back into reality.

"Hey."

She jumped, nearly spilling the milk she was frothing. She looked up from the jug to see a remorseful-looking James.

"Hi," she said, her eyes flicking between him and the milky whirlpool.

She was grateful to have something to focus on other than his eyes. The eyes that had bored into her the day before. And the night before.

And she'd just managed to get the dream out of her mind too.

"Do you have a break soon?"

"In about five minutes."

"Cool." He scratched his head. "Can we talk? When you have your break."

"Sure."

*   *   *

37

Ainslie made herself a coffee and clocked off for her break. James had sat at a corner table by a window. He was cradling his cup in his hands and studying the froth on top. Ainslie sat down opposite him. He glanced up, looking sheepish. When his eyes locked on hers again, flashes of her dream replayed in her mind. She forced herself to hold his gaze.

"What's up?" she asked, cutting to the point. "You speaking to me again?"

"That's actually what I wanted to talk to you about." James sighed and leaned forwards, resting his elbows on the table. "I'm sorry about yesterday. I acted like such a dick. I mean, I'm still gutted that you're retiring, and I really wish you weren't, but … I was being selfish. So, I'm sorry. And if this is gonna be our last year competing, then I wanna make it the best one ever."

Ainslie felt a wave of relief wash over her.

"I'm glad to hear that." A small smile crept onto her face. "I was starting to think you were jealous."

She immediately felt her cheeks burn. Had she really said that out loud?

"Jealous?" James shifted in his seat and smirked. "No way. You can keep Aidan all to yourself."

Ainslie pulled a face and kicked him under the table.

"So, are we good now?"

"Yeah, we're good," he replied, sipping his coffee. "You kidding? We're always good."

Ainslie pouted. "Look, I'll admit it'll be weird not skating anymore. And I'll definitely miss it."

"Well, we'll always be friends, yeah?"

"Of course!"

The very notion of them *not* being friends was absolutely heartbreaking. Ainslie had even started tossing around the idea of asking him to be her man of honour in lieu of a maid.

James placed his cup down with a clink, his expression changing, as if a storm cloud had cast a shadow over it. "What if Aidan doesn't want that?"

Ainslie frowned. She could hear it now. Aidan's gruff voice saying, "Well, if you're not skating anymore, why would you have any reason to see him?"

"Hey! Is this your fiancé?!"

The shrill voice cut through their conversation, and every muscle in Ainslie's body tensed up. One of her co-workers appeared at their table.

James just smiled. "No, I'm not. I'm her partner. James."

Ainslie noticed a look of confusion shoot across the girl's face.

"Skating partner," she said.

"Oh, cool! I'm Emily. Congrats on your skating thing!"

"Thanks." James raised his coffee cup in a half-hearted toast.

Emily bounced away to clear a nearby table. James raised his eyebrows.

"Now even non-skating folk are mistaking us for a couple. Bet Aidan would love that."

*　　*　　*

"Okay!" Sandra emphasised the word with a clap. "Now, I trust whatever was going on yesterday is in the past, and we can all move on with our lives?"

Ainslie stole a glance at James and noticed he was returning it. They both nodded.

"Good," Sandra said, "because if you wanna end up on that podium at Worlds next year, you're both gonna have to pull your heads in. We don't have time to waste on petty bullshit."

Ainslie looked down at her skates like a scolded child before following James to their starting position on the floor.

"You ready?" he asked.

"Let's do it."

She threw her leg over his hip and placed her hand on his chest, settling into their opening position. But it turned out she wasn't ready at all. As soon as she was back in his arms, her mind went back to the dream. With his hands on her body and his eyes locked on hers, she was reminded of how much she had craved his touch the night before. And how that feeling was bleeding so dangerously into reality.

The music began and they started to move through the routine, but Ainslie found herself getting distracted. Her mind kept wandering off to things she really liked about James. Physical things, like his bright smile or his kind, blue eyes. Intangible things, like his work ethic and his ability to make her laugh. The music abruptly shut off, pulling Ainslie out of her fantasy.

"Something still feels off." Sandra crossed her arms and stared the pair down. "I thought you'd sorted things out?"

"So did I." James glanced at Ainslie.

"Well, would you please take a minute and *actually* sort it out?" Sandra huffed, rolling away from them.

Ainslie raised her eyebrows. She hadn't realised her discomfort had been so obvious.

James turned to her. "Ains, what's wrong?"

"Nothing." She hoped she sounded believable. "I'm fine."

"Are you sure?" He placed a hand on her shoulder. "You're not still angry at me, are you?"

"No, of course not," she replied, tensing under his touch. "Look, I don't know what Sandra's talking about."

James looked unconvinced.

"Have you sorted it out?" Sandra called, rolling back over.

Ainslie nodded profusely. "Yes, I swear. It's all good."

Sandra squinted at her. "I hope so."

*　　*　　*

39

By the time the training session ended, Ainslie had a splitting headache. She was completely spent from putting all her energy into ignoring what James was unknowingly doing to her. All she wanted was to put a bit of space between them until she was able to get the dream out of her head, but before she had a chance to gather her things and make her escape, he'd caught up with her and offered her a lift home.

"I was just gonna walk …," she said, shifting nervously.

"I think we need to talk, though," he said, leading them to his beat-up little car.

They were barely out of the rink driveway when James piped up. "So, are you gonna tell me what's going on with you?"

"What do you mean?"

"Well, I thought we were all good after our talk at the café," he replied with a half smile, "but you've been acting weird all evening."

Ainslie scoffed. "I haven't been acting weird."

"Ainslie Jade Wynter," James said, raising an eyebrow, "how long have we been friends?"

"Nearly twenty years."

"Exactly. Therefore, I know when you're acting weird, and when you're acting normal, and tonight you've been acting weird."

"Maybe *you've* been acting weird."

"Nice comeback." He smirked.

It was becoming increasingly clear that Ainslie wasn't going to be able to avoid the conversation.

"Fine." She threw her hands up in defeat. "Things are changing, okay? And really fast."

James glanced at her out of the corner of his eye. "Yeah, they sure are."

"I'm broke." She counted her woes on her fingers. "And I'm gonna have to save up not just for Worlds but for a wedding. I'm gonna be *married*, which is crazy enough in itself. This is my last year skating, and it just feels … weird."

James didn't say anything.

"I know it'll be okay in the end," she said, leaning back on the headrest, "but right now, it's freaking me out."

"You know I'm here for you, right? You know that whenever you need help with anything, a shoulder to cry on, someone to complain to, I'm there. Consider me on call twenty-four hours a day, seven days a week. I mean, Aidan might be your fiancé, but I'm still your best friend."

"Hey." Ainslie turned her head to look at him. "Do you want to be my man of honour?"

James pulled a face. "Your what of what?"

"You know," she said, laughing, "like a maid of honour, but a man."

"A man of honour." James rolled the idea around on his tongue.

"Like you said, you're my best friend. There's no way you're not going to be involved in my wedding, and I don't like the chances of you being one of Aidan's groomsmen."

"Aidan is *not* gonna like the idea of you having *me* as a man of honour," James said, laughing.

"I don't give a shit!" she said, laughing as well. "It's not up to him, is it?"

They finally pulled up in Gadigal Avenue, and James turned in his seat to face her. "All right, I'll be your man of honour. It would be a privilege. Or even an honour."

Ainslie grinned. "It's gonna be great."

"Gimme a hug, Goose."

She reached over and embraced him, once more feeling that tug deep in her stomach.

"We're good, right?" he said as he drew away. "For real this time?"

"We're good," she replied, ignoring the pull. "We're always good."

*   *   *

That night, much to her chagrin, Ainslie had another dream. She was back in the car with James, and they'd just finished their earlier conversation. Only this time, instead of leaning across the car to hug him, she leaned across to press her lips against his. At first, he tensed under her touch, presumably out of shock. But seconds later, his hands were on her body, tangling in her hair, roving across the curves of her waist and hips, sliding between her thighs …

She woke with a start. Her face was on fire and her heart was pounding. She grabbed her pillow and flipped it over, punching it into submission. She threw her head back on it in a huff, praying that when she drifted back to sleep, her subconscious would give her a damn break.

CHAPTER 9

Over the course of the next several weeks, things began to return to normal. Ainslie and James were training every day, preparing for the new season, and they had both of their programs completed by late November.

As the Australian summer began to rear its ugly head, physical activity became more and more unpleasant, but it never derailed them from their game plan. The 2020 skating calendar wouldn't be released until the first of January, but they knew from experience that the New South Wales State Championships would be held in April. They were the only Senior Pairs team in the state, but they still needed to impress, and States was the first step on the journey to Worlds.

Ainslie was waiting for the 2020 calendar to be released before setting a date for the wedding, but they were hoping for next spring. Given the long lead-up, Ainslie's early stages of wedding planning mostly consisted of idly thumbing through bridal magazines, browsing the internet and drinking wine. And the more energy she put into planning, the easier it was to keep the intrusive thoughts about James at bay. Thankfully, he'd been staying out of her dreams too.

Ainslie quickly discovered that planning a wedding was a lot more stressful than she'd anticipated. There were a million things to do, many of which were going to cost a small fortune. She was picking up as many shifts at the café as possible, and her thriftiness had shifted into overdrive. She'd made a habit of running around the apartment, switching the lights off after Jaz. And she'd made a grand declaration that the air conditioning was not to be turned on until it hit forty degrees, but the temperature had been stubbornly peaking at thirty-seven.

She had also decided to put off telling Aidan about her man of honour idea. Even though she'd confidently declared that she didn't care what he thought, she knew deep down it would cause an argument. Things had been going so well between them since their engagement, she didn't want to risk putting a dampener on it. She made a mental note to tell him later, but she wasn't exactly sure when *later* would be.

* * *

Ainslie and James sat sweltering in the girls' apartment one Sunday evening, with the sliding balcony door wide open in a feeble attempt to combat the heat.

"I can't believe you still haven't told your parents you're engaged," James said, rolling up a bridal magazine and swatting at a fly that had flown in.

"You can't?" she replied without looking up from her laptop. "Don't you know me at all?"

"Goose," James said, sinking into the lounge beside her, "this is your *wedding*. If you don't invite your parents, you *will* regret it in the long run."

She narrowed her eyes at him. "I was *going* to invite them. I just hadn't found the right time."

"No time like the present," James replied, tossing her phone at her.

She caught it and groaned. "Seriously?"

"Do it! They like Aidan, don't they?"

"He's loaded." She raised an eyebrow. "Of course they like him."

She punched in her mother's number, her heart beating a little quicker as the phone rang.

"Hello, Ainslie," Meredith Wynter replied, her tone cold and unreadable. "What's the matter?"

"Nothing's the matter." Ainslie rolled her eyes. "What, can I only call you if something's wrong?"

"Well, you don't exactly make a habit of calling."

Ainslie glanced at James, widening her eyes and gritting her teeth. He lightly jabbed her arm in silent encouragement.

"Well," she said, shoving James with her foot, "I just wanted to let you know Aidan and I got engaged."

An uncharacteristically joyful sound came through the speaker and Ainslie nearly dropped the phone. She listened as her mother relayed the news to her father, who grumbled something inaudible.

"Your father says congratulations. I assume that means you're finally going to stop skating, then?"

"Um, yeah." Ainslie sighed sadly.

James cocked his head.

"Honestly, it's well overdue," Meredith said. "It was a great hobby, but it's time you grow up and live your life."

"Yes," Ainslie said through gritted teeth as she looked up at James again, "skating is a *great hobby*."

James pulled a face.

Ainslie struggled through the rest of the call before hanging up and dramatically sinking back in the lounge.

"I think she's happier about me not skating anymore than she is about me getting married." She sighed.

James winced. "I'm sorry."

"Forget it." She leaned forwards and tossed her phone on the coffee table before flopping back on the lounge and wiping the sweat from her forehead.

She looked across at James, who had a bridal magazine open in his lap.

"Hey." She smiled. "Thanks for helping me out with all this. I know it must be pretty boring."

"Boring? No way. I love picking out" — he glanced down at the magazine — "charcuterie boards."

Ainslie laughed. "You're the best."

He smirked. "I try."

*　　*　　*

Helping Ainslie with wedding planning was bittersweet. James enjoyed it, but only because it meant they could spend more time together before she stopped skating. When he actually stopped and took a moment to think about it, the shine went off the apple.

The extra time he'd been spending with her was also taking its toll on Rachel's patience. She thought the idea of him being Ainslie's man of honour was ludicrous and completely inappropriate.

"I can't believe Aidan would even allow that! I'll tell you right now, if you and I were getting married, and you wanted her as your best woman, there wouldn't *be* a wedding!"

"Are you serious?"

"Dead serious! Aidan is supposed to be the most important man in her life, not you."

"So, you're not big on the whole guys and girls just being friends thing then?"

"Be friends! I don't care!" Rachel had thrown up her hands. "But there has to be a line somewhere. I'm just saying that if I were Aidan, I'd be uncomfortable."

He could feel his relationship with Rachel straining under the weight of his friendship with Ainslie, and the worst thing was, he didn't really care anymore.

CHAPTER 10

It was an annual tradition for the Randwick Ravens Roller Skating Club to host what they called a Gala Weekend the week before Christmas. On the Friday night, the Randy Ravens Derby League would play an exhibition bout. The inline hockey teams would play an in-house game on the Saturday afternoon, and then that evening, the artistic branch would hold their gala skate.

Artistic skaters were invited to perform their own original routines to music of their choice. It was a holiday treat amid the madness of preparing for the competition season. Jaz had prepared a high-energy hip-hop routine. Lucy had an emotional, lyrical piece planned. Ainslie and James had managed to find a few spare moments in their busy training schedule to prepare a fun little number that was completely different from anything they'd normally do. It was cheesy and ridiculous, but they thought it would be funny to skate to the old Christmas classic "Baby It's Cold Outside". Ironically, of course, because the weather forecast for the day of the gala skate was forty-one degrees.

"Is Aidan coming tonight?" Jaz asked Ainslie as they got ready in the change room.

Ainslie put on a pair of earrings that looked like little Christmas presents. "He said he was."

"He's going to *love* your performance," Lucy said, her voice thick with sarcasm.

"What's that supposed to mean?"

Lucy raised an eyebrow. " 'Baby It's Cold Outside'?"

"What?"

"You know," Jaz said, "your normal programs are choreographed by Sandra, so you have no choice if she makes you do flirty shit. But *you* choreographed this one yourselves, and you *still* filled it with flirty shit."

"It's a joke! It's funny!"

"Yes, I'm sure Aidan will think it's hilarious," Lucy replied dryly.

Ainslie ignored the comment and tied a big red bow around her ponytail. So maybe the routine was a bit flirty, and maybe Ainslie enjoyed it just a little bit more than she should have, but it was *absolutely* tongue in cheek, considering it was, in fact, blisteringly *hot* outside. She primped her hair one last time, smacked her red lips together and flounced out to get her skates on.

Sometimes it was fun to pretend, just for an evening.

* * *

James could feel the temperature in the rink drop when Aidan walked in. The guy had the uncanny ability to command an entire room upon entry, and James had to admit, he was intimidating. He was clad in a grey suit and looked like he'd just finished work. He had his phone glued to his ear and was sharing strong words with whomever was unfortunate enough to be on the other end of the call.

As if on cue, the moment Aidan walked past the corridor that led to the change rooms, Ainslie emerged in her little red swing dress. James couldn't help but smile at how adorable she looked with her copper hair swept up into a ponytail and fixed in place with a comically oversized red bow. He watched as she quickened her pace, her short legs working overtime, trying to catch up with Aidan. She grabbed him around the waist and beamed up at him, but he threw her a courtesy wave and swatted her away, returning to his phone call. Ainslie's face fell. She marched past Aidan, thumping her skate bag down where James and Rachel were sitting.

"You look so cute, Ainslie," Rachel said with a smile.

"Thanks," Ainslie replied curtly.

"I'm looking forward to seeing you skate," Rachel added.

Ainslie looked over at her fiancé, who was still standing at the bottom of the grandstand on his phone, his voice now just below a yell.

"I'm glad someone is. I knew I shouldn't have invited him. Work is flat out for him at the moment."

"Too flat out to take two hours to watch his future wife perform?" James asked, shooting a judgemental look in Aidan's direction.

"Never mind," Rachel said, patting the grandstand beside her. "Here, sit with us. He can join us when he's done."

James had to wonder if Rachel had become more sympathetic towards Ainslie ever since he'd started to become distant himself. The thought nauseated him.

Aidan finally shoved his phone in his pocket and joined the group on the grandstand.

"Sorry, babe. I have court first thing on Monday morning, and my client is being a real piece of work."

"That was your *client* you were speaking to?" James blurted out. He immediately regretted it.

Aidan shot daggers at him. "Mate, what business is it of yours?"

Ainslie had busied herself with lacing up her skates and ignored the brief altercation. When she was done, she climbed down the grandstand. Aidan pecked her on the lips and patted her on the backside as she passed him.

"We should get warmed up." She glanced at James before flying down the side of the rink towards the warm-up area, far away from any prying eyes.

"You all right, Goose?" James asked, rolling into the warm-up area behind her.

Ainslie nodded silently, leg up on the barrier as she pushed into a gentle stretch.

"You're not, are you," he said, his voice flat.

"I just get so *irritated* sometimes." She grunted, reaching further into the stretch. "I was looking forward to tonight. I *always* look forward to bringing Aidan to things like this because I think maybe, *just maybe*, this will be the time he actually appreciates what I do. Maybe he'll be so impressed and amazed by my skating — by *our* skating — that he'll wake up to the whole thing and ..."

"Ains —"

"Why is it okay for me to come second to his work," she said, swapping legs, "but it's not okay for him to come second to my skating? He's probably gonna sit there the whole time, glued to his phone —"

"Ains," James said, "don't let yourself get upset now. We have a performance to give. Don't perform for him. Don't perform for me. Perform for yourself!"

She blinked up at him, and after a moment, she pursed her lips.

"You're right, Sunderland." She put her foot back on the floor.

"I'm always right." He smirked, raising his hands.

"Let's do this." She slapped her hands against his.

He caught them and squeezed them tightly. "That's the spirit!"

*   *   *

The pair skated a few laps in the warm-up area and practised some of their more challenging elements until Sandra's husband's voice came booming over the sound system.

"Welcome to the 2019 Randwick Ravens Artistic Gala," Tim said. "The performances will commence shortly. Please take your seats."

James and Ainslie weren't due to skate until the end of the evening, so they sat together in the skater's area, watching and cheering for their friends. Jaz's performance was a crowd-pleaser. Ainslie had been so focused on her own training, she hadn't even noticed how much Jaz had improved since she'd last watched her. Lucy's performance had the audience sitting in rapt silence. She always had a way of skating with such pure and raw emotion that anyone who watched her had no choice but to be moved. Ainslie didn't know many other skaters with that same je ne sais quoi.

Every so often, Ainslie cast her eye to where Aidan and Rachel were sitting. Rachel was transfixed on the skating, smiling and clapping along. Aidan looked bored out of his mind. Occasionally, he would ignore the performances altogether and stare at his phone.

Skate for yourself.

Ainslie repeated the mantra over in her head until James took her hand and stood.

"We're up," he whispered.

"Our final skaters for the evening," Tim said over the PA system, "are two of the strongest and most successful skaters in Australian artistic history. Individually, they're both amazing, but together, they're unparalleled."

Ainslie blushed the colour of her dress and glanced over at Aidan, who was, much to her relief, actually paying attention.

"They've been skating together for nearly twenty years and have countless national titles under their belts. They're currently ranked fourth in the world, an achievement no Australian skater has come close to in over three decades.

"Please welcome the incomparable Ainslie Wynter and James Sunderland."

*　　*　　*

They skated their program to perfection, telling the story of the song, flirty wordless banter bouncing between them. Their footwork was complex but looked effortless, and their daring lifts and throws had the audience cheering.

The music ended and they fell into their final position, James on one knee, Ainslie perched on his lap, the two of them cheek to cheek. It was corny as anything, but the crowd loved it. After a few moments, they rose and bowed to the audience, then exited the floor.

Tim thanked them and called the event to a close before playing JoJo's "Leave (Get Out)" to facetiously give the audience a hint to vacate the building. Ainslie let go of James's hand and flew off, retreating into the warm-up area.

"Ains!" James called, rolling after her.

Ainslie was sitting in a heap against the wall, aggressively unlacing her skates. She pulled one skate off her foot and flung it across the floor. James skated to the stray boot and collected it, just in time for her to fling the second one.

"Ainslie!" he said in a harsh tone, collecting her other skate. "What the *hell* is going on?"

"You didn't see?"

"See what?" He was genuinely flabbergasted.

"See *him*!" She spat out the words. "Sitting on his *fucking* phone! I don't even know if he watched any of it!"

James frowned and skated over to her, sliding down the wall to sit by her side. He didn't say anything. He just sat there while she sulked quietly.

"Who am I kidding?" She found his hand and mindlessly laced her fingers between his. "He's never gonna appreciate this part of me."

James felt his heart lurch in his chest when she held his hand. They'd just been holding hands out on the floor, but this was different.

Ainslie rested her head on his shoulder and spoke in a tiny voice. "What am I doing with my life, James?"

"What you love? What makes you happy?"

"Yeah, but my priorities are all wrong, aren't they?"

"What do you mean?"

"James, I'm a twenty-four-year-old woman dressed like a vaguely sexy Christmas elf with a bow the size of Queensland and no qualifications in anything except roller skating. I'm a university dropout, my parents are disappointed in me, and I'm engaged to a successful guy who I don't have any time for because my life is consumed by a sport that nobody's ever even heard of." She swatted away a stray tear in frustration. "I need to get my shit together, dude."

James was sure he felt his heart break in two. It was the inevitable moment. He'd seen it happen to every skating friend they'd ever had who'd retired to move on with their lives. The friends they'd promised to stay in touch with but never did. He knew it would happen to someone in his inner circle eventually, and given Ainslie's relationship status, he'd figured she would be the first to go. But he'd always held out hope that maybe things wouldn't change.

He wasn't ready for it to be over, but he didn't get a say in it. She was done, and this was it for them.

One more year.

"I think you should go, catch up with Aidan," he said finally, reluctantly untangling their hands.

They stood. Without skates, Ainslie was even shorter than him than usual.

"That was a great skate we just had," he said with a small smile. "Good job, Goose."

He patronisingly wiggled her giant bow, and she batted him away with a giggle. Then she wrapped her arms around his middle and held him. He squeezed her to his body, wishing he could stay there forever.

"Thanks for being my best friend," she mumbled into his chest.

"Yeah, well, I mean, your parents stopped paying me to hang out with you like ten years ago, but I thought I'd stick around." He laughed. "You kinda grew on me."

She socked him in the arm. "Way to ruin a nice moment."

"Any time."

*　　*　　*

They headed back out to the grandstand, James rolling along, Ainslie padding across the carpet in her socks. Rachel was beaming at them.

"You guys did so well!" She clapped. "I loved it!"

"What did you think?" Ainslie asked Aidan.

He smiled. Ainslie wasn't sure she bought it.

"It was so good, babe!" He kissed her on the head.

"You weren't on your phone the whole time, were you?" Ainslie raised an eyebrow. "Because I noticed when we were finished, you seemed distracted."

"Babe, I saw the whole thing! My client kept calling me the entire time. Literally, the second you finished, I had to answer. But I swear, I saw it all."

He took her hands and pulled her into a hug. Ainslie smiled, but his embrace didn't feel quite the same anymore.

CHAPTER 11

Ainslie lay in her bed on Christmas morning, staring at her ceiling and putting off getting up for as long as possible. Aidan had planned to pick her up around eleven, and she could hardly say she was looking forward to it. She would be far more in her element having her usual, simple Christmas with the Bannister siblings.

Ever since Jaz and her brother, Chris, first stumbled into Ainslie's life five years ago, it had become a tradition for them to spend Christmas together. The girls, in particular, always leaned on each other over the holidays (since James and Lucy would always be off celebrating with their *functional* families).

While Ainslie didn't have much to do with her parents, they at least acknowledged her existence. Jaz's situation was a completely different story. Jaz had always had a pretty tumultuous relationship with her parents, but when they found out she was a lesbian, it was all over. They told her they would've preferred it if she'd told them she had cancer or something because it would have been "easier to explain" to their friends. Jaz was out of their lives the next day, and Chris followed her right out the door.

This year, however, Aidan had insisted Ainslie join him at his parent's house instead. She'd only met Aidan's parents once before, and they were just as intimidating as she'd expected a couple of upper-class multimillionaires to be.

Aidan's father, Jacob Corbin, was a high-profile solicitor who owned the firm at which Aidan worked. He loved to start arguments about anything and everything, and playing devil's advocate was his favourite pastime.

Aidan's mother, Catherine Corbin, was a former supermodel who'd graced the covers of every big Australian magazine and had even made an international splash back in the eighties.

Aidan also had three younger siblings, Bradley, Isabel and Everley, who were twenty-five, twenty-two and nineteen, respectively. Everley was a sweet girl, albeit very spoilt. And Bradley was virtually a carbon copy of Aidan, just slightly shorter and less argumentative, and he mostly kept to himself.

But Isabel was awful. She was snooty and selfish and made absolutely no attempt to connect with Ainslie. When they'd first met, Isabel had looked Ainslie up and down before making a passive aggressive comment about her outfit. Then she had ignored her for the rest of the afternoon.

Ainslie massaged her temples. Just the thought of Isabel was enough to bring on a headache. Then she heard her front door creak open.

"Merry Christmas!" Jaz's shrill voice rang through the apartment.

That certainly wasn't going to help the headache.

Chris must have arrived, so Ainslie hauled herself out of bed reluctantly, threw on some socially acceptable clothes and trudged out to the living room.

"Merry Christmas!" Jaz sang again, running at Ainslie and scooping her into a hug.

Ainslie grunted as Jaz knocked the wind out of her. Chris folded the two of them up in a group hug, ruffling his sister's hair with his fist.

"Ugh! No!" Ainslie groaned. "It's way too hot for this much physical contact!"

"I can't believe you're leaving us on Christmas." Jaz pouted as she let Ainslie go and batted Chris away.

"You what?" Chris raised an eyebrow. "You deserting us on Christmas, Wynter?"

"Sure am, *Bannister*. I'm an engaged woman now."

Jaz let out a loud gasp. "We're never gonna have another Christmas together! You'll be married next year!" She pulled a face, and Ainslie rolled her eyes.

"Married, Jaz. Not dead."

"Might as well be."

"Well." Chris smacked his hands together and changed the subject. "Breakfast? I bought stuff for pancakes."

"The shaker-bottle kind?" Jaz asked before turning to Ainslie. "Because I wouldn't trust him in our kitchen with much more."

"Pfft. Coming from the girl who can't even hard-boil an egg."

Jaz punched him in the shoulder.

Ainslie sighed to herself before moving into the kitchen to warm up the coffee machine. *This* was the Christmas she wanted, not the afternoon of hobnobbing she was in for.

*   *   *

Chris placed a plate of steaming hot pancakes (the shaker-bottle kind) in the middle of the table and arranged an array of toppings around it. The girls took their seats and wasted no time piling their plates.

"Jason said you and James are retiring after next year," Chris said, stabbing a couple of pancakes with his fork and flopping them onto his plate.

Chris was good mates with James's brother, Jason, through hockey, so of course news of Ainslie's impending retirement had spread already.

Ainslie dropped her head and focused on pouring maple syrup over her stack. "Yep."

"That's a right shame. I always enjoyed watching you two skate. You can always make a comeback in a few years, though, yeah? People do that all the time."

Ainslie shook her head. "I don't really see that happening to be honest. I think once I'm out, I'm out."

"Can we talk about something else? This is way too depressing." Jaz frowned, aggressively squeezing the juice of half a lemon onto her pancakes. "It's bad enough you're retiring from skating, but I'm only just now realising what that means for everything else. I'm not gonna see you anymore."

"What are you talking about?"

"Think about all the skating friends we've had over the years. When they retired, have we ever seen them again?"

"Jaz, you aren't just my *skating* friend; you're one of my *best* friends, and I'm not gonna disappear off the face of the planet just because I get married. I'll probably be living twenty minutes across the city at Aidan's place."

Jaz's frown dissipated a little. "I suppose."

Ainslie reached across the table and squeezed Jaz's arm.

"We're basically family, Jazzy. You're like my little sister."

Chris reached over and squeezed Jaz's other arm.

"You're like my little sister, too." He smirked, and Jaz punched him again.

The rest of the morning passed in a blur, and Ainslie only grew more nervous about her Corbin Family Christmas.

*   *   *

As Ainslie curled her hair in the bathroom, her phone vibrated on the vanity.

Merry Christmas Goose! Hope you have a great day. Please try not to kill Isabel. I can't afford to bail you out.

She smiled and messaged James back.

Merry Christmas! Hope you have an awesome day too. Say hi to ur mum for me :) PS. I think Aidan could probably afford my bail.

I don't think he'd bail you out if you killed his sister.

You've never met Isabel :'D

Ainslie pursed her lips and sent another text.

And tell Jason and Rachel Merry Christmas from me too.

The response came back almost instantly.

Will do. But Rachel's not with us this year.

Ainslie frowned.
Well, that *certainly doesn't sound bad at all.*

CHAPTER 12

James wasn't at all surprised that the first words out of his mother's mouth when he showed up on her doorstep alone were, "Where's Rachel?"

Against his better judgement, he'd given Rachel a terrible excuse to get out of bringing her home for Christmas. He'd blamed his mother. He'd said she'd wanted this year to be just her and her sons. It was so pathetic, James couldn't imagine Rachel had actually believed him.

"Rachel couldn't make it," he said, lying to his mother's face.

"That's too bad." She pursed her lips before pulling him into a hug. "Come here, you. I've missed you like crazy!"

Once upon a time, Erica Sunderland had been part of the furniture in the skating community. She had been for years. But after her husband, Michael, died, she withdrew, not only from skating but also from almost everything. Michael's death had been sudden and traumatic, and even now, six years later, it haunted her from time to time.

Michael had been up a ladder, hanging Christmas lights on the roof, and he had fallen and hit his head. At first, he'd seemed all right, although Erica had suggested he get himself checked out by a doctor. He'd insisted he didn't need to, but the following morning when Erica woke up, he was lying beside her, already gone.

Erica blamed herself for not making him go to the hospital, and she'd been pretty reclusive ever since. She'd sought counselling and was working through her trauma, but she didn't really like to be too far away from home. She did, however, follow James's skating career religiously — via Rosa Charis, of course — and she never missed watching a competition if it was live streamed.

Despite James living in the inner city and Erica out in the suburbs in Campbellmead, James was actually quite close with his mother. But there was still one important thing he'd neglected to mention. The impending death of his skating career.

Jason turned up late, which was par for the course for him. As soon as he arrived, Erica put both him and James to work in her kitchen production line. James was in charge of peeling and chopping vegetables, as it was the task he was least likely to mess up. Jason prepared his famous Christmas pavlova, which he'd made every year without fail since he was fifteen.

"So, how's training going, James?" Erica asked, pulling the head off a king prawn.

"It's good," he said simply.

And it was, despite the melancholy hanging over it.

"I was actually thinking, maybe next year I should come to a competition. Maybe States," she added, "so I can finally watch you guys perform live again. It's been far too long."

"Well, if you want to, you should. Because it'll be the last chance you get."

Erica looked up. "What do you mean?"

"Next year's our last year competing."

Erica nearly dropped the prawn she was holding. "Why?"

"Ainslie's retiring." James emphasised the words with an aggressive chop of a sweet potato.

He hadn't meant for that to sound as bitter as it did.

"Why? Is she all right?"

"She's fine," James replied with another chop. "She's getting married."

"I bet you're thrilled about that." Jason smirked, whisking his egg whites.

"Shut up, Jason."

Erica shot Jason a look of warning before turning back to James. "So, you two can't keep skating ... why?"

"Because her husband-to-be won't let her." James dumped the chopped sweet potatoes into a bowl.

"Well, that's a shame." Erica sighed. "I miss Ainslie. Why don't you ever bring her down to visit?"

"She's not my girlfriend, Mum."

"Yeah, you wish," Jason muttered.

"Fuck off, Jason!"

"Hey! Watch the language!" Erica said. "And Jason, will you cut it out?"

As a teenager, Jason had always speculated that James had a thing for Ainslie, and he loved to rib him about it. It didn't help that "Jameslie" had always been a bit of a running gag in the Sunderland household. James and Ainslie had spent so much time together growing up, Erica used to joke about her being his future wife. But James had always had a feeling that behind all the jokes, his mother secretly hoped they would end up together.

"Is there ...," Erica said slowly, "anyone else you could skate with?"

"I mean, maybe?" James replied, popping a piece of carrot in his mouth. "But I don't know ... you skate with someone for nearly twenty years ... I don't think it'd be the same with someone else."

"Can't you just skate by yourself?" Jason asked, finally taking the conversation seriously.

"Yeah, I guess I could," James replied half-heartedly, "but I don't really enjoy skating by myself. Part of what makes it great is sharing it with a friend, you know?"

"So, you're going to retire too?" Erica looked disappointed.

"From *competing*, yeah. I still think I'd like to stay involved in *some* way, like coaching or something. I mean, Ainslie's getting her shit together. Maybe it's time I get mine together, too."

"So, do you think you might ... settle down with Rachel?"

"I don't think so," James said a little too quickly.

"Why not?"

"I don't know. I just don't think we're right for each other. We don't click as well as …" James caught himself. "As well as we should."

*   *   *

After lunch, James found himself standing in his childhood bedroom. Erica had practically kept it as a shrine to his skating career. Every single medal and trophy was still on display, coated in a thick layer of dust but still standing proud.

On the wall over his bed was a series of photos. There was one of him at about six years of age in his brand-new black artistic skates, which looked a little too big for him. He was beaming from ear to ear and proudly clutching a Learn to Skate graduation certificate to his chest. To the right of him was a tiny Lucy, wearing overalls and a timid smile, two black braids framing her moon face. To the left of him was an even tinier Ainslie. She was standing on her toe stops, stretching herself up as far as she could, trying to make herself as tall as her friends. She was wearing a huge, cheesy grin, showing off the gap where her two front teeth were missing. The trio hadn't really changed all that much, except James wasn't as grubby, Lucy was thinner, and Ainslie had a full set of teeth.

Another photo showed him and Ainslie, no older than twelve, standing on the top of the podium at the Australian Championships. That was their first gold medal on the national stage. James squinted at himself.

God, I was a gawky child.

The largest photo on the wall, and the one holding pride of place, was from six years ago. It was a candid shot the official photographer had captured just after their long program at Worlds that year. It was the first time they'd placed in the top ten. They were sitting on the kiss and cry lounge, Sandra in the middle with a hand on each of their knees. The photographer had snapped it the moment their ranking had been displayed on the screen in front of them. Ainslie's face was priceless. Her mouth was open in an ecstatic smile and her eyes were like saucers. James was looking across at her, his face lit up like the sun. He could see it written all over him.

Even then, he was so in love with her.

Of course, they'd always *loved* each other, but he always figured it was just a platonic kind of love. Perhaps it had been at one point, and obviously it still was on Ainslie's end. Apparently, for the last several years at least, he'd just done a stellar job of fooling himself into believing he only loved her like a friend.

James thought back to the moment in Sandra's office when he had first caught a glimpse of the obnoxiously large diamond ring on Ainslie's left hand, which thankfully she had been removing for training. In that moment, it had sunk in that she was going to spend the rest of her life with someone. And that someone wasn't him. All his animosity towards Aidan made more sense now.

A knock at his door startled him.

"Hey." Jason poked his head inside the room. "Sorry for giving you shit before."

"Yeah, it's fine."

Jason looked between his brother and the photo he was mourning over.

"Dude ..." He sighed. "You actually *are* in love with her, aren't you?"

James didn't see any point in denying it to Jason. "I just don't know how *not* to be."

Jason patted him on the back. "Time, my friend. Time is the only thing that's gonna help you. And distance, maybe."

Distance. The word stabbed him in the heart.

"Maybe retiring is the best thing for you. Can you imagine still skating with her when she has a husband? Do you know how shit that would be?"

James winced. "It'd be a fucking nightmare."

He looked back at the photo and sighed. Maybe Jason was right. The team of Ainslie *Corbin* and James Sunderland didn't quite have the same ring to it.

CHAPTER 13

Ainslie's palms were sweating as she stood in the shadow of the offensively large waterfront mansion in Vaucluse that the Corbin's called home. She'd been there before, but now that she was marrying into the family, somehow it seemed all the more intimidating. It didn't impress her as it probably should have. All it did was remind her just how out of place she was.

When she and Aidan were alone together, she could almost forget that he was wildly out of her league, but here, under the gaze of this massive home, all she could think about was the fact that she had about three hundred dollars to her name.

Of course, the building itself was nowhere near as terrifying as the people who were inside waiting for them. Ainslie wondered if the Corbins had some heiress or socialite earmarked as Aidan's bride. How disappointed they'd be when he tells them he will be marrying a roller skating barista.

She wiped her sweaty hands on her dress, and they headed towards the house.

Ainslie nervously wobbled on her high heels as she braved the steps up to the front door. Ironic. She could withstand the pressure of a World Championships and land triple jumps on roller skates, but the idea of Christmas with the Corbins was enough to turn her legs to jelly. She clung to Aidan's arm in an attempt to retain her balance.

They were met at the door by Catherine and her virtually immobilised forehead.

"Darlings!" She beamed at them with a blinding, porcelain smile and pulled them both into an embrace. "It's so wonderful to see you both!"

Her voice was shrill, and her mouth was way too close to Ainslie's ear when she spoke. She also smelled vaguely like alcohol already. Ainslie winced before pulling away and plastering a smile on her face.

Catherine led them through the double doors and into the foyer. The marble floor was so shiny, Ainslie couldn't help but wonder what it would be like to skate on. A modern and slightly abstract chandelier hung above their heads, the sun reflecting off it and scattering flecks of light around the place. The furniture was stark white, but not like the lacquered, chipboard junk that graced Ainslie's apartment.

Ainslie looked to her left, glancing into the formal living room, which was just as pristine as the foyer. The very idea of sitting on the immaculate settee in there was enough for Ainslie's palms to start sweating again. The only things breaking up the white were a glossy black grand piano in the corner and the largest Christmas tree Ainslie had ever seen inside a house.

"Aidan!"

Ainslie snapped back into reality as Everley came running down one of the two sweeping staircases that bracketed the foyer. She threw herself into her brother's arms, and he squeezed her tight. Aidan didn't visit his family home much. It wasn't that he didn't get on well with his parents. It was just that he was usually too busy. And when *he* was free, *they* were too busy.

He wasn't especially close with his siblings, but Everley was his not-so-secret favourite and always had been. She might have been the baby of the family, but that didn't mean she was any less accomplished than her older siblings. She'd seen more of the world than Ainslie ever hoped to, she used words Ainslie had never heard before, she was fluent in French and Spanish, and she played the piano like a virtuoso. She'd even been awarded a highly contested academic scholarship that was paying for her degree in fine arts (which sort of rubbed Ainslie the wrong way, considering the Corbins *hardly* needed the financial assistance).

And even though Everley was six years younger than her, Ainslie still found the young woman intimidating. But she was by far the least intimidating Corbin. Of course, being a Corbin meant she was completely out of touch with the majority of society, but somehow, she still managed to be endearing.

The same could not be said of Isabel, who'd just appeared on the first-floor landing. She gave Ainslie a visual once-over before sauntering down the stairs. Isabel was tall and dark-haired like Aidan and probably the most beautiful girl Ainslie had ever met. But she had a permanent scowl fixed on her face, and when she looked at Ainslie, it only deepened. She sashayed over to Aidan, completely ignoring Ainslie, and gave him a hug.

Seconds later, the doorbell rang. Catherine answered it, welcoming Bradley and his girlfriend inside. Her name was Imogen and she looked exactly like the kind of person Ainslie expected a Corbin to marry. Beautiful, well spoken, and by all accounts, filthy rich. Isabel squealed with delight and rushed to hug her. Clearly, Imogen had passed her test.

"Babe!" Isabel said. "It's so good to see you again! Oh, my God, I haven't seen you since that night at Tyler's!"

"Oh, my God, that was wild."

"We have to do it again soon."

Ainslie stood there in awkward silence, nervously shifting her weight from one foot to the other, while the two girls prattled on about some club they'd been to. She squeezed Aidan's hand a little tighter.

"Oh, it's so wonderful to have all my babies under one roof." Catherine gracefully held out her long, thin arms, gesturing at her brood.

"Where's Dad?" Aidan asked.

"Your father's out on the deck having a cigar," Catherine replied, her eyes narrowing ever so slightly, giving away only the smallest hint of disdain on her otherwise emotionless mask of a face.

She led them through the foyer and into the huge open-plan kitchen and casual dining area, the sterile, white motif continuing through the house. Glass bi-fold doors, which had all been pushed open, led out onto a deck that was larger than Ainslie's entire apartment. Beyond the deck was an immaculately landscaped garden, and beyond *that* was Sydney Harbour. Ainslie had to stop herself from audibly gasping when she saw the view. She'd forgotten just how picture perfect it was. Jacob Corbin laid his cigar in a crystal ashtray and stood, turning towards the house to greet his family at last.

Jacob looked exactly how Ainslie imagined Aidan would look in thirty years. He was tall (like all the Corbins) and still in fantastic shape. He had a strong jaw and salt-and-pepper hair, which was styled to within an inch of its life. He was wearing grey suit pants and a white shirt with the top few buttons open, the sleeves rolled up to his elbows. He swaggered into the house like the powerful patriarch he clearly was. Ainslie could tell where Aidan got his air of confidence from, though Jacob's was far more practised than his son's. While Aidan would still, on occasion, let his insecurities slip out, Jacob gave off the impression that he knew he was the most important person in the room and he didn't need to prove it to anyone.

He held out his hand to Aidan. "Son."

Aidan shook it as if they were making a business deal. "How you been, boss?"

Ainslie recoiled slightly at the term. Aidan's voice sounded a little less cocky than usual, and his demeanour had shifted to match. Ainslie hadn't spent a whole lot of time around Jacob Corbin, but clearly, he was the only person in the world who intimidated Aidan.

Jacob went around, shaking the hands of the men and kissing the cheeks of the women. Ainslie bristled when he leaned in to greet her. The smell of his aftershave mixed with cigar smoke was overpowering, and she wasn't sure, but she thought he lingered a little too long.

Catherine clapped her hands together once and announced that the cook had lunch ready. She led them all back through the hall and into the formal dining room, which sat just off the living room that Ainslie had glimpsed through the foyer. The long, glass table could easily seat twenty people, and it was laden with Christmas lunch. There were dishes full of colourful, roasted vegetables and every meat under the sun. There were trays of prawns and calamari and at least six different salads. The cook had even prepared a little seitan roast for Ainslie and Imogen (who also turned out to be a vegetarian).

As the family piled their plates high, Ainslie tried to keep a low profile. She wasn't sure when Aidan was planning on making the announcement, and her stomach was so full of butterflies, she barely had room for the meal. She'd taken off her ring and hidden it in her purse so she didn't give the game away early.

Jacob and Aidan were discussing a class action the firm was trying to secure. Catherine had already downed her glass of red wine and was signalling to a servant for another, and Ainslie was pretty certain the face she was trying to pull at her husband was a scowl. Isabel and Imogen were again talking about what-ever had happened at Tyler's (whoever that was), and Bradley and Everley were arguing about something. Ainslie wasn't sure what, but it sounded as if Everley was winning.

When everyone decided they'd had enough to eat, a servant appeared seemingly out of nowhere and began clearing the table. Ainslie shook her head a little. She couldn't believe she was in a house that had *servants*.

Jacob leaned back in his chair and let out a contented sigh. "That was one hell of a meal."

Aidan suddenly cleared his throat, and Ainslie felt her entire body stiffen. She blindly groped for his hand under the table, relaxing only slightly when she found it.

"Everyone," he announced, his voice a little less confident than Ainslie was used to, "I thought today would be a good day, with the family all together, to share with you some very important news."

Jacob sat forwards, listening intently. Catherine finally put her wine glass down. Isabel was doing her best to look uninterested but clearly still wanted to be in on the action. All eyes were on Aidan, and by extension, Ainslie. Her chest was flushing red and she silently prayed Aidan wouldn't notice how much her hand was shaking, although he must have because he gave it a gentle squeeze.

"I'm happy to announce," he said, far too slowly for Ainslie's nerves, "that Ainslie and I are engaged."

The room filled with gasps and squeals of joy. Catherine blinded everyone with her porcelain veneers, Everley was the source of the loudest squeal, sitting there, clapping like a seal, and Bradley gave Aidan a brotherly sock on the shoulder. Ainslie caught Isabel raising her eyebrows and pursing her lips, failing to disguise her opinion on the matter, while Imogen smiled politely. Jacob actually looked *proud*. Ainslie allowed her body to relax as she let out a long sigh of relief.

"Congratulations, son." Jacob raised his glass to them. "I wish you two all the happiness in the world."

*   *   *

The rest of the day went surprisingly well, much to Ainslie's relief. In the late afternoon, Catherine dragged her off to the living room to drink champagne and talk about the wedding. The woman had definitely had too much to drink, and just watching her sitting on that white settee with her champagne sloshing around in its flute was making Ainslie anxious. Catherine was rattling off names of designers and wedding planners and venues, all of which Ainslie knew would cost an absolute fortune. Suddenly she became very grateful for the champagne in her own hand.

Aidan, Bradley and Jacob had retreated to the back deck to drink old scotch together. Isabel and Imogen had made themselves scarce, and Everley joined Catherine and Ainslie in the living room, sitting at the piano to play Christmas songs.

Spending the day with the Corbins had really made the gravity of the situation sink in. *This* was going to be Ainslie's life soon. She was just a kid from

Campbellmead who made coffee for a living and couldn't afford to run the air conditioning during the summer. How the hell was she supposed to be a millionaire's wife?

Suddenly the word "wife" made her want to throw up, and she felt the seitan roast, mixed with the champagne, threaten to rise from her stomach. She'd performed in front of many audiences in her life — the crowds at Worlds had once been the most intimidating thing she'd ever faced — but this ...

Well, this was a whole new ball game.

CHAPTER 14

"See, that wasn't so bad," Aidan said as he threw his keys on the glossy console table near his front door.

His apartment resembled a slightly smaller version of his parent's house, just with a darker colour palette and various items of autographed rugby league memorabilia on the walls. Even though Ainslie had been there a million times, she was still nervous about touching anything. She sat down on his Italian leather lounge, taking in the view of the Opera House across the harbour. Once again, she had to stop herself from having a meltdown at the idea of this being her home soon. Aidan joined her on the lounge and handed her a glass of champagne.

"Cheers." He clinked his crystal flute against hers. "To you, my beautiful future wife."

Ainslie blushed and ignored the way her stomach lurched again at that word. "Cheers."

"I have something for you," he said, producing a little teal bag. "Saved the best for last."

Ainslie gave him a look as she took the gift. He'd already given her roses, chocolates, a designer handbag and a new dress earlier in the day.

She opened the little teal bag, and inside was that familiar, little teal box. She popped the box open and gasped when she saw it. A delicate gold necklace with a pendant in the shape of a roller skate on it.

"Oh, Aidan," she said, wrapping her arms around his neck. "I absolutely love it."

"This way, when you retire, you'll always have a little bit of skating with you."

Ainslie smiled. She'd also always have her Australian tracksuits, and her medals, and her memories … But she brushed it off. It was the thought that counted.

She handed him the necklace and turned her back to him, gathering her hair over one shoulder. He draped it around her neck and fastened the clasp.

"Perfect," he said, punctuating the word with a kiss on her shoulder.

He ran his hands up and down her arms and planted another kiss, just a little higher. Then he began trailing kisses all the way up her neck. A quiet moan escaped her, and she turned to face him. He captured her mouth with his.

"Merry Christmas, Aidan," she mumbled against his lips.

He silently scooped her up into his arms and carried her to his bedroom.

* * *

Aidan ran his hand over the slight curve of Ainslie's waist as she lay curled into his side. "So, I've been thinking about where we'll live once we get married."

Ainslie furrowed her brow and craned her neck to look at him. "We're not just gonna live here?"

"We could do," he said, playing with a lock of her hair. "But we couldn't stay here forever. What about when we start a family? It's no place for that."

Ainslie pursed her lips and propped herself up on her elbow. "Okay, I'll bite. What were you thinking?"

"Well," he said, lacing his fingers through hers and kissing her knuckles, "I was thinking, what if we had a bit of a sea change? We could get away from Sydney. Head south, get a gorgeous house in Brighton by the beach —"

"Melbourne?"

"Yeah, it's a great city. One of the most livable cities in the world. I think it would be a nice change for us. I could work from our Melbourne office."

Ainslie stiffened and withdrew her hand.

"And what about me?" she asked, her brow furrowing. "What would I do in Melbourne?"

"Once we're married, you won't have to work or anything. I'll be more than able to support us both."

"But I *like* working."

"Melbourne has cafés too, you know."

Ainslie was a little insulted, and it showed on her face.

"I don't mean it like that," Aidan said. "And if you decide you want to go back to university, you could do that in Melbourne, too."

"But my entire life is in Sydney. All my friends are in Sydney, my family is in Sydney —"

"And James is in Sydney." Aidan groaned under his breath.

Ainslie sat up, her face turning red. "What?"

"Well, you wouldn't want to be away from *him* now, would you?"

"Hey!" Ainslie pulled the sheet up, forming a barricade between them. "I didn't say anything about him. That was *you*, projecting. I don't particularly want to move away from *any* of my friends!"

"I have friends here too, Ainslie," Aidan said, his voice a little louder now. "But I want what's best for us and our marriage."

"I just don't understand how moving to Melbourne is what's best for our marriage!"

"Because if we were in Melbourne, we could start fresh." Aidan sat up too.

"Start fresh? So we meet new people together and only have mutual friends? I can't do anything on my own? Without your approval? I can't have a life outside our marriage?"

"Marriage is about being together."

"But it's not about isolating your spouse from everyone they know! Is that what this is about? Isolating me from my friends and family so you're all I have?"

"No, Ainslie —"

"Really? Because that sure is what it feels like!"

Ainslie climbed out of bed and began snatching items of her clothing off the floor.

"Why are you *really* so reluctant to leave Sydney, Ainslie? Honestly, is it because of him?"

Ainslie felt like pulling her hair out. She spun around to face him and let out a loud, exasperated groan.

"I can't keep having this fucking conversation with you! What is it, Aidan? Why are you so convinced I'd cheat on you?"

She wasn't sure she could take the moral high ground, considering the dreams she'd had. Or the feelings those dreams had evoked. But it wasn't like she had any intention of *acting* on those feelings.

He still hadn't answered her question.

"Well?"

But he just shook his head.

"I think I should go," Ainslie said at last, pulling the hem of her dress down around her thighs. "I'm gonna get a train home."

"You shouldn't get a train home alone this time of night."

Ainslie shot him a look over her shoulder. "I'll do what I like. We're not married yet."

*　　*　　*

Ainslie grumbled under her breath as she did the best she could to stomp along the footpath in her high heels. The night had grown chilly, and she shivered as she made her way to Gadigal Avenue from Green Square Station. Her hair was dishevelled by the wind that had whipped up, her lipstick had been smudged during the amorous encounter she'd had with Aidan moments before everything had turned to shit, and she was blinded by rage. And all she wanted to do was get home and sleep it off.

Out of the corner of her eye, she noticed a car slowing down beside her. Her heart started to race and she walked a little faster. She kept her eyes fixed ahead, her hands trembling as she silently prayed the car would move along. But it didn't. It just kept creeping along beside her. Her heart was now pounding in her ears, and goosebumps covered her skin. She was two seconds away from kicking off her shoes and making a run for it when she heard a voice.

"Ains?"

She knew that voice.

She spun towards the street, nearly falling off her heels. And she knew that car. The passenger window had been wound down, and James was peering at her from the driver's seat, his eyebrows knitted together in concern.

"What are you doing here?" Ainslie dipped down to look through the window. "I thought you were at your mum's place."

"I was, but I wanted to beat the Boxing Day traffic. What are *you* doing here? I thought you were at the Corbins."

Ainslie rolled her eyes. "Don't even get me started."

James frowned and unlocked the doors. Ainslie couldn't have been more grateful, and she wasted no time climbing into the passenger seat. She slammed the door shut, threw her head back on the headrest and heaved an exaggerated sigh.

"So," James said as he pulled away from the kerb, "what happened?"

"Would you believe another fight?"

"What was it about this time?"

"Strangely enough," she said, "not skating."

"That's a first."

"The day was actually okay!" she said, her voice unnaturally high. "His family were fine. They were *happy* for us. But then we went back to his place, and out of nowhere, he said when we're married, we should move to Melbourne."

James raised an eyebrow. "That's out of the blue."

"Yeah, I thought so too." Ainslie pushed her fingers into her hair and rested her elbow on the window. "He said he'd been thinking about it for a while. His dad's firm has an office in Melbourne. He said we should get a nice house there and start a family. I told him I didn't want to go, he got the shits, and ..."

She gazed out the window into the darkness.

"What?"

"He may not have brought up *skating*," she replied, "but he sure brought up *you*."

James pursed his lips and remained silent.

"He seemed pretty convinced that I didn't want to move to Melbourne because I didn't want to leave you." She sighed. "I mean, I *don't* want to leave you. I don't want to leave *any* of you guys."

"Hey," James said, glancing across at her, "do you wanna head home? Or do you wanna hang out for a bit? Because I don't really feel like heading straight to bed."

Ainslie glanced back at him. "Okay, I'm keen. Where do you want to go?"

"I have an idea."

*   *   *

James drove through the night, away from Ainslie's apartment. There was a park at the crest of a hill in Rose Bay that looked down over the rooftops, all the way out over the harbour. You could see the bridge from up there, but it was only a tiny little coathanger on the horizon. The two of them had stumbled upon the park several years earlier when Sandra and Tim had first moved to the area. They used to work out there before Sandra installed the gym at the rink.

Ainslie smiled as they climbed out of the car. "I almost forgot about this place."

It looked different at night. The lights of the city below and the moon beaming down from above cast an almost eerie glow across it, and as it was nearly midnight, they were the only ones there.

"Don't worry." James slammed the driver's door shut. "We don't have to do any push-ups."

They took a seat side by side on the swing set and gazed out over the city.

"So," Ainslie said eventually, "why didn't Rachel go with you to your mum's house? Are things okay with you guys?"

James dropped his head. "Actually, I've been trying to find the right time to end things."

Ainslie frowned. "When did this happen?"

James shrugged. "I don't know. It hasn't been rosy for a while. I just don't feel the same way about her as I used to."

Or as I do about you.

"What do you think happened?"

He glanced over and caught her profile in the moonlight. His heart ached. He knew exactly what had happened.

He shrugged again. "I don't know. Time goes on, things change. Eventually, you figure out who the most important people in your life are. Who you actually care about, and who's just there so you don't feel quite so lonely."

"You're only with Rachel because you don't want to be lonely?" She turned to look at him, and his gaze fell to his feet.

"Maybe." He kicked the dirt under his swing. "I don't know. I just don't think I can see myself spending the rest of my life with her. And I feel bad enough that I've led her on this long."

"When are you going to end it?"

"I wanted to wait until the new year." He sighed. "Didn't want to ruin Christmas."

"But then you'll just ruin Valentine's Day, and then her birthday, and then your anniversary." Ainslie shook her head. "There's never a good time to break someone's heart."

"Yeah, I know. I guess I'm just a coward."

Ainslie let out a warm laugh and began swinging a little. "You're not a coward. You're just a good person. You're caring and kind, and you don't want to hurt people."

James blushed. He was grateful it was dark.

"So, what are you going to do about this Melbourne thing?"

Ainslie sighed. "I don't know. I can ignore it and hope it goes away?"

James chuckled half-heartedly. "Yeah, that always works great."

She kicked up some dust as she slowed down her swing. "It's just … I feel like he's trying to isolate me so he can control me. Make it so he's all I have. Things would be so much easier if he wasn't so insecure about you and me being friends."

"People don't change easily, Goose. If he's insecure now, chances are he'll always be insecure. And sure, he can get rid of me if he likes, but I guarantee the second you make another friend who he deems takes up too much of your time, he's going to hate them, too."

Ainslie sighed heavily as she looked out over the city.

James followed her gaze, taking in the glittering view in front of them and doing his best to just enjoy her company and to not think too much about the fact that they were existing together on borrowed time. How many more moments like this would they have left?

James looked back at Ainslie, who was suppressing a yawn.

"Do you want me to take you home?"

Ainslie nodded, and the pair made their way slowly back to James's car.

*   *   *

On the drive back to her apartment, Ainslie closed her eyes, thinking about the day she'd had. After a while, she realised her time with James was the first time that day she'd actually felt completely relaxed. Being with James was just so easy. No drama, no walking on eggshells. Just company, comfort, familiarity. Just the two of them, together like peas in a pod.

She hadn't wanted to leave the park. She would have been more than happy to sit there with James forever. He'd completely and single-handedly redeemed her Christmas.

Being in Aidan's company and then in James's were polar opposite experiences, and that night — even if she knew she really shouldn't have — Ainslie had definitely preferred the latter.

"Hey," Ainslie said when they arrived at her building, "thanks for saving Christmas."

James smiled. "Not a problem."

She really didn't want to get out of the car.

"Have a good day tomorrow," she said.

"You too. Don't work too hard."

"Never."

"I might come by and get a coffee. When do you get off shift?"

"Two."

"Cool."

"Cool."

Ainslie couldn't shake the feeling that they were both stalling. As if they were waiting for something to happen, but they didn't know what. It didn't matter, anyway. Nothing was going to happen.

"Okay, goodnight." Ainslie opened the car door.

"Goodnight."

"Thanks again."

"You're welcome."

"Bye."

What am I doing?

"Merry Christmas, Ainslie," James said at last.

Ainslie smiled. "Merry Christmas, James."

*   *   *

When she finally collapsed into bed, she ran James's words over in her head.

Eventually, you figure out who the most important people in your life are. Who you actually care about, and who's just there so you don't feel quite so lonely.

She'd always been terrified of the idea of being alone, and she loved the feeling of being loved. Being loved, and having the odd argument, would have to be better than the alternative. And Aidan could offer her a comfortable life. Hell, more than just comfortable. *Extravagant* would be a better word for it. She'd never have to worry about her finances again.

But if she were to break it off with Aidan to see if she could have something with James, it would be a massive risk. What if it all went to hell? She wouldn't just lose her best friend, but her skating career would be ruined, too.

Hypotheticals didn't matter. James had never given her any indication that he liked her as anything more than a friend, anyway.

As she stared at her ceiling through the darkness, guilt gnawed away at her. She knew whose company she was missing, and it wasn't her fiancé's. She'd just argued with Aidan about there being nothing between her and James, but that night, it would have been so easy to slip up.

CHAPTER 15

James woke up on Boxing Day with his stomach in knots. He was conflicted. The night before had been so nice, but it had also been really weird, and even though he hadn't actually done anything, he felt incredibly guilty. Maybe it was the nostalgia from being in their old stomping ground. Maybe it was the fact they were both feeling a little sorry for themselves. But it had almost felt as if something could've happened between them. And he was ashamed to admit he wasn't sure he would've fought it if it had. The thought made him feel sick.

When he and Ainslie had been in the car, he'd had to remind himself who she was so he didn't instinctively kiss her goodnight. And unless he was reading the situation astonishingly incorrectly, it had almost seemed as if she'd felt the same way. It'd been too close for comfort, and he was starting to wonder if putting himself in any kind of vulnerable position with her was a mistake.

He reached over to his bedside table and retrieved his phone, unlocking it and opening his inbox. He stared at Ainslie's name on the screen and their previous messages. He chewed his lower lip, contemplating what to do. Eventually, he typed out a message.

> Hey. So sorry, got called into work. Won't be able to drop by. Have a good day.

He had to put a little space between them, for both their sake. A text came back almost immediately.

> K, no worries. Did you wanna go to the gym at some point?

He sighed.

> Not sure. Have to see. Got a few things to do.

> K. Let me know if you change ur mind. Ur coming to the NYE party right?

He'd forgotten all about the New Year's Eve party. For a minute, he contemplated not going. Aidan would be there. Aidan, plus James, plus copious amounts of alcohol … It didn't exactly sound like the recipe for a fun night. But seeing as he'd been at every single one of the girls' New Year's Eve parties for the last six years, he thought it might be more incriminating if he *didn't* show up. And he wasn't exactly thrilled by the idea of staying home while all his friends rung in the new year without him.

James was roused from his musings by the distant chime of the doorbell. He lifted his head off his pillow as if that would help him hear better. He couldn't hear any stirring from his housemates, so he threw on a shirt and went to answer it.

Rachel stood there, arms folded across her chest. Her usually full lips were pressed into a thin, straight line, and her dark eyes didn't look warm like they usually did. He was hit by a fresh pang of guilt when he saw her.

"Um, hi." He ran a shaky hand through his hair.

"Hi."

She didn't look angry. Or upset. She was wearing a poker face, and somehow that was worse.

There was an awkward moment of stillness between them before she blinked rapidly a few times, gave her head a little annoyed shake and said, "Well, can I come in?"

"Oh, yeah, sure. Come in."

Rachel brushed past him without so much as looking at him. She only went as far as the lounge and rested against it, looking as if she didn't want to get too comfortable.

"Do you want a drink or something?" James asked, just trying to fill the dead air.

"No," she said harshly. There was a beat of silence. "Thank you," she added, her voice a little softer.

James stood in front of her, looking sheepish.

"Look, I don't want to be here long." Rachel folded her arms. "If I don't say this now, I might change my mind, and I know deep down, I don't want to do that."

James looked at his feet and then back up at her eyes, signalling for her to proceed. He knew what was coming, anyway.

Rachel pursed her lips. "This isn't working."

James ruffled his hair ruefully, not sure what to do with his hands.

"You've been distant for months now, and Christmas was the last straw. I'm fed up with feeling like I come second. Second to skating, second to Ai—" She sighed. "No, this isn't about anyone except you. You and the fact that I don't think you love me anymore. Actually, I'm pretty certain you don't."

James heaved a sigh.

"Can you actually look me in the eye and tell me you still love me? Because I don't think you can."

James met her eyes and sighed. "I'm so sorry, Rachel."

She looked disappointed but unsurprised.

"I thought as much." She stood up straight and patted him on the chest. "I hope you find whatever it is you're looking for."

Then she walked towards the front door and slipped out of his house and out of his life.

James sighed and dropped his head. He was hardly surprised, but he still felt dejected. He'd wanted to end it anyway. It just so happened that Rachel jumped before she was pushed. His pride was a bit injured, but considering how he'd been treating her, he was kind of happy she got to have the upper hand at the end.

He trudged into the kitchen to make a coffee and then retreated to his room where he spent the rest of the day moping and ignoring messages from Ainslie. Mostly, she was just sending him memes. He figured she must've been bored on her break, but he wasn't exactly in the mood.

Eventually, she sent him an actual message.

Hey what are you doing tomorrow?

James groaned. The thought of seeing Ainslie, now that he was single and she wasn't, was extremely unappealing.

Got work. Sorry.

*　　*　　*

When James blew her off on Boxing Day, Ainslie just assumed he was busy, but now it had been three days since then, and he *still* hadn't contacted her. She was pissed. Christmas night had meant a lot to her, and now it seemed as if he wasn't even bothering to acknowledge her existence.

The other person she'd heard very little from was Aidan. She put that down to him being busy as well, and that was likely to be the case for him. They hadn't spoken in person since their argument on Christmas night, but at least they'd messaged back and forth a few times.

As if on cue, her phone vibrated in her apron pocket moments before she clocked on for her shift. She pulled out the phone and found herself feeling slightly disappointed that it was Aidan and not James.

We need to talk. I'll pick you up after work x

Ainslie huffed and shoved her phone back into her apron before taking her place at the coffee machine.

She spent her shift going through the motions. She didn't engage with any of her co-workers, and she was more brusque than usual with the customers. Two men had been living rent-free in her mind for some time, and at that moment, both of them were pissing her off.

Her mind kept drifting back to the park in Rose Bay, the moonlight in James's blue eyes and the way he'd looked at her in the car. Then she thought about Aidan and his plan to move them to Melbourne and how convinced she was that it was a thinly veiled attempt to force her into co-dependency. She thought about Aidan's text.

We need to talk.

Rarely did anything good ever come from a message like that, although he'd signed it with a kiss, so maybe it wasn't all bad.

As the day ticked on, the Sunday lunch rush served to take Ainslie's mind off her woes. She focused her attention on the seemingly endless list of coffee orders and on counting down the hours until she was able to get out of there and rest her aching feet. By 3 pm, she was so exhausted from having been so flat out that she'd almost completely forgotten that Aidan was picking her up. That was until she noticed him pulling into the car park.

On the rare occasion Aidan turned up to Ainslie's work, there was always a bit of commotion. His car alone gave everyone at her workplace reason to pause.

"Why the hell are you still working for me?" her boss had asked her one day as he greedily eyed the sleek, silver sports car slowly rolling into the car park. Ainslie had insisted that she still wanted to maintain some sense of independence.

Now more than ever.

Aidan didn't actually go into the café. Instead, he sat in his car until Ainslie finished her shift. She slid into the passenger seat, trying to avoid getting burnt coffee grounds all over the pristine leather. Aidan was smiling, which was a relief, although Ainslie thought she could see an uneasy look in his eyes.

"Hey." He leaned across the console and pecked her on the lips. "You smell amazing."

She raised an eyebrow. "I smell like coffee grounds."

"Mmm." He kissed her again. "My favourite."

He reached around the back of her head and slowly dragged the scrunchie out of her hair, letting it fall in waves. He twisted his hand in her locks and pulled her head gently towards his, kissing her deeper and harder. She let out a small moan as he gently pulled her hair, tilting her head back so his mouth could work its way along her jaw and down her neck.

Suddenly, she was acutely aware of the fact they were still in her work car park.

She managed to pull herself together enough to speak. "Aidan, this doesn't feel much like talking."

Aidan withdrew and kissed her lips once more. "You're right. Let's go for a drive."

*   *   *

They only drove a short distance from Ainslie's work, just over the other side of the motorway, in a similar direction to the one she'd driven with James on Christmas night. They drove down a wide, leafy street lined with old fig trees that reached across the road to touch each other, forming a canopy like a cathedral ceiling.

Aidan turned onto a narrower street, which snaked along the edges of Centennial Park. The street housed several grand old mansions. They were beautifully restored to what Ainslie imagined to be their original glory and were no doubt exorbitantly expensive. Ainslie had seen the homes every time she'd gone for a run around Centennial Park on particularly pleasant spring days. She'd always admired the houses and secretly fantasised about what it would be like to be able to afford one.

The homes looked out across the beautiful parklands and beyond towards the city skyline, and they were a hop, skip and a jump from the beaches.

Aidan pulled into a car space along the kerb.

Ainslie glanced at the houses and then at him. "So, what are we talking about?"

"What do you think?"

"Of what?"

"Of these," he said, gesturing at the homes.

"Of the houses? They're beautiful."

"How would you like to live in one of them?"

Her eyes grew wide and she had to force her jaw not to fall onto the floor of the car. "What?"

"Not right now," he added quickly with a laugh. "Don't worry, I haven't bought one. Yet."

"They're a bit of a commute to your Melbourne office, aren't they?" One of Ainslie's eyebrows quirked upwards.

Aidan hung his head and took a long breath.

"Ainslie, I don't care where we live, as long as it's together." He placed a hand on her leg and gave it a little squeeze. "This is a beautiful area, it's not far from your work, or from your friends. You could even still teach Learn to Skate if you wanted to. The rink's just down the road."

Now both of her eyebrows were raised. "Are you serious?"

"I'm serious." He smiled. "Really. I'm so sorry I spoiled Christmas. And sure, things will change when we get married, but I figured they don't have to change *that* much. Besides, I've always wondered what it would be like to live in one of these creepy old places."

Ainslie squealed and threw her arms around his neck, which was a bit of a struggle in the confines of the car.

"Thank you," she mumbled against his cheek. She couldn't believe how much lighter she felt. She pulled away slightly, hands still on his shoulders. "Also, did I really just hear you count the proximity of the rink as a plus?"

Aidan pursed his lips. "Yeah. I mean, when you retire, you won't have to be there every day, but I suppose it couldn't hurt for you to go to the odd session."

That was a huge step for Aidan. Even though the word "retire" kicked her in the gut, she was still grateful he was trying.

Ainslie cupped his cheek. "I love you."

"We could do it now if you like," he said, covering her hand with his. "Move in together, I mean. We're going to be married soon, anyway. Wouldn't you like us to have a place of our own? You could move into my apartment at first. And down the track, if any of these babies go on the market …"

Ainslie thought of Lucy and Jaz.

"I have a commitment to my lease for at least another six months. I wouldn't want to leave the girls high and dry. They'd need to either downsize or find another housemate and —"

"It's okay," he said, gently stroking his thumb along her bottom lip. "Don't stress. We can move in together whenever you like."

He replaced his thumb with his mouth, and Ainslie relaxed into his kiss. He rested his forehead against hers.

"I'm sorry," he said. "I really am. I hate that I upset you. And on Christmas Day. How can I make it up to you?"

Ainslie bit her lip and squeezed his leg. "I'm sure I can think of some fun ways."

Aidan chuckled. "Sounds good."

He gave her another quick kiss before starting the car and pulling out into the street.

Ainslie settled back into the passenger seat and breathed a deep, contented sigh. He wasn't a bad guy. Sure, he'd acted like a dick on Christmas, but he was clearly doing everything he could to make things right. And this was the first time he'd ever floated the idea of her still skating in some capacity once they were married. Maybe he was finally coming around.

They drove back to Aidan's apartment and picked up where they'd left off on Christmas night, *before* the Great Melbourne Fiasco. They fell into bed together, and Aidan came through on his promise to make it up to Ainslie.

"Are you coming to the New Year's Eve party?" she asked as they basked in the afterglow.

Given his social circle, Aidan always had many options when it came to ringing in the new year, but his attending the girls' rowdy flat party on Gadigal Avenue had been a tradition since they had first started dating.

"Of course," he said, running his hand up and down her back. "I'm going to have to be a little late, though."

She shifted her position, hooking one leg over him and lying on her front. She rested her chin on his chest so she could see his face.

"We landed that massive class action today," he said with a proud gleam in his eye.

"That's amazing!"

"And it's going to come with a very, very nice pay cheque," he said, squeezing her backside.

"Because you need a bigger pay cheque," she said, gesturing at the amazing view of the harbour outside his bedroom window.

"They should be paying me more, honestly," he replied, still mindlessly fondling her soft flesh, "seeing as they're expecting me to work late pretty much every day ... and it looks like I might have to work out of the Melbourne office a few days a week."

Ainslie smirked. "Maybe you shouldn't have just offered me a house in Randwick."

Aidan waved it off. "No, it'll be fine. It won't be forever. And it'll definitely be worth it for us in the long run."

Ainslie snuggled in beside him and rested her head on his chest. Ninety per cent of the burden she'd been carrying since Christmas had been lifted off her shoulders. The ten per cent that remained was the fact that her best friend had now ignored her for four days.

CHAPTER 16

By the time New Year's Eve rolled around, Ainslie hadn't heard from James in nearly a week. It was probably the longest time in their nearly twenty years of friendship they'd gone without speaking. She wasn't just annoyed anymore. She was worried. After Christmas night, he was the last person in the world she'd expected to ghost her.

She was sitting on the floor of her living room, feeling despondent, as she mindlessly inflated balloons with a helium canister. She tied one off and released it, letting it float to the ceiling. She was beginning to wonder if he would even show up for the party at all. It was usually all hands on deck for preparation, and on any other year, he'd have been there by now.

Lucy was cleaning the kitchen, preparing it for the onslaught of strangers who would no doubt be defiling it that evening. Jaz had picked up a trolley somewhere and was trafficking copious amounts of alcohol into the apartment.

"Where's James?" she asked, hauling another case of beer across the kitchen.

Ainslie shrugged. "Dunno."

"I would've thought he'd be here making himself useful," Lucy said, annoyed.

"You'd think so." Ainslie released another balloon and watched it bounce against the ceiling.

Lucy frowned and stopped what she was doing. "Did something happen?"

"Nope."

"You didn't have another fight, did you?" Jaz asked.

"Nope."

Jaz and Lucy shared an incredulous glance as Ainslie released another balloon.

"Well, anyway," Jaz said, heading back out the door, no doubt to buy more alcohol. "Tonight's gonna be wicked!"

Once Jaz was out of earshot, Lucy raised an eyebrow. "Sure. If by that you mean it's going to be loud and unbearable."

Lucy never was the biggest advocate for their parties. As the resident introvert, she'd made her opinion of them quite clear. The noise and the idea of having so many people in her house, touching all her things, sent her anxiety spiralling.

"We don't *have* to host them if you don't want to," Jaz had said once, reluctantly.

But Lucy had waved her off. "Oh, no. I'm not going to be the one responsible for ruining all the fun. Have all of you call me a buzzkill? Not a chance."

"I'm getting pissed tonight," Ainslie said, finally offering more than monosyllabic responses.

"Are you sure that's a good idea?" Lucy raised an eyebrow. "Last time that happened, it wasn't pretty. And I really don't want to have to put you to bed … again."

"This is my last New Year's Eve as an unmarried woman." Another balloon hit the ceiling. "I'm getting pissed."

Lucy held up her hands in surrender.

Ainslie neglected to mention the other reason she felt like drinking her woes away. She already missed James, and it had only been a week. That didn't bode well for her future as Mrs Corbin. Having a little too much alcohol was what she needed to forget all that. At least for one night.

The intercom buzzed and Ainslie jumped.

"Can you get that?" Lucy asked, elbow deep in the kitchen sink.

Ainslie climbed to her feet and trudged to the speaker.

"Hello?"

"Hey." It was James. "I brought snacks."

His voice evoked a fluttering in her stomach.

She buzzed him in. "Come on up."

Minutes later, he was sitting on the floor opposite her, helping inflate balloons and completely ignoring the elephant in the room. It was as if Christmas night had never even happened. Ainslie wanted to ask him why he'd been avoiding her all week, but she didn't want to talk about it in front of Lucy. Instead, she just sat there with him, inflating balloons in silence, until Jaz returned with more alcohol and began rattling off a list of people she'd invited. It sounded as if the entire skating club was coming.

"Jaz, if this place gets overrun with hockey players …," Lucy said threateningly.

Ainslie groaned. "If Jackson Hartley turns up, I'm gonna kick you off the lease."

"Ew, no! I didn't invite the guys' team. Well, except for Chris and Jason. Just the lasses." Jaz winked.

"Is Aidan coming?" James asked casually.

"Yes." Ainslie didn't look at him. "He'll be late, though. And I can't imagine he'll be partying too hard. He has to be at the airport at eight tomorrow morning to fly down to the Melbourne office."

"Jesus," Lucy said. "Does he ever stop?"

"No rest for the wicked," Jaz muttered, and Ainslie shot her a look of warning.

"Is Rachel coming?" Ainslie tried her best to match James's nonchalant tone.

"No."

Ainslie saw a suspicious glance pass between Jaz and Lucy. It must have been glaringly obvious that something was going on.

*　　*　　*

Music was thumping through the apartment, and the cheap disco light Jaz had bought online was throwing colourful shapes all over the walls. The small living area felt even smaller when at full capacity. James figured it would have to be a fire hazard. He leaned against the kitchen bench, people watching while sipping his beer half-heartedly.

There were a few artistic skaters he knew milling about, and some others were vaguely familiar. He assumed they must have either been derby players Jaz knew from her extremely brief foray into the sport several years ago or hockey players she knew through her brother. And there were a couple of faces he didn't recognise at all. Probably someone's co-workers. But the skating folk and the non-skating folk weren't really interacting.

How appropriate.

Jaz was trying to organise a beer pong match with a couple of the girls she'd invited. She seemed particularly interested in a short girl James didn't recognise. She was wearing a red flannel shirt and had her black, curly hair tied on the top of her head with a bandana.

Aidan had arrived well after ten, and by then, Ainslie was more than a little tipsy. James hadn't spoken to her since the guests had arrived. She'd been keeping to herself and seemed somewhat preoccupied with drinking, and as soon as Aidan arrived, all bets were off.

Now, she was sitting across Aidan's lap, holding her drink in one hand and using the other to play with his hair. She was completely inebriated and was alternating between whispering in his ear and kissing his neck. It might have been James's decision to put some distance between them, but he hadn't expected it to feel so shitty.

Lucy appeared beside him. "What's up?"

She leaned against the bench, sipping a lemon, lime and bitters. That was about as rowdy as Lucy ever got.

"Not a lot. What's up with you?"

She screwed up her nose. "Just trying my best to get through this stupid party without having a nervous breakdown."

"It's your house. You could just bail and go to bed."

"It's not like I'd get any sleep, anyway. We might as well just be wallflowers together."

"Fair enough."

They clinked their bottles together. Lucy shifted uncomfortably, as if she wanted to ask something.

"So," she said after a moment, "where's Rachel?"

"She dumped me." James took another swig of his beer. "Boxing Day."

Lucy sucked her teeth. "Ouch."

He shook his head. "It's not a big deal. I was gonna break it off soon, anyway. She just beat me to it."

"Are you okay?"

"I'm fine."

Lucy squinted at him. "You don't seem fine."

He had to change the subject.

"Who's that girl Jaz is hanging off?"

"I believe that's Cali."

"Cali …" He turned the name over. "She a derby player?"

"Hockey player."

"Right."

"I think Ainslie's going to be sick tomorrow," Lucy said, casting her gaze over to the lounge.

"That is if Aidan hasn't suffocated her by then." He sounded more bitter than he had any right to.

He cringed at the two, who were now sucking the air out of each other's lungs.

Lucy gave him a side eye. "That wouldn't happen to have anything to do with how miserable you look right now, would it?"

James frowned. "What? No."

"Oh, please," Lucy muttered.

"What?"

"Are you forgetting? Ainslie isn't the only one who's known you for nearly twenty years," Lucy said. "You think I haven't noticed the way you've been looking at her ever since she got engaged?"

"What, like a friend?"

Lucy laughed out loud. "Yeah, okay, if that's what you want to call it."

James put his beer bottle to his lips. "Look, maybe there was a time, years ago, when I liked Ainslie a little bit" —

Lucy raised an incredulous eyebrow.

— "but that's *so far* in the past. And now she's engaged to" — he gestured towards Aidan with his bottle — "that idiot."

"Okay, James," Lucy said, "you keep telling yourself that if it's what makes you feel better."

"Lu-cy."

"Ja-ames," she said, mimicking his whiny tone.

A few moments of silence passed between them, the air filled with the thumping bass of the stereo and the buzz of a dozen conversations.

"Sometimes, I wonder what would've happened if she'd ended up with you instead of him," Lucy said, thinking out loud.

James glanced at her. "Are you drunk, Luce?"

"On lemon, lime and bitters?" She scoffed. "Don't try to change the subject. And don't act like you've never thought about it. I'm not entirely convinced you don't *still* think about it. Ah, well." She downed the rest of her drink. "Hindsight really is twenty twenty, isn't it?"

James sighed and dropped his head.

Something caught Lucy's eye and she tossed her empty bottle in the bin.

"Hang on. I've got to go make sure those idiots don't fall off the balcony."

She hurried off to scold a group of people who'd congregated outside. Lucy really was the glue that held them all together. She'd always been the sensible one. She'd been that way since they were kids. James instantly missed her company, and standing alone in the kitchen made him wish he hadn't come after all.

Over on the lounge, Ainslie finally parted from Aidan, who stood up and sauntered to the bathroom. She sat upright, flattened her skirt and checked her phone. Then she caught James's eye, pouted, and pointed at him from across the room.

"You," she mouthed.

James instinctively looked over his shoulder before remembering he was standing in front of a wall. She was definitely pointing at him. She stood up and stumbled over, and he braced himself for ... he wasn't sure what.

"You," she said, collapsing against the counter. "You've been avoiding me all week, *Sunderland.*"

"Sorry, I've been busy." He wasn't in the mood to try to converse with her in the state she was in.

"Pfft, sure," she slurred.

"You're drunk, Ainslie."

She blew a raspberry. "Pfft. You are."

"Nice."

He'd been dying to speak to her all week, but not like this.

"I can't believe you," she muttered into her drink.

"What?"

"You," she said, raising her voice to compete with the loud music. "Christmas night. You were all sweet and nice and then boom! You ignore me for a week."

"I told you, Ainslie, I was busy."

"Busy." She scoffed, shaking her head. "No, you're a coward."

He raised his eyebrows. "Excuse me?"

He really wasn't a fan of Angry-Drunk Ainslie.

"You're a coward," she said, slurring. "If you would've just done something when you had the chance, maybe we wouldn't be in this mess."

James pulled a face. "What the *hell* are you talking about?"

"You ...," she said, thrusting a finger in his face, and then her expression softened, "and me," she finished sadly.

"One minute to midnight!" Jaz said from across the room.

The apartment erupted into cheers.

"Nearly midnight, then." Ainslie flipped her hair over her shoulder. "Better go off and find Aidan. He'll be wanting his New Year's kiss."

James suppressed an eye roll.

She pushed up from the bench and stood on her tiptoes. "Here." She planted a messy and uncoordinated kiss on his cheek.

"Happy New Year, *Sunderland.*" She patted him gently where her lips had been before stumbling away.

James was shocked, to say the least. There was no way she would remember that the next day, and he figured she probably wouldn't want to. He wasn't even sure *he* wanted to remember it the next day. He could still feel her soft lips on his cheek.

Someone had switched the television on, and the countdown had begun.

"Five! Four! Three! Two! One!"

James raised his drink to no-one in particular.

Aidan and Ainslie were joined at the lips once more, and Ms Red Flanno had planted a kiss on Jaz. Lucy appeared beside James again.

"Happy 2020." She planted a kiss on her fingers and transferred it onto his cheek with a gentle slap.

He winced. "Thanks for that."

"Cheer up, James. It'll be okay."

Except it wouldn't be. Because it was officially the last year of his career.

CHAPTER 17

After midnight hit, it didn't take long for the guests to lose interest and disperse, and after about an hour, the only people left were the girls, Aidan and James.

Lucy was already collecting empty bottles and dumping them with a crash into a garbage bag. James was lending a hand as best he could, but his energy was starting to wane. Ainslie and Aidan were still practically on top of each other, and Jaz was fast asleep on the lounge.

"Okay." Aidan slapped his knees and moved to stand up. "Let's go back to mine, babe. I gotta be up early."

He reached for Ainslie.

"Nuh-uh." James held up a hand. "You're not going anywhere. Not unless you've got someone who can drive for you."

Aidan glared at him. "You got a problem?"

"Have I got a problem with you driving home drunk? Yeah, as a matter of fact, I do." James folded his arms.

Aidan stood up and puffed out his chest. "Why don't you mind your own fucking business?" He strode towards James, a little wobbly thanks to his current state.

"Babe, don't," Ainslie said from the lounge.

"Mate, I couldn't give a shit if you drive yourself home," James replied. "But *she's* not getting in a car with you."

"You need to watch yourself." Aidan reeked of scotch, and he was standing uncomfortably close. "People might start thinking you're not such a good guy, after all."

James set his mouth in a line. "Either you stay here, or you drive home by yourself."

"Babe, just stay here," Ainslie slurred.

"Fuck this." Aidan threw his hands up and disappeared down the hall.

Ainslie stood up and slunk off after him.

"Wow." Lucy raised her eyebrows. "Alcohol brings out *such* a wonderful colour in him."

James sighed. "Was I really so out of line?"

"God, no."

Lucy put her hands on her hips, surveying the mess of the living room.

"I better put Jaz to bed. I'll deal with this tomorrow. You've had a bit to drink, yourself," she said, addressing James. "You can crash on the lounge if you like."

Lucy poked Jaz in the shoulder. She stirred slightly, but only enough to allow Lucy to haul her to her feet and lug her to bed.

Once the girls had left the lounge room, James settled into the lumpy lounge and tried to get comfortable. He kicked off his shoes and puffed the pillow Lucy had lent him. As soon as he was horizontal, the room began to spin. He closed his eyes. He hadn't had as much to drink as Ainslie or Jaz, but he'd had enough. And Ainslie's cryptic scolding was replaying in his mind. He couldn't figure out for the life of him what she'd meant by "you and me", and he wasn't planning on asking.

*　　*　　*

"Fuck me."

It was a groan of exasperation, not a request.

Somehow, it was morning already. James squinted and shielded his eyes from the bright sunlight that was blasting through the window. He glanced around the room, disoriented, and momentarily forgot where he was. He lifted his head from the lounge and saw Ainslie leaning against the kitchen bench, head in her hands, hunched over a glass of water and a box of paracetamol.

"Shouldn't I buy you dinner first?" he asked without thinking.

His throat was dry, and his voice was thick with sleep.

Ainslie raised her head slightly and winced. "Sorry. I didn't realise you were still here."

"I'm surprised you're the first one up." He sat upright and rubbed his eyes with the heels of his hands. "You were a mess last night."

"Aidan woke me up when he left," she said, dropping her head back into her hands. "He had to be at the airport by eight."

"I didn't hear him leave. I'm surprised he didn't smother me on his way out. I think he tried to fight me last night."

Ainslie laughed, but it morphed into a groan as she moved to switch on the coffee machine. "I don't remember much about last night."

"Yeah, you were pretty fucked up." James yawned. "I hadn't seen you that gone since the 2014 Nationals Dinner."

She furrowed her brow and pinched the bridge of her nose as the coffee machine poured espresso shots.

"Speaking of trying to fight people," she said, "did we … fight last night?"

"Well, I'm pretty sure a fight has to involve more than one person, so no, I don't think it could be called a *fight*. But you *did* yell at me."

She winced again and poured two cups of coffee. "I vaguely remember *that*. I was mad because you'd been avoiding me all week."

"Yeah …"

"In my defence," she said, trudging over to the lounge, coffees in hand, "you *have* been avoiding me all week. I know you said you were busy, but I don't know if I buy that."

"Rachel dumped me."

He neglected to mention the other reason.

Ainslie sighed, handing him a cup. "Fuck, I'm sorry."

"Don't be." He rested his head on the back of the lounge. "You knew I was gonna do it anyway."

"Yeah." She sat at the other end of the lounge and folded her legs underneath her. "But it still sucks."

"Still sucks."

James watched her as she took a sip of coffee. Her hair was pointing every which way, her eyes were glassy from lack of sleep, and she still had traces of old make-up smudged under her eyes. And yet, he still thought she was the most beautiful thing in the world.

"Why didn't you tell me?" she asked, licking her parched lips.

"It happened on Boxing Day. You'd just had a big fight with Aidan. I didn't want to bother you."

"Bother me? We're best friends. You wouldn't have bothered me."

James just shrugged and sipped his coffee.

"So, ah," Ainslie said into her mug, "I don't think I'm moving to Melbourne anymore."

"You're not?"

She shook her head.

"No," she said. "Aidan changed his mind. He said he didn't care where we lived as long as it was together."

James tried not to look too defeated.

"In fact," she added with a smile, "he even said we could move somewhere nearby so I'd still be near my friends and — get this — the rink. You know, if I wanted to go to a session or teach Learn to Skate or something."

"Oh." James raised his eyebrows. "How uncharacteristically considerate of him."

She pulled a face. "Shut up."

"I suppose he gave you that necklace too," he said, gesturing at the roller skate pendant.

Her fingers gently toyed with the chain. "He did."

"Seems he's finally decided to make an effort."

"James, don't start."

"Sorry."

Ainslie took another long swig of coffee and licked her lips again. It took everything in him not to stare at her mouth.

"Hey," she said, placing her mug on the coffee table. "Last night ... I didn't do anything stupid, did I?"

"I don't think so."

Ainslie scrunched up her forehead. "I didn't say anything else to you? Anything ... weird?"

"No," he said, chasing the lie with a sip of coffee. "Not that I recall."

She screwed up her face and pinched the bridge of her nose again.

"You sure? The last time I woke up this hungover, Lucy told me I'd streaked through the apartment."

James blushed and tried not to picture it. "Well, you definitely didn't do *that*."

"All right …," she said slowly. "Must've been a dream."

At that moment, Jaz emerged from the hall looking more presentable and alert than she had any right to.

Ainslie looked her up and down. "Excuse me. This is just rude."

"What?" Jaz walked to the kitchen and pulled a glass out of the cupboard.

"You had just as much to drink last night as me. Why aren't you suffering?"

"Because *I'm* not a lightweight." Jaz winked and took a swig of water.

Ainslie rolled her eyes.

"So, uh, Jaz." James folded his arms and grinned. "When were you gonna tell us about Cali?"

Jaz shrugged. "There isn't anything to tell."

Ainslie looked back and forth between the two. "Wait, who's Cali?"

"A hockey player," James said. "And the girl Jaz spent all last night hanging off."

"A hockey player? You know how I feel about hockey players. Present company's siblings excluded, of course."

Jaz squinted. "She's just a friend."

"Yeah, okay." James chuckled. "I could use a 'friend' like that."

Jaz picked up an empty plastic cup off the bench and tried to throw it at him. Of course, it was too light and didn't even come close to hitting him.

"Aaaaanyway," she sang, "what are you guys doing today?"

"Suffering," said Ainslie. "But nothing else."

"I was thinking we should go to Bondi, just the four of us like the good old days."

"There's no way I'm going to Bondi on New Year's Day!" Lucy's voice rang out from her bedroom.

"Oh, come on, Luce! We haven't had a day out just the four of us in ages. And once Ainslie gets married, we won't have any more chances."

Jaz pouted at Ainslie, who was wincing at all the shouting.

"Yes," Lucy said, appearing from the hall in a dressing gown, "but going to one of the most famous beaches in the world, on a public holiday, in the middle of summer, is probably the *worst* idea you've ever had."

"Come on, Lucy. Don't be such a mardy bum."

"Whatever."

"Well, I'm keen if you guys are." James slapped his knees.

Jaz clapped her hands together and looked at Ainslie, who pulled a face.

"Yeah, okay, fine," Ainslie said, "I'm in. Blistering sunburn might take my mind off my splitting headache."

*　　*　　*

Bondi on New Year's Day would be chaotic, but Jaz was still new enough to Australia to think going there was a stroke of genius. Lucy went along reluctantly but didn't hesitate to voice her opinion constantly of it being a terrible idea and looked smug when they got stuck in bumper-to-bumper traffic along the esplanade. They eventually found a parking space in a backstreet several hundred metres from the beach. Ainslie was hiding under an oversized hat and a pair of dark sunglasses. She looked like a corpse that the other three were puppeteering around.

There was scarcely room for any more people on the beach. The sand was littered with bodies lying prostrate on colourful towels. Some tanned, some not so tanned, all shapes, sizes and colours. The four grabbed some food from the Pavilion and eventually found an empty spot on the sand, sandwiched between a family of loud American tourists and an extremely bronzed, blond couple.

"This is absurd," Lucy said, grumbling when a child from the neighbouring family kicked up a spray of sand at them for the third time. "How is this in any way enjoyable?"

James peeked over his sunglasses at Ainslie, who hadn't touched her food, moved or spoken in nearly twenty minutes.

"You still alive over there, Goose?"

She lolled her head lazily to the side. "Just barely."

"You know," Jaz said, pinching a hot chip from Ainslie's untouched stash and popping it in her mouth, "no-one's ever told me where the 'Goose' nickname comes from."

James blushed. "It's stupid, really."

"It's not stupid," Lucy said. "It's actually very sweet."

James wondered if it was just the sun or if he was blushing even harder.

"Okay," he said, "but you need context, or it doesn't make sense."

"So, give me context?"

"It's stupid."

Lucy sighed. "It would make sense if you'd known Ainslie back when we were little."

Ainslie shot her a look.

"Back when we were about ten," Lucy said, "she used to chase him around constantly. At the rink, at school … just constantly. He'd make some comment, usually with the intention of provoking her, and she'd start chasing him around the place."

Ainslie pulled her hat down over her face.

"Honestly, in retrospect," Lucy said, smirking, "it was the most obvious schoolgirl crush I've ever seen."

A muffled groan emanated from under Ainslie's hat, and Jaz giggled.

"*Anyway,*" James said, taking over the story, already feeling awkward enough, "one year we were in Adelaide for Nationals, and the club went out on a daytrip to this wildlife park. We were all eating our lunch by a pond, and this goose came up and tried to steal my sandwich."

Jaz cackled.

"Like an idiot, I tried to save my lunch," James said, "and then it just started chasing me. I was completely freaked out —"

"You were screaming like a baby," Lucy said.

"Yes, thank you, Lucy." James narrowed his eyes at her. "Let's all laugh at my traumatic childhood experience. It chased me for a good five minutes before one of the rangers finally came and scared it off. Anyway, the next time Ains decided to chase me around the rink, one of the parents made a crack about the wildlife park goose, and then I guess it just became a rink in-joke."

"So, basically, his cutesy nickname for her came about because she was *really* annoying as a child," Lucy said.

Ainslie emerged from beneath the hat and shot her a threatening look. Jaz was still chuckling away.

"I mean," James added, "geese are also insanely loyal, protective and would bite the shit out of anyone trying to harm their friends or family."

He glanced at Ainslie. It appeared as though she was glancing back at him, but he couldn't really tell through her dark glasses.

"Man, I wish I could've known you guys growing up. It just sucks that it's nearly over," Jaz said. "I can't believe it's officially the last year we'll all be together."

Ainslie, who hadn't done much other than groan and glare at them for the duration of the whole goose story, finally piped up.

"Oh, my God! Can't we ever go five minutes without talking about that? Christ! Do we have to mention it every fucking time we hang out?"

She stood up from her towel and stomped down towards the ocean.

Jaz's face fell. "I'm sorry, I shouldn't have said anything."

Lucy waved her off. "It's okay. She's not exactly acting rational given the state she's in."

"I didn't mean anything by it. I'm just gutted she's gonna be leaving us. I know she says she's made peace with retiring, but … has she really?"

James shrugged. "She keeps saying she's come to terms with it, but I'm not sure I believe her."

"She changed a lot when she met Aidan, don't you think?" Lucy asked James, and he nodded in agreement.

"In what way?" Jaz asked.

"It's hard to explain," Lucy said, "but she used to be so bubbly and happy, and it was like the more time she spent with him, the more he drained her."

"He's the worst." Jaz frowned. "What does she see in him?"

Lucy shrugged. "Maybe she's just gotten used to having him around, and she's worried about being alone."

"She wouldn't be alone," James said. "She's got us. And she'd find herself snapped up by someone else pretty quickly."

Lucy gave him a look, and he kicked himself.

Probably shouldn't have said that.

CHAPTER 18

Ainslie's head was still pounding, but the cool sea breeze was mildly soothing. She closed her eyes and inhaled the salty air. She felt the warm sand underfoot and the cold foam rolling in to lap at her ankles. This year had come around far too quickly. When she first got engaged, it had felt like forever away, but the last three months had flown by in a blur. She was terrified by the thought of how fast the next twelve were going to go.

Out of the corner of her eye, she saw James plodding across the sand towards her. When he got to her side, he looked out over the ocean, not saying a word. She still had the faintest memory of dreaming about him the night before. She'd yelled at him and then kissed him on the cheek. It had felt so real.

They stood there for a few moments in silence, the tide pulling their feet deeper into the sand, the sea air whipping against their faces.

Eventually, Ainslie let out a sigh. "I seem to be cracking the shits a lot these days, don't I?" she said, the question more like a statement.

James smiled and dropped his head. "Kinda."

"Jaz makes it sound like once I get married, I may as well be dead."

James kicked at the sand. "I mean, you're not moving to Melbourne anymore. That's good, right? And you said Aidan told you one of the reasons was so you could be close to your friends."

"Yeah," she replied, "but it won't ever be quite the same, will it? We probably won't be able to have days like this, or parties like last night, or hang out like we did at Christmas …"

She glanced over at him, fishing for a response, but his face was unreadable.

"Sure." He bent down, picked up a rock out of the sand, and threw it into the ocean. "But if every time we all hang out ends in tears or yelling, it's not exactly going to be very pleasant, is it?"

"Maybe I'm just subconsciously trying to push you away. Make you hate me so it's not as hard when I'm gone."

James scoffed and put an arm around her shoulders. "Goose, there's no way in the world any of us are ever going to hate you. Least of all, me."

Ainslie felt a tear prick at her eye, and she was suddenly even more grateful to be wearing sunglasses.

"Hey. I'm really sorry about Rachel."

"Ah, she's better off without me."

"Are you kidding? She was lucky to have you."

"She didn't really have me, though, did she?"

Ainslie frowned. She wasn't quite sure what to make of that.

* * *

When the pair returned to their spot on the sand, Ainslie offered the others a wordless apology in the form of a small, slightly embarrassed smile. All was forgotten. There was no more talk about anyone's impending retirement or marriage, and Ainslie was finally able to bring herself to eat something. The more food and water she put into her weary body, the less she felt like a bear with a sore head.

Her hangover slowly faded, giving way to a slightly better mood, and by the time they got back to the apartment in the late afternoon, she felt relatively normal, if not a little sunburnt. That was until she heard the little pinging sound that indicated she had received an email.

She looked at her phone, and her heart rate picked up. The 2020 skating calendar was out. In the haze of her hangover, she'd completely forgotten today was the day she'd find out the dates for Worlds. And then they could finally set a date for the wedding. The thought made her a little woozy. Or perhaps that was still the remaining dregs of the hangover.

She stared at the screen, and the blue hyperlink taunted her. Once she opened it and knew the Worlds dates, the countdown to the end of her career would truly begin.

She'd told Aidan she didn't want to get married until after Worlds. Mostly because she wanted to have the stress of Worlds out of the way before she had to focus her energy on the stress of her nuptials, but she also didn't want to skate her last Worlds as Ainslie *Corbin*. It may have been a little irrational, but it just didn't seem like the right way to end the Jameslie era. She wanted them to be remembered in Australian skating history as Ainslie *Wynter* and James Sunderland.

She eventually lost her staring contest with the hyperlink, took a deep breath and clicked through. The first thing she checked was the Worlds dates. Final week of September. Their spring wedding could go ahead as planned. It was bittersweet. She smiled at the idea of the wedding, but now she finally knew the date of the last time she'd ever compete. If she hadn't felt like such a dried-up husk from spending the entire day in the sun, she might have cried.

She scrolled through the calendar, checking every single event to see if it was going to coincide with any birthdays, holidays or their anniversary. Almost every year without fail, something clashed, and it was guaranteed to cause a fight between her and Aidan. She caught a conflict almost immediately and groaned out loud. Valentine's Day. It was the Friday before the weekend of the pre-States league.

Shit.

There was no way Sandra would approve of her going out on the Friday night before a competition. Of course, the whole weekend would be a write-off too.

Shit. Shit. Shit.

90

She kept scrolling and checked the other dates. Miraculously, their anniversary, Easter, the June long weekend and both of their birthdays were all free. That was something, at least. She wasn't in the mood to fight about it, so she shot Aidan a quick message to let him know the Worlds dates, tossed her phone on the coffee table and filed the Valentine's Day news away for later.

CHAPTER 19

Most of the Randwick Ravens artistic skaters were given a couple of weeks off over the New Year period, but for the international grade skaters and Worlds hopefuls, there was no time to waste. The countdown was on. Routines were finished in structure, but there was still a lot of polishing to do. Ahead of them was months of fitness drills, strength training, footwork classes with Stephen (the club's dance coach), off-skate dance classes, yoga, stretching … The list seemed endless.

Ainslie could've used a few extra days to catch up on sleep after her New Year's Eve bender, but time did not permit that, and on the second day of January, she was trudging into the rink, ready for the first day of her final year, a fog of melancholy hanging over her head. She figured Sandra and James felt it too because as much as they tried to act normal during their off-skate lifts lesson, there was a sombre feeling in the air of the dance studio. Ainslie tried her best to seem as unbothered as possible, but at the end of the hour, as they headed downstairs to put their skates on, James placed a hand on her back and whispered, "Are you doing okay?"

"Yeah," she replied, pinching the bridge of her nose, "I'm just tired."

*   *   *

The main thing hanging over Ainslie's head was the Valentine's Day conflict. She knew she was going to have to tell Aidan sooner or later, but she was anticipating an argument about it, and that was the last thing she wanted. But with every day in January that went by, it only got harder to find a natural way to bring it up.

Ainslie soon felt the pressure of February bearing down on her, and she still hadn't said anything — not that it had been easy to get him alone for long enough to tell him. Aidan had spent every weekend since New Year's at the Melbourne office. The case he was working on had him run off his feet. Ainslie didn't know how he did it. The weekly interstate commute on top of his already hectic Sydney schedule must have been exhausting, but every Friday afternoon, he'd just kiss her goodbye and say he was racking up the frequent flyer points for their honeymoon (as if he needed them).

Maybe it was because he was enjoying the work (which Ainslie knew he did), or maybe he just didn't have the energy to pick fights, but things between the two of them were better than they had been in a long time. All the more reason why Ainslie didn't want to bring up the Valentine's Day problem and disturb the peace they'd finally managed to cultivate.

By the time February actually rolled around, Ainslie figured she couldn't really put it off any longer. She considered dropping the bomb in a text and hoping for the best, but when he invited her out on his lunchbreak one afternoon, she decided that maybe it was best to have the conversation in public. At least then, the tantrum might be more subdued.

They huddled together in a quiet corner of the coffee shop on the ground floor of Aidan's office building. Ainslie sat, picking at her salad, enjoying the weight of his arm around her shoulders and absolutely dreading what was bound to happen when she finally worked up the nerve to utter the words she needed to say.

"Hey," she said, her stomach churning a little, "I probably should've told you this sooner, but …"

He turned his head to look at her and furrowed his brow. "What's the matter?"

She swallowed hard, struggling to maintain eye contact. "I've got a competition the weekend of Valentine's Day."

Ainslie felt her body tense up as she waited for him to clench his jaw or roll his eyes.

But Aidan didn't even flinch.

"That's okay, babe. I'm probably going to be needed down in Melbourne that weekend, anyway."

"Oh."

That was all she could manage.

She was relieved it hadn't caused a fight, but the tension hadn't left her body. She knew he'd been required in Melbourne every weekend of 2020 so far, but she *had* sort of assumed he'd take *that* particular weekend off.

"We can do something extra special when this case has finished." He smiled and gave her a quick kiss.

"Yeah, of course." She offered him a weak smile in return.

God knows when that'll be.

"Well," Aidan said, wiping his hands on a napkin, "I've got to get back to work. What have you got on for the rest of the day?"

Ainslie chewed her lower lip. She knew exactly how she *could* get a reaction out of him.

"I'm meeting James at the rink at one thirty."

"Okay, babe," he said, kissing her on the head as he stood up. "Have fun."

Then he paid their bill and hurried back upstairs.

Ainslie frowned. Historically, a competition clashing with a holiday would be cause for World War III. And usually, any mention of James elicited a groan, at the *least*.

But now, nothing.

In fact, now that she thought about it, nothing since he had started working from the Melbourne office.

She should've been happy. Maybe he was finally coming around. She knew she should've been taking it as a positive step forwards in their relationship, but the smallest and most irritating of voices kept whispering in her head.

Why doesn't he care?

A sinister thought crossed her mind that maybe he didn't care if she spent time with James because *he* was spending time with someone else. She pushed the idea away. It was a stupid thought.

Jesus Christ, can't you ever just be grateful?

CHAPTER 20

The gym at the Randwick Rollerdome was for private, club use only. Nestled behind a wall of two-way mirrors, it looked out over the rink but was hidden from the prying eyes of the public. There were certain days when it would get overrun by hockey or derby players, but James and Ainslie knew exactly when they were able to have it all to themselves.

They jumped on side-by-side treadmills and booted them up.

"Race?" Ainslie said with a smirk. "Top speed, first one to tap out loses."

"Oh, you're on." James laughed, and they cranked up their machines.

The treadmills roared to life, and the pair pumped their legs as fast as they could. The gym was silent except for the pounding of their feet and the whirring of the belts. James glanced at Ainslie and couldn't help but grin. She had her eyes fixed ahead, steely and determined but with a hint of pure ecstasy behind them. She was breathing steadily and purposefully, but a trace of a smile gave her away. She was loving it. And he was loving watching her.

It was always a beautiful thing when her competitive side reared its head. It was one of the things he loved most about her. He knew that when she had her mind fixed on something, there was nothing anyone could possibly do to stop her. Never was she more beautiful than when she was completely lost in her passion for the sport.

For a moment, he found himself thinking about how she must do *other* things with that sort of passion too. He mentally slapped himself and focused on his own stride. He was growing tired, and it was only going to be a matter of seconds before she bested him. She would always best him. Every time.

He finally slammed the power button and slowed down.

"That's it. I gotta tap out."

"Thank God." She laughed, slowing her machine too.

"You always have to be the best, don't you, *Wynter*," he said with a smirk.

"We're a team, *Sunderland*. We're both the best."

They moved from the treadmills over to the squat rack.

"Hey," Ainslie said as she stepped up to the bar, "I know you probably don't want to talk about this, but I gotta get something off my chest."

James took on the role of spotter and moved behind her. "What's up?"

"It's Aidan," she said between squats. "He was kinda acting ... weird today."

"Weird how?"

She stopped squatting and looked at him in the mirror in front of the rack.

"I told him about our comp clashing with Valentine's Day, and he just ... didn't care."

"Maybe he's not that fussed about Valentine's Day. Not everyone is."

Ainslie raised an eyebrow. "Two years ago, we had a comp clash with his birthday, and he blew a fuse."

"So? That was his *birthday*. You know he's a bit of a narcissist."

Ainslie gave him a look. "Oi, don't start."

"Sorry."

"And, I don't know." She continued squatting. "I've been thinking about it, and he's been kinda … weirdly chill about *everything* since New Year's. Like, he's not picking fights or getting annoyed when I have to come to the rink …"

"Correct me if I'm wrong," James said, raising an eyebrow, "but isn't that a good thing?"

"Well, you'd think so, but it's just … really out of character, I guess?" she said as they swapped positions and James began squatting. "And …" She let out a heavy sigh and leaned against the neighbouring weight machine.

James stopped squatting and looked at her. "What is it, Ains?"

She sighed again. "I dunno. I guess I just got it in my head that he's been going to Melbourne pretty much every weekend since New Year's, and *something's* been putting him in a good mood … or someone …"

James frowned as anger flooded his body. "Do you think he's messing around?"

"No." Ainslie brushed it off as if the idea was ridiculous. "I mean … the case is paying the big bucks, and apparently, it's going pretty well … He's probably just riding the high of *that*."

James pursed his lips. "Honestly, Ains, I think it's a little weird that he's so predictably dickish that the very idea of him *not* being dickish is cause for concern."

She pressed her lips together and cocked her head. It clearly wasn't what she had wanted to hear.

"Look," James said, "maybe he's just finally decided to pull his head in. It's a new year. Maybe he's just happy *this*" — he stepped out of the squat rack and gestured between them — "is nearly over."

"Yeah, maybe." Ainslie pouted. "Wish I was happy about that."

"Well, I can't say I'm *thrilled* either," James replied. "Listen." He put a hand on her shoulder. "Maybe this is a good thing. Maybe he's changing for the better. But if you're worried, then I really think you need to be talking to *him* about it."

*   *   *

By the time Ainslie and James finished their off-skate conditioning, the rink was occupied by elite skaters of all disciplines. Strains of a waltz played over the loudspeakers as Stephen taught a Junior Dance couple. Sandra had Jaz on the jump harness, working on a triple Salchow, and Lucy was repeating her cluster sequence.

Not wanting to wipe anybody out, Ainslie and James decided to leave throws and lifts for another time and instead focus on their jumps and spins, taking turns and offering each other feedback. They sped around the rink side by side. James watched Ainslie out of the corner of his eye as she breathed in the warm summer breeze that was floating in through the open roller door. He could actually see her tension from the gym drop now that she had wheels under her feet. She peeled off to set up for an Axel. She warmed up with a solid single before looping back around for the double. With great speed, she launched herself into the air, rotated two and a half times and landed on one foot. She rocked up onto her toe stop a little.

"Nice," James said.

"Toed it."

"Yeah, but apart from that."

"Tessa Strong doesn't toe *her* Axels." She pulled a face as she rolled by him.

Tessa and her partner Antony had improved *a lot* before the last time Ainslie and James had gone up against them. And Tessa's jumps, in particular, had gotten annoyingly good, considering she'd once had a habit of underrotating them.

"All right, well, go and do it properly then," James said, teasing.

Ainslie shot him a steely-eyed glare and looped back around.

She grinned as she stuck the landing. "Beat that."

"I thought we were a team, *Wynter*," he said before speeding off to set up for his own jump.

He nailed it on the first try.

Ainslie applauded. "I knew there was a reason I kept you around."

"You mean it's not for my amazing charisma and dashing good looks?" He winked.

Her cheeks flushed a little. "I mean, those things certainly help."

He knew he shouldn't be flirting with her. Even if that was all it was. Even if she *did* flirt back. He'd never considered their banter flirting before, but now he was finding it difficult to interpret it any other way.

"Come on, Sunderland," Ainslie said with a single clap of encouragement. "Triple Salchow. Go!"

He flew off and lined it up. One, two, three revolutions and he wiped out, sliding backside first across the polished concrete.

"Oof." Ainslie winced. "You right?"

He dramatically rolled onto his back like a stuck turtle before leaping to his feet. "Yep."

"Hmm, I wonder if Dylan Porter from Queensland is in the market for a partner," Ainslie said, stroking her chin, the hint of a smile pulling at her lips.

"Why?" James smirked. "You think I could replace you with *him* when you retire?"

She narrowed her eyes at him and pouted. God, she looked so cute when she pulled that face. She was driving him crazy.

He backed up for another triple Salchow, this time landing perfectly.

"Ah, there's the partner I know and love."

James internally cringed at the L word.

They continued working through their jumps and spins, giving each other feedback here and there, laughing and joking, and "bantering" some more. James wanted to tell her just how much he would miss it. But she already knew. And he didn't want to spoil the moment by bringing up their expiry date.

CHAPTER 21

On Valentine's Day evening, just as he'd done almost every Friday since the beginning of the year, Aidan hopped aboard a flight to Melbourne. Ainslie and Lucy invited James over for a movie night, and Jaz covertly slipped out, presumably to go see Cali.

Lucy made popcorn, James provided the drinks (non-alcoholic, of course — they did have a competition the next day, after all), and Ainslie sat, curled up on the end of the lounge, barely paying any attention to the movie.

Aidan had promised to call her when he arrived at his hotel. He always did. She knew his flight got in at eight thirty, but it was pushing nine, and she hadn't even so much as received a text to say he'd landed safely. Ainslie had one eye on the movie and one eye on her phone as she anxiously chewed her thumbnail. When she checked her phone for the umpteenth time, Lucy kicked her with a socked foot.

"Want to try living in the moment, Ms Millennial?"

"What? I was checking the time."

"You have somewhere you need to be?" James asked, tossing a piece of popcorn in his mouth.

Ainslie glared at them.

When the movie finally ended, James stretched and announced it was time he went home.

"I'll pick you all up at seven tomorrow," he said as he collected his keys.

"Thanks for that," Lucy replied.

"Yeah, see ya." Ainslie barely processed what he'd said.

She still hadn't heard from Aidan, and the competition the next day was the furthest thing from her mind. Once she'd gone to bed, she decided she'd call him herself. She lay there, listening to the phone ring, patiently waiting for him to answer. Nothing except his voicemail. She hung up and tossed her phone onto the bedside table. It was unlike Aidan to forget to call her. They'd been doing the weekend long-distance thing for over a month, and he always called her. Besides, it was *Valentine's Day*.

She tried to convince herself that he must've just been tired and fallen asleep, but her mind kept teasing her with thoughts of what *else* he could be doing. She couldn't switch her brain off, and the more she thought about needing sleep, the more it evaded her.

*   *   *

The Randwick Rollerdome was bustling with that familiar competition atmosphere. Gangs of skaters in different coloured tracksuits all staked their claims along the grandstand, some mingling with each other, some not. The event coordinator and her team of roadies were hooking up computers and video screens. Stern-looking officials in navy blazers sipped coffee and chatted among themselves. Coaches paced up and down the side of the rink, surveying the floor.

The pre-States league was a necessary evil for skaters wishing to nominate for the State Championships, but it was quite a low-stakes affair. It wasn't a qualifier for anything, so placing and scores didn't really matter. It was more just an invaluable opportunity to get in front of judges before the first major competition of the season.

As the four of them were settling into the grandstand, Ainslie's phone vibrated in her pocket. She dug it out. One new text from Aidan.

Babe. I'm so sorry I didn't get a chance to call you last night. The traffic from the airport was absolutely shocking. By the time I got back to my hotel it was getting late and I knew you had a comp this morning, so I didn't want to call and wake you. I'm so, so sorry. Skate well today and I'll definitely make it up to you when I get back. Love you xo

Ainslie frowned. That was all well and good, but he hadn't mentioned falling asleep early, so it didn't really explain why he hadn't answered her when *she* had called.

She wanted to dwell on it, but she needed to keep her head straight for her performance later that day, so she shot back a brief response.

That's ok. Miss you. xo

She shook her head a little to clear it and looked around at the skaters from other clubs that had gathered around them. Jaz was regaling a few of them with some funny story about the time she had briefly dabbled in roller derby. Lucy had already fled down to the marshalling area by herself to warm up for her style dance.

Ainslie looked across at James. A grin was plastered across his face as he listened to Jaz recount the time she'd been knocked to the ground by three derby girls and had been unable to walk the next day (and — in her words — "not in the fun way"). It was in moments like this when it was most obvious to Ainslie just how different Aidan was from literally everyone else she knew. Things would have been so much easier if he was able to let loose every now and then. But he had never fit into their friendship dynamic. He'd never even tried to.

Jaz wrapped up her story just in time for the group to watch Lucy's style dance. Lucy skated clean and strong, putting down a solid performance for the first competition of the year.

Eventually it was Jaz's turn to warm up for her event. Senior Ladies Freeskating fell a little after midday, which was fortunate for Jaz because Ainslie was pretty sure she had heard her friend stumble back into the apartment *well* after midnight last night.

"What do you reckon Jaz was doing last night?" James asked as Jaz and the other Senior freeskaters sped onto the floor. Despite the late night, Jaz looked stronger than ever.

"I dunno." Ainslie smirked. "But I think she's got dark, curly hair and plays inline hockey."

James snorted.

Jaz's up-tempo industrial music definitely made her stand out from the others, most of whom had opted for film scores or classical pieces. Her triple Salchow was still a little underrotated, but the flick at the end was so fast it was barely noticeable.

Ainslie and James closed the session with their short program. They always were a drawcard, and the programmers knew that putting them on last was a sure-fire way to make people stay until the end.

Sandra had ended up choosing the Australian rock classic "Never Tear Us Apart" by INXS for their short program. It was sultry and bluesy and a complete crowd-pleaser.

Their scores were high, especially for the first competition of the year, and they left the rink feeling pretty satisfied with themselves.

*   *   *

The second day of the competition was much the same as the first. Ainslie and James's long program had the audience completely captivated. Those who recognised "Bolero" and remembered it from Torvill and Dean's Sarajevo 1984 performance watched with bated breath, waiting to see if the young pair would be able to fill the massive shoes of the legends who'd gone before.

When the music ended, it became clear that at the very least, they'd come awfully close. The crowd roared. Some people even rose to their feet (which rarely happened at so minor a competition), and Ainslie and James exited the floor with huge smiles plastered across their faces. Their grins only grew when they saw their score. It was a new personal best, a perfect way to begin their final season. Sandra clapped modestly, doing her best to conceal her pride with dignity. Ainslie and James threw their arms around each other and bounced up and down on their toe stops.

During the medal ceremony, Ainslie couldn't wipe the smile off her face. No amount of dud Valentine's Days could keep her from riding the high she was on.

Skating had always been her true Valentine, anyway.

* * *

That night, Ainslie, James, Jaz and Lucy all returned to the girls' apartment for a celebratory dinner, and afterwards, they split off to analyse the recordings of their performances. Lucy and Jaz holed themselves up in their rooms while Ainslie and James stayed in the living room, huddled around Ainslie's laptop.

Halfway through their review of the long program, a voice cut through the recording.

"Oh, my God, they are so cute."

Ainslie squinted and turned up the volume, trying to make out whose voice it was.

"I know, right?" said someone else. "It's so crazy to me that they're not a couple."

"They're not a couple?!" said a third voice.

Clearly, whoever was speaking hadn't realised how close they'd been standing to the camera. Ainslie glanced at James and caught him glancing back.

"No, they're just friends."

"Seriously? Honestly, why?"

"They've definitely slept together *at least* once." It sounded as if they were smirking, and the other two laughed.

Ainslie's cheeks started to burn.

"I actually heard she got engaged not long ago."

"For real? That sucks."

"Why does that suck?"

"I dunno, I guess I kinda shipped them."

"You can't ship real people."

The voices were finally drowned out by applause as the routine came to an end. The video finished, and the living room was filled with a deafening silence.

"Yikes," Ainslie said at last. "That was embarrassing."

"For us or them?"

"Both. Mainly us." Ainslie hoped her blush wasn't as obvious as it felt.

James shrugged. "Well, I can think of worse things to be accused of."

Ainslie's mouth felt dry, and she wanted nothing more than to change the subject.

"We did look good, though." She held up her hand for a high five.

"Oh, we looked amazing." He slapped her palm.

"What we did there," she said conspiratorially, "imagine it in four months at Nationals."

He bumped his shoulder against hers. "Imagine it in *seven* months at Worlds."

CHAPTER 22

The rational part of Ainslie's brain told her not to dwell on Aidan's Valentine's Day faux pas. It didn't seem worth it. But once the high of the pre-States league wore off, suspicion began burrowing its way back into her brain, and she spent the better part of February analysing his every move. It wasn't easy, considering they'd been struggling to find time when they were both free to see each other.

Aidan had still been as pleasant as ever, but Ainslie was starting to wonder if maybe he was bordering on indifference, which sent her mind spiralling down the rabbit hole.

Ainslie had also been thinking about James more than she probably should have. Every so often, she'd catch herself thinking about the remarks on the competition recording and blush. She realised this made her an incredible hypocrite, but she hadn't actually *done* anything. And after Valentine's Day (and taking into account all the other little changes in his behaviour), she was starting to worry that maybe Aidan couldn't say the same.

One Friday night in early March, when Ainslie was bored at home, she found herself sitting in bed, on her laptop, with her fingers hovering over the keyboard. She was fighting the urge to look up the company Aidan's father's firm was defending in the class action. Just to see if the case was legitimate. She didn't know what had gotten into her. She'd never imagined she'd ever be the sort of person to resort to cyberstalking her fiancé. But she couldn't help herself. She caved and typed the company name, along with Jacob Corbin's firm, into the browser.

The class action was real.

Ainslie closed the laptop and chewed at her thumbnail. She felt like an idiot. She was clearly overreacting, being just as irrationally jealous as she'd always accused Aidan of being.

Her phone rang beside her and she jumped.

Speak of the devil.

"Hey." She was more than a little surprised to be hearing from him on a Friday night. Normally he'd be on the plane by now.

"Babe! Great news. I'm free this weekend, and I'm planning on giving you the Valentine's Day you deserve."

A smile crept onto Ainslie's face, and her doubts began to fizzle out a little. "What did you have in mind?"

"Are you free tomorrow?"

"After training," she said. "I finish up around six."

"Perfect. What do you say to dinner and drinks at Quay and a night at the Shangri-La?"

From his tone, she could tell he was wearing a wicked grin on his face.

She bit her lip. "I'd say that sounds pretty nice."

"And then on Sunday, I've booked us a tour at Curzon Hall."

Ainslie nearly dropped her phone at the suggestion. "Seriously?"

"Seriously. Surely it's about time we book a venue, future Mrs Corbin."

Curzon Hall was an absolutely stunning wedding venue in North Sydney that Aidan's mother had given Ainslie a brochure for at Christmas. She'd fallen in love with it immediately, but the price tag was obscene.

Ainslie's stomach flip-flopped. If he was messing around with someone else, surely he wouldn't be this invested in wedding planning.

They chatted a while longer, and Aidan went into more *explicit* detail about his plans for their evening together. Ainslie couldn't help but blush. It felt like a huge weight was lifting off her shoulders.

*　　*　　*

Ainslie spent her Saturday morning shift and her afternoon training session distracted by the evening to come. It had been far too long since she and Aidan had been able to spend any real quality time together, and the idea of touring a wedding venue was exciting, if not a little bittersweet. Whenever Ainslie thought of her wedding, she found it difficult not to think about the fact that by the time it came around, her skating career would be over.

Aidan picked her up around seven thirty, showering her with flowers and chocolates as well as a diamond bracelet. They ate a lavishly expensive dinner at Quay and then checked into their luxury suite.

Later in the evening, as they basked in the afterglow of a long-overdue lovemaking session, Ainslie glanced up at Aidan.

"Why don't you come along to States this year?" she asked, drawing lazy circles across his chest. "It'll probably be the last opportunity you'll get to watch me compete. It would mean a lot if you could come. Plus, it's down the South Coast. We could get a little place on the beach. Might be nice to get away from it all. Spend some quality time together."

"Babe," he replied, stroking her hair, "I'm sorry, but I'm not going to be able to take the time off. Especially not after taking this weekend off."

Ainslie groaned. "When is this case going to end?!"

"Soon, babe." He pulled her in tighter. "It should be done by May. I hope. It's just been a really ... complicated one."

Ainslie let out an annoyed huff.

"I'm sick of this case," she said, sitting up a little, "taking up all your time. I barely see you anymore."

Aidan furrowed his brow. "Ah, I'm pretty sure we've had this conversation before, but about you and skating." His voice hardened a little. "From memory, you didn't like it very much."

"At least when I'm skating, I'm in the *state* for the most part. And at least I *call* when I say I will."

She mentally slapped herself for letting *that* slip out.

Aidan looked a little confused at first, and then his jaw tightened. "Is this about Valentine's Day?"

Ainslie folded her arms and doubled down. "Maybe."

She was all in now, anyway.

"I told you at the time," Aidan said, his voice low and controlled, "I fell asleep."

Ainslie's stomach dropped. Unless she was misremembering (and she was pretty certain she wasn't), that wasn't what he'd told her at all.

She snapped her head around to glare at him. "You did *not*."

Aidan looked even more confused.

"You said traffic was bad," Ainslie said. "You said you got back to your hotel late and didn't want to call and wake me up."

A storm cloud came over Aidan's features.

"Are you serious, Ainslie!" He threw himself out of bed and pulled his pyjama pants on. "I've been working my arse off every day for *two months* earning money for *us* so we can have the life *you* deserve, and you accuse *me* of messing around? It was one night, weeks ago. Forgive me for not remembering exactly *when* I got back to the hotel and *when* I fell asleep. If you haven't noticed, I'm exhausted!"

Ainslie wanted to disappear. Tears were beginning to form in the corners of her eyes, and she blinked them back.

"I'm sorry," she said, "I just … I don't know, I guess I just got it in my head … you're away so much —"

"For fuck's sake." He stormed over to the window and stared out over the city with his back to her. "You're acting like a crazy bitch. You've really been stewing over that for weeks? I didn't think you were one of *those* girls."

Ainslie dropped her head. He had a point, and she felt like an idiot. He was tired, and each weekend must've been blending into the last. But at the same time, she couldn't ignore that his story had changed. But she had no concrete proof that he'd done anything wrong. And he was so hurt.

"I'm sorry," she said in a tiny voice as she climbed out of bed. "This long-distance thing is … hard."

She walked over to him, wrapping her arms around his middle. She pressed her palms against his chest and rested her cheek on his back.

"I miss you," she whispered.

She felt him drop a little of his tension.

"It's not easy for me either," he said. "And it's made even harder when my fiancée doesn't trust me."

"I'm sorry," she said again, running her hands down his stomach. "Please forgive me. Please, let's not ruin tonight."

He slowly turned around, his eyes roaming up and down her still-naked body. A sly grin began to form on his lips.

"You know, you're lucky you're sexy," he said.

Ainslie's whole body flushed.

"Just remember how much this case is paying." Aidan ran his hands over the curves of her hips and squeezed her backside, pulling her against him. "Forget the South Coast for a weekend. When this is over, we can spend a month in Bora Bora if we like."

He dipped his head and kissed her, slowly and deeply, and now it was Ainslie's turn to release some of her tension.

"Besides," he said, "don't you normally have that … dress rehearsal thing at the rink before you leave for Nationals?"

"The Exhibition."

"Right. Well, I can come to that and see you skate."

The Exhibition was, in essence, a dress rehearsal that Sandra and Stephen held at the rink every year the night before the team left for Nationals. It was also a good opportunity for skaters' friends and family who weren't able to travel to Nationals to see what the skaters had been working on all year. Aidan had never been one to travel to Nationals. He wasn't able (or maybe, willing) to take that much time off work.

"You promise?" she asked, sliding her hands down his body, her fingers coming to rest at the waistband of his pants.

He pushed a lock of hair behind her ear and stroked her cheek. "I promise."

* * *

Ainslie was relieved that they'd managed to put aside their differences, but she still woke up the following morning with a small voice in her head saying, *Attack is the best form of defence.* And sure, he'd gone on the attack the night before, but maybe he just *genuinely* felt the need to defend himself. She recalled how angry *she* became when he accused her of things she hadn't done.

Ainslie tried not to let it bother her and did her best to simply enjoy their day out at Curzon Hall, although Aidan was spending an awful lot of time on his phone. While that was par for the course for Aidan, Ainslie wished he'd cut it out so they could take in their potential wedding venue properly.

"Babe, I'm just making sure everything's going all right in the Melbourne office," he said when she'd mentioned it.

"What, on a Sunday?"

He shot her a look, and she decided not to push it any further.

The lavish (and incredibly expensive) venue was about as close to a castle as Sydney offered. It was obscenely grand and surrounded by acres of lush, manicured gardens. The room they'd chosen for the reception was so large Ainslie couldn't even begin to imagine how they were ever going to fill it. She assumed that meant Aidan was planning on inviting every single high roller and socialite in Sydney.

The garden where the ceremony would be held was considerably cosier, complete with a white gazebo and fountains. The place looked like something out of a fairytale, but Ainslie had to admit, the entire affair felt wildly excessive.

Aidan put down the deposit without so much as blinking, and Ainslie nearly choked. She didn't know if there would ever be a time when she wouldn't be thrown off guard by his wealth. It made for a shocking contrast considering that earlier in the week, she'd had words with Jaz for spending too long in the shower and abusing the less-than-economical heat lamps.

*   *   *

As Aidan drove her back to her apartment on Sunday evening, Ainslie had one thing on her mind: Aidan's irregular behaviour. Sure, he had snapped when she'd accused him of fooling around, but that was understandable. But what still wasn't making any sense to Ainslie was why *other* things that would normally elicit a reaction from him were leaving him completely unphased.

Ainslie figured she must've gone off the deep end. Why she couldn't just leave well enough alone and trust him was beyond her. But something (call it paranoia or call it gut instinct) was still not allowing her to feel entirely confident about where she stood with him.

It was a little sick and twisted, but Ainslie knew if there was one thing that was guaranteed to set Aidan off, it would be the revelation that James was going to be her man of honour. They'd been in wedding planning mode all day, so it felt like the perfect segue.

She'd anticipated him hitting the roof. She'd prepared herself for the full inquisition, and she'd braced herself for the accusations and a patented Aidan tantrum. So she was more than a little surprised when she told him and he didn't even flinch.

"Sounds great, babe."

She squinted at him. "Are you sure you heard me correctly?"

She'd expected it to be like poking a sleeping lion, but Aidan just kept looking blankly ahead as he drove.

"I heard you."

"You're not mad?"

"Why would I be mad?"

Ainslie cocked her head. "Um, because you've always hated him."

He reached across the car and squeezed her thigh. "Well, last I checked, the groom outranked the *man of honour*, so I think we're good."

Ainslie frowned.

She should've been pleased — he didn't have a problem with it. But that *was* the problem.

The Aidan *she* knew *would've* had a problem with it.

CHAPTER 23

Training had been tracking along as normal. Ainslie and James had reviewed their pre-States performance with Sandra several times, which had unfortunately meant listening to whomever was making the inappropriate comments in the background over and over. Either Sandra didn't hear them, or she chose to ignore them. Frustratingly, every time Ainslie heard those comments, she was sent into another small tailspin.

"They're not a couple?!"

"Honestly, why?"

On the occasional long and lonely night when Aidan was in Melbourne, Ainslie found herself asking that same question. Sometimes she'd fall down the rabbit hole of trying to work out why nothing had ever eventuated between her and James even though there had been many times when it had felt like something could've, even long before she'd met Aidan.

She had been only nineteen when she'd met him. He was older and had seemed like the most sophisticated and interesting guy in the world. At the time, James had only been nineteen himself and was still a bit of a goofball. But she certainly didn't see him that way anymore.

She had to wonder, if she'd never met Aidan, *would* something have happened between her and James? It certainly wouldn't have been simple if something *had* happened, considering they had the weight of their entire skating career resting on their collective shoulders. They were just as much business partners as they were best friends, and Ainslie recalled the old saying about pens and the company ink. But there were some moments when she caught herself wondering if she'd made a very big mistake somewhere along the line.

The only way she could shut those thoughts out was to withdraw a bit. She couldn't quit James cold turkey — they still had to perform together — but perhaps she'd been playing her role a little *too* well. She was going to have to continue playing that role until Worlds, but she figured she ought not to enjoy it quite so much. Especially considering what she'd been accusing Aidan of.

Apparently, her plan to pump the brakes on her performance hadn't gone unnoticed by Sandra because after the final run-through of their long program the day before they left for States, the coach put a hand to her forehead and let out a sigh.

"I don't know. Something feels … off? You didn't sleep together, did you?" she said jokingly.

Ainslie turned bright red. "What?! No!"

Sandra waved them off. "Never mind. Maybe we're just having a bad day."

*   *   *

The following afternoon, Ainslie, James, Jaz and Lucy all climbed into James's beat-up little car and headed for the South Coast. Their bags were piled on their laps, their skates squashed in between their feet. Jaz and Lucy were crammed in the back like sardines, and Ainslie, up front, was in charge of the music. They wound down their windows as they hit the Mount Ousley descent at Wollongong and the coastline came into view. The hustle and bustle of the city was long forgotten, giving way to salty sea air and the sound of the ocean roaring in the distance.

"You guys ready to compete?" Ainslie asked, closing her eyes and basking in the sunshine streaming in through the car window.

"Yeah," Jaz said half-heartedly from under a mountain of luggage. "But last night, I couldn't land a triple Salchow to save my life, so there's that."

"Well, the last thing Sandra told *us* last night was that something felt off," James said.

"That's harsh."

"That's Sandra," Ainslie said. "She loves to instil a little fear right before a big comp. She thinks it will force us to pay more attention to whatever it is we're lacking."

"But what are you supposed to do with 'something feels off'?" Lucy asked. "That's not exactly the most constructive feedback."

Ainslie shrugged. "I dunno. I thought we felt fine."

That was a blatant lie.

"Same," James said unconvincingly.

*   *   *

The drive down to Shellharbour had been long, and after settling into the shabby little weatherboard weekender they'd rented, the four decided to take advantage of its veranda. The sun had set, and there was a chill in the air, but with the blankets they'd dragged out from the bedrooms and the hot beverages they'd prepared, the undercover nook made for a pleasant spot to spend the evening.

"What do you think your life would be like if you'd never started skating?" Jaz said, staring out into the darkness.

"Jesus, we're getting existential, are we?" Ainslie asked, sipping her tea.

Jaz winced. "Sorry, we don't have to talk about it if it's gonna make you upset —"

Ainslie waved it off. "It's fine."

"Well, for a start, I wouldn't have met all of you," Lucy said.

The others let out an exaggerated chorus of *aww*.

"Hold on," she added dryly. "I didn't say that would've been a bad thing."

Jaz grabbed the pillow she was resting her arm on and threw it at Lucy's head.

"But in all seriousness," Lucy said, collecting the pillow and fixing her hair, "there are so many great experiences I've had because of skating. Without it, I don't think I would've travelled as much as I have."

"I reckon if I hadn't started skating, I would've been an absolute disaster," Ainslie said, hiding behind her mug.

"Implying you're not one now?" Lucy said, earning herself another pillow to the head.

"If I hadn't had skating to focus on as a teenager," Ainslie said, "I reckon I would've been a complete train wreck."

"You were bad enough as it was," Lucy said. "Don't think I've forgotten the 2014 Nationals Dinner."

Ainslie shot her a look.

"Why? What happened at the 2014 Nationals Dinner?" Jaz's eyes widened, and a smile crept onto her face.

Ainslie groaned. "Don't tell her!"

"Oh, nothing." Lucy looked bemused. "Just a certain friend of ours got so wasted, she threw up all over the bathroom in the hotel foyer. I had to lie and tell the team manager it was food poisoning."

James chuckled into his hot chocolate.

"What are you laughing about?" Lucy cocked her head at him. "You were just as bad."

"All right, all right," Ainslie said. "The point is, I probably would've been *worse* if it weren't for skating."

"What about you, James?" Jaz asked, sipping her drink.

James looked thoughtful. "Well, skating brought you lot into my life. Which is obviously awesome. And like, I love all of you, but" — he looked at Ainslie — "I think there's just something about our friendship that's extra special, and I don't know if I would've ever formed that kind of bond with another person if it hadn't been for skating."

"Well, surely you will one day, if you eventually … get married or something," Lucy said. "Or at least I would hope so."

"Yeah, I guess."

"I dunno," Ainslie said. "I let him throw me into the air on a daily basis and count on him to catch my arse on the way down. I think we probably trust each other a lot more than some married couples do."

"Would you let Aidan throw you into the air?" Lucy asked.

"On skates? Absolutely not."

"What about not on skates?" Jaz smirked.

"Well, he'd have to be in the state for longer than thirty seconds now, wouldn't he?" Ainslie took another long sip of tea as an uncomfortable silence filled the air.

"I didn't really have a say in whether or not I skated," Jaz said eventually. "Me mam was so ice dance mad there was no way I was ever gonna be able to avoid it."

"I still can't believe you used to be an ice dancer," Lucy said.

"*I* can't believe *Chris* used to be an ice dancer," James added.

110

"I would've paid to have seen that," Ainslie said.

She'd only ever known Chris to be an inline hockey player, and the idea of him ever having been an ice dancer, considering his distinct lack of grace, seemed bizarre.

"Would you trust Chris to throw you in the air?" Lucy asked.

"God, no!" Jaz's eyes widened as though the entirety of her unsuccessful ice dance career was flashing before her eyes. "He was so bumble footed, I shouldn't have even let him do dance lifts!"

"All right, I've got one," Ainslie said. "What do you think you'll do with your life when you stop skating? We all know what I'm destined for, but what about you guys?"

"I've always thought it would be kinda cool to move somewhere a bit out of metro Sydney," James said. "Somewhere housing is more affordable. I think it'd be cool to try to establish a skating club of my own."

Ainslie blinked at him. "That'd be awesome."

"You could always come with." He stared into his drink. "Could always do with a business partner."

"Yeah, okay," Ainslie said, scoffing. "I'm afraid I'll be too busy being a trophy wife."

"Oh, boo-hoo," Jaz said jokingly, "Ainslie's going to be rich soon, her life must be *so* difficult."

Ainslie downed the rest of her tea. "Money isn't everything, Jaz."

James raised his mug to no-one in particular. "Sure helps."

*   *   *

They remained on the veranda, chatting a while longer, until Lucy checked the time.

"Well," she said as she rose to her feet, "I'm off to bed. Dance kicks off super early tomorrow. *As usual.*"

"Yeah, me too," Jaz said. "Also, I've gotta call … someone."

As soon as the girls were out of earshot, Ainslie smirked. "She's calling Cali."

James chuckled. "Oh, she's calling Cali for sure."

The pair sat quietly for a few moments, listening to the ocean breaking against the rocks. In the distance, a seagull who hadn't quite figured out it was bedtime yet let out a call. James glanced over at Ainslie. She looked pensive, as though she had a million thoughts running through her mind.

"Hey," he said at last, "are you doing okay?"

Ainslie shrugged. "Why wouldn't I be?"

James gave her a side eye. "Your comments seemed a little bitter, don't you think? Like the trophy wife remark? Or the one about Aidan never being in the state?"

Ainslie rested her head back on her chair and stared up at the stars.

"I dunno." She sighed. "This long-distance thing is a bit of a bugger, I guess. I asked Aidan if he wanted to come along this weekend to see us skate, and he said he wasn't able to get out of work. I was annoyed at first, but … I think I prefer it like this. Just the four of us, kicking back, talking about life and the future. Just like the old days."

James didn't say anything. Ainslie took a deep, shaky breath.

"Also," she added, "I guess I'm kinda bummed this is gonna be over soon. Three more comps. The countdown is really on now, isn't it?"

"Yeah. Sucks, hey?"

"Big time."

Ainslie looked into her mug, drumming her fingers against the ceramic. "That thing about starting your own club. That's really cool."

"Yeah." He gazed out into the darkness. "I guess I don't ever really *want* to move on from skating. It's not necessarily something you need to move on from. Someone has to stick around to raise the next generation."

She glanced up at him. The melancholy look on her face tugged at the deepest parts of him.

"I have to say," she said, "I'm a bit jealous."

Come with me then. Forget Aidan. Forget being a trophy wife. Come with me, and let's build an empire together.

"Offer's always open …"

She let out a weak laugh. "You know I couldn't."

James kicked at the floor and tried not to look too disappointed.

"You know, I'm glad to hear you still want to skate when I'm gone," she said. "I didn't want to be the reason you stopped doing something you love."

"I mean, I'll stop *competing*, sure, but as long as I have feet, I'll skate." He looked at her and sighed. "Won't ever be quite the same, though. Not without you."

Her eyes looked so different from how they'd once been. It was as if the last bit of fire left in them was seconds away from flickering out. In the distance, the waves still crashed on the shore, but all James was hearing was the small voice in his head, pleading with him to tell her he loved her.

Not a chance.

The moment lasted far too long, and then Ainslie spoke in the tiniest of voices. "God, I'm gonna miss you."

"I'm gonna miss you too."

James knew if they sat there any longer, one or both of them would cry, and that was the last thing either of them needed the night before a competition.

"It's getting late," he said, slapping his knees. "We've got a short program to smash tomorrow."

They both rose, the confines of the small veranda pushing them dangerously close. The way she looked up at him with her sad, tired eyes made him want to hold her in his arms and never let her go. She reached out and squeezed his shoulder.

"'Night, James."

"'Night, Ainslie."

CHAPTER 24

At eight the next morning, skaters from all over New South Wales were corralled inside the Nowra Leisure Centre. There was a handful of skaters from South Coast Rollers, whose numbers had been dwindling as of late. The South Sydney Club was there, clad in black and purple, and the Blue Mountains Artistic Club had grown significantly since 2019.

When the Randwick Ravens entered the venue, all dressed in black and white, a hush fell over the other clubs. It was difficult to ignore the looks coming from virtually everyone, some jealous, some curious. Randwick *was* the home of Jameslie, after all.

James could feel eyes burrowing into him as he and the girls walked into the stadium. There hadn't been much of a fuss at the pre-States league, but word must have travelled since then about how strong he and Ainslie had looked. He caught some people whispering to each other conspiratorially. He could only imagine what they were saying.

*　　*　　*

Lucy's event was first up, and she skated a strong style dance that left her in second place.

Jaz's warm-up had been a little worrisome. She'd looked uncharacteristically nervous, and Ainslie had been worried for a moment that she would choke, but somehow, she pulled her head together for her actual performance, much to everyone's relief.

Senior Pairs was the final event of the day.

Sandra meandered towards Ainslie and James as they rolled around the warm-up area.

"You ready?" she asked.

They glanced at each other and nodded.

"Now, we know you don't need to worry about your placing, but we still want to put the best performance we can out there," she said. "I want those judges going back to their home states and telling everybody that Jameslie is the best pairs team in this country."

Ainslie let out an extra-long exhale.

"You've just got to skate like you always do," Sandra added.

She must have dismissed their last training session as an outlier.

The pair took to the floor. The drawcard team, Australia's best hope for a Worlds victory.

Technically, everything was perfect. Performance-wise, it was good. But it wasn't *Jameslie* good.

"Okay," Sandra said when they skated off the floor, "not bad. But still ... something is just ... not working."

She looked as though she was trying to figure out what it was but couldn't.

James knew what it was but couldn't work out *why* it was.

Ainslie knew exactly what it was.

And why.

She'd held back.

She'd skated out there with James's hands all over her, and she couldn't stop thinking about Aidan and what she'd accused him of. And what he would've thought if he'd been there, watching her.

At some point, skating with James had started to feel like cheating.

It's not real! It's just pretend!

She'd been repeating that mantra to herself, over and over, but the problem was, it was starting to *feel* real. Especially when they shared moments like the previous evening, or like Christmas night. Moments when it felt as if they were standing on the edge of something.

And it was eating her up from the inside because she couldn't ignore the fact that deep down, she was starting to wish it *were* real.

*　　*　　*

The second day of States kicked off with Senior Ladies Freedance, and Ainslie, James and Jaz cheered as Lucy took the floor. Ainslie had no doubt that Lucy would be able to pull into first place. The girl who had bested her in the style dance had been awarded a pretty good score for her freedance, but Lucy had a look in her eye that Ainslie recognised: she was about to do something amazing.

The music began to swell, and she began to dance, and when Lucy danced, she danced from her heart. Her movements were so graceful and effortless it was easy to forget she was on skates. No-one owned the freedance quite like Lucy Huong.

Her routine ended in a flourish, and Ainslie and the others cheered as loudly as they could. Lucy returned to the marshalling area to await her score. When it came up, it was huge. More than enough to push her into the gold medal position.

"On ya, Luce!" Ainslie said.

"That was bloody brilliant." Jaz grinned, clapping ferociously.

After the event ended, James put a hand on Ainslie's shoulder.

"Hey, you wanna go for a walk?" he whispered.

Ainslie cocked her head. "Where?"

"The car park. Just wanna chat."

Ainslie felt uneasy, but she climbed down from the grandstand and they meandered outside. They mindlessly strolled along the perimeter with their hands in their pockets until James finally piped up.

"What do you make of this whole 'something being off' thing?"

Ainslie was a little taken aback, and her stomach tightened.

"What do you mean?" she asked, even though she knew the answer.

"You can't say you haven't felt it. I know I have."

"Felt what?"

"I don't know! I guess ... yesterday it just kinda felt like you didn't want to be skating with me."

Ainslie's face fell. "Seriously?" That couldn't have been further from the truth.

"Well, yeah," he replied. "We might've been physically in sync, but it felt like you weren't all there ... emotionally?"

"I don't know what you're talking about," she said, unable to look him in the eye.

"Ainslie ..." He was clearly losing his patience.

Ainslie let out an exaggerated groan and forced herself to meet his gaze.

"It was those comments, okay! The ones from the video from pre-States!"

James looked lost. "Huh?"

"The comments those girls made about us?"

Ainslie watched as the penny dropped.

"Ah."

"Look, don't get me wrong," she said, "I'm not physically disgusted by the idea of people thinking certain things about us —"

"Gee, thanks."

"But don't you ever find it ... uncomfortable? That people talk about us like that?"

James shrugged. "Well, sure. I mean, it's weird. But people have been making assumptions like that for *years*. You've always just brushed it off in the past."

Yeah, because it wasn't until now that I sort of, kind of, wished those assumptions were correct!

She mentally slapped herself.

"I'm *engaged* now," she said, dragging her mind back to Aidan. "I'm supposed to be getting married at the end of the year, and *everyone* knows it. I don't *want* people assuming things about me. Not things like that."

James sighed. "I get it. I really do. But it's not *real*. You know it. I know it."

Yeah, but what if it was?

She gave herself another mental reprimanding.

Ainslie put a hand to her forehead. She was starting to get a headache.

"I know ...," she said quietly.

"Look, Goose," James said, putting his hands on her shoulders, "we've only got three more shots at this. We want to go out on top, right?"

"Yeah ..."

"Then you're going to need to go out there this afternoon and act like you want to rip my clothes off!" he said jokingly.

She replied with a weak laugh.

Yeah, "act".

*　　*　　*

The Senior freeskaters were finishing their warm-up as James and Ainslie re-joined Lucy in the grandstand.

"How's Jaz doing?" Ainslie asked as she sat back down.

"Her warm-up was great. Looks like she got all the nerves out of her system since yesterday."

Jaz had been drawn last to skate the long program, and when the announcer called her to the floor, Ainslie nearly went hoarse from screaming. The music began and a hush fell over the crowd. Jaz made her first movements.

Her first element was a double Axel, and it was clean as a whistle. A huge smile spread across Jaz's face, and she sped off to the next element. There wasn't a single trace of the nerves she'd had during the warm-up the day before. Every jump was clean, every spin was fast. The triple Salchow was still slightly under-rotated, but it was on one foot.

Ainslie, James and Lucy all hollered from the grandstand as she hit her final position and the music ended. It was easily the best long program in the event. Jaz punched the air and beamed as she rolled over to Sandra, who was looking quietly confident.

When the scores finally came up, Ainslie let out a shriek. Jaz had done it. She'd won the long program by a mile and pushed herself up into first place overall.

"She's a bloody legend." Ainslie was so proud of her friend, she momentarily forgot about her own inner turmoil.

*　　*　　*

By the time the Senior Pairs event came around, the crowd was weary, although they seemed to be injected with fresh stamina as Team Jameslie was called to the floor.

Ainslie was thinking about one thing.

"Get out there and act like you want to rip my clothes off!"

She wasn't sure that little piece of advice had quite the effect James had in-tended. Mainly because now she couldn't stop picturing it.

It's not real. It's just pretend. It's not real. It's just pretend.

She repeated the mantra in her head, but when she was standing out on the floor, her leg wrapped around his hip, his eyes burning into her, imploring her to give him something — *anything* — in return … it didn't feel quite so pretend anymore.

And then that stupid music began to play. That driving drum line, beating a constant rhythm into her skull. That obnoxious flute, coaxing her along, temp-ting her to give in and play the role of seductress.

She couldn't.

It was too frightening. Too dangerous.

Too hypocritical.

116

They skated their routine and it was clean, as usual. But it still lacked something indescribable.

The music ended and James pulled her into their customary hug.

"I'm sorry," she whispered in his ear.

"Don't be. I get it."

But she could hear the disappointment in his voice.

A lump formed in Ainslie's throat as he took her hand and led her off the rink. It seemed like that patented Jameslie chemistry, the spark that had made them famous and that they were relying on to take them all the way to the Worlds podium, was gone.

CHAPTER 25

Ever since Aidan's blasé reaction to her man of honour idea, Ainslie had been stuck in a mental tug of war, trying to figure out if his response (or lack thereof) was something to be concerned about.

Aidan's class action had finally ended, and his trips to Melbourne had ceased, which Ainslie was grateful for. To make up for lost time, she'd been spending most of her evenings at his apartment. There hadn't been any more arguments since their night at the Shangri-La, but Ainslie couldn't help but notice how much time Aidan had been spending glued to his phone, and she was constantly fighting the urge to say something. Sure, it wasn't unusual for him to frequently use his phone for work, but Ainslie wasn't stupid. She knew the difference between an email notification and the sound of an incoming direct message.

She'd also noticed how when his phone wasn't in his hand, it spent an awful lot of time facedown, where she couldn't see the screen. And she'd definitely noticed how he turned it away from her every time she sat beside him.

Ainslie wanted to vent her concerns about Aidan to somebody. Mainly she just wanted someone to tell her she was overreacting.

She wouldn't normally bother Lucy with relationship drama, but Lucy *was* the most pragmatic one of her friends. Ainslie cornered her in the kitchen one morning to flag it with her.

Lucy leaned against the bench and folded her arms.

"Ainslie," she said, cocking her head, "this feels like something you should be talking to *him* about, not me."

Ainslie rolled her eyes dramatically. "Luce, I just need somebody to tell me I'm acting like a crazy bitch and that everything is fine."

"Don't call yourself that, Ains." Lucy's tone was sympathetic. "Look, I really want to be able to tell you that you have nothing to worry about … but honestly, from what you've told me, it does sound a little …"

"A little what?"

"Maybe I'm just biased because I don't like him."

"Lucy …"

Lucy let out a long sigh. "Honestly, I don't have the best feeling about it. I've never had the best feeling about him, full stop. The man is one giant, walking red flag."

It was exactly what Ainslie had feared hearing.

"So, do you think it's possible he's cheating on me?"

Lucy's gaze dropped to the floor.

Ainslie crossed her arms. "Well, do you?"

Lucy had been backed into a corner. "I'm sorry, Ains, but I wouldn't put it past him."

*　　*　　*

Late on the Sunday evening a week before she was to leave for Nationals, Ainslie sat curled into Aidan's side on his lounge while a movie played on his enormous television. She was hardly able to focus on it, though, not while Aidan's phone, facedown on the arm of the lounge, kept vibrating incessantly.

Ainslie had been trying her best to bury her worries and forget what Lucy had said. Lucy had always been wary of ... well, everyone, but after Aidan's phone vibrated for the seventh time in what could've only been two minutes, she couldn't hold it in any longer.

"God, you're popular tonight," she said, trying to sound casual.

She felt his body stiffen around her.

"It's the boys," he said. "I really clicked with a few of them down in Melbourne, so we started a group chat."

She really wanted to believe him.

"Huh. Not like you to be glued to social media."

Ainslie immediately regretted that one.

"Do you have a problem with that?" His voice had grown cold.

Her lower lip trembled, and she bit it to keep it under control. "No."

They spent the rest of the movie in tense silence, and when the credits began to roll, Aidan stretched his arms over his head and stood.

"You'd better be heading off, then."

"Are you really in such a hurry to get rid of me?" She'd intended for it to sound like a lighthearted jab, but instead, it came out sounding bitter.

Which, of course, it was.

Aidan pinned her in place with his gaze, clenching his jaw. His stare was so intense she had to look away. She dropped her head and noticed his hands were balled into fists, and a chill coursed through her veins.

"You're being really needy," he said.

Ainslie's throat felt as if it were about to close up. They weren't violent words, but they still stung. He moved towards the front door as though he was corralling her out of there.

Somewhere in the back of her mind, a small voice reminded her, *Attack is the best form of defence.*

She eventually found the courage to move.

"Sorry." Her voice sounded as if it didn't belong to her.

She grabbed her bag and moved towards the door, pausing beside him to see if he'd offer her a goodnight kiss. He pecked her on the lips, but his mouth was drawn in a tight line and he felt stone cold.

*　　*　　*

When Ainslie got back to her apartment, she couldn't help herself. She grabbed her phone and began scrolling through Aidan's social media. It wouldn't take long. He didn't post all that often, and it was mostly just business articles.

She felt like a woman possessed. If Aidan knew, he'd call her crazy, but she couldn't bring herself to stop. Then she noticed a recurring interaction.

A beautiful blonde woman named Sam Halliday had liked every single post he'd made since January. Ainslie chewed on her lower lip and clicked on Sam's profile. She lived in Melbourne, and it appeared she worked at Aidan's father's firm.

It's nothing. She's just another solicitor he met down there. Work colleagues, that's all.

But Ainslie couldn't ignore the churning in her gut. The act of liking social media posts on its own was fairly innocuous, but with everything else Ainslie had noticed, pieces were falling into place in the worst way.

CHAPTER 26

The week leading up to Nationals was set to be a hectic one. The Randwick Ravens Exhibition Skate would be held on Thursday evening, and the skaters would leave for the Gold Coast the following morning. Between packing and training, Ainslie thought it best to take the week off work so she could focus.

She spent most of the week with James, jumping back and forth between the rink and the gym and putting the finishing touches on their routines. The technical improvements had been going well, but Ainslie was still forcing herself to keep a lid on the chemistry they were so renowned for, which was making it difficult for her to muster the same enthusiasm and excitement she would normally have in the lead-up to a major competition. That and the fact that Aidan hadn't really spoken to her much since the whole "you're being really needy" fiasco.

Ainslie was hoping they'd be able to smooth things over before she left for Nationals just so she'd have one less thing to worry about while she was competing. She was relieved when he asked her over for dinner the night before the Exhibition Skate. Unfortunately, training ran overtime, and she turned up at his apartment forty minutes late and still in her training clothes, hair scooped into a sweaty, messy bun.

"I'm so sorry I'm late," Ainslie said when he answered the door.

Aidan looked her up and down. "You look like a mess."

"Cheers," she replied, moving past him into the apartment.

"No time for a shower?"

"We're going to be married in five months," she said, dumping her bag beside the lounge. "You're going to see me a lot worse off than this."

He raised his eyebrows, and Ainslie looked sideways at him.

"What?" She almost laughed. "You want me to get the rink stink off me?"

"I want you to get the *James* stink off you," he muttered as he turned towards the kitchen.

Now it was Ainslie's turn to raise her eyebrows. "Excuse me?"

"Nothing."

She chewed the inside of her cheek and kept her mouth shut. She disappeared into his bathroom, took a shower and changed, hoping her spare clothes were good enough for His Majesty. She couldn't work out why Aidan was making jabs about James again after such a long period of cordiality.

*　　*　　*

Aidan's irritability only got worse throughout the course of the evening, and all through dinner, he seemed only able to muster up monosyllabic responses.

"Are you okay?" Ainslie asked finally.

"I'm fine." The reply sounded more like grunting than speaking. "Just been a long day."

Ainslie took another bite and chewed silently. She studied him across the table. His jaw was clenched, and he wouldn't stop glancing at his phone. She was surprised to see it face up for once, although it wasn't like him to have it at the table.

He glanced at his phone one more time.

Ainslie couldn't help herself.

"You waiting to hear from someone?" She tried her best to sound nonchalant.

Aidan looked up at her, fury etched over his face.

Ainslie's palms began to sweat.

"Cut the shit, Ainslie. What are you implying?"

Ainslie opened her mouth to speak but Aidan didn't even wait for an answer.

"If you *must* know, I'm waiting to hear from a colleague."

Ainslie heard herself utter the words. "A colleague named Sam?"

As soon as she said it, her head began to pound. The little vein on Aidan's forehead pulsed furiously. She'd clearly struck a nerve.

A lump formed in Ainslie's throat, and she tried her hardest to choke it back as she asked, "Who's Sam?"

"Sam is a colleague." Aidan's voice was slow and calculated, and it was deeply frightening. "From Melbourne. Just one of —"

"The boys?" She was surprised by how steady her voice sounded. "Not Sam Halliday? The girl who keeps liking all your posts?"

She wished she could take it back.

He clenched his teeth, and his face turned bright red. He rose to his feet, slamming his fist down against the table, rattling all the crockery and knocking over his wine glass.

"Are you *fucking* kidding me, Ainslie?! You spend every waking moment with that *fuck* from the rink." He stared her down. "He's your fucking *man of honour*, which I *never* should've allowed in the first place, and you have the *audacity* to call *me* out for having a friend who's a woman?"

Ainslie wanted to throw up. Her heart felt as if it might pound right out of her chest. He stood across the table, towering over her. Ainslie had never been more terrified of another human being in her life.

"Last I checked, James likes all *your* posts too. Does that automatically mean *you're* fucking *him*? I didn't realise you were such a hypocrite."

Ainslie sunk a little further into her chair, hoping she could make herself so small she'd disappear. The inside of her head was like a whirlpool. And a voice in the back of her mind kept on screaming, *He's gaslighting you! He's being defensive because he's guilty!*

But there was no way she would be able to say that out loud, even if she wanted to.

Another internal voice chimed in.

You don't have solid proof. He's right about James. You are *a hypocrite.*

She couldn't think straight. All she wanted to do was get out of his apartment.

"I'm sorry." Her voice wavered. "I shouldn't have made assumptions."

"No." He glared at her, finally lowering his voice. "You shouldn't have."

Ainslie felt tears begin to roll down her cheeks, and she brushed them away as discreetly as she could. Aidan snatched up his phone and walked towards the living room, muttering curses under his breath.

Ainslie stood slowly, her legs shaking beneath her.

"I should go home," she managed to say.

"Yeah, that's probably a good idea," he said without looking at her. "I'll see you tomorrow at that … thing."

Ainslie furrowed her brow. "The Exhibition Skate? You're still coming?"

He shot her a look. "I promised, didn't I?"

Ainslie swallowed hard. She wasn't so sure she wanted him there anymore. In fact, she was starting to realise she didn't want him around *at all* anymore.

"Okay," she said slowly, not wanting to antagonise him any further. "I'll see you there, then."

Without another word, Ainslie grabbed her bag and slipped out of the apartment.

The second she was in the lift, the dam burst. Full, deep sobs wracked her entire body. She was on the verge of hyperventilating, and she was shaking from head to toe.

She couldn't keep on going like this.

CHAPTER 27

When Ainslie woke up the next morning, her eyes were gritty, and her head felt heavy. Last night, she'd gotten a glimpse of her future. If that was how Aidan was behaving now, in the early stages, when it was supposed to be all sunshine and roses, what hope was there for their marriage?

Sure, no relationship was perfect *all* the time, and she and Aidan had the occasional moments of bliss, but lately, it seemed as if every single time things were going well between them, one of them did something or said something that spoiled it.

Aidan had even managed to suck all the fun out of her skating, the *one thing* that had always brought her unparalleled joy. And her and James's scores had been suffering because of it. Ainslie knew there was no way they would get up on that podium at Worlds without their high performance scores. She had to do *something*.

Ainslie sat up and swung her legs over the side of the bed. Her decision had been made. No more holding back. No more worrying about what Aidan thought. There was no way she was going to let him steal her joy anymore.

*   *   *

Ainslie arrived at the rink around one that afternoon. Aidan had messaged to let her know he was planning to head over once he finished work, but Ainslie had given up caring by then.

As she walked into the rink car park, she spotted James lugging his skate bag out of the boot of his car. She felt a smile tug at the corners of her mouth.

When he noticed her, his face lit up. It caused her heart to swell and her stomach to do a little flip.

Fuck. I am a hypocrite.

"Goose!" He beamed. "You ready for Nationals?"

"Hell yeah, I am!" She couldn't help but laugh.

"That's the spirit!" He clamped his arm around her shoulders, and she let him.

She relaxed into his warm embrace as they walked into the rink together, and it was the first time all week that she'd realised just how much tension she'd been holding onto.

It felt so right, being tucked under his arm. James would never frighten her, or scream in her face, or leave her a sobbing, trembling mess.

The bar for men really is on the floor, if that's all it takes to win a woman's heart.

But Ainslie knew that James wasn't a bare minimum kind of guy. He did a lot more than just *not* frighten her. He made *everything* so much better. He'd always been there for her no matter what. He cared for her. He always had. He made her smile, and laugh, and blush furiously, and this was supposed to be their third-last skate together … and God, she was going to miss him so much it ached.

*   *   *

Ainslie stood at the entrance to the warm-up rink, looking out into the main area and scanning the crowd. It was nearly seven, and the grandstand was packed with supporters.

Lucy's parents were sitting at the top, her dad with his video camera at the ready. Jason Sunderland and Chris Bannister were sitting near them, chatting away. Aidan was sitting all the way at the opposite end of the grandstand, looking like he'd rather be anywhere else.

Ainslie felt a gentle hand on her back, and she jumped a little.

"Are you ready?" James was standing beside her, a warm smile on his face.

They were going to be opening the night with their short program and closing it with their long.

Ainslie shook out her legs one by one and took a deep breath. "Ready as I'll ever be."

James patted her on the back and ushered her towards the gap in the barrier as Tim called them to the floor.

The crowd erupted into cheers.

They stood in their first position, back to back, not yet touching. The opening strings of "Never Tear Us Apart" filled the air. Ainslie glanced into the crowd and spotted Aidan.

He was on his phone.

Rage flooded Ainslie's veins, and she gritted her teeth.

Fuck this. It's all or nothing.

The vocals kicked in, and the pair began their first movements, turning to face each other. Ainslie's eyes locked onto James's. And there it was. The iconic Jameslie fire had been reignited. Ainslie wasn't holding back. Not anymore. James looked a little startled at first, but it didn't take him long to pick up on her energy.

They took off at a slow, sensual pace, building with the music and eventually launching into their first element, a throw triple Salchow. Ainslie flew through the air and landed solidly on one foot. The crowd screamed.

A footwork sequence to the soaring sax solo. A death spiral when the music dropped to a pounding bass riff. A death-defying lift when the vocals hit a crescendo. They kept moving through the routine with ease, and grace, and that sizzling chemistry.

The music came to an end, and they hit their final position, breathing heavily.

"That … that was …" James wrapped her up in a hug. "We're back!"

Ainslie grinned. "Hell yeah, we are."

The cheers from the crowd continued until the two were off the floor completely. Sandra looked as if she'd been reborn.

"That's more like it!" She lovingly slapped both of them on the back. "I don't know what happened, or what you did to fix it. And frankly, I don't want to know. Just keep that same energy for the long program. And for next week!"

Ainslie couldn't keep the smile off her face.

"Did you want to go out and sit with Aidan?"

"Nah, I'm good."

"Do you think he watched?"

"Don't care." She grinned. "I skated that for me."

James grinned back and slapped her a high five. "Yeah, ya did."

CHAPTER 28

By the end of the night, the crowd was foaming at the mouth for more Jameslie, and Ainslie was dying to get back out there again. This was the big one. The routine they hoped would carry them all the way to the Worlds podium. It'd been so lackadaisical at States, Ainslie had imagined the international judges going back to their home states and telling everybody, "Oh, they're skating to Ravel's 'Bolero'. They have huge shoes to fill with that music. But I just don't think they cut it."

Ainslie pushed it out of her mind. She was determined to make tonight's performance a redemption skate, and Nationals was going to be next level.

*   *   *

The crowd roared as the final crescendo of "Bolero" rang throughout the building, but Ainslie couldn't hear the music or the people cheering.

All she could hear was her heart pounding in her chest and her heavy breathing. All she could see was James's face, so close to hers as they held their final position. No-one who witnessed that skate would be able to say that Jameslie's chemistry had flatlined. James lifted Ainslie upright and pulled her into a hug. They gave their final bows and rolled off the floor.

Tim announced that the Exhibition was over, and people began filing out of the building.

"Just —" Sandra made a chef's kiss. "You're back! I knew you could do it."

The coach walked off with her head held high and began packing down for the evening.

"That was awesome!" James was beaming as he folded Ainslie into another hug.

"I know, right! We're going to absolutely kill it next week!"

"Get your fucking hands off my fiancée."

Ainslie's heart dropped at the sound of Aidan's voice. It was absolutely boiling over with rage.

James let Ainslie go and raised his hands in surrender. He dropped his head and rolled backwards a little.

The skaters who were still milling about all snapped their heads around to watch the tall, dark-haired man in the expensive suit storm over to Ainslie and James.

"What the hell was that?"

"What the hell was what?" Ainslie crossed her arms defiantly.

"That." He gestured towards the rink. "That little … *display*."

"Um, our long program?" she replied innocently.

"You think I didn't notice?" His voice was just below a shout.

"Notice what?" Ainslie's volume rose to meet his.

"Notice *you*!" He finally lost what little restraint he had left. "And *him*!" He pointed aggressively in James's face.

Ainslie's mouth had gone dry. Her heart began racing as the fear from the night before came rushing back.

A few skaters nearby pretended they weren't listening as they hurriedly packed their skates away, clearly desperate to get out of there.

"You expect me to sit here and watch you do *that* and *not* think something's going on between you two?" He sneered.

"Aidan, I've told you a million times, there is *nothing* —"

"Oh, bullshit, Ainslie! You're not that good an actress!"

She wanted to throw something back in his face. The visits to Melbourne and the suspiciously good mood they left him in. The constant checking of his phone and his defensive response when she'd called him out on it. Sam Halliday and the attention she'd been paying him online.

Ainslie wanted to bring up all those things, but she couldn't. She was paralysed, caught in a state somewhere between rage and fear. Hot tears had begun welling in her eyes, and her bottom lip quivered. All the words she wanted to scream at him were jammed in the back of her throat.

"Come on, we're going home." Aidan grabbed her roughly by the arm, digging his large fingers into her skin.

Ainslie yelped in pain.

"Hey!" James said.

Aidan let go of Ainslie, almost shoving her away in the process, and turned his attention to James.

"You," he said through clenched teeth. "You're lucky you still have legs to skate with, you fucking dick."

"Mate, I think it's time you leave."

"Why don't you try to make me —"

"Hey!" The new voice belonged to Sandra. She was small, but she was mighty, and she was storming back over. "This is *my* rink, and if you don't leave right now, I'll have no choice but to have you physically removed."

Aidan was too proud for that. And as unhinged as he was acting, he respected power when he saw it. He ran his tongue over his top teeth in a sort of sneer and stood up straight.

"You know what? Fuck this. Fuck this whole sport. And fuck you."

His last words were directed at James.

"I'll be in the car," Aidan called to Ainslie over his shoulder as he marched out of the rink.

Ainslie's head was pounding. It felt as if time had stopped. James was staring at her as if he wanted to say something. Sandra wrapped an arm protectively around her shoulders.

Ainslie could still feel the imprint of Aidan's fingers digging into her arm. The sobs that'd been brewing in her chest rose up to her throat, and she finally lost control. She clapped a hand over her mouth to muffle the sound. She turned, shaking off Sandra's embrace, and raced down the carpet with her skates still on, past the grandstand and away to the safety of the change room.

*   *   *

James knew Ainslie needed space, but half an hour had passed since the Exhibition had ended, and he was worried.

"Lucy! Do you know where Ainslie is?"

"I think she's still in the change room —"

James started off before she could finish.

"— but I don't know if she wants to see anyone, though! She bit my head off when I tried to speak to her."

He ignored the warning.

He ran to the change room and knocked on the door, pushing it open slightly as he did.

"Ains? Are you decent?"

She replied with a sniff. "Yeah."

He opened the door and found her, skates still on, costume still in place, with her face buried in her hands and her shoulders heaving.

She raised her head and looked up at him. Her make-up was ruined, and her cheeks were streaked with tears.

"I'm so sorry," she said between sobs, dropping her head back into her hands.

"Hey, hey, hey," he murmured as he moved to sit beside her on the bench, "you don't have anything to be sorry for."

He wrapped an arm around her and squeezed her to his side.

"I'm so embarrassed," she said in a shaky voice, resting her head on his shoulder.

He held her tighter. "Don't be embarrassed. He should be the one who's embarrassed. He acted like a complete dickhead, and he had to do the walk of shame out of here."

"He's *always* going to be like this. It won't matter if you're around or not."

James held his tongue. He knew she was right, and he wasn't about to say he'd told her so.

"I can't do this anymore." Ainslie lifted her head and blinked up at him, her eyes red and weary. "I need to leave him, don't I?"

James looked at her. Her eyes were pleading with him. Sitting that close to her, he couldn't help but wonder what it would be like to kiss her. Part of him wanted to just give in and do it. Kiss her and tell her how he felt. Hold her and hopefully never let her go. Tell her that yes, she should leave Aidan and be with him instead.

But with them leaving for Nationals the next day, there was no way he was about to do something that stupid.

129

"I think you already know the answer," he said finally.

She dropped her head and sighed. "Yeah, I know."

*　　*　　*

Ainslie wiped her tears away and tried to focus on getting changed.

"Hey," Jaz said tentatively as she poked her head into the change room.

"Sorry about what you had to witness tonight."

"That guy has issues, my love," Jaz said, closing the door behind her. "Like anger issues, control issues, jealousy issues. Basically, every issue you want to avoid in an intimate partner."

Ainslie sighed. "I know, you're right."

"So, what are you gonna do?"

"I don't know."

Ainslie wasn't talking about the Aidan situation anymore. She knew exactly what to do about that.

Jaz sat down beside her.

"You know, I worry about you, Ains. I've always seen you as the big sister I never had. You're so cool, and funny, and brilliantly talented ..." Jaz sighed. "James and Lucy told me you changed a lot after you met Aidan. I know I haven't known you as long as they have, but I remember when we first met, you'd only just met Aidan, and even then you were so ... different from how you are now. And these last six or seven months ..." Jaz looked at the floor. "I know you probably don't want my opinion, and I know it's not my place to say it, but ... Aidan is toxic."

Ainslie zipped up her skate bag with an aggressive tug.

"I'm sorry," Jaz said quietly.

"I think Aidan's right," Ainslie said.

Jaz furrowed her brow. "What?"

"I think I'm in love with James."

Jaz's eyes widened slowly as her brain processed the words.

"Okay ... um, how long has this been a thing?"

"I don't know. I think I first realised it was on the cards a few months ago. But honestly ... probably ... when I think about it in retrospect ... always?"

Jaz exhaled sharply. "Well, that's kind of a big deal."

"Why? It's not like I can do anything about it."

"And why not?"

"Jaz," Ainslie said, "you know that sort of thing is a sure-fire way to ruin a perfectly good friendship."

"Only in books and movies. It *could* turn out to be the best decision you ever make."

"Well, then it could ruin a perfectly good skating partnership."

"Skating isn't everything! What if the reward outweighed the risk?"

"It doesn't matter. He doesn't see me that way. Besides, technically I'm still engaged."

Jaz rolled her eyes and groaned. "Are you serious? You're not actually still thinking about staying with Aidan, are you? After he publicly humiliated you and did *that* to you?"

Jaz pointed to Ainslie's arm, where a bruise was now developing.

"Jaz, please stop."

"You gotta stop making excuses for him, Ains. Honestly, I don't care if you hook up with James or not. All I'm saying is you need to leave Aidan. Tonight. Or you're going to be in big trouble."

"I know! I will!"

"Hey," James called from just outside the door, "your lovely fiancé is still sitting in the car park. He wants to know if you plan on leaving here at all tonight. Should I tell him to go fuck himself or …?"

"He's still here?" Jaz asked. "I'm surprised he didn't just drive off."

"I was supposed to be going to his place tonight. He probably wants to yell at me some more," Ainslie said to Jaz. Then she called back to James, "Tell him he can wait."

"Yes, ma'am."

"That's our lass." Jaz took Ainslie by the shoulders. "Talk to him. You know what to do."

CHAPTER 29

Ainslie felt powerful as she marched out of the rink towards Aidan's car. She didn't know if it was the pep talk from her friends or the adrenaline, but she knew exactly what she needed to do, and she was about to do it. But as she slid into the passenger seat and looked over at Aidan stewing behind the wheel, she felt all that confidence leave her body.

In silence, Aidan started the engine and began driving, the air between them thick with tension. She had to say it. She had to tell him it was over, and preferably before he drove all the way back to his house. Her heart was racing, and she had to sit on her hands to stop them from shaking. She clenched her teeth and focused all her energy on psyching herself up to speak.

Aidan was still silent. She thought back to the way he'd yelled at her. The way he'd grabbed her. The way he'd spoken to James. It didn't take long for her rage to begin drowning out her fear. She finally found the courage to speak, but unfortunately, it wasn't until they'd already passed the turn-off for her building.

"Are you proud of yourself?" She tried her best to sound tough, but her heart was still racing. "Making me look like an idiot in front of everyone?"

"Were we at the same Exhibition, Ainslie?" Aidan replied through gritted teeth. "Because the only person there who looked like an idiot was me. Standing back while I watched my *fiancée* with another guy's hands *all over her*."

Ainslie groaned.

"You know what, Aidan? You're right. You *did* look like an idiot," she said, "but not because of *me*. You made *yourself* look like an idiot. And whenever you make comments about me and James, every person who knows anything about pairs skating thinks you're an idiot!"

"Do *you* think I'm an idiot?"

"Yeah." She laughed in frustration. "When you go off like that, I do."

"Do you think I give a shit what a bunch of fucking *roller skaters* think about me?" Aidan said as he took the sharp exit for the Cahill Expressway a little faster than necessary. "Whatever. We only have three months of this bullshit left, anyway. Then you'll be done with skating, and that fucker will be out of our lives and out of *this* relationship."

Ainslie's heart was pounding in her ears as Aidan drove towards the Harbour Bridge. He looked like a wild man, his knuckles white on the steering wheel and his eyes burning with rage. She thought the vein pulsing on his forehead might burst. Her stomach was churning, she was sweating profusely, and her arm was twinging where he'd grabbed her. She braced herself.

She couldn't back down.

Not this time.

"Aidan," she said, trying to remain stony faced, "I will no longer be retiring at the end of the year. I have no desire to stop skating, and I'm sick of you telling me what I can and can't do."

Aidan just stared at the road ahead, his expression unchanging, and accelerated. He was well over the speed limit now. Ainslie grabbed onto the armrest with one hand and her seat with the other.

"You're fucking him, aren't you?" he said, his voice terrifyingly calm.

Ainslie's grip on the armrest tightened, and a chill ran through her.

"Aidan, please let me out of the car."

"See? You won't even deny it."

"Please." A sob threatened to escape Ainslie's lips. "Let me out."

He scoffed. "We're on the bridge! What the fuck are you gonna do? Jump off?"

Ainslie felt as if she was going to be sick.

"I *knew* you'd been messing around with him," Aidan said through clenched teeth.

"I've never done *anything* like that." Ainslie was trying to stay calm and not antagonise him further, but it was getting more difficult by the second. "If you're so convinced that I'm cheating on you, then that's *your* problem for being so insecure."

"What I'm hearing from you right now," Aidan said in a low voice, "is that you would rather skate with him than marry me. Is that what you're saying?"

He increased his speed even more as he took the exit off the bridge. Ainslie was relieved they were no longer driving directly over water.

"Aidan, please let me out of the car," she said again, ignoring his question.

"Answer me!" He smacked his palm against the steering wheel.

"Let me out of the fucking car!" Her throat turned hoarse as she held back the urge to cry.

"Not until you admit you're fucking him!"

"No! For the last time, I am *not fucking James!*"

Aidan went silent. Somehow the silence was even scarier than his yelling. At least when he was yelling, she knew exactly where she stood with him. But right now, her pulse quickened as she realised that Aidan was so incensed, so volatile, that she could be in real danger.

But much to her surprise and relief, he slowed the car down, took an exit at Milsons Point, and pulled into the shoulder of a backstreet.

He turned to face her, fury burning in his eyes, his jaw tight.

"You're a fucking liar. And I don't *fuck around* with liars."

Ainslie swallowed down the sob that was stuck in the back of her throat. There was no way she was about to cry in front of him.

"I can't do this anymore," she muttered as she unclasped the necklace he'd given her and pulled off her engagement ring. "I'm done."

Aidan sucked his teeth. "That's what I thought."

"Here." She handed him the jewellery, and he snatched it away.

"I hope you two are very happy together," he said with a snarl.

Ainslie rolled her eyes and climbed out of the car, her legs shaking beneath her.

"And don't be surprised if I don't drop everything to come to your fucking roller skating wedding," Aidan added.

"Whatever," Ainslie replied as she retrieved her bags from the boot.

She bent down and peered through the passenger-side window, feeling a little more confident now she was no longer inside with him. "Have fun with *Sam*, you dick."

With one final glare, Aidan sped off into the night and out of her life for good.

CHAPTER 30

Ainslie cupped a hand over her mouth and finally let out the sob that she'd been holding in. Just like that, a six-year relationship was over. It was the right decision, but her left hand felt oddly naked. She'd been rattled to her core and was still shaking all over, but at the same time, she felt as if the weight of the world had been lifted off her shoulders.

She looked around. Now she had a whole new problem. She was standing alone on the side of the road, somewhere in North Sydney. It was nearly nine, it was dark and cold, and she had to leave for Nationals in the morning.

She had to leave for Nationals in the morning.

Shit.

Aidan was supposed to be taking her to the airport.

Shit. Shit. Shit.

Jaz was getting a lift with Lucy and her parents, so there probably wouldn't be room in their car.

Ainslie wondered if it would be a stupid idea to call James while she felt vulnerable and lonely. But he was starting to look like her only hope. Besides, she'd really appreciate it if he could drive over and collect her from wherever it was that she was currently stranded.

"Hey, Goose." He sounded surprised.

"Hey." She tried not to sound as if she'd been crying.

"Are you okay?"

"Um, yeah. I was just wondering if you could do me a favour?"

"Of course."

"Can you come pick me up and take me home?" she asked, her voice cracking a little.

"Where are you?" He sounded worried, and she could hear his keys jingling already.

She looked up and down the dark street and caught a glimpse of the faint glow of Luna Park at the bottom of the hill. "I'm in Milsons Point."

"Milsons Point? What are you doing there?"

"Let's just say the break-up didn't go well," she said, brushing a tear from her cheek.

"Okay, um." He sounded flustered. "Just … find somewhere well lit and send me your location. I'll be there as fast as I can."

She hung up and shared her location with him, then she walked down towards Luna Park and sat on the steps beside the huge, grotesque face that served as its entrance. It was casting an eerie glow over the nearby harbour, and it appeared to be laughing.

Probably laughing at how stupid I've been.

It felt like the longest fifteen minutes of her life, but eventually, James called and told her he'd arrived. She found him pulled over in the street that ran behind the amusement park and climbed into his car. She flopped her head back against the headrest and let out a long, deep breath. He reached across the car and put a hand on her shoulder.

"Ains, are you … okay?"

"Can I please get a lift to the airport tomorrow?" she asked, ignoring his question. "Aidan was supposed to take me, and I really don't want to have to lug all my shit on public transport."

"Of course."

They drove back over the bridge towards Ainslie's apartment in silence. She wanted to get it all off her chest, but she needed a moment. The events of the evening were still swirling around in her head, and she was grateful that James wasn't pushing it.

When they turned into Gadigal Avenue, Ainslie finally spoke.

"Do you want to come up for a bit? The girls were going out for dinner with Lucy's parents and Chris. And if Jaz's latest post is anything to go by, they're not home yet."

"Sure," James replied, pulling into a car space along the street.

*   *   *

As Ainslie had said, the apartment was empty. James watched her as she headed straight for the kitchen and switched on the kettle.

"Tea? If we weren't leaving for Nationals tomorrow, I'd offer you something stronger. God knows *I* need it."

James shook his head. "No thanks, I'm okay."

Ainslie put her hands on the kitchen bench and dropped her head. "What a fucking night."

A long silence filled the air between them. James wanted to be there for her, but he was afraid to push it. She was clearly not okay.

"What happened?" he asked carefully.

Ainslie looked up at him and took a deep, shaky breath. She was white as a sheet, and her eyes were red rimmed and puffy.

"Aidan Corbin fucking happened, that's what."

James frowned. "Do you want to talk about it?"

She tilted her head back as if she was trying to stop more tears from falling. Then she closed her eyes and took another long, ragged breath.

"In a minute."

James stood up. "Look, you come and sit over here. I'll make you your tea."

She didn't argue. She just wandered over to the lounge as if she was in a trance and sat down. James moved into the kitchen and pulled a mug out of the cupboard.

"You know," Ainslie said, "last night …"

James stopped in his tracks and looked up at her. She was sitting cross-legged on the lounge and fiddling with her hands.

"Last night … I really thought he was going to hit me."

James nearly dropped the kettle as he was pouring. "What?"

"He didn't. But I swear to God, from the look in his eye … I think he wanted to."

James took the tea and carried it over to the lounge. He placed the mug on the coffee table and carefully sat down beside her.

She looked up at him with those sad, red eyes.

"And tonight …" She sniffed. "I thought he was gonna get us killed."

Her voice finally cracked, and she broke down in tears.

"Come here," James said.

She curled up against his chest, and James wrapped his arms around her. He listened quietly as she explained what'd happened. How Aidan had screamed and driven like a maniac before she'd demanded to be let out of the car. How he'd accused her of cheating and called her a liar. By the time she had recounted the whole story, she'd settled down a little.

Eventually, she slowly removed herself from James's embrace, wiping her eyes with her sleeve.

"I feel ridiculous for crying so much." She sniffed. "I know I did the right thing, but it just sucks, you know? Like, I don't regret leaving him, but I'm sad about what could've been … I dunno, it's stupid."

James put a hand on her knee and gave it a gentle squeeze. "It's not stupid, Goose. What you've just been through … that was *traumatic*. I'm pretty sure you have every right to *cry*."

Ainslie touched her arm where Aidan had grabbed her.

"How's your arm?" James asked.

She rolled up her sleeve. "It's okay."

James gasped at the light blue bruising. "It's not okay, it's assault."

She pulled her sleeve back down. "It doesn't matter, it's over now."

James pursed his lips, repressing the urge to say all the things he wanted to say about Aidan Corbin.

"You know what I realised tonight?" Ainslie asked, with a hint of a smile breaking through.

"What did you realise tonight?"

"After all this, it looks like 2020 isn't going to be our last season after all."

James wanted to crack a bottle of champagne and scream his joy from the rooftops at that revelation. Instead, he settled for a subdued smile.

A moment of silence hung in the air. James hated to see Ainslie hurting, but he was unbelievably grateful that she was safe and free from Aidan, who was clearly *so* much worse than James had ever realised. And even though he knew it was selfish, he was incredibly relieved not to be losing her anymore.

"Ains," he said finally, "you know what I think of Aidan, but I am truly sorry it didn't work out the way you wanted it to."

Ainslie brushed another tear away. "I just can't believe I wasted six years of my life on him. The red flags were there the whole time. I was just too *stupid* to see them."

"Listen to me," James said, taking both of her hands in his. "Don't you dare beat yourself up. You are the smartest, strongest, greatest woman I've ever met. And you're not too bad lookin' either," he added with a wink.

Ainslie sniffled. "You're too good to me."

"You're my best friend. You know I'd do anything for you."

James looked at her with a lopsided smile, and she let out a small chuckle. A few moments of silence passed between them, and their smiles seemed to turn into something else.

Something almost indefinable.

It took James a few moments to realise they were still holding hands. He couldn't help but notice how much he liked how it felt. They'd held hands so many times before, but this felt different.

"Honey, I'm home!"

The front door creaked open, and Jaz and Lucy shuffled inside. James quickly retracted his hands. He missed the feeling instantly.

"What's going on?" Lucy asked, placing her bag by the linen cupboard.

"I broke up with Aidan." Ainslie didn't elaborate any further.

Jaz looked relieved. "Oh, thank God."

James shot her a look.

"Sorry," Jaz muttered.

"It's okay," Ainslie said, slapping her knees and getting up from the lounge. "All of you were right. The guy's a dick."

James frowned. "That's putting it lightly."

Lucy excused herself to have a shower, Jaz put the kettle back on, and James grabbed his wallet and keys.

"Early one tomorrow," he said, turning to Ainslie. "I'll be around to pick you up at four thirty, okay?"

"Okay," Ainslie replied. "Thanks again."

He pulled her into a hug. "No worries."

Jaz cleared her throat.

"And thanks for coming over and keeping me company." Ainslie squeezed him a little tighter.

Jaz cleared her throat again, and Ainslie let go.

"See you tomorrow," Ainslie said.

"Bye."

*　　*　　*

As soon as Ainslie was sure James was well out of earshot, she turned to Jaz and threw her hands in the air. "Do you need a glass of water or something?!"

Jaz laughed. "What was going on there, huh?"

"What?" Ainslie said innocently.

"Don't think I didn't see you guys holding hands."

"He was offering me support."

"Support? Is that what you kids are calling it these days?"

Ainslie pulled a face.

"So now you've ended it with Aidan ...," Jaz said slowly, "and James is also unattached ... does that mean you're gonna —"

"Jaz ...," Ainslie said in a warning tone.

"Are you gonna tell James you're wildly in love with him?"

"Jaz, it's not that simple."

Jaz groaned. "Why not! You're best friends! You'd just be taking the next step."

"Well, for a start, it's been like ... an hour since the break-up. The body isn't even cold yet."

"And?"

"And what if I tell him, Jaz?" Ainslie lowered her voice so Lucy wouldn't hear from the bathroom. She didn't want anyone else's opinion on the matter tonight. "What if I tell him I have feelings for him, and he doesn't return them? Then I look like an idiot, and things will be super awkward."

"But what if he *does* return them? Then you'd have everything you ever wanted."

Ainslie sighed and put a hand to her forehead. "I can't. Not now, at least. *Maybe* when the season's over. And that's a *big* maybe. But I can't risk anything right now. We need to focus on Nationals and then Worlds."

"All right. Fair enough. But I really think you should tell him as soon as you can. He's a great guy, Ains. He's not gonna stay single forever."

"I know. Just ... give me time."

Ainslie retreated to the bathroom and had a long, hot bath, hoping to soak away some of the painful memories that Aidan had created for her earlier in the evening. Then she climbed into bed and listened to a guided meditation, but her mind was too busy to relax. It was taking her a lot longer to wind down than she would have liked, especially considering how early she had to wake up the next morning. Eventually, she fell asleep reading a book that she found shoved in her bedside drawer.

That night, she dreamed about James for the first time in months. But it wasn't heated and passionate and absolutely filthy like some of the others had been. It was different. She was just lying beside him, their fingers clasped together like they'd been earlier in the night, and he was smiling at her. His unmistakable blue eyes studied every line on her face.

"What?" she asked.

"I just love you so much," he replied, kissing her softly.

She jolted awake. But she didn't feel confused or frustrated like she'd felt after the other dreams. She just felt disappointed that it hadn't been real.

CHAPTER 31

When Ainslie's alarm went off at three thirty the next morning, she had no idea where she was. Her sleep had been intermittent and restless, and she had that horrible head fog that one gets when they've spent the better part of the night crying. It was certainly not an ideal way to feel on the day she left for her second-most important competition of the season. She rolled over and blindly palmed at her phone, hoping to hit the snooze button.

After about half an hour of dozing, a streak of light appeared in her doorway. She was vaguely able to make out Lucy's silhouette.

"Ains, you need to get up."

Ainslie responded with an unintelligible groan.

"Jaz and I are leaving now," Lucy said in a warning tone, "and James is going to be here in half an hour."

Ainslie grumbled a little more but eventually found the strength to drag herself out of the warmth of her bed and into a hot shower. As the water melted away her stiffness, she began to feel a bit like herself again.

Despite her weary eyes and the disaster that was the night before, she felt a satisfying sense of freedom. She was heading to Nationals with her friends. They would cheer each other on when they skated and make memories together on their days off. And at the end of the week, they would let their hair down at the Nationals Dinner, where Ainslie had every intention of drinking a little too much and dancing a little too enthusiastically.

And now, she had no-one to answer to but herself. A familiar flurry of excitement began to brew in her stomach at the thought.

*   *   *

It was only a short flight from Sydney to the Gold Coast and then a forty-minute bus ride from the airport to the hotel in Surfers Paradise where the team was staying.

Ainslie hoped that amid the madness of competing, she might find a few moments to get down to the beach. It was June — the middle of winter — so there was no way she'd set foot in the water, but a stroll along the sand and some fresh sea air would do the trick. She just needed to clear her head. All that'd been going through it since last night was the constant reminder that both she and James were single now.

So, are you going to do anything about it?

When all the skaters had arrived at the hotel, they were given their room assignments and briefed on what the week was going to look like. The team was then released to spend the day however they wanted, although they were strongly encouraged to rest up for state training the following morning. The younger skaters were instructed not to leave the premises without an adult guardian, but the older skaters had the freedom to go out as long as they didn't go alone. Ainslie, James, Jaz and Lucy dumped their luggage in their rooms and headed out to find the nearest shopping centre.

Surfers Paradise had an odd feeling about it in the dead of winter. In the summertime, it was probably one of the busiest tourist spots in the country, but in June, it was eerily quiet. The buzz it enjoyed during peak season was lying dormant, and the only tourists around seemed to be other skaters who were there for the championships. Ainslie had already spotted several familiar faces just in the time it took to walk from the hotel to the shops.

She was studying the nutritional information on a box of muesli bars when she was taken aback by a shrill voice.

"Jameslie!"

The voice sounded sickly sweet, and Ainslie knew exactly who it belonged to before she and James even turned around. Tessa Strong from Victoria. Complete with a fake smile emblazoned across her face. The team of Tessa Strong and Antony Bryce had come in second to Jameslie seven years in a row, and they were obviously bitter about it.

"Hey, Tess," Ainslie said, forcing a smile of her own. "Where's Tony?"

"Oh, Ainslie." Tessa laughed. "Not every pairs team feels the need to be constantly attached at the hip."

"Nice to see you too, Tessa," James said.

"Ainslie, I'm so sorry to hear your engagement didn't work out." Tessa's voice was saccharine. "But a bunch of us down in Melbourne heard this rumour …"

Ainslie groaned. "What rumour?"

"Well, word on the street is you left your fiancé for someone else." She shot James a look. "I think we can all guess who."

Ainslie sighed. "Tessa, that is the *least* creative rumour I've ever heard in my life. And also, very untrue."

Tessa looked unconvinced.

"That's what you guys always say, but …" Tessa put her hands up. "Look, I'm not trying to be rude. I'm just saying you could cut the sexual tension with a knife. Just do us all a favour and hook up already. Put *yourselves* out of your misery."

Tessa laughed as though what she'd said was the funniest thing that had ever been uttered before turning on her heel and walking back up the aisle. Ainslie's cheeks were burning.

"Well, that was super uncomfortable," she said.

"She's sick of always coming second to us," James said. "She's just trying to get inside our heads."

Well, it's definitely working.

*　　*　　*

Ainslie was grateful that state training was early on Saturday morning. It meant they had the entire afternoon and evening to relax and do as they pleased.

What she hadn't enjoyed, however, were the sideways glances and poorly hidden whispers as she and James had walked into the building. She could only imagine what people had been saying or how far the rumour Tessa had mentioned had travelled. As such, she had spent the entire morning trying to avoid skaters from the other states purely out of fear that someone was going to make another inappropriate comment and send her spiralling again.

After their training, she spent most of the afternoon kicking around the hotel with James, Lucy and Jaz before they walked to a nearby family buffet restaurant together for dinner. They found a quiet booth tucked away in a corner, and Ainslie offered to mind it while the others piled their plates.

"I'll grab you something," James said. "Veggie pasta, Greek salad and a diet coke? Oh, and cheesy bread?"

She smiled and made a finger-gun gesture. "You know me."

"I got you." He winked.

Ainslie noticed Jaz fail to hide a smirk as she flounced off with Lucy and James.

When they returned, James slid into the booth beside Ainslie and passed her a plate. He'd even gotten extra olives in the Greek salad, just how she liked. The small gesture made her heart glow.

"I honestly can't believe it's been a year since Perth," Jaz said.

"*I* can't believe this doesn't have to be my last Nationals anymore." Ainslie grinned as she popped an olive in her mouth.

The others let out a chorus of cheers in agreement. James put an arm around Ainslie's shoulders and pulled her into a side hug. She tensed a little at his proximity before remembering she had no reason to feel guilty anymore.

"You guys," she said, relaxing into his side, "I can't thank you enough for being my friends. Turns out you were right to hate Aidan. I guess you all saw the red flags, and I just ignored them because I was … in denial, I guess. But you lot are the best friends anyone could ask for, and I want you to know that I love you all to bits."

"We love you too, Ains," Jaz said, kicking her under the table. "And it's so awesome to see you this happy."

"Are you sure you're doing okay?" Lucy asked. "The whole thing was really intense, and for it to happen just before we left —"

"I'm fine," Ainslie replied, waving her off. "I think things were over long before Thursday night. His behaviour after the Exhibition just sealed the deal."

"We're so proud of you," James said, and Ainslie realised his arm was still around her. "You're an absolute legend, and that dickhead never deserved you."

Ainslie allowed herself to melt completely into James's embrace. She was so comfortable, nestled in beside him, and surely no harm could come from that.

143

"What's that you've got?" she asked, pointing at his plate.

"Mushroom ravioli."

"Is it good?"

"Here, have some, it's vego."

He stabbed a ravioli and offered it to her. She took a bite directly off his outstretched fork. Lucy and Jaz shared a sideways glance, which Ainslie ignored.

"Are you ready for tomorrow?" Ainslie asked the entire table, pretending not to notice Jaz still smirking.

"I'm pumped!" Jaz said, throwing a chip in the air and catching it in her mouth. "Honestly, I'm feeling so good about this."

"What about you, Lucy?" Ainslie asked. "You feeling prepared?"

"I think so," she replied cautiously, without elaborating.

"What about you two?" Jaz said. "You ready to make the country fall in love with Jameslie once again?"

James gave Ainslie a little squeeze. "Are you kidding? We've never been more ready in our lives. Right, Goose?"

He turned to look at her. He was already incredibly close with his arm still around her, but when he turned his head, he was *dangerously* so. She caught his eye and felt her heart race a little.

She smiled and dragged her gaze away from him, afraid of what might happen if she stared too long. "Right."

*   *   *

The four took the long way back to the hotel, wandering down to the beach and walking along the warm sand. It was dark, and the beach was illuminated only by the streetlights along the Esplanade. Jaz was on a pre-competition high, running around like a kid who'd had too much sugar. Lucy was the exact opposite. She'd fallen into one of her pre-competition funks, and it was clear from the look on her face that everything Jaz was doing was driving her up the wall. Ainslie was just strolling along the sand, falling into step beside James, feeling content and enjoying the cool sea breeze against her face.

"Do you reckon they'll ever allow same-sex partners to compete?" Jaz asked, bouncing off invisible walls. "Lucy, you could be my partner."

She swooped in, wrapping her arms around Lucy's waist and scooping her off her feet. She spun her around like a rag doll, and Lucy let out a shriek of protest.

"Put me down! There's a reason I do *solo* dance."

Ainslie wanted to laugh, but she knew Lucy wouldn't have appreciated that.

"Hey, can you guys do that thing?" Jaz asked, putting Lucy back on her feet.

"Gonna have to be a bit more specific, Jaz." James laughed.

"You know, that thing from the movie," she said, holding her arms out to the side like an aeroplane. "Where the lass like, runs, and then the guy picks her up like this."

She clumsily demonstrated what she was talking about.

"The thing from *Dirty Dancing*?" Ainslie laughed.

James scoffed, glancing at Ainslie. "Ch'yeah, we can do that, right?"

"Oh, easy," she replied cockily.

Ainslie took a few steps back, making enough space for her to have an adequate run-up. James stood, feet planted and arms outstretched.

Jaz laughed and began singing off key.

Ainslie took off into a little run before taking a flying leap towards James. He grabbed her by the waist and lifted her up over his head to the sound of Jaz's cheers. Ainslie stretched her arms out to the side, giggling like a schoolgirl. Moments later, James lost his balance and toppled over backwards, pulling Ainslie on top of him so she didn't fling headlong into the sand. They were laughing hysterically. They nearly butted heads in the process.

"You dropped me!" Ainslie play-scolded him, rising to her knees and brushing the sand off her. "That's it, Sunderland. You're fired."

"I'll drop you, all right." James chuckled as he tackled her. She let out a squeal.

"Would you two cut it out before you injure yourselves?" Lucy folded her arms. "You know if Sandra knew you were mucking around the night before you compete, she'd kill you."

"What, like you kill the vibe?" Jaz said, and Lucy marched off ahead of them in a huff.

"No, she's right," James said, climbing to his feet. "We should head off." He offered Ainslie a hand and pulled her out of the sand. "I'm not really fired, am I?"

"Of course not," Ainslie replied, hip-checking him. "Where am I gonna find a new partner at this hour?"

He hip-checked her back. "Guess you're stuck with me, then."

"Forever, it seems."

*   *   *

By the time Ainslie and Jaz meandered back to their room, Lucy was already in bed, sleep mask on, earphones in, presumably listening to rain sounds. She didn't move when they walked in, so Ainslie figured she was either already asleep or ignoring them. Ainslie grabbed a towel and her toiletries and made her way to the bathroom.

"Oi, you," Jaz whispered, one eyebrow raised. "What was *that* all about, huh?"

"What?"

"Oh, come on! You two were vibing tonight. Big time."

"What?" Ainslie said in an unconvincingly innocent tone. "No, we weren't."

"Are you serious?" Jaz scoffed. "The roll in the sand? The arm around you at the restaurant? He fed you off his fork, for God's sake. That means you've basically kissed now."

"Jaz, sh!" Ainslie cast a nervous glance towards Lucy's blanketed form. "We weren't acting any different from how we normally act."

"Exactly," Jaz replied, making finger-guns. "You two are bloody hot for each other, and you have been for years."

Ainslie turned bright red. "Jaz —"

"Ains, there's no use denying it, love. You've already told me you're into him, and honestly, that was pretty obvious tonight. It was *also* pretty obvious that the feeling is mutual, so are you going to do something about it, or not?"

"Look, I told you, maybe after Worlds, but definitely not now! The day before we're supposed to compete!"

"But you'll do something about it eventually?"

"Will you ever stop harassing me about it until I do?"

"No."

"You're a pain in my arse, Bannister." Ainslie smirked.

Jaz winked. "You love me."

Ainslie rolled her eyes, closing the bathroom door between them.

From the other side, she heard Jaz add, "But not as much as you love James!"

CHAPTER 32

Sunday morning was the day the championships officially got underway. The skaters competing that evening had their official practice at the crack of dawn. Then they would spend the day resting before the opening ceremony that night.

Despite Queensland's famously warm climate, inside the stadium was so predictably freezing in winter that Ainslie turned up wearing an entire doona wrapped around her shoulders.

"Did you steal that from the hotel?" James asked.

She nodded. "Yep. I remembered how cold it got from the last time we had Nationals here."

"Smart."

"Join me," she said, throwing some doona around him. "It's warm as toast in here."

James huddled under the doona, wiggling in close to Ainslie's side. He smiled a little when she seemed to do the same.

James had been happy with his and Ainslie's state training the day before, and it'd been so nice to see her back to her usual, bubbly self. He thought about how flirty they'd been with each other. Sure, they had always shared a bit of harmless banter, but the night before had felt different. There were times when it felt as if they were standing just a little too close to the line they'd drawn long ago. And they were peering off the edge together, both silently wondering if the other wanted to jump off.

They sat in the warmth of their blanket, sipping hot beverages and watching the Junior Freeskating official practice until Ainslie spotted their rivals.

She gasped. "Oh, shit. Here come Tessa and Tony. You reckon we can hide in this thing?"

She pulled the doona up a little higher, but they'd already been spotted.

"Hey, Jameslie!" Tessa called.

"You do realise we're two separate people, right?" James asked.

"Really?" Tessa cocked her head. "It's next to impossible to tell."

Ainslie rolled her eyes.

"Anyway," Tessa said, "one of my friends told me that the floor is way more slippery today than it was yesterday. Just in case you need to change wheels or anything."

"Thanks for the heads up," James said diplomatically, even though he and Ainslie knew perfectly well it was a tactic.

The Victorian pair flounced away.

Ainslie pulled a face. "Psych outs? Really? What are we, ten years old?"

James chuckled. "I feel like that statement would bear more weight if we weren't currently inside a blanket fort."

*   *   *

There were five teams in the Senior Pairs event, and they only had fifteen minutes for their official practice. Unsurprisingly, despite Tessa claiming otherwise, the floor was no different from how it had been the day before.

Official practice for pairs always tended to be a bit chaotic. Fifteen minutes, five teams, ten people all sharing the floor. There was a certain etiquette, which most of the teams followed, but Tessa and Antony usually liked to flout the rules. Either they had no concept of spatial awareness or they just didn't care. Ainslie guessed it was probably the latter.

Even so, the practice session went well, with no collisions or issues. All Ainslie had on her mind was getting out of there and getting back to the hotel so she and James could start their pre-competition rituals. Which mostly involved a nap, a healthy lunch and light stretching, followed by some sort of game to help them relax — usually whatever the hotel had available. Sometimes it was pool, sometimes it was foosball, but one of them always carried a deck of cards in their bag, just in case the hotel didn't have anything.

They'd nearly made it out of the stadium when a voice called Ainslie back. It grated in her ears. She'd recognise that voice anywhere. She spun around to see Rosa Charis, tall, tan and pristinely made up, as usual, grinning at her somewhat maniacally.

"Hi, Rosa."

"Listen, babes." Rosa placed a perfectly manicured hand on Ainslie's arm. "Can I borrow you for one sec?"

"My bus leaves in, like, five minutes —"

"It'll only be a minute, I promise," Rosa said, tightening her claw-like grip. "It's important, and I think you'll want to know."

Ainslie rolled her eyes. "Okay, fine."

"Sorry, just gotta steal your girl for a moment," Rosa said to James, squeezing his shoulder with her spare hand before pulling Ainslie down a small, empty corridor near the bathrooms.

"Listen. Babes," Rosa said. "Are you okay?"

Her tone had shifted to concern, but Ainslie wasn't sure it was genuine.

Ainslie furrowed her brow. "Yeah, I'm fine? Why?"

"Look," Rosa said, her voice laden with pity, "I heard about your break-up. It must've been so stressful coming here so soon after, but you've got to know people have been talking ..."

"Oh, I know."

I'm sure you've had your fair share to say too.

"You've heard the rumours?"

"That I left my fiancé for James? Yeah, I heard the rumours. They're not true."

148

"Oh, no, babes, that's not the rumour *I* heard."

Rosa had her sympathetic gaze down pat, but her tone gave her away. She was enjoying the drama far too much.

Ainslie squinted at her. "What rumour did *you* hear?"

"Babes," Rosa said, lowering her voice, "people have been saying your fiancé left you because you and James were having an affair."

Ainslie squinted even harder. "What people?"

"Oh, heaps of people. I've heard it floating around all day yesterday and today. I just thought that … you know … seeing as I'm kinda everyone's news source, that you might like to chat with me and clear things up."

Ainslie's face was on fire. Rumours that she had left Aidan for James were bad enough, but rumours that painted her as a cheater were infuriating.

"Listen," Ainslie said, trying to suppress her rage and steady her shaking voice, "for the record, my fiancé didn't leave me. I left *him*. And it wasn't because I wanted to jump into bed with James. It was because my ex was toxic and controlling and manipulative. It was because he humiliated me in front of my friends. It was because he *physically assaulted me* the night before I came here. So why don't you go back to your computer and tell people *that*, Rosa? Why don't you actually report on the *skating* for once, instead of people's personal lives? *Babes.*"

Ainslie turned around and stormed out of the corridor, feeling both angry that people were spreading rumours about her and incredibly pleased with herself for finally giving Rosa Charis a piece of her mind. Rosa was left with her mouth hanging open. It was probably the quietest she'd ever been in her life.

*   *   *

Ainslie was initially worried that an altercation with Rosa would leave her in a bad mood, but it had actually left her feeling incredibly powerful for the rest of the day as the adrenaline continued to pump through her body.

"You should've seen it," she said to James as they played pool very poorly in the hotel games room. "Her face was absolutely priceless."

"I'll bet," he replied, sinking the white ball by accident. "Do you think there were actually rumours like that going around? Or do you reckon she was just trying to get a rise out of you?"

"Who knows," Ainslie replied after making a very pathetic shot. "Wouldn't surprise me, though. But I'm not going to waste time thinking about it. We've got a competition to win."

James sunk one of Ainslie's balls by mistake and winced. "Thank God it's not a pool competition."

"Yeah, we definitely shouldn't quit skating."

CHAPTER 33

The grandstand was packed to the rafters with spectators and skaters. Music was pumping through the speakers, and the stadium was draped in green and gold, ready for the competition to begin. There was a familiar buzz in the air that only came from the opening night of a championships, and Ainslie had a stomach full of butterflies and a head full of hairspray.

All the competitors were gathered on the warm-up court in their various uniforms, milling about and catching up with their interstate friends until the event coordinators began ordering them to stand in their respective teams. Jaz would be the only one of the four to march with New South Wales, and she gave the others a sad wave as they went to go march with the rest of the 2019 Australian team.

"Next year," Ainslie mouthed as she gave her a thumbs up.

The opening ceremony was always a bit monotonous, although the march-past part was fun enough. Ainslie, James and Lucy marched together at the back of the pack, Lucy shaking her head at the other two, who were photobombing the Juniors in front of them.

Once they completed a lap of the competition floor, the competitors sat cross-legged on the cold timber while the important people made speeches and took oaths. The 2019 Australian team was congratulated on their performance in London, and James and Ainslie were even awarded male and female Skater of the Year, respectively, for coming fourth place.

Once the championship director finally declared the competition open, the skaters marched off the floor the way they had come. A dance troupe from a local performing arts school entertained the crowd while the athletes in the first few events got ready. Then, after the floor was swept, the program finally kicked off.

Lucy headed to the marshalling area to prepare for her style dance while the others sat in the grandstand and watched the quartet events.

"Should we form a quartet?" Jaz asked.

"We'd be awesome as a quartet," James said.

"Maybe when we retire from solo and pairs, we can do quartet," Ainslie said. "We're all pretty busy as it is."

"We'd beat this lot," Jaz said a little too loudly.

Ainslie punched her lightly on the shoulder as a disgruntled parent turned around and shot her a dirty look.

After the quartets had finished competing, Lucy and the other Senior solo dancers were up. Ainslie, James and Jaz hollered in the grandstand as she raced around the floor in her cute little rockabilly get-up. Lucy wouldn't have been caught dead wearing something like that in any other context, but for her rock-and-roll themed style dance, it was perfect. She ended the event in second place, just behind Amelia Benson from Western Australia and just ahead of Rebecca Davies from New South Wales. But it was close, and it would all come down to the freedance.

By the time Jaz had to head down to the marshalling area, the freezing cold was settling into the venue. Ainslie's stolen doona made a reappearance, and she and James cocooned themselves inside it once again.

"Do you think Jaz has her head together today?" James asked.

"I think so. She was pretty happy with her official. She always has been the one of us least likely to have a meltdown."

"True. Her warm-up at States was probably the first time I've ever seen her get close to losing it.

"But she made a bloody good comeback."

"Maybe she put pressure on herself because she thought it was her last chance for us all to go to Worlds together."

"Yeah, maybe." Ainslie smiled as she realised that that was no longer the case. "That's one thing we can thank Aidan for, then."

His name hung in the air like a bad smell, but huddled under the warmth of the blanket, pressed in close to James's side, Ainslie didn't care. In fact, she was so distracted by how close he was sitting, she didn't even notice that Jaz's event had started warming up. Ainslie and James cheered as Jaz flew around the floor, looking strong and fast, not a trace of her States warm-up nerves in sight.

"She looks good," James said.

"God, I hope she can do it. It would be so fun, the four of us at Worlds together."

"Well, none of us have qualified yet."

"Yeah, but you and me and Lucy are going into Nationals as hot favourites. Jaz is an underdog."

"Everyone loves an underdog."

"I don't know if John Greaves loves an underdog," Ainslie said, glaring over at the panel of judges and spotting the crotchety old man in question.

She'd once overheard John Greaves say that Jaz would never make it as an artistic skater because no matter what, she'd always "look like an ice dancer".

"Meh, John Greaves doesn't know anything," James said.

"Well, he likes us."

"He likes *you*." James chuckled. "And he likes the tight little bodysuits Sandra puts you in."

Ainslie slapped his leg under the blanket. "Ew."

"You know I hear he has a thing for redheads ..."

"Gross."

"I mean, he has a point. The bodysuits are pretty nice ..."

Ainslie screwed up her nose and slapped his leg again. "James Sunderland, don't let people hear you talking like that. What *will* they think?"

"What they already think anyway?"

She narrowed her eyes at him. "Cheeky."

Ainslie sat there for the next few moments, trying to concentrate on Jaz's performance. She felt like the worst friend in the world — all she could think about was what James had just said. Was he joking? He could've just made the crack about John Greaves. He didn't need to add the bit about *him* thinking her tight bodysuits were nice. Her mind was racing, trying to work out what it all meant until finally, a tiny voice in her head scolded her.

It's just banter. It doesn't mean anything.

Jaz skated a clean short program, and Ainslie and James cheered as the placings were displayed, revealing that she'd finished the event in second place. The conclusion of Senior Freeskating meant it was time for the pairs to make their way to the marshalling area.

Ainslie and James waddled down the grandstand, still cocooned in their blanket.

"Hi, Jameslie!"

Ainslie tensed at the sound of Tessa's voice as she flounced past them.

"I thought you said earlier that you were two different people?" Tessa laughed heartily.

Ainslie pulled a face and yanked the blanket off.

James shivered. "We have to be cold because Tessa's a smart arse?"

"Let's just beat them again. That'll be payback enough."

Every little snide comment was another distraction Ainslie didn't need. She was still trying to ignore the fact that James may or may not have just admitted to being attracted to her.

*   *   *

They entered the marshalling area, where all the other teams were already running, stretching and doing off-skate lifts. There was a distinct feeling of tension as they walked in. Maybe Ainslie was just imagining it, but it felt as if all eyes were on them.

The thirty minutes prior to their event seemed to pass by much faster than any regular thirty minutes, and before they knew it, all five teams were circling around in the corner of the competition floor like pairs of vultures, waiting for the announcer to call them out.

The second the event was announced, Ainslie and James shot out of the proverbial gate, closely followed by Tessa and Antony. The three other teams kept safely to the back of the pack, and all five pairs tore around the rink at top speed to the sound of applause.

Ainslie heard a group of people scream out "Go Jameslie!" in a perfect chorus.

She'd bet money on Jaz being the one leading them.

Their warm-up was strong and seemed to end far too quickly. Ainslie and

James would be the third pair to skate, just after Tessa and Antony. They rolled around the warm-up court while the first two teams skated. They never did like to watch their competitors.

"You feeling good?" James asked.

Ainslie shook out one leg and then the other. "Yep, you?"

"Better than ever."

When Tessa and Antony took to the floor, applause emanated from the other side of the divider that separated the marshalling area from the competition floor. Ainslie and James's casual conversation turned into nervous chatter as they tried to drown out the sound. When the music came to an end, James and Ainslie slipped through the divider and found Sandra.

"I want to see a nice, strong landing position from you, Ainslie, on the throw Salchow, okay? Hips under." Sandra put her hands on her own rear end and thrust her pelvis forwards to demonstrate. "And James, make sure your edges in the footwork sequence are nice and deep. Please, no jumped turns! Let's not throw away easy marks." She swatted him gently with the back of her hand. "And most of all," she said, grinning, "have fun with it. Energy. Chemistry. Let's go."

Ainslie took a deep breath and nodded her head. James stretched his shoulders.

Tessa and Antony's marks came up. They were good. Very good. Sort of intimidatingly good.

Sandra gave them one last pat on the back as they moved closer to the edge of the competition floor. "Go give 'em some of that special Jameslie treatment."

The announcer's voice rang over the speakers. "Please welcome to the floor, representing New South Wales, Ainslie Wynter and James Sunderland."

James held out his hand and Ainslie took it. They raised their hands together and exploded onto the floor. The crowd was roaring. They slowed to a standstill in the middle of the stadium, faced each other and shared a silent nod. Then they assumed their positions. The crowd fell silent in anticipation, and suddenly … strings. The music began, and the building filled with the sensual voice of the late Michael Hutchence.

They began to move together. So in sync, so emotional, so passionate. Ainslie was trying with all her might to focus only on her movements, but her mind kept threatening to wander back to James and how he made her feel so alive when they skated together.

But there was no time for that. Next minute, she was flying through the air in the throw triple Salchow. Sandra's tip proved futile, and Ainslie tipped slightly forwards on the landing. It was toed, and she very nearly put her hand on the floor, but she saved it. Nothing career ending, but she was pretty certain Tessa and Antony had skated perfectly clean.

She shook it off and focused on the next element, side-by-side double Axels. Now *they* were clean.

Then she was up in the air again, soaring high above the crowd, held firmly and securely by the familiar arms beneath her. She dismounted with grace and ease, and they danced their way through their footwork sequence. They moved through their other elements, the error from the Salchow long forgotten. Everything else was perfect.

They hit their final position. Ainslie's back pressed against James's chest, his arms wrapped around her waist, holding her close. He held her there for a few moments longer than she had expected, and she hoped that maybe he would never let go. He dropped his head a little, and amid the eruption of cheers, she heard him whisper in her ear, "That was amazing. Great work!"

His breath on her neck made her shiver, and his lips were so close to her skin she thought she felt them brush against her. But, as if she were being pulled from one of her dreams, he turned her around and drew her into one of their customary, just-friends, end-of-routine hugs. He released her so they could take their bows, and she instantly missed his arms around her.

They skated over to the kiss and cry lounge, which really only had room for two. Sandra sat on one end, and James sat beside her, pulling Ainslie into his lap. Ainslie was barely able to cope anymore with the closeness, the touches and the shameless flirting. She'd promised herself that *if* she planned on telling him how she felt, she wouldn't do it until after Worlds. But she was starting to think she wasn't going to be able to wait that long.

Their results came up. The technical score suffered a little bit thanks to the Salchow, but the program components were phenomenal.

Place 1.

They'd done it.

Tessa and Antony were close behind, but that didn't matter. They still had the long to go, and "Bolero" was hopefully going to blow everyone away. James wrapped his arms around Ainslie's waist and squeezed her. She let out an involuntary squeal of joy, and Sandra patted her on the knee.

"Nice work," Sandra said. "Even if you didn't listen to me about your hips."

"I don't think old mate Johnny minded your hips for a second," James said, patting Ainslie on the offending hip.

She elbowed him in the ribs, the two of them laughing as they pulled themselves out of the lounge.

Ainslie smirked. "You need to behave yourself."

And you need to stop flirting with me unless you intend to follow it up with some action.

* * *

That night wasn't kind to Ainslie. She was still incredibly wired from their skate when they got back to the hotel, and she struggled to switch off, even after taking a long, hot bath. When she did finally manage to fall asleep, she was rudely interrupted only hours later. She jolted awake, glancing at her phone and realising it was three o'clock. Her heart was pounding, and she was drenched in sweat.

"For fuck's sake."

"Shut up," Lucy muttered from the next bed.

"Sorry," Ainslie whispered.

She flopped back down on the pillow, her entire body on fire. The last dream she'd had about James had been so sweet and wholesome. Still not ideal, but at least she could look him in the eye after. But this dream had been the furthest thing from sweet and wholesome. It had been wild and red hot and far too explicit. She rubbed her eyes, trying to shake the image of what her brain had made her see, how it had made her *feel*.

She got up and splashed her face with cold water, her hands still shaking, and stared at herself in the mirror. She looked about as red as she felt.

Girl, you are in way over your head.

CHAPTER 34

When Ainslie's alarm went off a few hours later at five thirty, she knew it was going to be a long day. She had to be at the stadium by seven for official practice, and they wouldn't skate their long program until eight that night. And she was already exhausted. She just hoped she would be able to act normally around James after what they'd done in her subconscious a few hours ago.

That dream really was the last thing she needed the night before competing, but she knew she'd brought it on herself with all the flirting they'd done the day before. She was just going to have to suck it up and pretend she wasn't constantly replaying it in her mind and wondering *What if?* Because this was it, the day they'd been waiting for. The culmination of the last nine months. If they skated that night exactly as they'd skated at the Exhibition, a performance so convincing that it had destroyed an entire relationship, then there'd be no doubt that they would be selected for Worlds.

Ainslie could barely wait for the Nationals Dinner on Friday evening, when she could put on the little red dress she'd brought, grab a glass of wine (or six) and be handed that coveted ticket to Barcelona. Her mind kept wanting to run ahead to the end of the week, but the more rational part of her brain kept reminding her that Tessa and Antony were sitting right on their tail. It was the closest anyone had come to dethroning Jameslie in years. They'd still qualify for Worlds in second place, but Ainslie hadn't worked her backside off all year for silver. She hadn't blown her personal life to pieces for silver. And she certainly wasn't holding herself back from everything she had ever wanted for silver.

*   *   *

Ainslie and James began their early-morning warm-up by running a few laps around the warm-up area. Ainslie ran in silence, her mouth drawn in a straight line, eyes fixed ahead as her shoes thumped against the wooden floor. James glanced over at her.

"You okay?"

"Never better," she said plainly, not daring to look at him.

Tessa had made a snide remark when they had arrived about how she and Antony were "coming for them", and Ainslie had been seething ever since. What Tessa didn't know was that what she had said was exactly the sort of comment guaranteed to light a fire under Ainslie and kick her desire to win into overdrive.

She and James did a few off-skate jumps and lifts, then they stretched for a few minutes before lacing up their skates and rolling around the warm-up area. Jaz was already out on the floor, finishing up the last few minutes of her official practice, and Ainslie and James pulled up to the gap in the divider and watched her.

Jaz had improved so much over the course of the last twelve months. Six years earlier, she'd never even tried on roller skates. Now, here she was, sitting in second place after the short program in Senior Ladies Freeskating. She just had to keep it together and put down a clean performance in the long. She flew past them and shot them a quick, cheeky grin, and Ainslie cheered.

Jaz rolled around the corner, setting up for her triple Salchow. One, two, three. Clean. Completely checked.

Ainslie screamed and jumped up and down on her toe stops. "Yes, girl!"

"That was clean!" James's jaw dropped. "Has she done that before?"

"No. She's been underrotating for months!"

"You know, Sarah Grey's triple isn't clean. And Laura McLaughlin's is only really a double and a half."

"If she can nail that, as well as skate everything else clean, she could do it."

The sound that signified the end of official practice for Senior Ladies rang through the stadium, and Ainslie and James headed into the marshalling area.

The announcer called over the microphone, "Senior Pairs. You have fifteen minutes."

James and Ainslie pushed their way to the front of the pack like they always did. Hand in hand, they skated two laps of the rink at top speed. The spectators and other skaters who were still hanging around applauded as they flew by.

There was clear tension between the two top-ranking teams. It wasn't unusual for Tessa and Antony to refuse to give way to anyone, but they seemed to be going out of their way to obstruct James and Ainslie in particular. Ainslie had once suggested she and James be more like that, but he had sternly said no. It was too dangerous. He wasn't about to let his pride cause either of them to get injured. He couldn't imagine launching Ainslie into an overhead lift and being too stubborn to stop if someone got in the way. That was a sure-fire way to end up in the emergency room.

They began to run through their program item by item, pausing between each to discuss and repeat things. They got to the final lift, and James launched Ainslie above his head. She felt secure up there. He began rotating, and she changed her body position. On the third rotation, he saw Tessa flinging towards him in a travelling camel out of the corner of his eye. He tried to control his panic as he called out, "Down!"

Ainslie clearly hadn't heard him. Meanwhile, Tessa was gaining on them.

"Down!" he called, louder this time and brought Ainslie down suddenly. It was either that or get wiped out by Tessa.

She fell a little awkwardly, but he caught her securely in his arms and lowered her feet to the ground. They scooted out of Tessa's way just in time for her to centre her heel camel.

Ainslie glared daggers at her.

"Sorry!" Tessa called as she finished her spin.

"Are you okay?" James asked Ainslie, his hand on the small of her back. "Again."

They skated another lap to set up for the lift once more. This time, no-one set up their spin to interfere with them. Ainslie dismounted perfectly, her four wheels hitting the floor with a satisfying thud.

The fifteen minutes of practice flew by in a flash, and when it was done, Ainslie angrily rolled off ahead of James and started taking her skates off aggressively.

"Are you sure you're okay?" James asked, sitting beside her and unlacing his own boots.

She nodded silently.

He'd known her long enough to be able to tell she was a little shaken. The almost-fall had raised his heart rate considerably, so he could only imagine how scary it must have been for her up in the air.

"Sorry again for that little mishap," Tessa said as she padded past them in her socks. "You're okay, though, right? It didn't shake you too much?"

"All good," Ainslie replied, forcing a diplomatic smile.

Tessa padded away to the change rooms.

"That was civil of you." James raised an eyebrow.

Ainslie chuckled. "Good thing you can't read my mind."

*　　*　　*

The skaters headed back to the hotel with strict orders to get some food, debrief and rest before they would have to leave for the stadium at six. Ainslie and James picked up some lunch and retreated to the peace and quiet of James's room for their pre-competition rituals. They set up a picnic and sat cross-legged on his bed. It didn't take long for Ainslie to launch into an impassioned rant about Tessa. A knock on the door interrupted her, and James got up to answer it.

"Hey, James." It was Paula, the team manager.

Paula Kemp was a short, round woman in her late forties who'd been taking on various team management roles in the Australian artistic roller skating world for years. She was good at her job, and she took it very seriously, often too seriously. Particularly when it came to micromanaging the adult skaters who craved a bit more freedom.

"Just letting you know the bus is leaving from the back entry tonight." Paula caught a glimpse of Ainslie sitting on the bed. "Ainslie, you know you're not supposed to be in here."

"We're just hanging out," Ainslie said, her mouth full of sandwich.

"Well, do it in a common area. You know girls and guys aren't allowed in each other's rooms. Rules are rules. I don't need you setting a bad example for younger skaters."

Ainslie groaned and hopped off the bed. Being micromanaged by Paula was her least favourite part of team travel. She also didn't like the implication. She'd *just* managed to get the notion of fooling around with James out of her head.

158

CHAPTER 35

The stadium was absolutely buzzing. All the high-profile events had their second (and final) parts scheduled for that night, and the atmosphere was electric. The hum of a hundred conversations filled the air as Ainslie and James claimed their spot in the grandstand. Lucy was already in the marshalling area, all made up and looking like a princess, ready for her freedance. Ainslie caught a glimpse of her rolling back and forth, hands on her hips, eyes down. Jaz was pacing up and down the hall by the change rooms, keeping warm before her long program.

"Lucy looks focused," Ainslie said.

"Lucy's always focused," James replied.

The first group of Senior solo dancers took to the floor for their warm-up and then were called back out one by one. There was a variety of performances. A lot of musical theatre numbers, a lot of swing music, a few ballads here and there.

When the second group went out for their warm-up, Ainslie screamed at the top of her lungs for Lucy. She looked ethereal. She was practically floating on a cloud out there.

Lucy was last to skate. Amelia Benson was second to last and was in fine form, as usual, and Ainslie felt a familiar case of sympathy butterflies in her stomach as her friend was announced. But she needn't have worried. Every time Lucy stepped onto the floor at a competition, the anxious little girl Ainslie had known from childhood was forgotten.

The second her music started, Lucy completely transformed. From her first movement, the crowd was enthralled, and with every flourish, she conveyed raw emotion, drawing every single note into a perfect extension. Every turn was crisp, every edge was pure and deep. As Lucy danced, Ainslie's heart raced as she silently willed her to skate her best, as if she could control her performance from her seat. But she didn't need to. Lucy was breathtaking.

Ainslie was so fixated on her friend, she didn't even notice that she'd grabbed James's hand and was squeezing it. He was squeezing hers back.

The music came to a crescendo, and Lucy hit her final position. The crowd erupted into cheers, and Ainslie finally noticed she was still clutching James's hand. She let it go as if it were red hot against her skin, blushing a little as she realised what she'd done. It felt ridiculous considering how many times they'd touched hands, but it reminded Ainslie of where his hands had been in her dream the night before. She banished the thought from her mind and jumped to her feet, cheering for Lucy as she exited the floor.

Ainslie and James nervously waited for the scores to come up. After what seemed like an eternity, the screen sprung to life. Her scores were high. Then the screen displayed her position.

Place 1.

Ainslie screamed. Lucy had done it! She'd beaten Amelia Benson! She was going to Worlds as Australia's best!

* * *

Ainslie and James passed Lucy on their way to the marshalling area, and they practically crash-tackled her.

"You did it!" Ainslie cried. "You did it! You were amazing!"

Lucy's eyes were red, and she looked as if she was about to cry, but she couldn't wipe the smile off her face.

"Thank you," she whispered, squeezing her friends tightly.

"Congratulations, Lucy," James said, patting her on the back.

"Good luck, you two. Not that you'll need it."

* * *

As Ainslie and James ran their warm-up laps, Ainslie started to feel her nerves kicking in for Jaz. She knew how badly she wanted to qualify, and Jaz had worked harder than anyone.

Ainslie kept herself focused on her warm-up until she heard them call Jaz to the floor. She raced to the gap in the divider. James jogged over and stood just behind her. He was standing far too close for comfort, and he had his hand resting absent-mindedly on her shoulder.

Jaz's music started, and she took off like a bull out of a gate. She looked strong. She launched into her opening jump. The double Axel. A little wobble on the landing, but it was still on one foot. Ainslie's heart nearly leaped out of her mouth, and James squeezed her shoulder a little. Jaz skated an upbeat transition and headed into her combination spin. It was fast. Ainslie lost count of how many revolutions she did on her heel camel.

Good thing I'm not a technical specialist.

Her invert was so low it was frightening, but she pulled up from it with pure strength. Ainslie was thoroughly impressed. Jaz skated her next few elements. First jump combination. Solid as ever. Triple toe loop. Clean. Next jump combination. Perfect. Solo spin. Amazing.

Ainslie's mouth was hanging open as she watched her friend skate the performance of her life. Apart from the wobble on the double Axel, she'd skated to near perfection. Jaz lined up for her final element. The triple Salchow. One. Two. Three. *Perfect.* Ainslie screamed and reflexively grabbed onto James.

Jaz hit her final position, and the crowd cheered. But no-one quite as loudly as Ainslie.

The scores came up. They were high. But were they high enough?

Ainslie's heart nearly stopped completely. And then Jaz's placing came up. Place 2.

It wasn't enough to beat Sarah Grey, but it was enough. It was all she'd needed to qualify for Worlds.

Jaz came off the floor, and Ainslie and James engulfed her in a group hug.

"Girl, you did it!"

"I can't believe I stuffed the Axel, though. Bugger," Jaz said, but it didn't stop her from grinning from ear to ear.

"Plenty of time to perfect that by *Worlds*!" James said, socking her lightly on the shoulder.

"Two events down. One to go." Jaz smacked James on the back and winked at Ainslie. "Go get it."

*   *   *

Jameslie was the second-last pair to skate. The event somehow managed both to pass too quickly and to drag on interminably. By the time they were called to the floor, Ainslie's body was pumping with adrenaline.

They stood in their first position, and she took a deep, even breath, trying to ready herself. Then she made the mistake of looking too deeply into James's eyes again. He was gazing back with the look they'd practised so many times before. Now all it did was remind her of every little moment they'd shared throughout the week, every wonderful thing he'd ever done for her, everything he'd done the night before in her dream. Her heart fluttered.

She'd come too far to let that look derail her now. Once, it would've crippled her, but now she knew that if they wanted to win, she had to focus all her energy on one place and embrace it. Make it part of the performance.

So what if people talked? Why not really give them something to talk about?

The opening strains of "Bolero" started to wind through the air. Their first movements had always been intimate and sensual, but for the first time since Sandra had choreographed them, Ainslie gave herself full permission to relish the start of this routine. If all they were ever going to do was dance around the point and flirt with each other, then why not have a little fun pretending?

Ainslie's hands slid down James's chest. His palm ran the full length of her thigh as she extended into an arabesque. Then he was pulling her back in, hands on her hips, his gaze fiery and dangerous. Ainslie wondered whether everyone in the stadium could feel it or if it was all in her mind.

Their first element was the throw triple Salchow. Ainslie's hips weren't a problem anymore. All four wheels hit the floor at the same time as she stuck the landing. Next, they moved on to their side-by-side combination spin, then their combination jump, then their Militano lift. They focused their energy on each element as it came, but during the transitions in between, their energy was directed most potently at each other.

The constant drumbeat of "Bolero" pounded through the stadium, the melody building along with the tension between the two skaters. As the music reached its crescendo, they vaulted into their final spin pancake lift. Ainslie watched the stadium swirl around her as they flew together across the floor, her breath momentarily taken away. James lowered her into the dismount, and she felt her wheels touch down. She beamed. That was the last element, and they'd nailed it.

The music came to a climax, and they hit their final position, Ainslie dipping low, James holding her around the waist. Just the two of them, it seemed, in a big empty stadium. Eye to eye, nose to nose, their lips so close it was almost unbearable.

Okay, snap out of it. It's over.

But James's gaze was so intense, and both their mouths were agape as they took quick, shallow breaths. How easy it would be to just close that little gap between them. If someone had lit a match nearby, the air would have ignited. The crowd seemed to be frozen as well, waiting with bated breath to see what would happen next.

Ainslie almost felt disappointed when James finally lifted her upright and whipped her straight off her feet and into a hug. The applause from the audience was deafening. When he finally set her back down for their bows, Ainslie's legs felt so wobbly, she thought she might collapse. She was grateful when he put his arm around her as they rolled off the floor, even though doing so only served to make her even weaker at the knees. But at least she could use his body to prop herself up.

"That was intense," Sandra said, grinning and fanning herself. "I think the judges are going to need a cold shower after that one."

Sandra was clearly joking, but Ainslie was starting to think that *she* was going to need a cold shower too. The performance had felt far too real.

James and Sandra sunk into the kiss and cry lounge, Ainslie once again dropping into James's lap. It was a risky move, particularly considering how tight his pants were.

After what felt like an age, their scores appeared on the screen. Their technical score was excellent, but the program components were through the roof. The crowd cheered again, and James wrapped his arms around Ainslie.

Tessa and Antony were yet to skate. The rival pair stood with their noses in the air, ready to take the floor. They shot James and Ainslie a sour look before they took off.

James, Ainslie and Sandra vacated the kiss and cry and stood at the back of the marshalling area to watch the other pair's performance. It was strong, and they'd definitely improved since the year before. Their jumps were high, their lifts were inventive, and their spins were fast. James glanced at Ainslie, who was chewing nervously at her thumbnail. Every technical element Tessa and Antony skated was perfect, but their performance and chemistry? It didn't even begin to come close to Jameslie's.

Tessa and Antony finished their performance and awaited their marks in the kiss and cry. Ainslie's heart was pounding, and she squeezed James's hand.

The technical marks came up. They were high. Really high. Ainslie couldn't even remember her and James's technical score. For a moment, she wondered if they'd been beaten. Her heart was in her throat. Then the program components came up. They were nowhere near her and James's. She swallowed hard and waited for the ranking.

Place 2.

James punched the air, and Ainslie squealed. It was close this time, but they'd still done it. And they'd looked amazing doing it. James scooped Ainslie into a hug and flung her around like a rag doll. She was nearly crying with laughter.

"We did it, Goose! We're going to Spain!"

He set her back on her feet, and for a split second, she caught his eye. It occurred to her that if they were in a cheesy eighties figure skating movie, that would've been the moment he kissed her. And she wanted him to, more than anything. Instead, he just patted her on the head and smiled. She scrunched up her nose and lightly shoved him.

*   *   *

Ainslie felt as if she were floating on air as she and James made their way back to the grandstand.

"Hey, you guys." Jaz came bounding up the hall towards them, keeping her voice low. "Did you hear? Sarah Grey has been done for doping."

"What?" Ainslie and James replied in unison.

"She got randomly drug tested. Some supplement she'd been taking came up with a banned substance. She's likely to cop a four-year ban, and she's been disqualified."

"Fuuuuuuck, that sucks," James said. "But, wait ... that means ..."

"You're the Senior Ladies champion!" Ainslie said. "Lucy's got her gold. So do we ... Three for three!"

Ainslie couldn't believe they'd all actually qualified for Worlds. And not only had they all qualified, but they'd also done it as national champions.

CHAPTER 36

"How do I look?" Ainslie asked, twirling around and checking herself out in the mirror.

The fabric of her little red dress swirled around her thighs as she moved.

"Gorgeous, as always," Lucy replied as she put on her earrings.

Friday night had come at last, and after a week of competing and supporting, Ainslie was more than ready to celebrate.

"Who are you trying to impress, Ains?" Jaz smirked.

Ainslie grabbed Jaz's hand and lifted it to her lips. "Only you, Jaz. You know you're the only one for me."

Jaz rolled her eyes. "How do *I* look?"

"Proper gorgeous, love," Ainslie replied in a poor imitation of Jaz's accent, and then she kissed her on the hand.

"Are you excited, Jaz?" Lucy asked, smoothing down her hair with her palms.

"I'm trying to play it cool."

"You've never played anything cool in your life," Ainslie said, laughing.

Jaz ignored her. "But, yes, I am chuffed to bits!"

Ainslie checked herself in the mirror one last time. She primped her hair and smacked her lips together. She looked good, but not half as good as she was feeling. For the first time since she'd broken up with Aidan, she had a spare five minutes to really reflect on how free she was now. And how amazing it felt.

Then there were all the moments she and James had shared since the break-up, which kept replaying in her mind. How he'd comforted her and made her laugh when all she'd wanted to do was cry. All the times he'd touched her, a hand on the small of her back, an arm around her shoulders, their fingers brushing together. Not to mention the electricity when they'd skated. She didn't know if she was just delusional, but it almost felt like if they shared enough of those moments, perhaps eventually they would evolve into something else.

Wishful thinking, probably.

The girls promptly left their room and headed to the lift. A door opened halfway down the hall and James emerged. Ainslie's heart leaped in her chest a little. He looked gorgeous (as usual) in his own effortless way. He also smelled ridiculously good, and Ainslie felt her throat go dry.

"Hey." He smiled. "You ladies are looking lovely tonight."

As he said it, his eyes lingered on Ainslie for perhaps a little too long, and she felt her stomach flutter.

The four loaded into the lift, which was already almost at capacity. Ainslie found herself pressed awkwardly between James and the lift buttons, and it made her feel unsteady. Being close to him had never been a problem before, but as she inhaled the scent of his soap and cologne, she couldn't help but imagine what it would be like to have that scent all over her. She shivered at the thought.

He looked down at her, and she prayed he couldn't read her mind.

He smiled. "You excited?"

She forced a smile of her own. "Yeah."

"Your hair looks nice," he said as he casually coiled a lock around his finger.

Ainslie swallowed hard. "Thanks."

Are you trying to kill me?

She pictured him shoving her against the lift wall and kissing her. Then she had to wonder if she could manifest it if she thought about it hard enough.

*   *   *

Down in the function room, groups of people were already milling about, and the atmosphere was buzzing. The room was decorated with black and gold balloons, and dozens of round tables with white tablecloths were dotted around a parquet dance floor. A DJ had already set up his table in the corner and was playing some soft background music. Red velvet lounges had been arranged in clusters around the back of the room in case people wanted to escape the revelry of the dance floor. A photo booth stood in one corner, and a seemingly endless queue of teenagers had already formed. Standing like a beacon of light in the otherwise dimly lit room, a bar ran the length of the far wall.

Ainslie, James, Lucy and Jaz headed straight there and began planning their evening.

"Do you guys want to split a bottle of wine?" Ainslie asked.

"Sure," said Jaz. "But first, cocktails!"

Jaz was not messing around.

They collected their drinks and made their way to their table, waiting for the formalities of the evening to begin. Jaz sipped an obnoxiously coloured beverage while Lucy sloshed her straw in and out of a ginger ale. James poured two glasses of red wine for himself and Ainslie.

"You know, I was shattered because I thought this was going to be your last Nationals," Jaz said, pouting at Ainslie. "But now, we can celebrate! To many more!"

James raised his glass. "A toast."

The others all looked at him and followed suit.

"To Goose!" he said, pulling her into his side. "We all love her, and we're all super happy she's not retiring anymore. Or marrying an arsehole. No-one more so than I."

He clinked his glass against Ainslie's, and she blushed.

"Ladies and gentlemen," the MC announced from the stage, "it's that time of the evening when we announce the 2020 Australian team."

Ainslie felt James squeeze her tighter, and she tensed up again. The announcer read the names of the Junior team and then moved to the Seniors.

"Lucy Huong, Senior Ladies Solo Dance."

Everyone applauded, and the other three hollered as Lucy headed to the stage.

"Jayne Bannister, Senior Ladies Freeskating."

James and Ainslie screamed at the top of their lungs as Jaz, looking embarrassed for probably the first time in years, ducked her head and followed Lucy.

"Ainslie Wynter and James Sunderland, Senior Pairs Freeskating."

Ainslie beamed. James grabbed her hand, squeezed it in his, and pulled her towards the stage.

After the entire team was announced, they all stood on the stage together, posing for a team photo. Tessa caught Ainslie's eye, and even though she had been selected too, she was looking bitterly at Ainslie and James. A couple of younger skaters who were standing near the stage were also looking right at them and whispering something to each other. Ainslie wondered if her and James's skate was still the talk of the town. Or perhaps they were just wondering why their hands were still entwined. Not that she was complaining, but Ainslie had to wonder the same thing.

*   *   *

With the formalities over, all Ainslie wanted to do was hit the bar, grab some more drinks, and maybe dance the Nutbush in a tipsy stupor. She returned to their table, snapped a quick selfie with her selection letter and went to post it on social media.

What appeared at the top of her feed made her stomach drop, and she felt all her excited energy leave her body like a rush of air. A post from Aidan. In the madness of the week, she'd forgotten to unfollow him. There he was, a smile emblazoned across his face, his arm draped around a beautiful blonde woman. The woman was familiar.

The photo wasn't captioned, but the first comment on it told the whole story. A comment from a user called @sam.halliday.

So good to be seeing more of you now! Can't wait to have you here full time. Six months long distance is far too long. Love you xo

Ainslie frowned. Six months. She glanced at the location tag. Melbourne. She dropped into her chair. She licked her lips and grabbed her glass of water, taking a swig to try to remedy her bone-dry throat. She'd suspected it, sure. But to have it finally confirmed … She felt sick. But it didn't take long for the nausea to boil into rage. She was just about to throw her phone across the room when she felt a gentle hand rest on her shoulder.

"Wanna dance, Goose?"

She turned around and looked up at James, her eyes beginning to water. She held out her phone for him to see.

He fell silent for a moment before sinking into the chair beside her. "Oh, Ains."

"I don't even know what to say." She sighed.

"I do," James replied, placing his hand on her knee. "He's a piece of shit who never deserved you."

"You know what?" Ainslie shoved her phone back into her bag. "I don't feel like dancing anymore. I think I'm just going to sit over there in the dark alone. And get drunk."

"Not alone," James said, patting her knee. "I can sit with you if you like."

"That's sweet, but you don't have to. I don't want to drag you down with me."

"Hey, what are friends for, right?"

Ainslie smiled weakly.

Sure. Friends.

CHAPTER 37

James and Ainslie meandered over to the bar to refresh their drinks before retiring to one of the red lounges in a dark and quiet corner. Most people were on the dance floor, and those who weren't were either at the bar or lining up for the photo booth. Ainslie crossed one leg over the other and took a long sip of her drink. James shifted uncomfortably, leaning forwards and resting his elbows on his knees. He cradled his wine glass in his hands and took a deep breath. He glanced over at Ainslie. She looked so beautiful. She always did.

"Ains," he said, "I know you probably don't want to talk about it, but I just wanted to say again how proud of you I am. For standing up to Aidan like you did. That was really brave of you. And I know it couldn't have been easy."

She dropped her head, and a small smile crossed her face. "It was easier than you might think."

"And I just want you to know," he said, "that even though I hated Aidan … so much" — Ainslie let out a weak chuckle — "I'm truly sorry about how it all turned out."

"Yeah." She sipped her drink. "Me too."

The silence that hung in the air between them wasn't as comfortable as it usually was. James couldn't figure out what to make of that.

Ainslie was the first to break it. "Love. Am I right?"

James sighed. "Yeah."

"It's got to be better than this," Ainslie said quietly. "It's not all just some lie they tell us when we're kids, is it?"

James stared into his drink. "I guess we just haven't found the right people yet."

Ainslie slouched back on the lounge. "How the hell are you supposed to know who the right person is?"

"I don't know," James replied, leaning back with her. "But I like to think if you find the right person, you just … know?"

She swirled her drink in her glass and watched it whirlpool.

"Easier said than done. For six years, I thought Aidan was the right person. And now in hindsight … how stupid was I?"

"You're not stupid."

"Are you kidding? He never supported me. He screamed at me. He *scared* me. And he accused me of being unfaithful, even though *he* was seeing someone else. And I thought *he* was the one? Maybe it isn't so hard to figure out. Maybe I'm just an idiot."

"Stop."

"He's the arsehole," she said, "and yet now he's happy with someone else. Meanwhile, here I am, alone and miserable."

"Listen," James said, shifting himself to face her. "You're never alone. You've got me. You've got the girls. And you've got Sandra."

"You know what I mean," she muttered. "I liked having somebody to love. Somebody who loved me back. But I guess he never actually loved me, did he? Not really."

Ainslie finally lifted her head and looked at him. Her eyes were filled with such sorrow, he swore he felt his heart break. He didn't want to overstep, but it felt as if she was calling out to him. He couldn't help it. He slipped his arm around her shoulders and pulled her into a side hug.

"So many people love you, Goose. You don't need Aidan."

"I know. You're right," she replied, swatting away a tear.

"I hope you know you deserve the world, Ainslie Wynter," he said earnestly. He could've sworn he saw her blush.

"Thanks, James."

"Any time."

*　　*　　*

James stood and went to buy them more drinks.

As soon as he was out of her sight, Ainslie's body released some of its tension. He'd never had quite that much of an effect on her before, but he looked so good, and he smelled so good, and the things he'd been saying were so beautiful and honest. She almost allowed herself a sliver of hope that maybe that night might actually be the night something happened. She didn't want to be the one to leap first, but she was pretty certain that all she needed was for him to give her the smallest opening, the slightest indication that he could care for her as more than a friend, and she'd jump right in.

He was back before she'd had a chance to gather her thoughts properly, and he handed her a glass of lemon, lime and bitters. She was grateful for that. The last thing she needed was more alcohol. As slightly buzzed as she was, she knew better than to get *completely* drunk around him. Drunk Ainslie had a habit of doing stupid things.

He sat back down beside her, and if she wasn't mistaken, it was just a little bit closer than he'd been sitting before he left. His leg brushed hers, and she felt a pull inside her to do something.

Say something. Anything. Just tell him how you feel.

But the words refused to form.

"Do you think Stephen realises how ridiculous he looks right now?" she said instead.

She nodded to where the usually dignified coach was dancing, looking more uncoordinated than was to be expected.

James chuckled. "For a top dance coach, he really doesn't have a lot of rhythm out there. I hope the irony isn't lost on him."

Ainslie laughed. "I think he's probably had one too many gin and tonics to even remember what irony is."

As their conversation flowed, the volume of the music around them built, and they seemed to huddle closer together on the lounge. At some point, James's arm had even managed to creep back around Ainslie's shoulders. And that pull inside her wasn't going anywhere. The warmth of his body beside hers … she needed it closer. The smell of his soap and cologne … she needed to be bathed in it. His ruffled blond hair looked so incredibly soft … She imagined herself raking her fingers through it, maybe tugging it gently and holding on for dear life as he …

She nibbled her lower lip and pretended to focus on the words he was saying, but she was silently praying to whatever divine force would listen that he'd be the one to make the first move just so she wouldn't have to.

Eventually, the conversation petered out into silence. The silence was the worst. When there was silence, there was nothing to distract her.

"I'm sure that girl will be good for Aidan," Ainslie said simply to have *something* to say. "He's probably relieved he doesn't have to put up with me anymore."

"Hey," James said, squeezing her a little tighter to his side. "No-one has to *put up* with you."

His eyes flickered away from hers, down to her lips, and back again. Ainslie's stomach tightened.

"For as long as I've known you," he said, crooking his index finger and gently lifting her chin with it, "it's only ever been a pleasure."

Ainslie's heart began pounding. Was it actually, finally, happening? Just one finger to her chin was enough to send waves of nervous anticipation through her. She was absolutely dying to know what else those fingers could do. His eyes were so kind, and he seemed to gaze into her soul.

She dropped her eyes to his lips, hoping to give him some kind of hint. It felt as if they were frozen in time, both of them waiting to see what the other was going to do next. Ainslie couldn't stand it. There was no way she was about to let this moment pass her by. She placed a hand on his thigh and squeezed lightly in a silent and impatient invitation.

Ever so slowly, James moved in closer. First, just their noses brushed together, and then he pressed his lips so softly, so tentatively, against hers. Ainslie felt dizzy, and it was definitely not from the wine she'd drunk. She'd never felt more sober in her life. He was gentle, as if he were afraid he'd break her if he went too far. But his kiss ignited a spark inside her, setting off a fluttering deep in her belly and a heat between her legs.

She'd told herself she only needed a small indication, and this was one pretty clear indication.

James suddenly pulled away. His cheeks were the colour of Ainslie's dress, and he looked absolutely mortified.

"I— I'm so sorry. That was so out of line. Look at me, being all weird. That was so inappropriate, I'm so —"

"Shut up, Sunderland." She grabbed him by the front of his shirt and pulled him back to her, crushing his lips with hers.

There was no caution coming from him this time. Clearly, he'd just been patiently waiting for permission. His hands now roamed, one moving to tangle itself in her hair, the other travelling bravely across the small of her back. Ainslie's skin was aflame, and desire was pulsing through her entire body. She pawed at his shirt, feeling his taut muscles under her hands. She'd touched him so many times before, but there had always been a safe layer of lycra there. Now she craved the feeling of his skin on hers.

After what felt like a glorious eternity, they finally came up for breath.

One of his hands was still coiled in her hair. One of hers was still pressed to his chest.

James's breath was heavy. "What …? What are we doing, Ains?"

"What I've wanted to do for ages," she said, her voice low and husky.

He raised his eyebrows. "Ages, huh?"

"Apparently."

Everything was happening so quickly, but there was so much heat in his gaze as his eyes searched her face, Ainslie thought she might just combust on the spot. It was the same heat she'd seen in his eyes so many times before in her dreams. But this was real.

She suddenly realised that her hand was now resting dangerously high on his thigh. They couldn't stay there. They'd already gone too far. If someone had seen them …

Then he said the words she'd been dying to hear for far longer than she cared to admit.

"Do you … want to get out of here?"

Ainslie nodded furiously, and he grabbed her hand, dragging her from the function room, both of them silently praying — unbeknownst to each other — that this wouldn't end up being the stupidest idea they'd ever had.

CHAPTER 38

"I hope Paula doesn't see us," Ainslie said, giggling as James dragged her towards the lift.

"God, she didn't like it when you were just *hanging out* in my room."

"She's not gonna like what's about to happen." Ainslie bit her lip and pulled him into the lift.

When they were safe inside, James took her by the shoulders. "Are you definitely sure you want to do this?"

In the back of his mind, he knew if they got caught, there would be hell to pay, but in that moment, his mind had taken a leave of absence and his dick was standing in for it.

Ainslie rolled her eyes dramatically and responded in the affirmative, pulling him into another rough, heated kiss. James wrapped his hands around her, groping at her tight behind through the thin fabric of her red dress. She ground her hips against him, and he groaned into her mouth. He felt her lips curl into a smile.

The lift stopped at the third floor, and they sprung apart just in time for a group of hotel guests to step inside. James's face was burning. His hands were aching to touch her again but they were currently preoccupied with trying to conceal the situation going on in his trousers.

The rest of the lift ride felt interminable.

By the time they arrived at the fifth floor and stumbled down the hall to James's room, he was on fire. He fumbled with the key card, too distracted by Ainslie's hands on his hips to manage it properly. She whispered something filthy in his ear, and he dropped the card on the floor and swore.

When he finally managed to unlatch the door, he pulled Ainslie inside and pushed her up against the back of it. He pinned her there, holding her hands above her head. She blinked up at him with a sly look in her eye.

She bit her lip.

"Well," she said, her voice sultry and like nothing he'd ever heard from her before. "You got me in here. What are you going to do with me?"

A low growl escaped him, and he lifted her right off her feet. He propped her firmly between his body and the back of the door, and she squeezed her thighs around his hips. Her hands moved to the front of his shirt, and she began unbuttoning it as urgently as if she were digging for treasure. She grazed her fingernails down his chest, and he shivered. He kissed her again, his tongue hot against hers. She smelled like vanilla, and she tasted like wine. His lips trailed down to her neck, his teeth skating gently across her soft skin. She let out a sound that was somewhere between a moan of pleasure and his name caught in her throat.

"Oh, God. James, I need you right now."

Another jolt of electricity shot through him as she claimed his lips with her own once more. And then the gravity of the situation truly hit him as he realised he didn't have any protection.

Shit.

He'd never been one for casual hook-ups, and it wasn't as though he'd been expecting *this* to happen. Especially not at Nationals, of all places.

He disengaged from their kiss.

"Ains, wait."

He reluctantly pulled away and studied her. Her eyes were wild, and her pink lips were swollen and slightly parted as she gasped for air. Stray strands of her hair fell around her face. She looked confused, and frustrated, and a little worried.

"I don't ..." He was barely able to get the words out. "I don't have ... any ... protection. Do you?"

"No." She brushed her hair out of her eyes. "It's not like I was planning on getting laid at Nationals."

"Shit."

"It doesn't matter," she said breathlessly. "I can just take a pill tomorrow ... I mean ... if you don't mind ..."

"I don't mind. As long as you are *absolutely* sure?"

She nodded. "I am."

"You don't think this is the stupidest idea we've ever had?"

"No." She shook her head impatiently. "Now shut up and give it to me."

*   *   *

Ainslie had always known that James was strong (he did lift her over his head on a daily basis, after all), but the sheer power he'd exuded as he'd hauled her across the room towards his bed was a surprise. But quite a pleasant one. She'd always pictured him as the gentle type, like he'd been when he'd first kissed her downstairs. The candles-and-roses type, the gallant romantic. But his primal strength, the power and control that he was exercising, while seemingly out of character, was turning her on like nothing else ever had. It was a side of him she never thought she'd see, and she was loving it.

He dropped her to the mattress, shrugged off his now unbuttoned shirt and kicked off his shoes. Ainslie licked her lips as her eyes roamed greedily across his body. She'd seen him shirtless before, but it was all about context. She'd never seen him like *this* before.

She could feel the heat building between her thighs and she sat up, slipping the thin straps of her dress off her shoulders. She shot him a fiery stare, silently daring him to rip it off. He didn't waste another second. He grasped the hem of her dress, and in one swift movement, the garment was off her body and on the floor alongside his shirt.

He climbed on top of her, covering her body with his, and she delighted in the feeling of him crushing her to the mattress. His skin against hers felt so perfect, and she ached for more.

His mouth moved to her neck, and he nipped at the soft skin there. Ainslie lolled her head back to grant him better access, and a moan escaped her lips. He trailed his kisses across her collarbone and down the curve of her breast.

He reached behind her, lifting her slightly off the bed, and unclasped her lacy bra before tossing it on top of the ever-growing pile of clothing. He drank in her body with his eyes, and the look on his face was so hungry, so desperate, that it caused Ainslie's skin to flush bright red. He resumed his work, his kisses venturing down her newly revealed skin.

Ainslie was certain that at any second, she would wake up. It *had* to be another dream. She reached down between their bodies, fumbling for his belt. She managed to focus long enough to unbuckle it, unbutton his trousers, and shimmy them and his underwear off his hips. He wasn't making it easy, though, what with his lips continuing their delicious exploration from one breast to the other.

He withdrew from her long enough to kick his pants and his briefs the rest of the way off. Then he hooked his fingers in the waistband of her underwear and dragged them slowly down her legs.

Nothing was separating them now. Years of friendship had been lain completely bare.

Lying there under the burning heat of his gaze, Ainslie wondered if she should be feeling awkward or embarrassed, letting her best friend see and touch all of her. Because she wasn't. It felt so right, as if it was something they should've been doing for years. They'd both wasted so much time chasing affection here and there, completely ignoring what had apparently been so obvious to everyone else.

They were made for each other.

Once again, James covered her body with his, and Ainslie gasped at the feeling of all of him against all of her. Her head was spinning as he resumed kissing her neck as if she were the air he needed to breathe. She ran her palms across his back, feeling his muscles ripple under her hands.

His skin was soft and gentle like she'd always imagined it would be, but it was radiating a heat that was igniting her entire body. She breathed him in. It was such a familiar, comforting scent. A scent she'd known for years that had always made her feel safe.

She hooked one leg up around his hip, positively aching for him to finally touch her the way she needed to be touched. She found one of his hands and guided it down her body. He didn't need any guidance after that.

His touch was so precise, so expert, as he sweetly manipulated her. Her eyes lidded, and her tongue darted out to wet her lips. Energy pulsed through her entire body, and she rocked her hips against his hand, coaxing him onwards. She inhaled sharply through her teeth and put her lips close to his ear.

"Please," she said through ragged breaths.

She was more than ready. She needed to know what it felt like to have him inside her.

He raised his head and looked at her, his blue eyes locking onto hers. Those familiar, sweet eyes that were now burning with desire for her. His gaze was so intense that she struggled to hold it.

"You're definitely sure?"

She crinkled her brow as she tried her best to focus on forming the words.

"Yes! God, yes."

He didn't take his eyes off hers as he, painfully slowly, pushed inside her. The pressure was absolutely delectable, and a long, strangled moan escaped her lips. He rested his forehead against hers, and she wrapped both legs around his waist, moving in time with him. She chewed on her lower lip as she felt the intensity build, and she clung to him as if her life depended on it. He quickened his pace, making an exquisitely carnal sound that originated from somewhere deep inside him.

"Oh, God." She gasped, trying her best to keep her voice down.

Her breath was coming faster now, and the heat was building as she climbed higher and higher until she was teetering on the precipice. She pushed her fingers into his hair and held on tight. Moments later, her whole body was wracked with sensation, and she completely came apart around him. Her mouth fell open as a cry threatened to escape her lips, and he silenced it with another kiss as he followed her over the edge.

*   *   *

When they finally came crashing back to earth, they lay side by side for a long moment, staring at the ceiling. James was trying to comprehend what had just occurred. How had they gone from chatting in a function room to lying naked together in his bed?

The room was silent except for their heavy breathing. Eventually, James turned his head towards Ainslie and noticed she was already looking at him. He felt the corner of his mouth twitch, and the next thing he knew, they both burst into peals of laughter. What else could they do? They'd just changed *everything*.

"Do you think we just ruined our friendship?" he asked.

"I think I'm okay with it," Ainslie replied, "if it means we get to do *that*."

"Did *that* really just happen?"

"I think so."

"Oh, my God." James raked his fingers through his hair.

"Who would have thought you were so good in bed, Sunderland?" Ainslie asked, laughing, her eyes still hazy with bliss.

"Oi," he said, play-scolding her, his cheeks flushing. "You sound surprised."

He wrapped his arms around her and pulled her closer, pressing his lips to the top of her head. He savoured the feeling of her body moulded against his, marvelling at how perfectly they fit together. He buried his face in her hair and breathed her in again, worried that at any moment, he'd wake up, and it would've all been a dream. He squeezed her tighter to make sure she was actually real.

At last, they'd finally crossed the line. And that night, both James and Ainslie fell asleep with a smile on their face for the first time in a very long time.

CHAPTER 39

Ainslie was woken up the next morning by noises of people moving in the hotel hallway. Rays of sunlight were peeking through the blinds, and when her eyes first flickered open, she was completely disoriented. She wasn't in her room. She knew that much because Lucy wasn't there shaking her head in silent disapproval and stomping around the place, packing her things. It only took her a second to realise she had a person wrapped around her. Then all the events of the night before came flooding back. The kind, quiet words spoken in the corner of the function room, the way James had looked at her as if she were his entire world, the feeling of her heart leaping in her chest when his lips had first touched hers, the way he'd made her feel with his hands and his mouth and …

Good God.

She heard him breathe a contented sigh behind her, and she buried her face in her pillow in an attempt to silence the happy squeal she was dying to let out.

So, the night before *hadn't* been a dream. She still couldn't quite believe it, even though he was there with her, just as real as she was. She tried to ignore the fear that was niggling away in her stomach, a tiny part of her that was terrified that what had happened was just a fling. What if when he woke up, he regretted it? What if he'd only brought her back to his room because he'd felt sorry for her? They could never go back from this, and she didn't want to. She wanted to be with him more than anything. And after last night, it certainly seemed as if he wanted the same thing.

She heard him stir, and when she felt him squeeze her tighter, her fears began to melt away.

"Good morning, Goose," James whispered into her ear, his voice thick with sleep.

"Good morning," Ainslie replied, unable to wipe the grin off her face.

James lazily nuzzled at her neck with his nose, and she shivered.

"That was not quite how I expected the Nationals Dinner to end," he said as he nipped her skin with his lips.

"It usually ends with a hangover and regret," Ainslie said, rolling over to bring herself nose to nose with him. "I have to say, this was much better."

"I'll say." He smiled and kissed her sleepily. "But, I've got to ask."

Ainslie's heart nearly stopped.

"What exactly does this mean? For us?"

"I mean … what do you want it to mean?" she asked, her voice shaking a little.

"Well, you know," he said, sounding just as nervous as she felt, "you were upset about Aidan last night and like … was this just to get your mind off him? Was this just like a rebound thing … for you? Because … it kind of meant a lot to me, and I was worried that maybe you'd … regret it."

"Hey," Ainslie said softly, running a finger along his lips. "What happened may not have been planned, but I certainly don't regret it. You know how unhappy I've been. And last night … well, I was happy."

James smiled.

"I was more than happy," she said with a laugh. "I was fucking elated."

James grinned and took her by the waist. He pulled her closer, drawing another long, luxurious kiss out of her. She relished the sensation and gave herself over to him. This was exactly where she wanted to be. She wrapped her arms around his neck and pulled him on top of her. He traced his fingers up her ribs, still kissing her. Ainslie's arms never left his neck, and she clung to him as if she were afraid he'd disappear if she let go.

"Ains," he said, "we've been friends for such a long time, and I can't believe it took me so long to realise it, but —"

A frantic pounding on the door cut him off.

"Shit," he muttered.

"What do we do?" Ainslie mouthed.

Getting caught in such a predicament was not on Ainslie's list of things to do that day. If they were discovered, Paula would blow a fuse. It would be the scandal of the year. Who knew what the consequences would be? People had been kicked off teams for less. Their position on the 2020 Australian team could be at stake if she were to find out.

Ainslie flew out of bed, taking the blanket with her. She bolted into the bathroom as James struggled into his tracksuit pants. She pressed her ear against the door and listened.

"James! Have you seen Ainslie?" Lucy's voice was muffled.

Ainslie heard the door click open.

"Hey, Luce, what's up?"

"I don't think Ainslie came back to our room last night. She seems to have disappeared."

"Uh … no, I haven't seen her. She was upset last night and wanted to leave the dinner. She said she was going for a walk. I think down to the beach? To clear her head … But she said she was going back to her room after …"

Ainslie rolled her eyes. He was rambling, and that lie was only going to stress Lucy out further. Suddenly, Ainslie's stomach dropped as she remembered her dress, which — unless James had thought to move it before he'd answered the door — was still lying in its place on the floor, where it had been flung the night before. That would definitely be incriminating. She squeezed her eyes shut, hoping that she could mentally make it disappear. Either that or that Lucy just wouldn't notice it.

"Maybe check down in the dining room?" James said, not sounding anywhere near as casual as Ainslie would have liked.

"You don't seem very concerned. Check-out is in an hour, and all her stuff is strewn about our room. If you see her, tell her I'm not packing for her."

"I will. I'm sure she's fine." James sighed. "Just ... let me get dressed. I'll meet you down at breakfast, and I'll help you look for her."

"Fine."

Once the door was closed, Ainslie burst out of the bathroom.

"You're such a terrible liar," she said, chuckling, sweeping her dress up off the floor and waving it in his face.

"Oops."

"Now, I'm going to have to sprint down the hall and hopefully not get busted by Lucy the bloodhound." Ainslie threw her dress over her head.

"So, I guess this is our little secret for now," James said.

"Well, you know we'd be in the shit for doing this on a Nationals trip. I mean, Paula was ready to crucify me for eating lunch in here."

"True."

"We'll keep it hush for now. Until we figure things out." She tousled her hair. "Sandra probably doesn't need to know right now, either."

Ainslie put her shoes on and noticed James watching her with a smile.

"I'll pack my things and get changed," she said. "Meet you back here in ten, and then we'll go down to breakfast." She placed her hand on the doorhandle. "I'm going to run."

"We're probably not going to get any time alone again until we get back to Sydney," James said. "But we need to finish that conversation."

"Tonight. When we get back." She pecked him on the lips. "See you in a bit."

Ainslie turned to leave, but James pulled her back to him, wrapping her up in his arms and kissing her one more time. When he finally released her, she was breathless.

"Bye," she said, but it came out no louder than a whisper.

She stuck her head out the door to check if the coast was clear, then she ran full speed down the hall.

Ainslie's heart pounded as she fumbled with her key card. She muttered a prayer under her breath that no-one would spot her, hair a mess, make-up smudged, still wearing the same clothes as the night before. The longer she stood in the hallway, the more her earlier elation became overshadowed by the fear of being caught with her proverbial pants down. Her panic was making the key card even more difficult to handle. Eventually, she managed to jam it in the door and slip inside to safety.

"Busted!"

Ainslie nearly jumped out of her skin.

Jaz was standing in the middle of the room with her arms folded and a smug grin painted on her face. Ainslie felt her face flush, and she took a moment to think about if she should even bother trying to conjure up a lie.

"I ... sorry," she said. "I went for a walk after dinner ... went down to the beach ... I fell asleep —"

God, I'm a worse liar than James.

"Bullshit! That is a walk of shame if ever I saw one."

"I'm not quite sure 'shame' is the right word for it," Ainslie said as a telling smile slowly began to creep across her face.

Jaz squealed so loudly Ainslie grabbed a pillow off the bed and threw it at her.

"What on *earth* happened last night?" Jaz said, finally lowering her voice. "Don't think I didn't notice you leave together."

Ainslie blushed furiously. "Do you think Lucy noticed? Or Sandra? Or Stephen?"

"I don't think so. Sandra and Tim left early, Stephen was drunk, and Lucy was faffin' about this morning, worrying about not being able to find you, so I don't think she noticed." Jaz furrowed her brow. "Actually, she said she was going to go ask James if he'd seen you ... Were you ...?"

"Hiding in his bathroom naked."

Jaz cackled. "Oh, my God, this is amazing!"

"You can't tell anyone!" Ainslie said as she lobbed another pillow.

"What— Not even Lucy?!"

"Especially not Lucy! There's no way her anxiety would be able to cope with keeping a secret this big. I didn't even want *you* to know."

"Well, it's too late for that now, so you may as well spill." Jaz was bouncing off the walls. "I've been invested in this relationship for years! I thought maybe you'd tell him you fancied him. I didn't think you were gonna go off and shag him."

Ainslie somehow turned redder. "Oh, my God, it was ..." She couldn't even find the words.

"How did it even happen?"

"Well, I guess this is what started it all." Ainslie pulled out her phone and found the photo of Aidan and Sam Halliday.

Jaz scanned the post and pulled a face. "Are you kidding me? What a cockhead."

"I was devastated by this last night." Ainslie frantically picked up the pieces of her New South Wales uniform and carried them to the bathroom. "But when I woke up this morning, I was like, *Aidan who?*"

"Okay, but how did you go from that" — Jaz gestured at Ainslie's phone — "to that?" She gestured at Ainslie's state of dress.

"One minute we were just talking," Ainslie said, slipping into the bathroom to change, "and then things got really intense. And then he just ... kissed me."

"He kissed you first?! See, I bloody told you he was into you! Did you tell him how you feel?"

"I didn't really get a chance to *tell* him," Ainslie called through the door, "but I *showed* him, if you know what I mean."

Jaz snorted.

"But this morning, it was like he was going to tell me something important," Ainslie said, "but then we got interrupted by bloody Lucy banging on the door."

"God, she's a buzzkill. Well, what do you think he was going to say?"

"I don't know."

"I mean, from what you're telling me, I doubt he was going to say he just wanted to be friends."

"Jaz, this is real." Ainslie lowered her voice as she re-emerged from the bathroom. "He said it meant a lot to him. This feels like the real thing. Like, when we were together, I was like, *Why haven't we been doing this for years?*"

Jaz smiled. "Well, you look happier than you've looked in a long time."

She felt it, too, as if she were on a cloud.

"But seriously, though, don't tell anyone," Ainslie said. "The last thing we need is to get our arses handed to us by Paula for ... *fraternising* on a Nationals trip."

"Fraternising?" Jaz smirked. "Is that what you kids are calling it these days?"

Ainslie shoved all her belongings into her suitcase. She sat down hard on the bag and managed to zip it up. After doing one last check of the room to make sure nothing had been forgotten, she and Jaz headed out. Halfway down the hallway, James emerged from his room, dragging his suitcase behind him. He glanced at Jaz and then at Ainslie. He looked like a deer caught in headlights.

"She knows," Ainslie said.

"What? How did you ...?"

"Oh, please, neither of you are as slick as you think you are." Jaz slapped him on the back. "Nice work, mate. You bagged yourself a babe. Don't worry, I won't tell."

"Yeah." Ainslie glared at Jaz as they got in the lift. "You bloody well better not."

*　　*　　*

The New South Wales team were already in the dining room eating their breakfast. Sandra and Stephen were sitting at a long table with the Randwick skaters in the far corner of the room. Lucy was sitting alone at the end of the table, looking restless and agitated.

"Found her, Luce," James said innocently, and Lucy looked relieved.

"You had me worried, Ainslie," Lucy said. "What happened to you last night?"

The memory of what had *actually* happened to her the night before passed through Ainslie's mind, and she prayed she wasn't blushing.

"Sorry. Some personal stuff went down and ... I just needed some time alone, so I went for a walk. I just sat on the beach to clear my head, and ... I guess I must have fallen asleep ..."

Lucy narrowed her eyes. She hardly looked convinced. Ainslie had to wonder if Lucy could read her mind because all she could think about was the incredible sex she'd had the night before and how she was absolutely dying to get back to Sydney to do it again.

"Ainslie!" Paula's voice snapped her out of her reverie.

Ainslie winced and turned around to see Paula sitting at the table behind her.

"You know you're not supposed to leave the hotel grounds alone while under the care of the team."

"I know. I'm sorry."

Paula being under the impression that Ainslie went off the premises alone was far better than her knowing what she had *actually* done.

"Forget it," Paula said, waving her off. "Go and get some breakfast."

Ainslie was happy to get out of there before she dug herself any deeper. She grabbed breakfast from the buffet and sat opposite James. The two of them ate in relative silence, occasionally trading knowing glances while the others chatted away. Ainslie was pretty sure they didn't look suspicious, but she couldn't help but feel as if everyone knew something was going on.

She was also finding it quite difficult to be around him, pretending that nothing had changed when everything was different now. It was all she could think about. Where were they going to go from here? It felt like the beginning of something amazing, and she still couldn't quite believe it was real.

She also couldn't believe how long it had taken for her to admit it to herself. It had always been James. Obviously. Aidan had never made her as happy as James did, even when they had been engaged. James had always treated her better. She felt like an idiot for ever choosing Aidan over James, and she was so incredibly thankful that she hadn't left it too late to change her mind.

She picked up her phone and sent a quick, covert text message.

I can't wait for us to be alone again x

James's phone was on silent, but the screen lit up, and she watched as his eyes flicked towards it. He put his coffee cup to his lips in an attempt to hide his reaction. He lifted his gaze up to her and smiled.

"Me neither," he mouthed from behind his cup.

Sandra clinked her teaspoon against her glass, and Ainslie jumped.

"Let me just say," Sandra said, "well done, everyone, for your outstanding performances this year. You all made me and Stephen extremely proud. While for most of you, this is the end of the competitive season, for others, this marks the start of your Worlds journey. Congratulations to Ainslie and James, Lucy and, of course, a huge congratulations to Jaz for her first-ever selection."

Jaz blushed and did a little victory dance in her chair.

"And you two …" Sandra waggled her finger at Ainslie and James.

Ainslie's paranoia made her clench every muscle in her body.

"At the beginning of the year, we thought this would be our last Worlds together," Sandra said. "And even though the circumstances that changed that weren't the greatest, I just want to say I'm incredibly happy that Team Jameslie will live to see another season."

Ainslie felt James's foot brush against her leg under the table and she glanced at him.

He winked. "Go Team Jameslie."

*   *   *

The flight back to Sydney was only two and a half hours long, but it felt like the longest flight of Ainslie's life. She was sitting next to James and absolutely bursting to be able to speak to him alone, but she had Lucy sitting on her other side. So instead, she sat there, half paying attention to a movie, half chatting about Barcelona, trying as best as she could to distract herself.

It wasn't easy, however, especially when James inconspicuously slid his hand across the seat, bridging the small gap between them, and brushed his fingers against hers. Ainslie's breath hitched at the slight touch, and she immediately felt ridiculous. How were they going to skate together if every time he touched her, she turned to putty? At one point, much to Ainslie's relief, Lucy got up to go to the bathroom.

"I want to finish that conversation from this morning," James whispered, turning to face her.

"Me too," she replied, "but we can't talk here with everyone around."

"No." He frowned. "How about we meet at the park near your place? Around five. And we can talk. Alone and uninterrupted."

Ainslie nodded. "Sounds like a plan."

"I can't wait." He smiled before checking no-one was looking and stealing the briefest of kisses.

By the time Lucy returned from the bathroom, they'd broken apart and had their eyes fixed ahead on their screens. Ainslie wasn't paying any attention to the film, though. She just stared blankly at the screen as the ghost of his kiss still lingered on her lips, so full of the promise of what was to come.

CHAPTER 40

The apartment on Gadigal Avenue was a flurry of action for the rest of Saturday afternoon, much to the chagrin of Lucy, who was trying to enjoy a book on the lounge. Jaz was practically bouncing off the walls with excitement. She only sat still once Lucy suggested she put her energy to good use and start researching Barcelona. Every so often, she'd loudly announce any skerrick of Catalan trivia she happened across. Lucy just sat quietly in the corner, looking mildly irritated and trying her best to block her out. The only person being more annoying than Jaz was Ainslie.

Ainslie could tell she was driving Lucy up the wall, but she couldn't help it. The butterflies in her stomach were in a frenzy, and she kept asking for the time every five minutes.

"You have a phone. Use it," Lucy said after Ainslie enquired for the umpteenth time.

"What's got you all worked up, Ains?" Jaz smirked.

Ainslie shot her a look of warning. "Nothing. I'm just … wired."

"Okay?" Lucy said over her book. "So go for a run."

As if on cue, Ainslie's phone vibrated on the kitchen counter. She nearly fell over a chair as she bounded over to check it.

I'm downstairs.

She stifled a smile. "You know, I think I might."

"Can you grab some milk while you're out?" Jaz asked, a knowing look on her face.

Ainslie narrowed her eyes at her.

"You little shit," she mouthed.

*　　*　　*

Green Square Park was an oasis in an otherwise concrete jungle. It bloomed with lush grass and colourful flowers. Ducks frolicked in the humanmade pond, the white and grey apartment buildings on Gadigal Avenue and the adjoining streets looming around it. Dusk was just beginning to fall, and an orange-and-pink glow was being cast over the neighbourhood, the final traces of warmth setting with the sun.

James was waiting for Ainslie with his shoulders hunched against the cold and his hands pushed deep into his jacket pockets. His heart raced a little as he mentally prepared for what he was about to say.

When he saw Ainslie emerge from her building, wrapped up in a cosy, over-sized jumper, his stomach filled with butterflies. As she got closer, he could see her cheeks were flushed pink from the cold, and her smile was lighting up her whole face, which just caused him to smile too.

"Hey," he said, reaching a hand out to her.

"Hey." Her smile somehow grew even brighter.

Ainslie gingerly took his hand, and he laced his fingers tightly through hers, pulling her into a kiss. He folded her up in a warm embrace, wrapping his coat around her to protect her from the cold evening air.

"I've been waiting all day to do that again," he said.

"Me too."

James kept Ainslie cocooned in his jacket as they began strolling side by side, walking slowly around the pond.

James had never felt nervous around Ainslie before. It was a strange feeling. But of course, he'd never been moments away from baring his soul to her. He knew he had to do it. Suck it up and tell her everything, tell her exactly how he felt. He'd waited long enough already, and if the night before had been anything to go by, he didn't think he had anything to worry about. Less than twenty-four hours earlier, she'd looked him dead in the eye and practically begged him to have his way with her. And now she was walking beside him, her fingers entwined with his, looking so very content.

He took a deep breath. It was going to be okay.

"So," he said finally, "I should probably finish telling you what I started telling you this morning."

He glanced at her, and she looked nervous, which in turn made him feel *more* nervous.

"A few months ago," he said, "when you came to training and told me you were getting married, I lashed out like a complete dick."

"Yes." Ainslie pursed her lips. "I remember that very well."

"Anyway," he said, "I realised something that day. Something I think I'd always known deep down. And in hindsight … it couldn't have been more obvious."

They finally stopped walking, and James sat down on a park bench. Ainslie sat down beside him, still holding his hand and looking at him intently. He kicked the dirt and looked down at his feet.

"Did you know I had a crush on you before you met Aidan?" He laughed weakly.

He saw Ainslie smile out of the corner of his eye.

"No, I didn't."

"I never said anything because I was scared." He dragged his eyes away from the ground and forced himself to look at her. "I thought it'd just freak you out and ruin everything. And our friendship is the most important thing in the world to me.

And you have to know that us being just friends would *never* be a consolation prize for me. But when you got engaged, I realised that for some reason, I'd been holding out hope that maybe one day I'd get the courage to tell you … That day at the rink, I acted like a dick because I realised I'd missed the boat."

Ainslie didn't say anything. She just stared at him. He wondered if he looked as vulnerable as he felt.

"I know this might sound completely ridiculous," he said, "because it's just *so* quick, but …"

Somehow his heart was both on his sleeve and stuck in his throat. The words he wanted to say were stuck in there as well. Ainslie gently placed her hand on his knee, silently encouraging him to continue. He took a long, deep breath. There was no going back now.

"I think I'm in love with you, Ainslie," he said, studying her face for any hint of a reaction. "Or rather, I *know* I'm in love with you. If that wasn't already obvious from last night."

She cupped his cheek in her hand.

"You know, I'm pretty sure I've always loved you," he said.

He barely had a chance to get the last word out before her lips were on his and she was kissing him deeply and hungrily. She didn't even need to say anything. He was pretty sure she was telling him everything he needed to know. After what felt like an eternity, she slowly withdrew, her hand still holding his face.

"It doesn't sound ridiculous at all," she said. "I spent the last six years thinking I knew what love was. I think I'd been conditioned to believe it's all hard work and compromise. But now, in just under twenty-four hours with you … it's so incredibly simple."

James thought his heart might explode. The corner of his mouth twitched into a half smile.

"So … what you're saying is …"

Ainslie blushed. "I … I love you, too."

He pulled her back in, wrapping her up in his arms and kissing her again. He felt her lips curl into a smile. She slipped her hands inside the front of his jacket, clutching him by his waist and pulling him closer. He cocooned her up in his arms, wishing they could freeze time and stay in that moment forever. But eventually, they had to come up for breath.

"Can you imagine what Aidan would say if he found out about this?" James said.

"I can't believe you're thinking about *him* right now," Ainslie said, laughing. "I also can't believe he was right all along."

James laughed along with her. "He and *literally* everyone else we know."

"I guess we used the 'just friends' defence so often we started to believe it."

"Friends was good," James said, "but this … this is everything."

"So," Ainslie said, gazing up at him as they remained huddled together on the park bench, "what is 'this' then? Officially?"

"Well," he said, squeezing her tighter, "I guess you would be my girlfriend now, wouldn't you? Or … partner?"

"I mean, I've been your *partner* for nearly twenty years now." Ainslie chuckled.

"Well," he replied, "now you're my *partner* in every sense of the word."

"I like it," she said, crinkling her nose and beaming.

"But I think you're right about not telling Sandra yet," he said with a frown.

Ainslie pouted. "Yeah, I can't imagine she'd think of this as anything other than a distraction. Especially this close to Worlds."

"So, *secret* partner then," James said. "Just until after Worlds."

"Well, it's not a secret from Jaz," Ainslie said, giggling. "I think she's more excited than either of us are."

James smiled and pushed a lock of hair behind Ainslie's ear. "Oh, I don't think that's possible."

*   *   *

Ainslie could've stayed on the park bench wrapped in James's arms forever, but even as she cuddled into the warmth of his jacket and body, the cold was really starting to set in, and she shivered.

"I told Jaz I'd get some milk," she said. "Care to accompany me to the shops?"

"I'd love to."

"Then do you want to come back to ours?" Ainslie asked, hoping not to sound too eager but absolutely dying to get him back in bed. "You could have dinner with us?"

"Sounds like a plan."

After a quick supermarket run, the two returned to the girls' apartment. It was hardly unusual for James to pop around, and Lucy barely batted an eyelid when they walked through the door together. Jaz, on the other hand, smirked at them from the lounge, and Ainslie shot her a threatening glare.

As Ainslie went about making dinner, James did his best to assist, though he was fairly hopeless in the cooking department and was one stupid question away from Ainslie kicking him out of the kitchen for good.

She was chopping carrots when she noticed Jaz staring at them. Ainslie locked eyes with her and gave a carrot one swift and particularly aggressive chop, hoping her threat would translate. Jaz just stifled a laugh and went back to her laptop.

The four ate dinner, and Lucy seemed to be as in the dark as ever, no thanks to Jaz's continued smirking. Ainslie was relieved when Lucy yawned and announced she was going to bed.

"I've got an early start tomorrow," Jaz said, "so I should probably turn in as well."

Once the girls were safely away in their rooms, James turned to Ainslie.

"All right," he said, leaning in for a kiss goodnight. "I better be off."

Ainslie stopped him in his tracks, laying a finger gently upon his lips.

"Or you could stay here?" she whispered.

"Really?" he whispered. "With the girls home?"

Ainslie shrugged. "Why not? It's not like they go in my room. Plus, they both have work tomorrow morning, and you and I have the day off. They'll be gone before we get up, and they won't even know you were here."

"Well, I'm convinced."

"I thought you might be," she said as she grabbed him by the hand and pulled him into her room.

CHAPTER 41

For the second morning in a row, James woke up entangled in sheets with his best friend. Their first night together had been urgent and desperate, as if they both thought it might be the only chance they'd ever have. But the second night had been different. They'd taken their time to explore one another completely and learn all the intimate things they didn't already know about each other. There was no need to rush, and they didn't need to worry about being caught by team management. They both knew that they had all the time in the world now.

They'd fallen asleep huddled under Ainslie's cosy doona, protecting each other from the chilly winter night. Now she lay draped across his chest, her copper hair tousled about the place, his arm going numb underneath her. He watched as her shoulders rose and fell upon her gentle breaths. He smiled to himself and toyed with a lock of her hair. He gazed out the window, over the city, not wanting to move and wake her up. He couldn't hear any noise coming from the apartment, so he figured Jaz and Lucy must have left for work. The stillness of the moment was so perfect he wondered if they could get away with never leaving the bed.

Eventually, he felt her stir, and she raised her head lazily. She looked up at him through half-lidded, tired eyes and let out a contented little huff.

"Hey," she said sleepily.

"Hey."

"I could get used to this," she said, her voice a purr as she repositioned herself to face him better.

"Me too."

"We don't have to leave for the rink until four. We have the whole day to ourselves."

"Let's stay right here."

"I like the sound of that," she said, leaning in and kissing him good morning.

He wrapped his arms around her waist and pulled her on top of him.

"You smell like coconut," he mumbled between kisses.

She giggled. "Is that a good thing?"

"Are you kidding? I want to eat you up."

He buried his face in the crook of her neck and rolled her over. She let out a shriek, and James hoped he was right about the girls being gone already.

"Your hair is so soft," she said as she pushed her fingers into his hair and tugged ever so lightly.

An unholy sound escaped his lips, and he felt his face turn bright red. She pulled a face that told him she was definitely going to use that against him in the future.

He pulled back and looked at her. "Are you trying to kill me?"

She smiled provocatively. "I never noticed that your eyes have a little green in them," she said, brushing his hair away from his face. "How have I never noticed that before?"

He lifted her chin and ran his thumb along her bottom lip. "Your lips are really soft. And I really enjoy kissing them."

"The feeling's mutual." She kissed his thumb before rolling him back over and climbing astride him. "I really enjoy doing other things too."

He ran his hands up her thighs. "Hmm, like what?"

She blinked down at him innocently. "You know what."

"I know." The corner of his lips quirked upwards. "But I want to hear you say it."

"How about some of our more … intimate skating moves," she said, running her hands across his chest. "But with no clothes on."

He laughed. "That's … weirdly hot."

He marvelled at her as she sat atop him, the morning sun bathing her skin in a golden glow, her hair falling down her shoulders like Lady Godiva. Just days ago, it would have been a distant fantasy.

"Have I ever told you how *incredibly* sexy you are?" he asked, running his hands over the curve of her hips. "I've thought so for quite some time."

"So, Greaves isn't the only one who likes my tight little body suits." She smirked.

He gave her backside a little squeeze. "I prefer what's underneath them."

She ran her hands up his arms and leaned down, kissing him again.

"Do you think it's going to be weird?" he asked. "Training together now?"

"It doesn't have to be," she said, shrugging. "Nothing has really changed, has it?"

"Are you kidding? You can hardly say that while you're like *that*." He gestured vaguely at her state of undress.

"We've both had these feelings for a while now. It's just that now we've acted on them … twice."

"And what if our chemistry was so good because of all the unresolved sexual tension?"

"I mean, it could've been." A cheeky smile began to spread across her face as her hands returned to his chest. "But I don't think the sexual tension is going anywhere for a while yet." She leaned down, pressing a kiss on his chest. "Not when every time I look at you, I picture you like this." Another kiss, a little to the left of the first. "Who knows? Maybe it will make our chemistry better?"

"I hope so." He smiled as she kept trailing soft, warm kisses down his body. "Because there's no way we're going back to the way we were."

"It's not going to be easy, though," Ainslie said, continuing her way down his stomach, "being around you and pretending I don't want you."

"I mean, *I've* had a lot of practice in that department," he said, feeling his arousal grow.

"Sandra would be so mad," Ainslie said, giggling. "She'd definitely consider this a pretty major distraction from our training."

"Oh, but you're such a good distraction."

Her kisses were dangerously low down his body now. She bit her lip and shifted even lower.

"Would you like me to *distract* you one more time before we get breakfast?"

"Yes, please."

*　　*　　*

The two spent the better part of the day holed up in Ainslie's bed, distracting each other a few more times and only really getting up to go to the bathroom or to get food. At about three thirty, they reluctantly dragged themselves out from between the sheets and got ready to go down to the rink.

They headed over to Randwick via James's house so he could get changed and grab his skates.

The two of them arriving at the rink together wasn't unusual, but Ainslie's guilty conscience got the better of her when Sandra flashed them a smile.

"Afternoon, guys."

"Afternoon," they replied in unison.

Ainslie knew it was incredibly unlikely that Sandra knew about them. In fact, it was virtually impossible. But it didn't stop her from feeling paranoid.

"Do you think she knows?" she whispered to James when Sandra was out of earshot.

"How would she possibly know?" he asked, laughing.

She knew it was irrational, but she'd spent the entire day in a state of total euphoria, and she felt like a completely different person. So she had to wonder if she looked different too.

"I dunno," she said. "Do you think she can tell we've spent the whole day in bed together?"

"She's not a mind-reader," James whispered, "but she isn't deaf either, so maybe keep your voice down. Just act normal, and no-one will be any the wiser. We've just got to get through today. It'll only get easier, I'm sure."

Ainslie wasn't sure about that at all.

*　　*　　*

Ainslie headed to the change room only to discover Lucy was already there. She was halfway through putting her hair up into a bun.

"Hey," Ainslie said, trying to sound as casual as possible, and in so doing, not sounding casual at all. "How was work?"

"Fascinating and fulfilling, as usual," Lucy replied dryly. "What did you get up to today?"

Ainslie's mind flicked back to earlier in the day, replaying some of the different

191

things she and James had *gotten up to* together. Her mouth went dry, and she checked herself out in the mirror to make sure she wasn't blushing.

"Nothing much," she said, as naturally as she could manage. "Just hung out around the house."

She fled into the safety of a toilet cubicle, hoping her paranoia would pass before her pairs lesson.

* * *

"Time for a debriefing," Ainslie said when Sandra called them over.

"Not our first for today," James whispered with a hint of a smile.

Ainslie swatted him on the arm and tried not to laugh.

"Okay, you two," Sandra said as they rolled up to the barrier. "Firstly, good job at Nationals. You did it, but it was close this time."

Sandra brought up the results on her laptop.

"Tessa and Antony have improved a lot since last year," she said. "They were nipping at your heels with the technical score, and it's the little things. For example, they got a Level 4 for their footwork sequence, and you only got a Level 3. We can tweak things to lift the technical score. But your program components ... skating skill and transitions, very good. Choreography, excellent. And these performance marks?" She tapped the screen. "That's our silver bullet. I've got to say, it was probably the best performance I've seen you put down. When I think about where we started with this routine and how far we've come ... I think you finally convinced me that you wanted to tear each other's clothes off."

Ainslie felt her cheeks turn red. She knew it was just a throwaway joke, but for a split second, she thought Sandra might actually know, after all. Thankfully, the joke didn't hang in the air too long, and Sandra continued with her critiques. Ainslie soon realised that once the shoptalk began and they were focused solely on skating, everything felt ... normal.

Sandra put them to work as she sifted through both programs with a fine-toothed comb, making changes and adding flourishes where necessary.

Ainslie was incredibly relieved to discover that sleeping with James hadn't seemed to have negatively affected their working relationship. If anything, it had improved it. They weren't acting anymore. There was no barrier between them. They'd both seen each other at their most vulnerable, and all their inhibitions had been forgotten.

* * *

James looked over at Ainslie and watched as a single bead of sweat rolled from her temple, down the column of her neck. It snaked its way along her collarbone and disappeared between her breasts. He'd never envied a bead of sweat before. His palms began to grow clammy as he thought about how badly he wanted to trace its path with his tongue. Her lips were parted as she gasped for breath, and her brow was furrowed as she listened intently to Sandra's instructions. He couldn't shake the memory of the last time she'd made that face. The night before. When she was writhing beneath him, her legs clamped around his waist.

Jesus Christ.

He shifted his weight from one leg to the other, trying to ignore how tight his pants had become.

Sandra's voice cut into his daydream. "I'm sorry, James. Is there something you'd rather be doing?"

God, yeah.

Clearly, he wasn't being as covert as he thought he was. And he'd *literally* just told Ainslie to act normally.

Ainslie was smirking at him. He wondered if she could read his mind.

"Sorry," James muttered, and Sandra rolled her eyes.

"As I was saying," Sandra said, "I want to see one more run-through of the long program before we wrap things up. Ainslie, for the love of God, watch your hips on the landing of the triple Salchow, all right?"

Just the very mention of Ainslie's hips was enough to cause James's mind to wander again. He mentally slapped himself.

He wiped his increasingly sweaty palms on his pants before taking Ainslie in their opening position. For the first time in his life, he was grateful to have his manhood held down by a dance belt.

*　　*　　*

Sandra seemed happy with their improvements, and the rest of the training session went as normally as could be expected. James managed to get a hold of himself, but Ainslie definitely noticed the struggle, and she'd been doing her best to push his buttons. By the time Sandra finally dismissed them, he had only one thing on his mind.

As they headed down the hall to the change rooms, he pulled Ainslie into a gap between some lockers, trapping her between his body and the wall.

She looked up at him and ground her hips against his. "I knew I'd gotten you all hot and bothered back there."

He responded with a frustrated grunt and kissed her roughly and relentlessly, hands roaming to all sorts of dangerous places, pulling her hips harder against him.

Then came a sound they neither needed nor wanted to hear.

"Ahem!"

They snapped out of their embrace and whipped their heads around at the interruption. Ainslie heaved a massive sigh of relief when she saw it was only Jaz. James was bright red.

Jaz folded her arms. "You guys are really going to have to be more careful if you don't want to get busted by Sandra."

Jaz was right. It had been incredibly stupid and risky. But it was also incredibly hot.

Ainslie could barely wipe the smile off her face as she fled into the ladies change room, Jaz following close behind.

"Well, well, well," Jaz said, "I'll take that to mean your little talk last night went well."

Ainslie casually pulled her singlet off over her head. "I don't know what you're talking about."

"Ainslie! Don't leave me hanging! You're the only straight couple I care about! You should consider that an honour!"

Ainslie was absolutely relishing every moment of torturing Jaz, but she couldn't hold it in any longer.

"Jaz," she said, "to say it went well would be the understatement of the century!"

Ainslie explained everything that had happened during their talk in the park. How he'd lashed out about Aidan because of jealousy, how he'd told her he was in love with her and always had been, how she'd told him she felt the same way. Jaz interjected with squeals throughout the entire story.

"And today was *so perfect*," Ainslie said dreamily. "We just hung out all day, then came to training, and things felt … normal."

"Normal," Jaz said with a smirk. "Except now after training, instead of getting coffee, you get felt up behind the lockers."

Ainslie pulled a face and threw her drink bottle at Jaz, who caught it at the last second.

"But seriously," Jaz said, "I don't think I've *ever* seen you this happy. I think that means you're onto something good."

"I've never felt like this before," Ainslie said, lowering her voice. "I know it might sound crazy because it's so quick, but I honestly feel like James is who I'm meant to be with. Like, forever."

"Quick?" Jaz cackled. "You've known each other for *twenty years*. That's hardly quick."

"You know what I mean."

"It doesn't sound crazy. You two are soul mates. It's just that *literally* everyone else in the world figured it out before you idiots did."

CHAPTER 42

The next few weeks were hectic. Ainslie and James's relationship was blossoming into something beautiful, but their training regime had shifted into overdrive, and even though they would've liked to have spent every waking moment making up for lost time, they were required at the rink almost every day. They'd managed to not allow their relationship to get in the way of their training, but unfortunately, their training kept getting in the way of their relationship.

One late Saturday afternoon, Ainslie had a leg thrown up on the barrier. She pushed into the stretch, feeling it deep in her hamstring.

"Hey, are you free tonight?" James asked, rolling up beside her and grabbing his foot in a quad stretch.

"Sorry," Ainslie said, smirking, "I have a boyfriend."

"He's a very lucky guy," he replied, not so subtly checking her out as she stretched.

"Keep it in your pants, Sunderland."

"Seriously, though," James said, lowering his voice, his tone shifting, "do you want to finally go out tonight? Our first *official* date?"

"Of course I do," she replied, matching his volume, "but I thought you had to work."

"Swapped shifts. Had to get my priorities in order."

Ainslie raised an eyebrow. "Paying your rent isn't a priority?"

"Hey, Wynter, do you want to go out or not?"

"Yes." She beamed. "I do."

"Great. I'll pick you up from your place at seven thirty, okay?"

Ainslie was a little distracted by the sight over James's shoulder. The sight of Sandra near the music box, glaring at them. There's no way she could've heard them over the music, but Ainslie felt conspicuous anyway.

"Dude, Sandra's looking right this way."

"So?" He shrugged. "She's probably just wondering why we're talking instead of training." He leaned in close and whispered. "Talking about how I want to rip that stupid leotard clean off your body."

Ainslie pursed her lips. "Don't start this game. You know I *always* beat you."

"Bring it on."

Ainslie bit her lip and whispered, "I like how your butt looks in those tight pants. Makes me want to sink my teeth into it."

James sucked his teeth. "Not sure if that's hot or terrifying. I think it's both. She still looking?"

Ainslie glanced over James's shoulder. "No."

He stole the quickest of kisses. "Seven thirty. Your place."

*   *   *

Their training session had been long and exhausting, and Ainslie had struggled to stay focused. Her mind kept wandering off to thoughts of later that night. Their first official date. She felt strangely nervous. This was *James*. Her best friend. She didn't really have anything to be nervous about, but as she stood in front of her mirror straightening her hair, her stomach was a whirlwind of butterflies.

She gave herself a final once-over in her full-length mirror and tried to calm her nerves, wondering if she should do a shot. That probably wasn't the best idea.

She'd chosen a little black dress that hugged her slight curves in all the right places. She knew James didn't care what she wore; he'd seen her at her very best and her very worst. But even so, she wanted to make sure she gave him a real treat.

She ventured from her room, preparing herself for an onslaught of questions.

"Flippin' 'eck!" Jaz said from the couch. "You look bloody hot!"

"Too hot," Lucy said, smirking. "Where are you off to?"

"I have a work thing," Ainslie replied simply.

"When you say work thing ...," Jaz said, an evil grin spreading across her face.

Lucy lowered her book to join in the ribbing. "You look like you have a hot date."

"Why yes, Ainslie," Jaz said, folding her arms, "you *do* look like you have a hot date. Anyone we know?"

Ainslie glowered at Jaz, her red lips forming a thin line.

"I *don't* have a hot date. It's Amber from work's birthday, and we're going into the city for drinks."

"Whatever you say." Jaz winked.

Lucy just looked bored and returned to her book.

*   *   *

Ainslie's stomach was doing backflips and her heart was pounding the entire way down to the foyer, but as soon as she stepped out of the building and saw James's face, her nerves eased, and her pulse quickened for a different reason. There he was, leaning casually against a lamppost in the moonlight, wrapped up in a dark grey overcoat. He looked so effortlessly handsome, it made Ainslie want to skip the date and take him straight back up to her room.

"Well, don't you look positively cinematic," she said, smiling.

When he smiled back, she felt all her remaining nerves leave her body. He stepped out from under the light of the lamp and closed the gap between them.

He reached out and stroked her cheek with his thumb. "You look so beautiful."

"So do you," she said, her skin tingling where he touched her. "I mean, not beautiful, but ... yeah, I guess beautiful. Or rather, handsome if you prefer —"

He cupped her cheek in his palm and stopped her rambling with a kiss. She wrapped her arms around his waist and buried herself inside his coat, enjoying the warmth of his body.

She pulled away reluctantly. "Can't we just skip the date and head straight to ... after?"

James laughed out loud. "I love the enthusiasm, and we can definitely do that later. But right now, I have plans."

"I hope they weren't outdoor plans." Ainslie eyed the starless sky and the black clouds covering the moon. "Because it looks like it's going to pour."

"Never mind," James said. "If worst comes to worst, we can just do your plan."

*   *   *

Ainslie had her hand on James's leg as he drove towards the inner city. He thought his face might split in half from all his smiling.

"Where are you taking me?" she asked, giving his leg a little squeeze and peering expectantly out the window.

James kept his eyes on the road and grinned. "You'll see."

The glowing embers of the city lights began to crest over the horizon, and soon they came into view of St Mary's Cathedral. James could pinpoint the exact moment when Ainslie figured out where they were going.

She let out a sudden gasp. "Don't tell me ..."

James grinned.

Beneath the steps of the cathedral was Cook + Phillip Park, and on the edge of the park, under the ancient fig trees, was Ainslie's favourite restaurant. It was a vegan Chinese restaurant that sat under a glowing canopy of fairy lights.

James had taken Ainslie and Lucy there one Saturday night not long after the girls had moved in together to welcome them into city life. He'd been looking for a place specifically to cater to Ainslie's vegetarianism. She'd loved it so much she'd had her next couple of birthdays there. But once she got serious with Aidan, they stopped going.

The host led them to a table outside, under the sparkling canopy. The winter air was bitterly cold, but it was cosy beneath the portable gas heater. James couldn't take his eyes off Ainslie. In the glow of the fairy lights, she somehow looked even more beautiful. Her copper hair appeared to be throwing flecks of gold, and the deep green of her eyes sparkled under the flickering candlelight of the table's centrepiece.

She caught him staring and reached across the table to take his hands. "I can't believe I'm actually on a date with you. That's so weird."

He raised his eyebrows. "Weird is one word for it, I guess."

"Good-weird, of course." She squeezed his hands. "It is crazy, though, to think that a month ago, this would've been nothing more than a fantasy."

James smirked. "A month ago, you were fantasising about us being on a date?"

"A month ago, I was fantasising about a lot more than just us being on a date," she said out of the corner of her mouth. "I suppose there's no harm in confessing to that, now you've seen me naked."

"Wait, what?"

"Nope, I'm not giving you any more details," she said. "It's way too embarrassing."

"You can't just say something like that and then not elaborate. Come on, Wynter. Spill."

Ainslie gave him a look. "Okay, fine, I may as well. You're stuck with me now."

James settled back in his seat and folded his arms, a smug grin on his face.

"Okay, so it all started the night we had that fight at the rink when I told you I was engaged," she said, her cheeks turning pink. "That night, I had a dream. A kind of ... spicy dream."

James bit his tongue and tried not to laugh. "Go on."

"Then I kept having similar dreams over the next several months, until eventually —"

"I made all your dreams come true," he said, taking a victorious sip of his water.

"Shut up, Sunderland." Ainslie laughed, kicking him under the table.

James lowered his voice and leaned forwards. "Why don't you tell me every single dirty dream you've ever had about me, and we'll work our way through them together?"

"Well, I must warn you," she replied, wrapping her lips a little too seductively around the straw in her glass and taking a sip. "Some of them are pretty filthy."

*　　*　　*

"Now," James said as they climbed back into his car, "as much as I love and appreciate that dress you're wearing, you're going to want to wear pants for this. I brought you a pair. They're in there." He pointed at a green enviro bag that was sitting at her feet.

"Pants?" she asked, pulling out a pair of black leggings. "You want me to put pants *on*? I don't think you quite understand how this whole 'date' thing works, Sunderland."

"Just put the damn pants on, Wynter," James said, laughing. "I'll be more than happy to remove them later, but right now, you gotta trust me."

Ainslie wiggled her way into the leggings as James parked his car up a back-street in Bondi. As they walked down the hill towards the beach, Ainslie caught a glimpse of what they would be doing and squeezed his hand.

"Oh, you're kidding me!"

"I'm just glad it hasn't rained yet," James said, glancing at the dark skies overhead. "You up for it?"

Lain out before the Bondi Pavilion, right on the beachfront, was a pop-up outdoor ice rink. Ainslie had liked an article on social media about it a few days earlier, and James had made a mental note to include it in their first date plans. It was lit from all angles with floodlights, and dance music was pumping through the chilly night air.

"I'm up for it," she replied. "But I haven't been ice skating since I was twelve."

"Oh, so we won't be showing off our throw triple Salchow?"

"That'd be a no. If we break something, Sandra will literally kill us."

They lined up and received their stiff, blue plastic hire skates and teetered out onto the rink. The second Ainslie stepped on the ice, she nearly fell flat on her face. James caught her reflexively.

"Why is it so different?" she said, a whine to her voice.

"It's a different sport," he said, laughing. "You can't be the best at everything."

Ainslie narrowed her eyes at him. "Who do you think you're talking to, Sunderland?"

She had that look in her eye that told him she was up for the challenge, and after about half an hour of working her way through all the single jumps, she was trying to jump an Axel. James watched on, hopelessly enamoured by her drive and passion but also genuinely afraid she was going to injure herself.

The fifth time she went sprawling across the ice on her backside, he pulled her up off the ground and managed to drag her away from jumping. They spent the rest of the session simply gliding around together hand in hand until their feet were too sore from the rentals. They left the ice rink arm in arm with wind-flushed cheeks and huge smiles on their faces.

CHAPTER 43

"So," James said as he slid into the car and turned to Ainslie, "I have one more thing planned before we do your thing."

"My thing?"

"Making your dreams a reality," he said with a smirk.

"Oh, right." Ainslie blushed.

They drove a short distance from the beach and turned down a familiar residential street towards the park in Rose Bay where they'd spent Christmas night.

"Our spot," Ainslie said quietly.

"I like to think of it that way." James smiled.

They pulled a couple of blankets from the boot of the car and set up a spot on the hill where they could overlook the whole city. The wind was bitterly cold against James's face, but he couldn't have cared less if he'd tried. Ainslie huddled into his side, the pair of them enveloped in a blanket, not unlike how they'd been at Nationals. How different things were now.

"I had all these grand, romantic ideas for tonight," James said, staring out over the city lights. "Ideas that I can't afford, of course. I wanted it to be absolutely perfect because you deserve nothing less, and ... you know ... you're used to ... a millionaire taking you out. But at the end of the day, I realised I just wanted to spend the night hanging out with my best friend. My best friend who I also get to make out with."

"It *was* perfect," she replied, cupping his cheek with her hand. "And please don't compare yourself to ... him. I'm *so lucky* to have you, and I'm so glad you're my best friend. Forget money. There's no-one in the world I would rather hang out with than you. Or make out with, for that matter."

James smiled and brushed his nose against hers. She closed the gap between them with a kiss.

"So," he said, wrapping his arm around her shoulders, "tell me something about yourself that I don't know."

"You've known me since I was five," Ainslie said, laughing. "I think you know everything there is to know."

"Come on. There has to be *something* you've never told anyone. Not even me."

Ainslie gazed off for a moment, contemplating an answer.

"Okay," she said finally. "Do you remember the Summer Skate Camp back in 2013, when my room got busted by Paula for having alcohol? And Kristen Lewis from South Coast Rollers took the fall for it?"

James tried not to laugh. "It was yours, wasn't it?"

"Of course it was."

James cackled. "And you never fessed up?"

Ainslie shook her head guiltily. "I still feel terrible about it, and I've been avoiding Kristen at competitions ever since. God, I was naughty back then."

"Naughty *back then*?" James nudged her. "That's coming from the girl who hooked up with her skating partner on a Nationals trip three weeks ago?"

"And you loved it."

"I did."

"Okay." She elbowed him. "Your turn, then."

"Okay." James pursed his lips. "The day we met, you called me — and I quote — 'a stupid butt'."

Ainslie burst into peals of laughter. "Oh, my God! Did I really? Were my insults really that brutal?"

"You were a *mean* five-year-old!" James said, laughing along with her. "I mean, it *was* because I accidentally knocked you over when we were practising scissors, so maybe it was a little bit justified."

"It was *absolutely* justified," she said. "But that's not a secret."

"No," he said, "the secret is that I wanted to be your friend, and it really hurt my feelings when you were mean to me."

Ainslie giggled. "Seriously?"

"Yep." James pouted.

"Oh, that is so adorable! I'm sorry." She planted a kiss on his cheek and whispered in his ear. "If it's any consolation, I don't think your butt's stupid now. In fact, I really like it."

Ainslie poked his hip with her finger.

"It wasn't that you thought I *possessed* a stupid butt," he said. "I think you were more implying that I *myself* was the human embodiment *of* a stupid butt."

"Oh, my God, Sunderland. Just take the compliment," she said, groaning, and wrapped her hand around the back of his neck, pulling him into another kiss. He chuckled against her lips.

"Okay," she said, "I have another one."

James blinked at her expectantly. Ainslie took a long breath. This one must have been a doozy.

"Okay," she said. "When we were around sixteen, there may have been a brief window of time when ... I had a crush on you."

"Are you kidding me?"

Ainslie bit her lip and shook her head.

"Why didn't you say anything?"

"I was sixteen! I was a dumb arse! We were friends, and I ... I was scared you wouldn't like me back."

"Oh, I definitely liked you back."

"Well, why didn't *you* say anything?!"

"I was also sixteen! And also a dumb arse!"

"So if we'd just been brave enough," Ainslie said, "we could've been together for like, nine years by now?"

"I guess so."

"God, that sucks," Ainslie said sadly. "We lost all that time? Just because we were both sixteen-year-old dumb arses."

"Hey." James cradled her face in his hand and stroked her cheek with his thumb. "We have all the time in the world now." He touched his forehead to hers, and their noses brushed again. He closed his eyes, enjoying the closeness.

Ainslie was the first to break the stillness, closing the gap between them, pressing her lips to his again. She drank him in slowly. He entangled his fingers in her hair and slipped his free arm around her waist, pulling her closer. Her hands slid into his coat and around his middle.

Out of nowhere, a deafening clap of thunder rocked the entire city, and they both jumped at the sound.

"That was a bit of a mood killer," James muttered.

"Doesn't have to be," Ainslie said, her voice a purr, kissing him again.

Then the heavens opened, and the rain that had been threatening all evening finally fell in sheets.

"Goddammit." Ainslie dropped her head in a feeble attempt to shield herself from the rain.

They climbed to their feet and hurriedly collected their blankets. James grabbed Ainslie's hand, and they ran towards the car. Dripping wet, they threw themselves inside. James cranked up the heater and turned to Ainslie. Her hair was drenched and hanging limply around her face.

He winced. "Sorry about the rain."

"Rain on our first date." Ainslie shook her head in mock disapproval. "How dare you?"

She rubbed her arms and shivered.

"You're freezing," he said, glancing hopelessly at their rain-soaked blankets.

A wicked grin spread across Ainslie's face. "Well, why don't you keep me warm?"

Before he had the chance to say anything more, Ainslie had clambered over the gearstick and straddled him. He reclined his seat to give her more room as she placed her hands on his shoulders and bit her lip. He ran his hands across the small of her back and over her backside. Now he was regretting having given her the pants earlier.

Ainslie flipped her damp hair over one shoulder, leaned down and drew him back into another long, deep kiss. The rain drummed away on the roof of the car, and she peppered soft kisses across his face and neck, running her hands across his chest, sparks igniting where she touched him. He was so lost in her that he didn't even notice she'd undone the buttons of his shirt.

"Was this in one of your dirty dreams?" he asked breathlessly between kisses.

"This is better."

James ran his hands along the tops of her thighs, pushing the boundaries of the short skirt of her dress and cursing her goddamn leggings.

She must've been able to read his mind because she put her lips close to his ear and hissed, "Still think the pants were a good idea?"

He moved his mouth to her neck, pressing hot kisses down to her collarbone. He slid the strap from her dress off her shoulder, making room for his lips to venture down further as he caressed her through her lacy bra.

"God, James," she said, "I need you right now."

He was about two seconds away from giving her exactly what she wanted, but instead, he pulled all his focus together and reluctantly withdrew from her. His eyes were a little unfocused, and God knows his pants were a hell of a lot tighter than they'd been five minutes ago.

"What is it?" Ainslie asked, her face all pink and flustered.

"As much as I *don't* want to ask you to get back in your seat," he said, "I can think of more appropriate and comfortable places to continue this."

With the girls home, Ainslie's apartment was out of the question, so they decided to head back to James's instead, knowing full well that his housemates didn't care a bit about who he brought home.

Ainslie climbed back into her seat. She pulled the strap of her dress back up onto her shoulder and placed a hand perilously high on his thigh. James gripped the steering wheel and focused all his attention on the road ahead, trying his best to ignore her touch burning into his leg. Honestly, if she moved her hand any higher, he'd have no choice but to pull over.

*   *   *

They were barely locked in James's room for five seconds when he put his hands on Ainslie's shoulders and sat her on the edge of the bed.

"First things first," he said, "let's get rid of these bloody pants."

He slipped his hands under her dress and hooked his fingers in the waistband of both the damp leggings and her underwear. He peeled them off her laboriously slowly.

"Your turn," she said, practically panting already. "Pants. Off. Now."

"Yes, ma'am," he replied, his hands flying to his belt.

He discarded his trousers beside Ainslie's leggings. She wiggled herself out of her dress and threw it on the pile. His eyes appreciatively scanned her figure for a moment before he play-tackled her to the mattress. He crushed her to the bed, and she wrapped her arms around him, clinging on for dear life. He slid his hands up her now bare thighs and buried his face in the crook of her neck. Ainslie inhaled sharply as his lips, teeth and tongue began working their magic.

"Just remember," she said, gasping, "if you leave a mark, I'm going to have to hide it from Sandra."

"Well, then," he said, his lips brushing against her ear, "I'm just going to have to leave a mark somewhere she can't see, aren't I?"

A fluttering filled her belly, and heat pooled between her thighs at those words. It only intensified as his mouth began travelling down her body. Her eyelids fluttered closed, and she let out an involuntary moan as he worshipped her completely.

Somehow Reality James was even better at this than Fantasy James had been. She wasn't sure why she was surprised. Perhaps she had thought it was too good to be true. They were always so compatible as friends and teammates, and a small part of her had worried that maybe they just wouldn't be compatible as lovers. But if the sounds that she was making were anything to go by, sexual compatibility was definitely not a problem.

*   *   *

"My housemates are going to have questions," James said breathlessly as they crashed back onto the bed, spent, and sweaty, and perfectly satisfied.

"Well, they won't be questions about your ability in bed, that's for sure," Ainslie replied, running a hand through her completely dishevelled hair.

James let out a tired laugh.

Ainslie was still seeing stars. She thought she'd known what pleasure and intimacy was. With Aidan, it had been ... fine. But with James ...

Holy shit.

Maybe it was because James wasn't selfish like Aidan was. Maybe it was because he always made sure to go the extra mile. Or maybe it was because *this* was love. Actual, real, deep love. Not the imitation love she'd been receiving from Aidan for the last six years.

She rolled over into James's side and brushed her lips against his. "I love you, James. So much."

"I love you so much, too, Ainslie," he whispered.

"And not just because you have the ability to make me see the face of God," she added.

James laughed and pulled her closer. "So, good first date then?"

"The best first date of my life. And I hope it's the last first date of my life."

As soon as the words were out, she panicked. Was it too soon to say something like that? Too forward? What on earth would James think of it? Just when Ainslie was silently hoping he hadn't heard her, a warm smile spread across his face.

He squeezed her a little tighter and planted a kiss on her forehead. "Me too."

CHAPTER 44

As wonderful as their first date had been, it quickly became apparent to both Ainslie and James that they were going to have to wait quite a while before they could have a second one.

Worlds preparation had been going exceptionally well, but Sandra had been driving them like never before. She'd been increasing the difficulty of all their elements, and they'd been taking extra footwork classes with Stephen. Sandra had also given them a strict off-skate schedule, which included hours in the gym and dance studio. Ainslie barely had time to scratch herself between all the training sessions.

Then, of course, there was work. Most weeks, Ainslie would squeeze in five days at the café. She scrounged away every cent she could as the deadline for payment of her Worlds fees came screaming towards her, and by the time she'd finally paid up, her bank balance was looking rather sad.

While she was spending a lot of time training with James, there didn't seem to be a lot of time for their newly discovered extracurricular activities. This, of course, made it a whole lot easier to keep their relationship under wraps.

When they *did* get a chance to spend time together at Ainslie's place, it was never questioned. James's presence in the apartment wasn't exactly unusual, even if he had been there a little more often than normal.

One August afternoon, after Ainslie clocked off work for her lunchbreak, she noticed a group text that had come through from Sandra about an hour earlier. It'd been sent to her, James, Jaz and Lucy.

Hi guys,
I've got a parent/teacher interview at Rosie's school
tonight. Tim was going to go but he has the man flu.
You've all been working really hard recently so why not
take the night off as a treat.
See you tomorrow,
Sandra.

Ainslie quietly punched the air. It was all she could do to stop herself from breaking out into a fully-fledged victory dance. She quickly called Jaz.

"Hiya," Jaz said.

"Hi. Did you see Sandra's text?"

"Yeah, I did. It's great, right? It means I can go to the work party I thought I was going to miss."

"You're going out tonight?" Ainslie said hopefully.

"Yeah, I even managed to talk Lucy into coming. Figured you might want the apartment to yourself … if you catch my drift."

Ainslie could hear the smirk in her voice.

"You convinced Lucy to go?" Ainslie said, still suppressing her urge to do a victory dance. "You really are a miracle worker, Jaz Bannister. I could kiss you right now."

"I got you. But you definitely owe me."

"I don't have any money, but I promise you I'll give you a great big hug. What time are you leaving?"

"Like, seven?"

"And when is it expected to finish?"

"I dunno, midnight?"

"Fantastic," Ainslie said, grinning. "Text me when you're on your way home."

"Will do. And I will hold you accountable to that hug, by the way."

Ainslie hung up and quickly shot James a message.

> You see Sandra's text? The girls are going out tonight. Do you want to hit the gym in my building? Afterwards you can come back to my place and give me another workout ;) Love you xx

James replied in the affirmative almost instantly.

*   *   *

"We've got the whole place to ourselves tonight," Ainslie said, pulling two clean bowls out of the dishwasher.

"Are you sure?" James asked, sticking his head down the hallway.

"Yep." She nodded as she opened a bottle of wine and poured them each a glass. "Lucy and Jaz aren't expected to be back until midnight, and hopefully," she glanced up at him and winked, "we'll be in bed by then."

James moved behind her and placed his hands on her hips, trapping her between his body and the kitchen bench. He nuzzled her neck with his nose and began pressing warm, soft kisses across her skin. Even though Ainslie was definitely keen to let him continue, she was also really hungry. She turned herself around in his embrace and cupped his cheek in her hand.

She put her lips so tantalisingly close to his, but instead of kissing them, she simply said "Go get changed, our food's going cold" and patted his cheek.

"Tease."

"I promise I'll make it up to you later." She smacked him on the backside as he shuffled off to change.

Ainslie set up a nest of pillows and blankets on the lounge and placed their meals and wine on the coffee table. She ducked into her room and changed into a t-shirt that she'd stolen from James. It was practically a dress on her.

"Hey, is that mine?" he asked, looking her up and down when she returned to the living room.

"I pinched it."

"It looks better on you, anyway." He put his hands on her waist and pulled her into a kiss. "Actually, it probably looks better *off* you."

Ainslie bit her lip and resisted. "Dinner first. We really should refuel before our second workout."

* * *

It was only a simple second date, with none of the pomp and circumstance of the first. Just takeaway, wine and a cheesy movie, all while snuggled up on the lounge under a blanket.

But it was perfect.

For the first time since they'd gotten together, Ainslie felt as if they were a normal couple, doing normal couple things, and momentarily forgot that they were still technically sneaking around. She snuggled in beside James with her head on his chest and his arms wrapped around her, his fingers playing with her hair. She felt so safe and so content, and she couldn't help but long for the time when they didn't have to be so secretive anymore.

When the credits of the film rolled, James kissed the side of her head.

"This is nice," he whispered, his lips brushing her ear.

Ainslie shivered at the gentle touch and smiled. "I think we should make the most of our time alone."

"Finally."

He laid her down on the lounge and nuzzled into her neck, kissing his way across her throat and along her jawline until his lips returned to hers. She wrapped her arms around him and kissed him back fervently, running her palms across the lean muscles of his back.

She felt his hands slip under her shirt. His warm fingers grazed lightly up her stomach before venturing higher and caressing her breasts. His thumb brushed across one of her nipples, and the sensation sent a shudder through her entire body.

She grabbed blindly at the hem of his shirt, separating their lips briefly as she pulled it up over his head. She pushed her fingers into his hair and tugged it gently, the way she knew he liked.

"Why haven't we been doing this for years?" she mumbled between kisses.

"I don't know, but let's never stop."

"Okay."

Ainslie was seconds away from suggesting they relocate to her room when she heard the worst possible sound she could've heard at that moment.

"Oh, my God!"

Ainslie and James both snapped their heads around so synchronously, it was almost comical.

Standing in the kitchen was Lucy, her arm thrown up in front of her face as if she were shielding her eyes from the sun, and Jaz standing slightly behind her, blushing and trying not to laugh. It was as if time had frozen for a moment, and Ainslie was pretty sure her heart had stopped beating.

Pulling herself back to her senses, she lightly shoved James. He snapped back into reality and leaped off the lounge, scrambling to retrieve his shirt while also trying to conceal the situation going on in his pyjama pants.

"What on *earth* is going on?!" Lucy said, lowering her arm and checking if everyone was decent.

As mortified as Lucy was clearly trying to sound, Ainslie could see the faintest trace of a smile threatening to break through her otherwise serious expression. James had turned bright red and sat uncomfortably, fumbling to put his shirt back on. He looked like a child who'd just gotten caught with his hand in the biscuit tin.

Lucy waved her arms at the sight before her. "Is this … a *thing* that's happening?"

"Yeah," Ainslie said finally, her cheeks absolutely on fire. "Yeah, it is."

"Well, how long has it been going on?!"

"Nearly two months," James murmured.

He appeared to have lost the ability to look people in the eye.

"Nearly two months! Wait a second … Nationals was two months ago … Did this …?"

Ainslie watched and waited as Lucy did the mental math.

"You didn't," Lucy said with a gasp.

Ainslie nodded. "We did."

Lucy pointed at Ainslie. "So when you didn't come back to the room after the dinner, you were …"

"Yes!" Ainslie and James said in unison.

"Bloody hell," Jaz said, finally letting out her laughter. "This is amazing!"

"Why aren't *you* more surprised?!" Lucy snapped at her.

Ainslie dropped her head. Jaz looked bashful.

"I kinda … already knew," Jaz said with a shrug.

"What?!"

"I busted Ainslie after she did the walk of shame back to our room the next morning," Jaz said.

"You've known since June?! Why did nobody tell *me*?!"

"I didn't even want *Jaz* to know!" Ainslie said. "She just happened to catch me! We didn't want *anyone* to know! Not yet, anyway."

Lucy shook her head in disbelief and sat down on the lounge opposite them.

"Why didn't you want anyone to know?" Lucy asked, finally lowering her voice.

"We didn't want Sandra to find out before Worlds," James said. "We don't want her thinking it's going to distract us or anything."

"Okay," Lucy said slowly. "I was shocked at first, and I probably didn't need to see … that" — she gestured at the two of them — "but let's be honest, I'm hardly *that* surprised."

"Well, duh!" Jaz said, beaming. "We all knew this would happen *eventually*. Everyone who can *see* knew this would happen eventually."

Ainslie narrowed her eyes at her.

"I mean, she's not wrong," Lucy added. "There's a reason why people always mistake you two for a couple. It's because you *look* like a couple, you *act* like a couple, and now I guess you *are* a couple, so …" Lucy glanced at James, who immediately looked away. "I don't think James is ever going to look me in the eye again."

"What are you guys doing home this early, anyway?" Ainslie said. "Oh, and thanks for the heads up, by the way, *Jaz*."

"Hey," Jaz said, throwing her hands up, "I messaged you! Not my fault you were too busy defiling our lounge."

"The party was awful," Lucy said with a groan as she stood and headed to the kitchen. "I don't know why I let you talk me into going." Lucy glanced up at Ainslie and James and raised an eyebrow. "Although, *now* it makes sense."

Lucy proceeded to fill the kettle with water. "Everyone except me and Jaz were drunk. And these horrible old men kept hitting on Jaz for some reason."

"They only want what they can't have." Jaz flipped her hair dramatically.

"All right," Lucy said, pouring herself a cup of tea. "This has been one bizarre evening, so instead of completely spoiling your night, I'm going to just forget everything I saw here and go to bed."

"Me too," Jaz said, standing up and ruffling Ainslie's already messy hair. "Don't be too loud, if you know what I mean."

Ainslie dropped her face into her hands, completely mortified.

"And please don't do anything gross in our common living areas!" Lucy called over her shoulder. "And if you already have, then I don't want to know!"

A brief moment of incredibly awkward silence hung in the air. Ainslie was worried that the night was ruined until she heard a small snort escape from James. The snort turned into a chuckle, which turned into a laugh, and then she was laughing too.

"Well, at least we don't have to sneak around Lucy anymore," James said, shrugging.

"You know, I'm actually glad," Ainslie said. "Tonight's been really nice. And now we can do it more often."

They left their little nook in the living room and relocated to Ainslie's bedroom.

"Now," Ainslie said, "where were we before we were so rudely interrupted?"

"I remember," James said as he practically tackled her onto the bed. She landed on the bed with a laugh, his body pressing hers into the mattress.

She grabbed him by the waist and smiled. "I'm so happy this is — as Lucy put it — a *thing* that's happening."

"Me too," he said, grinning. "Best thing to *ever* happen."

CHAPTER 45

With Jaz and Lucy both in the know, things certainly became easier for Ainslie and James, at least at the girls' apartment, though Ainslie was worried that if they got too comfortable around the house, they'd forget that Sandra still wasn't supposed to know and accidentally expose their secret at the rink.

Ainslie also hadn't realised how much she would enjoy telling people. It was nice not to have to hide, and it was nice to see how happy Lucy was for them (once her initial embarrassment of catching them in the act had worn off).

James and Ainslie also figured that if Lucy and Jaz, two people ingrained in their skating lives (and who saw Sandra on a nearly daily basis) knew, then there was one other person they could tell. Someone who they knew would never spill the beans and who would be absolutely elated to hear about it.

So one Sunday evening, the pair jettisoned off straight from training to James's old house in Campbellmead to visit his mum.

When Ainslie was growing up, Erica Sunderland had been like a second mother to her. She was always a lot kinder, warmer and more encouraging than either of Ainslie's own parents. After Ainslie fell out with her family, Erica was still there, offering her love and support and motherly comfort.

Ainslie had seen a lot less of James's mum in the years since his father had passed away, but Erica always liked and commented on everything Ainslie posted on social media. And whenever Ainslie saw she had a message from her, it brought a smile to her face.

*   *   *

Ainslie couldn't wait to catch up with Erica again, and she was even more excited about telling her the news.

"Maybe have your phone ready to call triple zero," James said as he pulled into the driveway of the old brick suburban. "Mum might just have a heart attack when we tell her."

"You think?"

"Are you kidding? She's been waiting for this for years. You know, after I first introduced her to Rachel, she said to me, 'She's nice, but I've never understood why you don't just go out with Ainslie'. I told her, 'Well, for a start, she's dating someone else'."

Ainslie chuckled. "Did she really say that?"

"It wasn't even the first time. Let's just say that if arranged marriages were a Western tradition, my mother would've had us hitched years ago."

Ainslie laughed. "Okay, good. So at least I know she's not going to be living up to the toxic mother-in-law stereotypes."

"Oh, definitely not. I think she loves you more than she loves me."

Ainslie hadn't even bothered to tell her parents. She'd just sent them a cold text message a couple of months ago saying her engagement was off. Her mother had tried to call her several times afterwards, but she'd been ignoring her. Ainslie knew her mother, and *she* would *definitely* have lived up to the toxic mother-in-law stereotypes.

James put his hand on Ainslie's back and knocked on the door, and the two were almost instantly barrelled over.

"Hey, kids!" Erica cried as she pulled them both into an enormous bear hug. "Oh, it's so good to see you! Especially you, Ainslie! Oh, it's been way too long, sweetheart."

Erica captured Ainslie's face between her hands and planted a kiss on her forehead. Ainslie giggled.

"I told you she loves you more than me," James said.

"There's plenty of love to go around," Erica said, squeezing her son's cheeks together and kissing him on the nose.

James blushed, and Ainslie giggled. Everyone could use a mum like Erica Sunderland.

*   *   *

Erica ushered them through the hall and into the living room, her silver curls bouncing along behind her. She'd already laid out afternoon tea. Mismatched novelty mugs sat on the small coffee table, ready for the English breakfast to be poured. Beside them sat a small wheel of camembert, some crackers and a packet of assorted cream biscuits.

Ainslie smiled at the humble spread. It reminded her of those afternoons long ago when Erica would pick them up from school and bring them back here so they could have a snack and do their homework before she would ferry them off to the rink. There was a time when Erica and Ainslie's mother would alternate in that responsibility, but Ainslie had always preferred it when it was Erica's turn.

Ainslie snatched up a biscuit and glanced around the living room. She hadn't been there in years, and it looked as if nothing had changed at all. Childhood photos of James and Jason lined the bookshelves, and a beautiful portrait of Erica and her late husband, Michael, hung above the brick fireplace. There were several professional action shots of Ainslie and James, their entire career laying out visually before them.

"Mum," James said casually, as he popped a cracker in his mouth, "I thought you might like to know, I'm seeing someone new."

A kind smile spread across Erica's face, and the lines around her eyes deepened. "Oh, really! That's exciting!"

"Yeah, it's pretty serious," Ainslie added. "They're practically glued at the hip. But I approve of her. She's really cool."

"Yeah, you'd really love her," James said.

"Well, when do I get to meet her?" Erica asked, eyes flicking between the two of them.

She looked as if she was trying to process something, and Ainslie wondered if she'd already figured it out but was managing her expectations in case she was wrong.

"Well, you kinda already have," James said.

Erica furrowed her brow. "Is she from skating?"

"Yeah," James said, popping another cracker into his mouth with a practised air of nonchalance.

"Well, why didn't you bring her with you!" Erica cried, exasperated.

"I did," James said, still casual as ever.

Ainslie gave a little smile and a wave.

Erica fell silent for a moment. Her eyes darted back and forth between them a few times before the penny finally dropped.

"Are … are you serious?" she asked cautiously. "Because if you're joking, I'm going to kill you both."

James pulled Ainslie to his side. "Yeah, we're serious."

Erica shrieked. Ainslie winced as the sound split through the room.

"I can't believe this! I knew it! I always knew it! And I was suspicious from the second you started talking about it. I just didn't want to get my hopes up!"

The older woman flew to her feet and pulled them into another hug. Ainslie's heart was so full. She glanced at James, and he looked as if he felt the same.

"So, what happened, angel?" Erica looked at Ainslie as they sat back down. "Last I heard, you were engaged."

Ainslie sucked her teeth. "Yeah, that didn't quite work out."

"Well, it's his loss," Erica said, patting her on the knee, "and my gain." She winked.

"I mean, I think it's actually more *my* gain …," James said, and his mother waved him off. "And we're not telling anyone yet, Mum. So *please* don't go posting anything incriminating on social media."

"I'd never. But why not?"

Ainslie explained the situation, and Erica nodded along and swore herself to secrecy.

"Well," Erica said and clapped her hands together, "I hope that I'll get to see more of you, Ainslie, now that you're practically my daughter-in-law."

"Easy, Mum," James said, turning beet red. "It's only been two months."

Ainslie giggled.

Erica ignored him. "You're staying for dinner, yes?"

"Sure."

"And why don't you stay overnight, head back home in the morning?" Erica added as she flitted from the living room to go and get dinner underway.

Ainslie glanced at James.

"Do you want to say here?" he asked. "Or do you want to leave tonight?"

"*I* want to fool around in your childhood bedroom," she whispered.

James pursed his lips and let out a long exhale. "Sixteen-year-old me just punched the air so hard."

CHAPTER 46

August was flying by at breakneck speed. Sandra had been keeping her skaters so busy it felt as if Nationals had only been mere days ago. But Worlds was bearing down on them, and before they knew it, they were a month out from boarding the plane to Barcelona.

Tensions were high, especially around the apartment. As Worlds raced closer, Jaz had somehow managed to evolve into an even more energetic version of herself. On the opposite end of the scale, Lucy had begun retreating inside herself and snapping the heads off people who tried to get inside her bubble, which was par for the course for Lucy in the lead-up to a big event. It was her way of coping with stress and always had been, so the others knew not to take it personally.

James had been hanging around the apartment a lot more since Lucy had discovered their secret, but there hadn't been any more opportunities for proper dates. There simply weren't enough hours in each day.

As for Ainslie, she was exhausted. She'd been training her backside off and selling her soul to the coffee shop to pay for it, and it was all beginning to catch up with her.

*   *   *

"Okay, Team Jameslie!" Sandra clapped her hands together once and came to a stop in the centre of the rink.

Ainslie and James joined her. Ainslie pinched the bridge of her nose and wrinkled her brow. A fresh wave of exhaustion had come over her after their last run-through, and it was making her feel a little nauseated. She was well acquainted with being tired, but this was next level. And she'd been feeling it on and off for pretty much all of August. She wondered if she should get a blood test or something. Maybe her vegetarianism had finally given her the iron deficiency Aidan used to warn her about in his condescending tone as he dug his way through a steak. She shook out one leg and then the other and tried to regroup.

"Let's do one more run-through of the long program," Sandra said, "focusing mainly on performance but also paying attention to the changes we've been finalising. Then we'll call it a morning, okay?"

Ainslie nodded and let out a sharp exhale, trying to ignore the slight upset in her stomach. She made fists with her hands and drummed them on her quadriceps, trying to massage out her sore muscles.

James placed a hand on her lower back. "You good?"

"Yeah," she said, but her voice wavered.

Ainslie breathed through her fatigue as "Bolero" began to drum its way through the rink. The motions had become second nature to her, but the performance was still as fresh as ever. Even when she wasn't feeling one hundred per cent, Ainslie found it easy to embrace the theme of the routine, especially seeing as performing it was the most intimate thing they'd had time for in recent weeks.

The drums began to build, and the music slowly climbed to its crescendo as they skated towards their final lift. The ascent was smooth, as usual, and it felt as strong and steady as it always did. James held her in place with both of his hands until she was secure in the air. Then he began rotating. He released one of her hands, and she pulled herself into her position.

*   *   *

One moment, everything was fine. Normal. The lift they'd done countless times was going off without a hitch.

Then the next moment, all the wheels on James's left skate came screeching to a halt.

It felt as if he'd hit a brick wall. A bolt of panic shot through him as he realised what was happening, but it was happening so quickly there wasn't any time to react.

His panic was rapidly replaced with hopelessness as he realised he was letting Ainslie fall.

And not just fall, but careen towards the floor.

James hit the ground first, landing straight on his knees. He felt a ripple of pain shoot up his legs, but nothing incapacitating. A split second later, a sickening thud reverberated through the rink as Ainslie hit the ground.

She slid across the floor, and the plastic hockey shield rattled violently as she hit the barrier. James's knees were aching like nobody's business, but he couldn't care less. He looked over to where Ainslie lay limp on the ground. If Ainslie ever fell and didn't immediately get up, that meant it was serious.

She wasn't moving. And there was blood.

"Oh, my God." The words got caught in his throat on their way out, and his voice was raspy and weak.

He scrambled to his feet, ignoring the two huge holes he'd torn in his pants. He darted towards Ainslie and dropped down by her side.

"Ains." His voice sounded as if it didn't belong to him. "Can you hear me?"

There was no response.

His heart started racing, and it felt as if all his blood had rushed to his skull and was swirling around in his ears.

Then he saw it. A gash in the back of her head.

He reached for her, but Sandra bellowed across the rink, "Don't move her, just in case she's hurt her neck."

216

James pulled his hands back, startled.

"I'll call triple zero," Sandra added, looking grim.

Lucy came speeding over and dropped down beside him. She looked as white as a sheet.

"What happened?" she asked.

"I ... don't know ...," he said. "I ... I think I hit something."

Lucy stood up and immediately began surveying the area.

James turned back to Ainslie. "Ains? Ainslie? Goose? Can you hear me?"

Nothing.

All he could see in his mind's eye was his mother's haunted face all those years ago. All he could think about was how her voice had sounded when she'd told him his father had died.

Head injury. Fall from a ladder. Insisted he was fine. Gone. He's gone. Dad's gone.

James was starting to feel as if *he* was about to pass out at any moment.

"Ainslie?" he said, and his voice cracked completely. Tears began to blur his vision as Jaz rushed over and handed him a towel for the blood.

Ainslie let out a weak murmur and slurred, "James? What happened?"

Her eyelids fluttered open, and she blinked up at him in a daze. The weight of the world lifted off his shoulders. He heaved a sigh of relief, but a small voice in his head reminded him she could still be in danger.

Dad seemed okay too, remember?

He held the towel to her head, and she winced.

"You're okay, Goose," he whispered, stroking her cheek. "We had a fall, but you'll be okay. Sandra's calling an ambulance."

"I feel sick."

"Can you move at all?"

She tried to sit up slowly. But as soon as she was upright, she slumped back down. James caught her and held her against him.

"I don't think I broke anything," she muttered, clutching a hand to her stomach, "but I definitely feel like I'm gonna be sick."

"You're going to the hospital," James said. "We need to make sure you're all right."

"My head's killing me," she slurred.

She rested her head on his shoulder, and her eyes drooped.

"Hey," James said, lifting her head off him. "I'm not letting you go to sleep on me, Goose. You're concussed out of your mind."

He held her face and looked into her eyes. Her pupils were wildly unfocused, as if she were a million miles away. James kept holding the towel to her head as he rubbed her back with his free hand. He pressed his lips to the top of her head. He didn't even care anymore if Sandra saw. All he cared about was getting Ainslie to the hospital.

"James!"

He turned around to see Lucy rolling over, holding something tiny between her thumb and forefinger.

He squinted. "What is it?"

"A stone," she replied, flicking it over the barrier and out the roller door. "Must've been walked in from outside."

"For fuck's sake," he muttered.

He felt his blood begin to boil. Such a tiny obstruction, but it had the power to cause so much damage. He couldn't even fathom the idea of losing the best thing to ever happen to him because of a piece of debris the size of a pinhead.

After what seemed like an eternity, the sound of an ambulance siren came into earshot. James wished he could find comfort in that sound, but he was too terrified of what might come. He wanted to scream, but he seemed to have lost all ability to produce sound. He took his skates off hurriedly, and Jaz fetched his shoes for him as the paramedics loaded Ainslie into the ambulance.

"Are any of you joining us?" a paramedic asked the group.

James leaped forwards and climbed into the back of the ambulance.

"I have to finish up here," Sandra called, "but I'll come down after I'm done."

"We'll take Ainslie's stuff home," Jaz said. "Make sure you call us when you know how she is."

"Of course," James replied, feeling a little woozy.

"Hey," Lucy said, her voice firm, grounding him. "She's going to be okay, James."

"Yeah ... I know."

And he really wished he did.

CHAPTER 47

Ainslie had always loathed hospitals. She'd been fortunate enough to have avoided them for the most part, and she'd been glad for it. Just the thought of hospitals made her skin crawl. The chemical smell of disinfectants, the bright, sterile fluorescent lighting, the bitterly cold air conditioning. Something about it all set off anxiety deep in her gut.

As she was wheeled through the corridors, she struggled to keep her eyes open. The lights overhead were absolutely blinding, and all she wanted to do was take a nap, but a nurse kept saying, "Stay awake, darl."

She still felt woozy, but she was grateful that so far, she'd resisted the urge to vomit. Her head was throbbing, and even though the paramedics had patched up her wound, she could still feel blood oozing from it. The rest of her body was still vibrating with the dull ache that came with falling eight feet straight into concrete, and she was trying to avoid moving for fear of exacerbating it. Nothing felt broken, but she was pretty certain she was going to be covered in enough bruises to make up for it.

The next hour or so was a blur as nurses ferried her from room to room. She was vaguely aware that James was somewhere nearby. Sometimes he was made to wait outside the room, but the knowledge that he was around, even when she wasn't quite sure where he was, was comforting.

Ainslie surrendered herself to the expertise of the doctors and nurses as they pricked her with needles and wrapped a blood pressure cuff around her arm. They X-rayed her ribs and performed an ultrasound, which she thought was odd, but she guessed it was to check for any internal injuries.

She wasn't really paying a lot of attention to what was being done to her. She was too busy thinking about Barcelona. Worlds. And the fact that they were supposed to leave in a month.

She was also thinking about James and how terrified he'd looked when she'd come to. She hadn't seen him look like that since his father had died. She wasn't stupid. She knew he must have been thinking about him.

And she still had no idea what had happened. She knew it was an accident, but it was unlike James to just trip over his own skates.

The nurses finally found Ainslie a bed on a ward. The air was filled with groaning and the incessant beeping of machines. On the upside, her bed was nearest the window. It wasn't much of a view; all she could really see was the building next door. And she still had blue curtains pulled partially around her for privacy, but at least the window made her feel a little less claustrophobic.

She'd been given painkillers, and they were finally starting to kick in. She wasn't feeling quite so drowsy anymore, either. She was still tired, but she no longer felt as if she was about to black out at the drop of a hat.

James was sitting in an uncomfortable chair beside her, stroking the back of her hand with his thumb. He looked as tired as she felt, and if the redness around his eyes was anything to go by, he'd definitely been crying.

"How are you feeling, Goose?" he asked quietly.

Ainslie smiled weakly. "A bit sorry for myself."

"Yeah …," he said softly as he carefully brushed a lock of hair behind her ear. "I'm not surprised."

"What happened?"

"I tripped over a tiny, little stone. Lucy found it. No bigger than a pinhead. I'm so sorry, Goose."

"Hey, it's not your fault. It was just an accident."

She studied his face. He had tears in his eyes. She knew him well enough to know where his mind had been.

She squeezed his hand. "Are *you* okay?"

"Yeah, I'm okay," he said, managing a smile. "I was just a bit scared."

"Did you hurt yourself?"

"Nothing major," he replied. "Ruined my pants, though."

Ainslie chuckled weakly.

Footsteps came clicking across the linoleum floor, and the blue curtain opened. A doctor in navy scrubs stepped through, a pile of paper on his clipboard.

"How are you feeling, Ainslie?" he asked, casting an eye over his notes.

"A little better."

"How's the pain?"

"Better."

"Good, good." The doctor raised his gaze from his clipboard and looked between the two of them. "Figure skaters, huh?"

Ainslie raised an eyebrow. "More or less." She didn't have the energy to get into the whole ice-figure-skating-versus-artistic-roller-skating thing right now.

"Dangerous sport," the doctor replied. "I'm sure you'll be glad to hear you haven't broken any bones."

Ainslie allowed herself to breathe a sigh of relief. That would've been the last thing she needed a month out from Worlds.

"We want to keep you in overnight, just to monitor your head injury and manage your pain. You're doing fine, but we want to keep an eye on you to make sure you *stay* fine, okay?"

Ainslie nodded.

The doctor shuffled his papers. "There is another thing that we found on one of your scans."

His tone had shifted, and Ainslie didn't like it one bit. He'd lowered his voice and stepped closer. Ainslie felt James's hand tighten around hers.

"Is this your partner?" The doctor gestured at James.

Ainslie nodded.

"Okay," the doctor said, sounding oddly sombre. "I'm sorry that I have to tell you this, and I imagine it's probably going to be quite a shock. But I'm afraid that it appears you have experienced a missed miscarriage."

The words hit Ainslie's ears, but they didn't seem to penetrate into her brain.

"Basically, what a missed miscarriage means is that the foetus has stopped developing, but your body has not *physically* miscarried yet. In your case, the foetus appeared to be about six or seven weeks old when it stopped developing."

Ainslie's head was spinning. The doctor was still saying things that she was only half processing.

"I think I can probably guess, but were you aware that you were pregnant?"

Ainslie's eyes were wide, and she'd forgotten how to form words. She shook her head, and James squeezed her hand tighter.

"Now," the doctor said, "it's unusual for a fall to cause a miscarriage this early in a pregnancy, although your fall was quite severe. It's much more likely that your body silently miscarried beforehand."

Ainslie was only partially aware of the doctor staring at her sympathetically. All that was running through her mind was how exhausted she'd been and how she'd been feeling a bit off. She'd put it down to stress and over-training. But she'd been *pregnant*?

Then she remembered that very important little thing she'd meant to do the day after their night on the Gold Coast. She'd been so caught up in everything, and they'd been in such a rush to get home, she'd *completely* forgotten to go to the chemist.

The doctor apologised and told them he'd give them some time alone, and then he slipped away between the curtains. Ainslie and James both sat in stunned silence for what felt like an eternity.

When Ainslie had woken up that morning, it'd been a normal day. Now she was in hospital feeling worse for wear, with stitches in the back of her head. And she'd just found out that not only had she been pregnant but also the pregnancy had failed. Wave after wave of emotion crashed over her. Confusion, shock, anger at herself for being so careless in the first place.

Of *course* they weren't ready to have a baby. The thought hadn't even crossed her mind. And yet, here she was, her heart heavy and her head spinning. And she couldn't even cry. She just felt hollow. She'd lost something she hadn't even known she'd had — something she didn't even know if she wanted — and yet the grief was so visceral, she thought she might just throw up. But maybe that was because of the concussion. She didn't know anymore.

James was still squeezing her hand, and she looked up at him. He looked devastated.

"I don't know what to say." His voice wavered. "I'm so sorry."

She tugged on his hand, wanting nothing more than to be near him. He moved closer and wrapped her up in his arms as best he could, avoiding the cannula in her hand.

She buried her head in his chest. "No, *I'm* sorry."

He rubbed her back. "You have nothing to be sorry for."

"I should've known. I missed a period, and I didn't even think twice about it. I've never been all that regular, and I've always been useless at tracking them. If I'd known …"

James pulled away slightly and looked into her eyes, still holding her around the shoulders. "You couldn't have done anything to stop it. You heard the doctor. It probably had nothing to do with the fall."

Ainslie gazed out the window, unconvinced.

"It's always going to be in the back of my mind, though," she whispered. After a moment, she shook her head slightly. "It just feels so strange," she muttered, turning from the window and looking back at him. "I feel like I'm missing a part of myself, but that's so stupid because I didn't even know. And I can't even cry! Why aren't I crying?!"

She collapsed into his arms.

"It's okay, Goose," he said softly as he stroked her hair. "It's not stupid. It's okay. You're still in shock."

"If I *had* known," she said, "and I'd told you I was pregnant, what would you have said?"

"I would've been surprised. And scared as hell. But I would've been excited too. Because the only person in this world that I could love as much as I love you would be a tiny little version of us."

James didn't even bother to fight his own tears anymore, and Ainslie envied him.

*　　*　　*

The doctor returned about an hour later to take Ainslie through her options on how to proceed, whether naturally or assisted. Everything was happening so quickly, and the entire conversation frightened her a little as he explained the different procedures. It was more than Ainslie had planned to deal with that day.

The doctor told them about the grief counselling and chaplaincy services the hospital provided and then disappeared back onto the ward. After he left, Ainslie looked at James. He hadn't stopped holding her hand, and she didn't want him to. She loved him so much she couldn't comprehend it. She didn't even know it was possible to love someone that much — so much it made her want to laugh and cry and scream all at the same time. She was done with hiding it. If she'd learned anything in the last couple of hours, it was that life is too short.

"We should tell Sandra," she said. "About this. About us. I don't want to sneak around anymore. I want everyone to know how much I love you."

James smiled the most genuine smile he'd managed to since arriving at the hospital. "I agree."

He stroked her cheek and kissed her softly.

Only seconds later, his phone chimed.

"Speak of the devil," he said.

Sandra had arrived and was in the foyer.

"Can you please tell her?" Ainslie asked, squeezing James's hand as he stood up. "I just … I don't think I can. I really don't want to relive it."

"Of course," he said, kissing her one more time. "Do you need anything?"

"Maybe some tea?"

"Consider it done."

*　　*　　*

James paused for a moment in the hallway outside Ainslie's room, leaning his back against the cool wall. He knew in his rational brain that it had just been a horrible accident, and the doctor *had* said it was unlikely that the fall had caused the miscarriage. But James had *seen* the fall. It'd been brutal. He didn't know much about pregnancy and miscarriages, but he couldn't imagine a fall that severe would've been *good*. The thought had clearly crossed Ainslie's mind too. What if the doctor was wrong? What if the fall *had* caused it? Then, if it hadn't been for a tiny little stone on the floor, there could've been a little him or a little Ainslie in a few months' time. James was finding it difficult not to blame himself.

He'd almost been a *father*. He had no idea if he would've been ready for that, and of course, their career would've been put on hiatus. But at the same time, the idea of having a child with Ainslie warmed his heart.

But none of that mattered now.

He pushed away from the wall and started walking, using the time it took to reach reception to try to compose himself. He didn't want to look as if he'd been crying, but he had a feeling that as soon as he explained what had happened to Sandra, he'd have no choice in the matter. He wanted to be strong for Ainslie's sake, but his heart weighed a tonne.

He found Sandra loitering around the main foyer, looking antsy. The second she saw him, she darted over.

"How is she?"

"She's okay …" He managed to get the words out without his voice cracking, but he could tell Sandra saw right through him.

"What's wrong, James?"

He could see the concern in her eyes.

"She's all right." James ran a shaky hand through his hair. "She's going to be bruised, and she has a pretty decent concussion, but she didn't break any bones."

"Well, that's good news." Sandra squinted at him. "But I can tell something's wrong. I *know* you, and I know when you're not telling me the truth."

James took a deep breath and told her about the miscarriage.

Sandra's mouth fell open. "Are you serious?"

"Yeah." His voice was wavering. "She didn't know she was pregnant. The doctor doesn't think it was the fall, but I don't know …"

Sandra slowly shook her head. "Oh, my God, the poor thing." She looked straight into James's eyes, her gaze burning into him. "James, is there something else you want to tell me?"

Something inside him told him she already knew. He dropped his head.

"It was mine … ours." His voice was barely above a whisper.

Sandra didn't look surprised. "How long has it been going on?"

"Since Nationals."

"You know, I had a feeling," she said, a bittersweet smile hovering at the corners of her lips. "Something seemed different about you two."

James stared blankly at her. "You knew?"

"I know everything," Sandra said, placing an index finger on the side of her nose. "You seemed so much closer. I mean, you were always close, but you were practically inseparable. It's been doing wonders for your chemistry."

"Are you serious? We didn't want you to know because we thought you'd think it would *ruin* our chemistry."

"Well, it might have," Sandra said, "if it'd just been physical. But you two really love each other, don't you?"

James smiled weakly. "Yes, ma'am."

Sandra dragged him into a hug. She was almost two feet shorter than him, so it was quite the sight.

"I'm so sorry, honey," she whispered, rubbing his back. "But you need to know that you never have to keep anything from me. I always have been, and always will be, Team Jameslie."

CHAPTER 48

Ainslie looked relieved when James returned with Sandra and a plastic mug of tea. James hadn't liked the thought of leaving her alone, even if it had only been for about ten minutes.

Sandra's maternal instincts kicked in as soon as she saw Ainslie. She rushed over and sat on the edge of her bed, wrapping her up in a hug. She held her quietly for a moment, and James placed Ainslie's tea on the table by her bed.

"She already knew about us," he said with a hint of a smile.

Ainslie's eyes widened. "Really?"

"Yep." Sandra winked. "Nothing gets past me. Ever. And don't worry, you have my blessing."

"We thought you'd be mad," Ainslie said.

Sandra pulled a face. "Why would I be mad? You're both adults. You can do what you like. But honestly, it makes sense. The two of you go together like peas in a pod."

An announcement came over the sound system, warning them that morning visiting hours were almost over.

"Feel better, honey. I'll see you soon." Sandra kissed Ainslie on the cheek before giving James one last hug and then leaving.

James squeezed Ainslie's hand. "Afternoon visiting hours start at two, so I'll be back then, and I'll bring the girls."

"Okay." She gave him a small smile.

"Do you want me to tell them, too?"

"Yes, please," she said quietly, nodding. "I wish you didn't have to go."

He stroked her hair. "Me too."

He would've loved nothing more than to hide out in there, but he could hear a nurse rounding up visitors and kicking them out.

"I love you." He kissed her once on her forehead and then on her lips.

"I love you, too."

She looked so melancholy as he slipped out between the curtains, and he resented having to leave her. The doctor had said she'd be fine, but James was still worried that if he left, somehow something would go wrong. He was definitely going to need a distraction between now and two o'clock.

*   *   *

Jaz ushered James inside the girls' apartment. "How is she?"

"Not the best."

225

Lucy emerged from her room, concern etched across her brow. She froze when she saw James. "Oh, God, what is it?"

"Well, she didn't break anything. But …" James sighed. He could understand why Ainslie didn't want to keep reliving it. "It turns out she's had a miscarriage."

Jaz gasped, and silence filled the space between them.

Lucy's eyes went wide, and she pressed her lips together. Eventually, she spoke again.

"Oh, James … I'm so sorry."

She pulled him into a hug and nearly squeezed the life out of him. She just kept repeating how sorry she was. Jaz joined in, wrapping one arm around James and the other around Lucy. It felt odd for the three of them to be there together without Ainslie, as if their friendship chain was missing a link.

"Thanks for letting me drop by," James said. "I really didn't feel like going back to an empty house and stewing in my guilt alone."

"You can't feel guilty for this, James," Lucy said. "You and Ainslie signed up for a lifetime of bruises and bumps when you decided to skate pairs."

"I know that," he replied, "but this wasn't just a bruise or a bump, was it? She's *lucky*. What if she'd hit her head just a little harder? Or in a different spot? People *die* from head injuries all the time. My *dad* …" He tried to push down the sob in his throat that was threatening to escape. "If something had happened to her … it would've been because of me."

"James," Jaz said, taking him by the shoulders. "You hit a rock! You can't control that. You've been skating pairs for nearly twenty years, and this is the first time you've had a fall this bad."

"But is it worth it? In the end? We skate, and we love it, but what's the cost when something like this happens? Sure, the doctor said the fall probably didn't cause the miscarriage, but what if it did? I'm pretty sure Ainslie has it in her mind that it did. That *kills* me. For the first time in way too long, skating is not my top priority anymore. *She is.*"

"James Sunderland, don't you dare use this as an excuse to quit," Jaz said. "You know that's not what Ainslie would want."

"Look, James," Lucy said, pouring him a cup of tea. "It's going to be a process. You're grieving a loss, and that's okay. And no-one wants to feel responsible for their partner being in pain, but it was just one of those things. It was a horrible, freak accident, and it will take time to move past it. But you *will* move past it. And you need to let it make you stronger."

They were right. Ainslie was resilient and tenacious, and he couldn't imagine her letting this setback get the better of her in the long run.

"Sooooo," Jaz said, "does this mean Sandra knows now? About you two?"

James scratched his head. "Turns out she'd figured it out for herself."

"Are you serious? Are you saying you could've been public this whole time?"

"Well, we can go public now," he said, shrugging.

Lucy chuckled. "Rosa Charis is going to have a field day."

CHAPTER 49

Ainslie was due to be discharged the following morning. When James arrived to pick her up, he was told that during the night, nature had run its course, and she'd spent the next several hours in the throes of pain. It was comforting to know she'd been in the right place should she have needed medical attention, but he was furious he hadn't been able to be there with her. Especially when he finally arrived at her bedside and saw how traumatised she looked.

Apart from the dark circles under her eyes from lack of sleep, Ainslie was as white as a sheet. Her eyes were glassy and red and distant, and she didn't have much to say. The mental image of her writhing in agony all night, without him, tore him apart.

Because of what had happened overnight, her discharge was delayed until later in the afternoon. On the positive side, James was able to stay with her until then. Perhaps the nurses had taken pity on the wretched-looking young couple and didn't have the heart to ask him to leave after visiting hours ended.

Ainslie had been quiet the entire time, and she didn't say anything as they drove home, either. She sat in the passenger seat staring wistfully out the window, her head resting on her hand. She seemed a million miles away.

James wondered if maybe he'd overstayed his welcome. Maybe she just wanted to be alone. As much as he wanted to stay with her, he also wanted to give her space if she needed it.

He parked outside her building and grabbed her bag for her, then walked her to her door, still in silence.

He kissed her on the forehead. "I'll see you later, then."

She blinked up at him, her eyes misty. "You're leaving?"

Her voice was quiet and shaky, and it cut him to the core.

"I mean, I don't have to," he said. "You just seemed quiet, and I thought you might want some space …"

"Please, can you stay with me?" She heaved an uneven sigh. "The girls are at work, and I don't want to be alone."

A sad smile spread across his face, and he pulled her into a hug. She wrapped her arms around his middle and clung to him.

He rubbed her back and muttered into her hair. "Neither do I."

Ainslie shuffled down the hall to go take a shower, and while she was gone, James took it upon himself to turn down her bed, pile up some pillows and set up a nice, comfortable nest for the two of them. He cued up a movie on her laptop and went to the kitchen to prepare some food.

He thought he heard something, but it was half drowned out by the kettle boiling. He clicked off the jug and listened carefully. Quiet sobs were emanating from down the hall. He walked to the bathroom and gently knocked on the door.

"Goose? Are you all right?"

Stupid question.

When there was no response, he cracked the door open. Ainslie was sitting on the closed lid of the toilet in her underwear and t-shirt, her face buried in her hands. Her shoulders were heaving as she finally let out the sobs that had been evading her for the last twenty-four hours.

His eyes widened when he saw the bruises on her legs. He kneeled down in front of her, and she wrapped her arms around his neck, clinging onto him like a frightened child. He held her tightly as she let out deep, heart-wrenching sobs into his shoulder. He rubbed circles into her back and let himself cry with her.

There they were. Sitting in the cold bathroom. Two hearts completely broken, sharing each other's pain. It had been a chaotic, tragic and abrupt ending to their honeymoon stage.

When Ainslie finally loosened her grip on him and withdrew, James cradled her face in his hands, brushing away a stray tear with his thumb.

"Do you still want to have a shower?"

Ainslie nodded, her lower lip quivering.

He gently took the hem of her shirt between his fingers and pulled it over her head, careful to avoid her stitches. He audibly gasped when he saw the black and blue bruises down her ribs and hips. He traced his fingers across the marks, his touch as light as a feather. He gingerly placed kisses upon every one, working his way up her body before rising to meet her face to face and kissing her lips. He removed the rest of her clothing before removing his own and leading her carefully into the shower. He soaped up a loofah and gently helped her wash her aching body, making sure he stole a kiss whenever he could.

They held each other some more, they cried some more, and by the time they were out of the shower and into their pyjamas, James felt a little bit better. He hoped Ainslie did, too.

James led her to the nest he'd made in her bed. Ainslie huddled down in the blankets, and he climbed in beside her.

"I love you. So much," he said. "And if I've learned anything these last two days, it's that I need to tell you more often."

"I love you, too. So much." Ainslie yawned and curled herself in beside him, nuzzling her nose into his chest. "Thank you for taking such good care of me."

"It's honestly what I live for."

James pulled the blanket over them and held her in his arms until he felt her breathing ease into the peaceful rhythm of sleep. He kissed her forehead and closed his eyes. Even as sleep evaded him, he did his best to rest, listening to her soft sounds, a gentle reminder that she was safe beside him.

CHAPTER 50

The dream was so vivid.

The panic as she realised she was falling. The feeling of weightlessness as she flew through the air. The sound of her bones crunching as she slammed into the ground.

It jolted Ainslie awake, and she let out a sound that was somewhere between a gasp and a cry.

"Goose?" James asked, his voice laden with worry. "Are you okay?"

She pulled herself closer to him, snuggling in under his arm as he wrapped it around her. "You know how I said I didn't want to relive it?"

He stroked her hair. "Bad dream?"

She nodded, clinging to the front of his shirt. Her pain was easier to deal with when he was beside her, and she didn't want him going anywhere.

Outside, the sun was rising over the city. Ainslie knew she'd fallen asleep quite early the previous evening — she must've slept all night. God knows she'd needed it.

"Do you want to go out for breakfast this morning?" she asked.

"Are you sure you're feeling up to it?"

"I think the best thing for me right now would be to go out and get some fresh air and sunlight."

In all honestly, Ainslie would've been happy to lie in bed moping for the foreseeable future, but Worlds was looming on the horizon. And she was thinking about Barcelona, and her recovery, and how she only had one month until they left. And now, half of that month was going to be spent with her sidelined by doctor's orders.

*   *   *

It'd been a while since they'd been to The Bean together, and Ainslie, while still tired and melancholy, had felt physically well enough to walk the short distance there.

"Do you know what I just realised?" James asked, reaching across the table and taking her hands in his.

"What?"

"This is our first time out in public as an official, non-secret, proper couple. Emphasis on the non-secret."

Ainslie giggled for the first time in a few days. It sounded strange to her ears, but it felt nice.

They ate their breakfast and talked about what the setback meant for them. Ainslie wasn't thrilled about her two-week forced break so close to Worlds, and even though she was so exhausted at that moment that she couldn't have possibly imagined putting skates on, that didn't stop her from grumbling about it.

"Ains, you have to listen to your doctors."

"I know! But we only have a month left until we leave, and we're not going to get on the podium if I take longer than two weeks off."

"Goose," he said, taking her hands in his again, "two days ago, my biggest concern was getting on the podium at Worlds, but now, my biggest concern is you and your wellbeing. Physical and mental. There are always going to be more competitions, but there's only one Ainslie Wynter."

Ainslie cocked her head and smirked. "Are you saying you don't care if we bomb at Worlds?"

"Not as long as we bomb together."

*　　*　　*

The next two weeks were a challenge for Ainslie.

During the first few days, she was grateful for the rest, but by the end of the first week, her feet were itching to get back in skates. Physically, she was feeling a lot brighter thanks to the downtime, but mentally … she had her good days and her bad days.

Some days, she'd feel almost completely back to her normal self. Other days, she barely wanted to get out of bed. James had been amazing through it all. He was at her apartment nearly constantly, and she was incredibly thankful to have him around all the time.

He'd integrated into the apartment dynamic so smoothly, it felt as if he'd sneakily moved in there. Ainslie was hardly surprised by how much she was enjoying sharing her living space with him, and she'd decided she wouldn't mind them having a more permanent arrangement.

Every night, they'd huddle on the lounge and watch TV together before heading to bed and falling asleep in each other's arms. Every morning, James would get up early to make her coffee and breakfast and bring it to her in bed.

She'd told him he was spoiling her, but he'd just shrugged and said, "Yeah, that's the whole point."

Some nights she slept peacefully. Other nights she would dream of crashing into the concrete and wake up shaken. The worst dreams were the ones where she was holding a baby. She usually woke up crying from those. But no matter the dream, James would always wake up as well, as if he had an internal alarm. Then he'd hold her and stroke her hair until she fell back to sleep.

*　　*　　*

James had been training alone, which was odd to see. He and Ainslie were such a package deal that it didn't look right, him being out on the floor by himself.

And even though she was banned from skating, Ainslie never missed a training session. She sat on top of the barrier, watching James and the others practise, offering encouragement and feedback if anyone asked.

One Saturday afternoon, she was sitting on the barrier feeling particularly sorry for herself when it occurred to her that she couldn't remember the last time she'd actually watched James train alone. She was able to take proper notice of how much his skating skill and artistic impression had improved. And his triples were so strong now, it was kind of a turn-on. A weird turn-on, but a turn-on nonetheless.

She watched Lucy skate her freedance. It'd been stunning at Nationals, but now it was polished, and refined, and truly Worlds ready.

Jaz stuck a solid triple Salchow in the far corner of the rink. No-one would've been able to guess that only two months ago, she had been struggling with it.

God, my friends are talented.

Ainslie tried to ignore the jealous pang in her stomach she felt as she sat and observed her friends preparing for the biggest competition of the year. All while she was relegated to the barrier.

"How are you feeling?" Sandra pulled up beside her, and they both watched James's combination spin.

"I've been better," Ainslie said, mindlessly kicking her heels into the barrier. "Feel pretty useless at the moment. Being benched sucks."

"You don't need to come here every day if it upsets you."

Ainslie shook her head. "No. I think I need this. I already have enough FOMO as it is without not being here at all." She nodded towards James. "He's looking good."

Sandra smiled. "No matter what happens at Worlds, I hope you know how honoured I am to be your coach. You kids really are something special."

James came skidding over to the barrier.

"You guys talking about me?" He raised an eyebrow as he took a swig from his drink bottle.

"Only good things," Sandra replied.

He put his hands on Ainslie's knees. "How are you doing?"

"I'm okay. You're looking good out there, Sunderland."

"I ain't shit without you, Wynter." He smirked. "Wanna go for a ride?"

Before Ainslie could even respond, he'd scooped her off the barrier and rolled away with her in his arms.

"I swear to God, if you drop her, I'll kill you!" Sandra called after them.

Ainslie enjoyed the feeling of the wind on her face and James holding her. She wrapped her arms around his neck and let him twirl her around the rink. She giggled, not caring a bit if the others saw.

Eventually, he rolled back up to the barrier and sat her on top of it, placing his hands on her waist and kissing her, perhaps a little too enthusiastically, considering where they were.

Ainslie smiled. "I had a dream once, not too unlike this."

James smiled back. "Yeah, so did I."

CHAPTER 51

By the time her two weeks' rest were over, Ainslie couldn't get on the rink fast enough. She laced up her skates in record time and darted out onto the floor, feeling a little wobbly after her time off.

"Are you sure you're okay to skate?" James asked, touching her arm.

"Of course I'm okay," she said a little too defensively and then patted his hand apologetically.

"Ainslie," Sandra called, "we'll start with jumps, okay? Work your way through the singles, then doubles, then you can get back into triples if you feel comfortable."

If I feel comfortable? I've got Worlds in two weeks. I bloody better be comfortable.

She sped around the rink, getting used to the feeling of wheels underneath her again. Slowly, and one by one, she picked off all her single jumps. Then the doubles. They were practically second nature at this point in her career, so she was hardly surprised she still had it.

Then she set up a triple toe loop.

At the last second, she baulked. Ainslie never baulked.

She shook it off and set up a second time. Once again, she baulked. She growled under her breath and pounded her fists on her thighs.

"Are you okay?" James asked, coming up beside her.

"I'm fine," she said, but she didn't sound so sure.

"Goose," James said, taking her by the shoulders, "you've got this. You've done it a million times before."

She nodded along in agreement, patted him on the arm and skated around for another attempt.

Third time's a charm.

But it wasn't.

"Fuck!" she said as she pulled out of the jump once again.

James rolled up beside her and put a hand on her shoulder. "It's okay."

"It's *not* okay!"

She saw the shock and hurt in his eyes and immediately regretted her words.

"I'm sorry," she said softly, taking his hand in hers. "I'm sorry. It's just … I'm just …" Her quivering lip was betraying her brave façade. "I'm going to let you down …"

"Ainslie Wynter," James said as he pulled her into a hug, "you're never going to let me down."

"It's just the first day back, Ainslie," Sandra said as she rolled towards them. "You've still got two weeks. You've still got it in you, I know."

But a new kind of panic had already begun to set in. What if she *didn't* still have it in her? Sandra must've seen the worry in her eyes.

"How about we go through both routines with the music?" Sandra said. "You can do whatever elements you feel you're able to, okay? Just go easy and communicate with each other."

Ainslie nodded, nervously rubbing her arm. She was going to have to get over her fear, and fast.

Sandra put on their short program music, and they marked out their routine. Ainslie replaced her triples with doubles but was able to spin without any problems. She called off the throw triple Salchow and the lifts, but they completed their footwork sequences and focused on their skating skills and artistic impression. When the music ended, James patted her on the back.

"Good job, Goose."

She nodded, but she didn't say anything.

The pair had a quick drink and a stretch before Sandra put on their long program music. They took their places and began the familiar opening movements.

Ainslie jumped the double Axel and was pleased with the small victory, but she baulked on the triple flip and turned the other triples into doubles again. Her spins were fine, but again she called off the lifts.

She was beginning to make her own blood boil. She knew it was only the first day back, but she only had *fourteen* days. Every day she wasted baulking just lowered their chances of that podium finish. And if she was certain about one thing, it was that the longer she put off doing the scary elements, the harder it would be.

They rounded the corner, skating the transition that came before their final lift.

The lift.

"Do it," Ainslie called, not allowing herself a moment to overthink it.

"Are you sure?"

"Yes! Do it!"

They prepared for the lift in the same way they always did. They locked eyes for a moment before entering, and a look of pure trust passed between them. Ainslie launched herself, and James lifted her high above his head. She was solid, her position strong in the air even though her heart was racing. They rotated, changed position, and began the dismount. It was a perfect landing, and all four of Ainslie's wheels struck the floor with a clean and satisfying thud.

Ainslie beamed at James, and he beamed back. They didn't even finish the routine.

"You did it!"

"Nailed it!" Ainslie cheered, holding up both of her hands.

James slapped her a double high five. Lacing his fingers between hers, he captured her hands and pulled her into a kiss.

He rested his forehead against hers. "I'm so proud of you, Ainslie."

"Okay, let's keep it PG," Sandra called from the music box, but she was smiling from ear to ear.

Once the lift was out of the way, it was as if Ainslie had broken the seal on her fear. After taking a moment to gather herself, she managed to jump a triple toe loop and a triple Salchow, much to everyone's excitement. She and James performed the offending lift a few more times to really solidify it before trying all their other lifts as well.

Ainslie decided to put off the throw jumps for a couple more days. Her right hip had really started to ache. It was the one that had taken the most impact in the fall, and it was also her landing hip, so it was hardly surprising that it was sore. But instead of getting hung up on it, she focused on all the successes of the day, and by the end of the training session, she felt a whole lot better about the entire situation.

"Before you two leave," Sandra said, as they all took off their skates, "can we have a chat up in my office?"

Ainslie and James looked at each other. It wasn't like Sandra to call impromptu meetings.

The pair made their way upstairs ahead of their coach and sat in her office in nervous silence. But when Sandra sat down opposite them and smiled kindly, Ainslie relaxed a little.

"Okay," Sandra said. "I didn't want to have this conversation earlier because I knew you were both really going through it."

Ainslie furrowed her brow.

"I just have to know," Sandra said, "why on *earth* did you think you weren't able to tell me about this relationship?"

She almost sounded hurt. Ainslie fiddled with her hands.

"I don't know," Ainslie said. "We were just worried. I guess we thought you'd think it would distract us from our Worlds prep. Which, now in a roundabout kind of way, it did."

"And we know you didn't exactly have the greatest experience competing with someone you were also in a relationship with," James said.

Sandra scoffed. "You two are absolutely nothing like Luke Browning and me. Mostly because *you*," she said, glancing at James, "aren't a complete arsehole."

The pair chuckled, and Sandra continued speaking. "Listen, I'm more than happy for this" — she gestured between them — "to happen. But I want you to know there are always going to be risks. Skating with a loved one is hard work. You're doing fine at the moment, but you've been together, what? A few months? Honeymoon stage. In the long term, it's hard."

Ainslie nodded. "I know." She glanced across at James and placed a hand on his knee. "But I think it's worth it."

"You know, we had a real crash course in adult relationships in the last two weeks," James added as he took Ainslie's hand. "It would've been nice not to have it a month out from Worlds, but I think it forced us to grow up a little."

"Look at you two," Sandra said, smiling. "You were babies just yesterday. I still remember how hard it was to get you to touch each other in the early days … I see that's not a problem anymore."

Ainslie and James chuckled, and Ainslie blushed.

"So," Sandra said, "I'm very happy for you two, and I wish you all the best. But let's keep things open and honest between us in the future, okay? The relationship between the three of us here is just as much built upon trust as any other. Now," Sandra said and clapped her hands together. "That's not the only thing I wanted to talk about."

Ainslie felt her nerves kick up again.

"We leave for Worlds in just under two weeks. Ainslie, you did well today to get over some of your fears, but I know it's not going to be easy. Tomorrow, you can work on triples and throws, and it might not be a problem. But maybe you'll have a bad day and not feel like you're up to it. We're just not going to know."

Ainslie didn't want to think about not being up to it. That wasn't an option.

"Recovering mentally is often a lot harder than recovering physically," Sandra added. "And personally, I think it's far more important. I know you guys had a goal to get on the podium this year, but I want you to know that it's more important to me that you're healthy, happy and safe. Let's be honest, losing two weeks of training a month out from Worlds is less than ideal. But whatever happens in Barcelona, I want you to know that I am incredibly proud of you. As skaters, and as people."

Ainslie felt a warmth in her chest, and she smiled. "Thanks, Sandra."

Sandra leaned back in her chair. "Did I ever tell you about the big fall I had when I was younger?"

Ainslie raised an eyebrow. "Not in detail."

"Ah, the details. All anyone remembers is how Luke dumped me for a gold medal. Anyway," she said. "We were doing a reverse layover camel. We mistimed it, and I copped his skate right under my chin. That itself knocked me rotten. Then, of course, I fell over backwards, landing on my arm and splitting the back of my head open."

James winced. "Shit."

"Tell me about it. I was in hospital for a week. I ended up with a broken jaw and a broken wrist. I had ten stitches in my head, and I'd sprained my neck. A real solid injury. It happened two weeks before Nationals, so we were *definitely* out for that. And I was gonna be a write-off for the rest of the season. But before we skated as a pair, we'd both skated singles, so Luke just got approval from New South Wales to go to Nationals and skate alone. It was that year he went to Worlds by himself and came home with gold for Australia. He also came home with Marianne Perkins, but that's another story."

"Yikes," Ainslie said and winced. "I'm sorry."

"Ah, don't be," Sandra said with a sly grin. "You two are world number four. His best skater is an off-brand talk show host who gets her best viewing figures by talking shit about *my* best skaters."

*　　*　　*

It didn't take Rosa Charis long to hear the latest news to come out of New South Wales.

Ainslie and James were making dinner one night as Jaz mindlessly scrolled through social media.

"Hey, you guys!" Jaz called. "Have you seen Rosa's latest post?"

"No," Ainslie replied, drying her hands.

"You guys are the stars of it," Jaz said in a singsong voice.

Ainslie let out a dramatic groan. Lucy looked up from her book.

Jaz started reading the post aloud. " 'After years of vehemently denying that they are anything more than friends, New South Wales pairs team Ainslie Wynter and James Sunderland are *finally*' — 'finally' is in all caps, by the way — 'a couple off the rink as well as on.' "

"Well, at least she's reporting the truth now," Lucy said.

" 'The pair changed their relationship status just days after a serious training accident that landed Ainslie in the hospital and off skates for two weeks. There is some speculation that the two had been in a relationship for much longer, with some sources claiming to have seen them together at the Nationals Dinner in June.' "

"Who on earth are 'some sources'?" Ainslie asked.

"They say she has eyes everywhere," James said ominously.

"She goes on to say," Jaz added, " 'Two weeks off from training a month out from Worlds is a huge disadvantage, and we wish Ainslie all the best with her recovery.' "

"At least she was nice about it," Lucy said.

"Yeah, real nice," Ainslie said, scowling. "Now everyone's going to be feeling sorry for me."

"Would that really be so bad?" James asked.

She looked at him sideways. "The last thing I want is to get to Barcelona and have *Tessa Strong* thinking she can use my trauma as a weapon in her head games arsenal."

"There are so many comments," Jaz said, laughing. "Amanda Dickinson said, 'About time'. Your mate Tessa said, 'I knew it!' That coach Lisa Brown from Queensland said, 'Isn't this old news? Haha. Just kidding, congrats you crazy kids'."

"Funny how everyone's commenting on your relationship status, and yet no-one seems to care about the whole *accident that landed you in hospital* thing," Lucy said and frowned.

Ainslie waved a hand. "It's fine. I really don't want to have to relive it every

237

time someone sees me and asks if I'm okay. As for us," she said, patting James on the cheek as she walked past him, "let 'em talk!"

*   *   *

Later that night as they lay in bed, Ainslie rolled on her side and propped herself up on her elbow.

"Can I ask you a question? You can say no."

James looked at her quizzically and smiled. "As if I'd ever say no to you."

"You know …," she said, absent-mindedly playing with the fabric of his shirt, "technically, our lease says we can have four tenants on it."

He laughed. "That's not a question."

She suppressed a smile, and it ended up being a happy little pout.

"Ainslie Wynter, are you asking me to move in with you?"

"Maybe," she replied coyly. "If you wanted to."

"Of course I want to." He put a hand on her waist and pulled her close. "Do you think the girls would mind?"

"You've practically lived here for the last two weeks," she said. "They'd just be happy if you finally started paying rent."

"True."

"So …," she said. "James Sunderland, will you officially be my roomie?"

James pulled her into a kiss. "Ainslie Wynter, literally nothing would make me happier."

CHAPTER 52

The trip from Sydney to Barcelona via Dubai was going to take a little over a day. Ainslie and James had been roused from their peaceful sleep well before dawn by Jaz and Lucy arguing in the hall over whether or not Jaz should have packed her orthotics in her hand luggage. (Needless to say, Lucy and her sensible over-preparedness had won.)

Even though their flight wasn't until eight, they had to be at the airport three hours early, and as soon as they'd checked in and found their gate, the four of them had flaked out on the floor drinking overpriced coffee while they had waited to board. A few people had clocked their Australian uniforms and asked what sport they were playing. When they had replied with "Artistic roller skating", they'd been met with blank stares and a polite "Oh, well, good luck!"

The four were seated together in the centre section of the plane, and Jaz had fallen asleep the second they were in the air. Ainslie envied her. She never could sleep on planes.

Lucy had already cracked open her book, although Ainslie knew her well enough to know she probably wasn't actually absorbing the content as much as she was trying to distract herself from the pressing urge to keep the plane in the air with her mind. She'd always been a nervous flyer.

James was scrolling through the in-flight entertainment on the little screen that was embedded in the seat in front of him.

Flying long haul for Worlds was always a challenge. Sitting in a cramped space on little to no sleep for twenty-four hours and getting off the plane with jelly legs didn't exactly fill one with a lot of enthusiasm to compete. For far-flung trips like this one, they always arrived a week before their event so they could recover from the jet lag and get their muscles functioning properly again.

Ainslie rested her head on James's shoulder and closed her eyes. With sleep evading her, resting her eyes was going to be as good as it would get. It wasn't just the early morning that had Ainslie weak and weary. She owed much of that to the events of the past month, in particular the last two weeks. After the pep talk Sandra had given them that first day back, Ainslie had pulled her aside and told her that while she appreciated the concern, she didn't want Sandra to go easy on her. She didn't want to be the reason they didn't do their best at Worlds.

Sandra had raised her eyebrows, shrugged and said she would, but only if Ainslie was sure.

"I am," Ainslie had replied. "I don't want to let James down."

Sandra chuckled. "I don't think there's anything you could *ever* do to make that boy think of you as anything less than perfect."

After that, they'd jumped back into training right where they'd left off before the accident. Sandra had suggested they both pare back the gym work as they got closer to leaving just so their bodies had time to recover. But Ainslie had still gone right home and done a workout in their living room.

James had stood over her as she lay on the floor doing crunches. "You're supposed to be resting."

"I'll rest when I'm dead."

"You'll be dead when Sandra finds out you're not resting."

The ding of a flight attendant call button roused Ainslie, and she sleepily lifted her head off James's shoulder. She made a little humming sound as she looked around, a little disoriented.

"I can't believe it," James said. "Is that Ainslie Wynter, sleeping on an aeroplane?"

She noticed that the movie he'd started watching only moments ago now had the end credits rolling.

She rubbed her eyes. "I was asleep?"

"Sure were. I must have the magic touch."

She smirked. "Or I'm just really tired."

*   *   *

Once they touched down in the UAE, they barely had time to race from one plane to the next. Ainslie felt fairly delirious by that point. Her two-hour nap on James's shoulder was all the sleep she'd managed. James and Lucy looked just as wrecked as she was feeling. Jaz, on the other hand, had slept for a decent chunk of the Sydney to Dubai flight and had rediscovered her energy.

The second flight was only about half as long as the first, but somehow it felt longer. They all made sure they spent some time getting up, walking around and stretching. Puffy ankles were always a risk after a long-haul flight, and Ainslie wanted to avoid them as much as possible.

By the time they finally touched down in Barcelona, they were running on about nine hours of sleep between the four of them, and the only reason that number was so high was thanks to Jaz's six-hour nap on the first flight.

When Ainslie stepped into the bright, filtered sunlight of the terminal, she felt a little dazed and confused. She wasn't sure what day it was, and she couldn't tell without checking a clock whether it was morning or afternoon. But it was all par for the course when it came to international travel, and Ainslie was used to it.

They all gathered their luggage (no-one's bag had gone missing, thankfully) and waited outside the terminal for Paula to arrive with their minibus. Ainslie sat on top of her suitcase and rested her chin in her hands, fighting the urge to fall asleep.

CHAPTER 53

The hotel where the Australian team was staying was only a short drive from the airport. Once they arrived and met with the other state contingents, Paula handed out their room assignments. She then gave everyone half an hour to have a shower and get changed before they were to meet back in the foyer.

As everyone dispersed, Paula tapped Ainslie and James on their shoulders.

She lowered her voice. "Before you two head off, can we have a quick word in my room, please?"

The pair shared a quizzical glance and followed Paula up to the suite she was sharing with Sandra and Stephen. Ainslie and James sat side by side on the hard leather lounge, and Paula sat opposite them in a matching leather armchair as if she were about to interview them for a talk show. Ainslie studied her body language. She was struggling to look them in the eye, and she kept fiddling with her hands and shifting uncomfortably. Ainslie had a bad feeling she knew what the talk was going to be about.

"So," Paula said finally. "Hi."

Ainslie narrowed her eyes a little. "Hi?"

Paula clasped her hands together and leaned forwards in her chair. "Look," she said. "There's no way to go about this without it being ... a little awkward ... but it *does* have to be said."

Ainslie peeked at James out of the corner of her eye, trying to see if he looked as uncomfortable as she felt. He did.

"There are certain protocols," Paula said, "that I, as your team manager, have to remind you of and that you have to abide by while travelling with the team."

Ainslie's eyes widened. She wished the lounge would swallow her so she didn't have to have this conversation.

"It's been brought to my attention that the two of you are in a relationship now. Which is great, by the way. Congratulations. But as your team manager, I am obligated to remind you that there are certain rules regarding things like ... being in each other's rooms, sneaking out after dark ..."

Ainslie's face contorted into a look of sheer horror. She glanced at James again. He was bright red. So was Paula, for that matter.

"I know you're both adults, and I know you're teammates, but while you're under my care, you are required to follow these rules, and um ..." Somehow, Paula's face got even redder. "Just remember, there will be consequences if I find out ... there's been any ... shenanigans."

"Say no more," James blurted.

Oh, God, please say no more!

Paula seemed to relax a little. "Okay, good. As long as you catch my drift."

"Oh, we catch it all right," Ainslie said. "With both hands."

"I'm sorry this has been awkward," Paula replied. "But let's forget about it and move on. See you downstairs in" — she checked her watch — "twenty-two minutes."

The pair left Paula's suite and made a beeline for the lift in silence. As soon as they were safe inside, Ainslie buried her face in her hands and squealed.

"Oh, my God, that was *humiliating!*"

"What does she think we're gonna get up to?" James said and laughed. "You're rooming with the girls, and I'm rooming with Tony. Not exactly prime conditions for *shenanigans.*"

"*Shenanigans.*" Ainslie cackled. "Oh, my God, I can't believe she said *shenanigans.*"

*   *   *

After twenty minutes, the entire team had reconvened in the foyer.

It was an annual tradition at Worlds; Paula would take them all out on a walk around the neighbourhood as soon as they arrived. Partly, it was to show the team where the local amenities were, but mostly it was to get them all outside in the sun and keep their minds off their jet lag for at least an hour.

Paula herded them like sheep through the maze of narrow streets in the Gothic Quarter and then hustled them out into the clearing of La Rambla. The thoroughfare was lined with restaurants and bars, and it was currently bustling with lunchtime patrons. They found a quaint restaurant where they could all enjoy some tapas and a rest.

As soon as their backsides hit their chairs, Tessa Strong, who'd placed herself opposite Ainslie and James, slapped her hands on the table and grinned.

"You guys!" she said in a singsong voice. "What did I tell you?"

They both looked at her blankly.

"Um … congratulations?!"

"Um, thanks?" Ainslie gave her a less-than-enthusiastic smile.

Not because she wasn't still blissfully happy, but because she couldn't tell if Tessa's well wishes were actually genuine. Tessa had spoken so loudly it brought the whole table to attention. Suddenly, Ainslie and James were the focus of the entire team.

"So, how did it happen?" Amanda Dickinson asked expectantly.

Ainslie certainly wasn't going to answer *that* truthfully. Not with Paula in earshot.

"Oh, you know," she said, "it just … happened."

Amanda didn't look satisfied with her response.

"How long? Were you like, secretly together at Nationals? Because your long program was so freaking hot," Amelia Benson said, fanning herself.

James blushed. "No, it was after Nationals."

"So like … did you *always* know you'd get together eventually?" Riley Stuart from South Australia asked. "Because I'm pretty sure *we* all did."

Everyone at the table laughed. Even Ainslie had to smile.

"Not *always*," Ainslie said. "But it has been the most natural thing in the world, hasn't it?"

She looked at James, and when he smiled back at her, she momentarily forgot they were being interrogated.

"Well," he said, slipping his hand under the table to find hers. "I mean, *I* was definitely always in love with *her*. It just took her a little longer to figure it out."

That was met with a chorus of "aww"s.

Ainslie felt her heart leap, and she squeezed his hand. She hoped that now they'd given the people what they had so clearly wanted, they'd drop it. If the circumstances had been different, she would've been perfectly happy to sit there and talk about how the greatest love story the Australian artistic skating community had ever seen came to be. She would've revelled in the jealous looks from the others, the looks that were absolutely green, because she'd done it; she was not only one of those rare exceptions who'd managed to score herself a skating partner but also one of those even rarer specimens who'd fallen in love with them.

It was only mere months ago that she would've given anything to have the freedom to shout from the rooftops that yes, she loved James Sunderland more than she'd ever known it was possible to love another person. But it had only been a month since their accident, and she was exhausted, and jet lagged, and she still had a small twinge of pain in her right hip. And she was still grieving. She hadn't really had time to process everything.

She'd recovered physically, for the most part. But she'd been so busy training, she hadn't had the time to speak to anyone about it. She knew for a fact that James's mum had been through something similar and would've been there at the drop of a hat to support her. And the one person who'd been making her fitful nights bearable was the one person who, for the duration of the trip, wasn't allowed to be there for her when she needed it the most. It hadn't even occurred to her until their conversation with Paula that she would have to deal with her nightmares alone for the next two weeks. It should've been obvious, really. She knew the rules. But it hadn't even crossed her mind.

*　　*　　*

After tapas, Paula led them down to the beach. The shops and restaurants had closed for siesta, and Ainslie figured she was still looking for things to keep the skaters occupied.

Jaz bounded ahead with the four girls who made up the quartet team, Lucy was catching up with Amanda (with whom she shared an affinity for peace and quiet), and Ainslie and James hung at the back of the pack, hands interlocked.

The effort required to trudge through the soft sand only further depleted their already dangerously low energy stores.

"Are you okay?" James asked. "You seemed quiet at lunch."

"Yeah," Ainslie said, sighing. "It just occurred to me that I have to be all alone with my thoughts every night. Which I'm sure will be a real treat."

"Yeah, it's a bit shit. But if you need to call or message me, you know you can. Any time."

"And wake up your roomie? Yeah, okay."

"I'll put my phone on vibrate and tie it to my head, if need be." He smiled. "And we can always try to sneak out if we absolutely have to. Let's face it, we got away with a lot worse at Nationals."

"I hate feeling like this," Ainslie muttered. "Feeling so bloody needy, and sad, and tired all the time. And feeling like a naughty twelve-year-old for having the *audacity* to want to spend time with my partner."

"Jameslie!" Paula called from the front of the pack. "Please keep up with the group, thank you!"

All eyes flicked to them. Ainslie swore she could see some smirks and suppressed giggles. She rolled her eyes as they picked up their pace.

"I feel like a sideshow."

"Yeah, it's gonna be a long two weeks."

*   *   *

When ten o'clock hit, the skaters were finally given permission to go to sleep. Lucy and Jaz crashed almost immediately, but Ainslie found herself lying in her cold, small bed, staring at the ceiling. She hadn't thought she would have any trouble dropping off considering how exhausted she was. But now, she was overtired and wide awake. And even though she resented how needy it made her feel, she was missing the warmth of her usual bedfellow. When midnight came and went and she was still wide awake, she grabbed her phone and sent James a message.

You awake?

He replied almost instantly.

Yeah. You ok?

Can't sleep.

Me neither. Wanna talk?

Roof?

*   *   *

They met ten minutes later in their pyjamas by the light of the rooftop pool.

"I hope Tony doesn't wake up and find you missing," Ainslie said.

"Tony and I have an understanding. I don't ask him any questions when he disappears with some random Italian guy. He doesn't ask *me* any questions when he wakes up and finds me missing."

They snuggled together on a banana lounge. The sky seemed starless thanks to the lights of the city, and the breeze was cool on Ainslie's skin. She rested her head on James's chest and listened to his heartbeat. He absent-mindedly ran his fingers up and down her back, and she sighed happily.

"If someone told me last Worlds that in twelve months' time I'd be here with you, I would've laughed in their face," James said. "But secretly, I would've hoped they were right."

Ainslie smiled sleepily. "Me too."

"Really? Even a whole year ago?"

"Yeah. I mean, I did a pretty good job lying to myself about it for six years, but I have always loved you."

James squeezed Ainslie a little tighter and planted a kiss on the top of her head. She breathed deeply and peacefully beside him. It would have been so easy just to nod off. After a few moments, she spoke again.

"Did you know," she said quietly, "if I got pregnant when I think I did, we'd be around about the twelve-week mark by now?"

James held her tighter. "This week, we'll skate for her."

"Her?"

"I like to think she was a girl. Mainly because I much prefer the idea of a tiny little you running around over a tiny little me. Just ask my mum."

Ainslie let out a weak but genuine chuckle, and they fell back into a long, companionable silence. James quietly stroked her hair for a while as the events of the last few weeks replayed in her mind. Eventually, he broke the silence.

"Maybe we shouldn't have come here."

Ainslie lifted her head and looked up at him, confused. "What?"

"Everything happened so quickly after the accident. There wasn't any time to process it all. I know you're still hurting. I know *I* am. I mean, can either of us *really* say we're in the best headspace right now to compete at Worlds? Let alone get on the podium?"

"No. But I didn't want to let you down."

He stroked her cheek. "You're never, ever going to let me down, Ainslie. If anything, I feel like I've let *you* down."

"How?"

"By making you feel like you had to pull everything together in record time so we could be here."

She pursed her lips, trying to control the wave of emotion that was threatening to crash over her. "I guess we're both just a big old mess, aren't we?"

"Seems it," he replied with a half smile. "But there's no-one I'd rather share my mess with than you."

*　　*　　*

They fell asleep in each other's arms on the banana lounge. It would've been a disaster had their jet lag not saved the day and woken them both up at three in the morning. Ainslie felt even sorer from having fallen asleep in such an uncomfortable position. She stood up from the lounge and winced, drawing a large circle in the air with her knee to stretch out her hip.

James sat up and placed his hand on her offending hip. "Are you okay?"

"Yeah. I've just had this twinging since the fall."

He gingerly lifted the hem of her pyjama shirt and placed a kiss on her right hipbone.

"I'm sorry," he said as he placed another kiss, a little to the right of the first. "I wish I could make it better."

He planted a trail of kisses from her aching hip across her stomach. Ainslie shuddered as all her emotions finally came to a boil. James looked up at her, concern etched across his brow. He stood, still holding her hips. She couldn't stop her lip from quivering, and tears had begun to cloud her vision.

"You *do* make it better. You're the only thing that can."

He held her face between his hands and peppered kisses across her cheeks, kissing away every tear and then meeting her lips with his at last. She wrapped her arms around his middle and pulled him closer to her, finding comfort there like she always did. She kissed him hungrily, wishing she didn't have to ever leave his side again. She wanted to stay up on the roof forever, sharing each other's space, holding each other close.

James pulled away reluctantly. "We'll be in the shit if Paula finds out we're out here."

"You said yourself," Ainslie said, the hint of a smile starting to shine through her sadness, "we got away with a lot worse at Nationals."

James chuckled. "Using my own words against me, I see."

Ainslie let herself laugh and gave him another tight hug. There would be hell to pay if Paula found out, and unlike at Nationals, they were now on her radar.

"No, you're right," Ainslie said. "I guess we should go back to our rooms."

"Yeah."

"You better text me the *second* Tony disappears with some Italian guy," she added with a wry smile.

He wrapped an arm around her shoulders as they headed for the lift. "Oh, don't worry. You'll be the first to know."

CHAPTER 54

Lucy's eight-thirty alarm pierced the silence of the morning, and Ainslie had every mind to pick up her friend's phone and launch it across the room.

After she'd returned to her room in the early hours of the morning, she'd lain staring at the ceiling for a while before fatigue had gotten the better of her, and she'd finally drifted off into a dreamless sleep.

The abrupt wake-up call had her feeling a little disoriented, but once she remembered where she was, she was able to appreciate how much better she felt. She was still tired, but she didn't feel quite so on the verge of having a breakdown.

She took a hot shower to help wash away the aches caused by spending part of the night napping on a banana lounge. As she let the water warm her and wake her up, she began to feel a bit more like herself again.

The day before had been one of her bad days, most likely exacerbated by her jet lag. She'd needed the sleep, she'd needed the cuddle, and she'd needed the talk with James. Now, in the light of a new day, things didn't seem quite so bad.

*   *   *

The girls headed down to the dining room, where Ainslie piled her plate high with scrambled eggs and tomatoes. She made herself a strong coffee and slid into the chair beside James.

"Morning," she said, pecking him on the cheek.

"You look a bit brighter today," he said, putting his arm around her shoulders and giving her arm a little rub. "Did you have a good sleep?"

She nodded lazily and pulled her chair a little closer to him.

Amanda smiled as she stabbed her fork into a rasher of bacon. "I know you're probably sick of hearing it, but you two are so stinking cute."

"I know, right?" Ainslie smiled and took a sip of coffee.

She winced. It tasted like dishwater.

"But for real, though," Amanda added. "I heard about your accident."

"I'm pretty sure everyone did," Ainslie replied, "but no-one wants to talk about *that*."

"Were you guys okay?" Amanda asked, lowering her voice. "Pairs falls scare the shit out of me."

Ainslie dropped her gaze down to her plate, and James took over.

"Yeah, it was pretty severe. This one had a pretty bad concussion." He gently stroked Ainslie's hair where the stitches had been. "Definitely scared the shit out of *me*. And there were a lot of bruises. But no broken bones, thankfully."

"Shit," Amanda said and screwed up her nose. "Thank God it wasn't worse."

Ainslie just nodded down at her breakfast. She wasn't about to ruin her good mood by going into the finer details of how everything had actually been *so much* worse.

A shrill voice sliced through the air of the dining room.

It was a voice that made Ainslie's blood pressure skyrocket. She turned to see none other than Rosa Charis, waving as she sauntered over to the cluster of tables that the Australian team had claimed. She was wearing a full face of make-up and didn't have a hair out of place. She certainly didn't look as if she'd just gotten off a long-haul flight mere hours ago. She stopped at another table and made small talk with a group of Queenslanders.

Amanda looked around the table. "Any of you know Rosa was coming this year?"

Ainslie shook her head. "No. I don't care anywhere near as much about her business as she cares about mine."

Ainslie may have been in a better mood than she had been the day before, but she wasn't quite at the point of being in the mood to talk to Rosa. She lowered her head and pretended she was invisible, hoping to remain unnoticed by the Queen of Gossip herself. But moments later, Rosa was standing at their table, one hand resting on the back of James's chair, the other perched on her hip.

"Hey, you guys!" She sounded as perky and chipper as ever. "How are we doing?"

They all mumbled their responses. Ainslie ignored her.

"You excited to get out to country training today?"

She was met with a muttered, off-key chorus of, "Yes." She was trying so hard to get a conversation out of them it was painful.

"When did you get in, Rosa?" Amanda asked, clearly trying to make things less awkward.

"Oh, I've been here all week. I have family in Valencia, so I went down to visit them. Then I just popped up here, and now I get to spend the whole championships with you guys!"

"Awesome," Ainslie muttered under her breath.

"And you guys!" Rosa's voice was sickly sweet as she swung around to face Ainslie and James. "Look at you! What did I tell you? Match made in heaven."

She ruffled James's hair with her long, thin fingers. He bristled, and Amanda stifled a laugh.

"Lucky girl." Rosa winked at Ainslie. "This one's such a cutie."

She then swanned away.

Ainslie pulled a face. "Yikes."

"What the hell was that?" Jaz asked.

"I have no idea," James said, trying in vain to fix his hair.

"I guess she ran out of ways to antagonise me and decided she needed to change tact," Ainslie said.

"Why does Rosa have it in for you, in particular?" Amanda asked.

Ainslie shrugged. "I have no idea."

"Jealousy?" Jaz asked. "Because you've been more successful than her?"

"Lots of people have been more successful than her," Ainslie said as she sipped her watery coffee.

"It's definitely jealousy," Lucy said. "But I have a feeling it's not your skating success she's jealous of."

Ainslie squinted at her. "What do you mean?"

Lucy looked back and forth between Ainslie and James. "You haven't guessed?"

The pair stared back blankly.

"Okay. I can't be sure, but I think it probably has something to do with a little incident that happened at the Nationals Dinner in 2014."

Lucy had the entire table's attention. Ainslie's brow was fixed in a furrow of confusion.

"Don't you remember? Brisbane, 2014. We were nineteen. And back then, those two could drink with the best of them." Lucy nodded towards James and Ainslie. "We were all just hanging out on the dance floor, singing along to terrible music, and Rosa comes bumbling over. Maybe she was a little tipsy, I don't know. But she would've been what? Twenty-three, twenty-four?"

"Oh, God," James said, his eyes going wide. "We don't need to hear this story."

Jaz was smiling and chewing on a piece of croissant. "Yeah, we do."

"Anyway," Lucy said, "she came over to us and was being really inappropriate with James. It was very awkward, and he was *not* into it. At the time, we thought it was kinda funny until she tried to make a move."

James had turned bright red.

Jaz looked riveted. "What kind of move?"

"Like. A *move*."

"Oh, my God, I remember that!" Ainslie grabbed James's arm, and her eyes lit up as she revelled in his discomfort. "That was so weird!" Her expression changed back to confusion. "But wait, what's that got to do with me?"

Lucy pursed her lips. "Well, James freaked out and rejected her in what was possibly the most humiliating moment of the century, right in the middle of the dance floor. In front of everyone. Rosa, being an *extremely* overly confident twenty-something, flatly rejected by a nineteen-year-old ... Let's just say her ego took a massive blow. I think some people even caught it on camera, and I'm pretty sure it did the rounds on social media."

If Jaz had had popcorn, she would've been shovelling fistfuls of it into her mouth. James looked as if he wanted to disappear. Ainslie still looked a little befuddled.

"Fast forward to about an hour later," Lucy said, glancing at Ainslie and James, "and *these* two are throwing back the beers like there's no tomorrow. Plus, there was the little fact that they were always *constantly* flirting with each other."

"No, we weren't," Ainslie said.

"Yes, you were. So, they were flirting in that little bickering, bantering way they used to do. And by this point, they're completely hammered, and I'm the only one still capable of making rational decisions. So, they disappear for a bit, and I find them a little later, in the photo booth, seconds away from a complete make-out session."

Jaz spluttered out a laugh. Ainslie nearly spat her coffee across the table.

"Wait," James said, "I don't remember this part of the story."

"I'm not surprised," Lucy replied. "I told you, you were hammered. So, I pull them off each other because I figured it wasn't something they would've been down for had they been sober. You know, I was worried it would cause all sorts of drama if they did anything stupid. So, I sent James to bed, put Ainslie to bed myself — not before she threw up all over the bathroom in the hotel reception — and pretended none of it ever happened. But before we left, I saw that Rosa had witnessed the whole thing. So, I can only assume that as a cover-up for her humiliating rejection, she started telling people that the reason James shot her down was because he was secretly already spoken for."

Ainslie's stomach clenched. Her good mood had died sometime during that story.

Now she was beginning to see red.

"Are you serious?"

Lucy shrugged guiltily. "I don't know what else to tell you."

Ainslie's face was on fire, and she could feel a crushing pressure between her ears.

"Are you saying that potentially, we could've gotten together *six years ago*?" Ainslie asked, trying to keep her voice down. "Like, before Aidan? Before I wasted *over half a decade* of my life?"

"Ainslie, there's no guarantee that the two of you drunkenly hooking up at nineteen would end up as picture perfect as this has," she said, gesturing between the two of them.

A tiny voice in the back of Ainslie's mind told her that Lucy had a point, but she didn't want to hear it. All she was hearing was that she and James could've had an extra six years together if Lucy hadn't seen fit to interfere. She could've avoided the heartache that being with Aidan in those final months had caused. Her entire life could've been different.

"Why didn't you ever think to tell me about this?"

"And what would you have done? No offence, Ainslie, but you weren't exactly the most *responsible* teenager …"

"What?" Ainslie was yelling now. "So irresponsible that I'd *what*? Go and get pregnant a couple of months out from Worlds? Well, oops, I still managed to do that at twenty-five, so I guess I'm not exactly the most responsible *adult* either. Good thing it didn't work out then, huh?"

Ainslie stood and stormed out of the dining room.

*   *   *

James watched Ainslie's retreating form, and an uncomfortable hush fell over the entire Australian team. There was no doubt everyone had heard what she'd said.

All eyes were on James, and he was frozen in silence. Lucy was biting her lip and trying not to cry. The excitement had drained from Jaz's face, and Amanda looked as if she'd just put together the pieces and realised what Ainslie had meant by "it" not "working out". Her eyes were so sympathetic and sad that James wanted to disappear even more now than he had during the Rosa Story. He excused himself from the table and ran after Ainslie.

He caught up to her in the foyer and gently took her by the arm. He was relieved and surprised to see she wasn't crying.

"Well, that didn't go so well now, did it?" he said.

"I can't believe her," Ainslie said, spitting out her words in anger. "She's always so high and mighty. Always thinking she's so much better than me because she doesn't drink, or swear, or drop out of uni, or make *irresponsible* decisions ..."

James folded her into his arms and rubbed her back.

"Don't be mad at Lucy," he said.

"Why not?!" she said into his chest. "Because of her meddling, we lost *six* years."

"Goose," he said and took her by the shoulders, "she was only doing what she thought *we* would've wanted. I mean, we were pretty adamant about being *just friends* back then. We can't ever know if things would've worked out well if we'd done something. But the way it *has* worked out — even if it took a little longer — it's been so awesome, hasn't it?"

"Yeah," she muttered. "Apart from that one little thing."

"Yes, apart from that."

"Did I just announce to the whole team that I ...?"

"You did," he said, frowning.

"Shit." She put a hand to her forehead. "So much for keeping it quiet. I really didn't want to give anybody any fuel to get inside my head."

"Ains, if anybody decided to use *this* to get inside your head, then they aren't just trying to psych you out," James said. "They're straight up shitty people. Borderline evil."

Ainslie sighed and nodded. "No, you're right." She pulled a face. "God, it's gonna be pretty awkward, facing everyone after that little outburst."

"It's definitely going to turn into a story they tell their friends for years to come."

Ainslie screwed up her nose. "Thanks. That makes me feel so much better."

CHAPTER 55

When Ainslie boarded the shuttle bus to the country training venue (half an hour after what would later become known as the Breakfast Incident), it seemed as if no-one knew how to talk to her anymore. Some of the team looked as if they'd worked out what had happened and kept shooting her sad, sympathetic smiles. Others whispered among themselves, seemingly still trying to figure it out. Jameslie was definitely going to be the talk of the championships, just not for the reason they'd intended.

Before they'd boarded the bus, Ainslie and James had managed to pull Amanda aside and explain what'd happened. She'd hugged them both tightly and promised to nip any rumours or false information in the bud should she hear anything floating around.

Ainslie and James sat quietly on the bus, ignoring the din around them. Ainslie rested her head on James's shoulder and did her best to get in the right headspace to skate. Lucy and Jaz were sitting across the aisle from them. Lucy was in the window seat looking sheepish, resting her chin on her hand and doing all she could to avoid looking at Ainslie. Jaz looked a little caught in the middle. It wasn't the first time Ainslie and Lucy had fought. They'd been friends for twenty years and were polar opposites, after all. Ainslie knew that eventually, they'd get over this little speed bump, too, but she wasn't in the mood to talk to her just yet.

*   *   *

The drive to the venue was only ten minutes long, and thankfully, by the time they arrived, everyone was too preoccupied with shaking out their jet-lagged legs to be bothered with Ainslie's personal life. And no-one more so than Ainslie herself. She'd become surprisingly good at compartmentalising things over the course of the last twelve months, and she knew that once she had her wheels under her, things would feel normal again.

Her first few steps onto the unfamiliar rink were shaky. The floor was made out of a hard plastic tile, and it took a lot more effort for her to push across than when she was on the smooth painted concrete they were used to. Ainslie felt as if her leg muscles had atrophied as she bogged heavily across the skating surface, trying out all her edges and doing her best to find her feet. Sandra kept reminding her that it was a normal feeling after having spent hours cramped in a plane not too long ago.

"It's just the first country practice," the coach said after Ainslie complained about feeling shaky for the fifth time. "It's never been about running programs or jumping triples, you know that. Just roll around and try to get your movement back."

Even with the reminder, Ainslie still felt a little panicked by how much difficulty she was having moving around the rink. And that slight pain was still gnawing away at her hip. She was pretty certain it was being exacerbated by the excess pushing that was required to make her wheels move across the sticky floor.

"How's it feeling today?" James asked, rolling along beside her and placing a hand on her right hip.

"It's okay." The tremble in her voice threatened to give her away. "Just a twinge."

"Let me know if you need to rest."

She frowned and placed her hand over his and then pulled it from her hip, still holding it, and stretched her arm out so they were poised to skate together.

"We don't have time to rest," she said, taking off at as fast a pace as she could manage.

James fumbled to catch up before he fell into stride beside her. They pushed around the floor in a figure eight, first forwards, then backwards, before coming to a stop beside Sandra. Ainslie's breath was heavy, her legs were gelatinous, and her hip was sore. She dropped her hands to her knees and took deep, stabilising breaths.

"This isn't good," she said. "I feel like shit."

"Come on, Goose. We always feel like shit after the first country practice."

Ainslie pursed her lips and did a few standing hip circles, trying to suppress the pain.

"You're going to be fine," Sandra said and placed a hand on her shoulder. "We'll get through this the same way we got through the rest of this bloody year. One day at a time."

*   *   *

Country practice was finished by midday, and Ainslie left the session feeling disheartened that she hadn't done anything more than roll around. James and Sandra kept reminding her that she'd felt the same way every year she'd been to Worlds, and it had always worked out just fine in the end. But she wasn't hearing it.

She hadn't spoken to Lucy all morning, but she'd watched her practise. She'd looked really strong, which made Ainslie irrationally annoyed. She really didn't want to go the entire championships without speaking to Lucy, but she'd gotten to a point where she didn't know how to bring up the issue again. Jaz had also looked quite good at country practice, if not a bit nervous. It was her very first major international competition, after all, so Ainslie had expected her to be a bit jittery. But she'd seemed to be having a good time.

On the trip back to the hotel, all anyone could talk about was how their training had gone. Ainslie was just pleased to hear they'd apparently stopped talking about her. She was also relieved to hear that most of them were talking about how rusty they'd felt and how difficult the floor had been to work with.

"*I* was pretty happy with how *we* did. I thought the floor was fine."

Ainslie knew that voice belonged to Tessa without even turning her head.

*   *   *

It wasn't until day four that Ainslie finally managed to shake her jet lag completely, and by country practice that day, she was finally feeling like herself again.

She still hadn't spoken to Lucy much, save for a few pleasantries. Lucy hadn't apologised, either, so they were at an impasse. The tension was unpleasant, and Ainslie didn't want it hanging over her head for her competition, so she vowed to resolve it all before her first official practice.

Much to everyone's excitement, that day's country practice was at a different venue. This time, it was in a small, two-court basketball hall, and when Ainslie stepped out onto the boards, she felt like a brand-new woman. After skating on plastic tile for the last few days, being on timber was like a dream.

"Look at you," James said, a warm grin on his face. "You look like yourself again."

"I feel like myself," she said and smiled as she rolled steadily around the floor, feeling out the new surface.

They warmed up and finally had a go skating both of their programs in full. They were squashed into two courts when they would normally use three, and they were focused much more on technical elements than performance, but they skated clean and with confidence. When they finished their long program, Ainslie beamed and squeezed James in a big hug. That was all she'd needed. One solid practice to prove to herself that she still had it in her.

*   *   *

Even though Ainslie was thrilled with how training had gone, her hip was still a little tender. James, Lucy and Jaz were planning to do another grocery run, but Sandra had instructed Ainslie to go back to the hotel and rest.

"Go to your room and ice it. Take some paracetamol, and we'll book you in for a massage this afternoon."

She was sitting on her bed, icepack pressed to her hip, laptop across her knees, watching the videos of their run-throughs that Sandra had recorded that morning. They'd looked good.

The sound of a key card and the clicking of the door unlatching dragged her attention away from the screen. She raised her head to see Lucy slipping inside.

"Oh, hi," Lucy said sheepishly.

"I thought you went to the shops."

The air in the room felt cold.

Lucy chewed her bottom lip. "I was actually hoping to talk to you."

Ainslie snapped her computer shut, and Lucy caught a glimpse of the icepack. A look of concern crossed her face. "Are you all right?"

Ainslie winced as she shifted her position on the bed. "I'm fine. Just a little twinge. Probably something to do with being launched at full speed into concrete a month ago."

Lucy looked as if she was holding back tears. She hurried over and sat on the edge of Ainslie's bed.

"Ainslie, I'm so sorry," she said. "I can never undo what I did, but I just feel terrible. You'd insisted so many times that the two of you were just friends, and I thought I was saving you from ruining everything. And then you met Aidan, and he was so awful, and if I'd known you and James would be so happy together ..."

Ainslie shook her head. "Luce, you couldn't have known. Hell, *I* didn't even know."

"And I'm so sorry for what I said," Lucy said, tears welling in her eyes. "What I implied. I never meant to insinuate anything. You're not irresponsible. You're fearless, and brilliant, and you're my best friend, and I hate that I hurt you."

Ainslie sighed and held out her arms. "Come here, Luce."

Lucy wrapped her arms around Ainslie and kept murmuring her apologies into her hair.

"Listen," Ainslie said, patting her on the back, "my hormones have been completely off the rails the last couple of weeks. Everything has either been making me cry or pissing me off. And let's be honest, I *am* pretty irresponsible, like ... ninety per cent of the time."

Lucy smiled a little through her tears.

"Besides," Ainslie said, "I didn't need to have a complete meltdown in front of everyone, either."

"I think you were justified," Lucy said, brushing away a tear.

"Didn't need to invite the entire Australian team to my shit show, though, did I?" Ainslie said, the corner of her mouth quirking up into a half smile.

Lucy allowed herself to laugh. "Guess not."

"Look," Ainslie said, "the 2014 Nationals thing was ... a shock. But there's no way to know how things would've gone if we'd done something that night. I mean, people say everything has its time. Maybe we weren't supposed to be together until now."

"You two are so perfect for each other," Lucy said, sniffing. "And it's so wonderful seeing you so happy. Especially after everything you went through with Aidan."

"It all worked out in the end." Ainslie shrugged. "For better or worse."

Lucy wiped away another stray tear and groaned. "I hate fighting."

Ainslie smiled. "Me too. Let's not do it again."

Lucy looked at Ainslie, the furrow of worry returning to her brow. "Are you sure your hip is okay? Are you going to be able to skate on it?"

"Luce," Ainslie said, "I've come this far and been through so much bullshit this year, there's no way in hell I'm not skating now. Even if it's a fucking disaster."

CHAPTER 56

"Are you nearly ready?" Lucy was standing by the door, tapping her foot impatiently.

She was dressed in full Australian uniform, hair neat and straight, lanyard with her competitor pass safe around her neck.

"I'm looking for my pass!" Jaz cried, throwing items of clothing all over her corner of the room.

"Why didn't you just put it on the bedside table?"

"Would you two settle down?" Ainslie dropped to her knees and produced the lost pass from under Jaz's bed. "It's right here."

Jaz looked embarrassed. Lucy looked as if she wanted to kick someone up the backside.

Ainslie laughed. "Let's start a tally of all the times Jaz loses her pass this trip. Then, at the afterparty, that's how many drinks she has to have."

Lucy rolled her eyes. "Let's not encourage her."

Jaz chuckled. "I'm already up to seven."

*   *   *

It was finally opening night, and the bus to the stadium was buzzing with excitement. Paula walked up and down the aisle, handing out clip-on koalas for the skaters to gift to the other nations. It was somewhat of a tradition, an olive branch from the Australian team. And each year when it became known that the Aussies had clip-on koalas, skaters from the other delegations would clamour to get their hands on one.

Paula had taken them on a tour of the venue a couple of days earlier so they could learn the layout and get their bearings. The massive stadium had been hollow and empty that day. The event had yet to be bumped in, and the only people who had been milling about were a handful of volunteers. But when the skaters arrived on opening night, the venue was ready for them.

The shiny white floor had been laid. Barriers had been set out around the perimeter, displaying the logos of the sponsors who were partnering with the championships. Tables had been set up for the officials, and streams of spectators were beginning to flow into the stands. Several local news stations had parked their vans out on the back loading dock.

In the soccer field next to the stadium, hundreds of competitors from all over the world were being corralled into groups. A handful of exasperated volunteers were pacing up and down along the crowd, trying to communicate in a combination of Spanish, Catalan and English that the skaters needed to line up in alphabetical order by country.

Towards the front of the crowd was Australia, loud and proud in their green and gold. The Juniors stuck to the front of the pack, bursting with excitement as they clicked away, taking photos of themselves with their clip-on koalas. The Seniors kept to the back, some joining in on the revelry, others standing stoically in small cliques as if they were too cool for that sort of nonsense. Jaz was bouncing around, handing out koalas to the nearby Argentinian skaters. The entire area was vibrating with excitement and anticipation.

Just before eight o'clock, a hush fell over the crowd as the muffled sound of someone speaking on a microphone emanated from inside the stadium, indicating that it was time to begin. Volunteers barked orders about which direction to walk and where to stand once they were inside, looking pretty pleased with themselves for having wrangled so many over-hyped athletes in one place.

A fanfare began playing over the speakers inside, and the crowd slowly pressed forwards. Jaz sprang off with a skip in her step. Lucy ducked her head, prematurely hiding from the television cameras. Ainslie found James's hand and threaded her fingers between his.

"Here we go," she said, only loud enough for him to hear. "This year, our year?"

James lifted their entwined hands to his lips and kissed her knuckles. "It already is."

One by one, each nation was called into the stadium. Each new delegation was met with the sound of thunderous applause. When Ainslie stepped inside, the sheer size of the crowd took her breath away. She'd been to many World Championships before, but this one, without a doubt, had the biggest crowd she'd ever seen. And one of the loudest. She couldn't help but beam with pride, a smile that warmed her entire body. The joy and honour of representing her country caused her heart to swell in her chest. She'd made it. She was here, surrounded by all her best friends — all the people she loved most.

Amid the racket of the crowd, the blinding lights of the stadium and the love she felt all around her, Ainslie began to feel the worries of the last month melt away. The melancholy thoughts that'd been keeping her up at night were being drowned out by the upbeat music and the roar of the crowd. She'd gone through hell to get there, and in that moment, she couldn't have been happier.

*   *   *

After the formalities of the opening ceremony had finished, the skaters were ushered out one door and back in through another. They filed into a roped-off section of the stands, where they could watch the opening entertainment. The show had only been going for five minutes when Paula's head appeared at the end of their row.

"Ainslie, James, Tessa and Tony, the bus for you is leaving in five minutes."

Ainslie pouted. The pairs had their official practice at the crack of dawn the following morning, so they were being chauffeured home for a relatively early night with orders to have dinner and go straight to bed.

*   *   *

Back at the hotel, the dining room was mostly deserted, and the dinner buffet was looking rather thin. Ainslie piled her plate with what little food was left available, and she and James found a quiet spot in a corner, away from where the staff had begun sanitising tables and stacking chairs.

"Are you excited for tomorrow?" James asked, pouring them both some water.

"I am now," Ainslie said and smiled.

"You weren't before?"

"I was stressed, and nervous, and hormonal," she said, stabbing a cherry tomato with her fork, "but after tonight, I'm pretty pumped."

"Well, we're as prepared as we'll ever be. We've worked hard. Now we just need to leave the whole of 2020 out there on the floor."

"Hey, you guys."

The voice was unusually timid, considering who it belonged to.

Ainslie looked up to see Tessa and Antony standing beside their table, looking forlorn.

"Hi," Ainslie replied cautiously.

An awkward silence hung in the air until Tessa finally sat down next to Ainslie. She teetered on the edge of her chair, almost as if she was preparing to make a clean getaway if she needed to.

"I know this probably doesn't mean much coming from me," Tessa said, "and I know we've all been rivals for years, but I just wanted to let you both know how genuinely sorry I am."

Ainslie felt her eyebrows raise, almost of their own accord.

"I'm really sorry to hear about your accident, and I'm really sorry to hear about … what happened," Tessa said, lowering her voice a little. "When stuff like that happens, you realise just how insignificant skating competitions really are in the big scheme of things."

"Nothing like personal tragedy to give you a little perspective," Ainslie said, glancing across at James.

"Like I said, I know it might seem strange coming from me, and you probably think I have some ulterior motive, but I don't. I just wanted to offer my condolences."

Ainslie wasn't sure she had heard this properly. She blinked a few times, waiting for some kind of punchline. When it didn't come, she softened.

"Thank you, Tessa," she said. "I actually really appreciate it."

Tessa smiled warmly. "I mean, I'd still love to beat you guys, but I'm not a complete bitch."

Ainslie forced her smile to stay on her face, and James raised his eyebrows as the other pair left to get their dinner.

Ainslie pursed her lips. "Only Tessa Strong could offer such a nice sentiment and then completely ruin it two seconds later."

James shook his head and laughed. "She really is something. I don't know what, but … something."

*　　*　　*

After they'd eaten dinner, they headed upstairs to turn in.

"Tomorrow's the day," James said as they arrived at the door to the girls' room.

"Tomorrow's the day."

"We did it, Goose," he said, cradling her face in his hands. "We got here. And whatever happens, I love you to bits."

He kissed her softly.

"I love you, too. More than Tessa loves shit-stirring."

James let out a low whistle. "That's a lot."

"I know." She smiled and pulled him into a hug. "Goodnight, James."

He planted a kiss on the top of her head. "Goodnight, Ainslie."

CHAPTER 57

The shrill ringing of Ainslie's alarm cut through the darkness of her hotel room at five the following morning. Lucy and Jaz stirred and groaned in their beds, rolling over and pulling their blankets over their heads. Ainslie reached out in the pitch black, slamming her hand down on the phone in an attempt to snooze the alarm. Instead, she knocked it off the bedside table and under the bed. Muttering an expletive under her breath, she dragged herself out of bed to retrieve the still-shrieking phone. There was no point snoozing it now she was up. The phone vibrated in her hand, and a text from James appeared.

Morning Goose! Today's the day!! x

Ainslie rubbed her weary eyes, unable to match his early-morning enthusiasm. There were far too many exclamation points in that text for 5 am.

Even a hot shower didn't do much to wake her up, and, still half asleep, she applied her make-up for her official practice in the terrible fluorescent lighting of the bathroom. She fixed her hair into a sleek bun, pulled on her official practice costume and threw her Australian tracksuit over the top, doing her best not to wake her sleeping friends, who didn't need to be up until a much more reasonable hour. She grabbed her competitor pass and dragged her skate bag to the door as quietly as she could, then slipped out of the room.

*　　*　　*

Paula and Sandra were already eating breakfast when Ainslie got to the dining room. Tessa, Antony and their coach were huddled away in a corner, eating alone.

"Good morning, sunshine," Paula said, sounding far too chipper.

Ainslie did her best not to scowl at her.

"How did you sleep?" Sandra asked.

Ainslie yawned into her elbow. "Yeah, not bad."

"Morning, sleepyhead." James appeared at her side with two plates of food.

He handed her the one with no bacon and gave her a quick kiss good morning. Since the Breakfast Incident, Paula had been a lot more lenient with them. Ainslie was still pretty sure she didn't want them messing about in each other's rooms, but at least she wasn't calling them out in public anymore.

"Are you two ready for today?" Paula asked, her mouth half full of masticated eggs.

"As we'll ever be," James replied.

Ainslie just nodded sleepily.

Once she had some caffeine in her bloodstream and some food in her belly, she felt a hundred times better, and by the time they boarded the bus to the venue, she only had one thing on her mind. Their short program.

She couldn't believe the day had actually arrived. Somehow, London 2019 seemed like only yesterday while simultaneously feeling like an eternity ago. So much had happened in the last twelve months, and so much had changed since the last time they had stepped onto the world stage … No wonder time felt meaningless — 2020 had been complete chaos.

But the day had arrived, and they were back in the green and gold. Barcelona 2020. The climax of the year that was supposed to be theirs. The year they'd once thought would be their last. The year they got on the podium. Ainslie wasn't quite sure that was such a realistic goal anymore.

*   *   *

As Ainslie entered the stadium, she felt her pulse begin to quicken. A heady cocktail of excitement and adrenaline pumped through her veins as they walked into the warm-up area. The early-morning sun was coming in through the high windows in streaks, slowly warming the otherwise chilly building. It felt like a completely different stadium from the one they'd been in the night before. Without the atmosphere of the crowd, and the athletes, and the revelry, it seemed eerily quiet. The calm before the storm.

Ainslie and James had been drawn tenth to skate, which meant they would be training in the second of three groups. Tessa and Antony had been drawn third and wasted no time warming up off skates so they were ready to go in Group 1.

Sandra led Ainslie and James into a quiet corner of the warm-up area. She took Ainslie's hand in her left and James's in her right. The pair joined hands, completing the circle, and Sandra cast her gaze between them.

"All right, team," she said. "We've talked a lot about how much you've overcome to get here, but today we forget all about that. All that matters is today. Short program. You've done this routine a million times now, and I know what you're capable of."

The pair nodded along.

"So," Sandra said, "we focus, we relax, we show them how we do it in Australia. May the spirit of Michael Hutchence be upon you."

The pair chuckled at the reference to their music.

"I'm so bloody proud of you." Sandra squeezed their hands, her lips twitching into a smile. "Now, go. Warm up. Chop chop!" She clapped her hands twice for emphasis, and the pair turned on their heels, shooting off to run laps of the warm-up area.

As they ran, Ainslie caught a glimpse of their competitors out of the corner of her eye, but she never gave them the satisfaction of watching for too long. It was a power move to pretend you were undaunted by your competition. She spotted the Spanish pair that'd pipped them at the post the previous year. A fresh rush of adrenaline hit her just from seeing their smug faces. And she caught a glimpse of the two Italian teams who'd placed first and second. They'd been furiously competitive, leaving Spain and Australia in the dust.

A voice rang out over the loudspeaker announcing that the first group of Senior Pairs could take the floor for their official practice. The warm-up area cleared of the first five teams, and Ainslie watched Tessa and Antony disappear between the divider and out onto the floor.

She began to feel that familiar fluttering in her stomach, the one she both craved and resented. She focused on their off-skate lifts to take her mind off it, and it wasn't long before Sandra appeared beside them and told them it was time to get their skates on.

*   *   *

They stood in the marshalling area hand in hand and listened to Sandra's final comments. Ainslie was only half paying attention. She was preoccupied with glancing around to see who was in the building. A few officials were sitting up high, observing the practice. Unmanned cameras were set up around the perimeter. A few random competitors were dotted around the stands, some paying attention, some just there because they'd been dragged down early to support their teammates.

Ainslie squeezed James's hand.

"Are you ready?" she whispered as the voice over the speakers called Group 1 off the floor.

Then the announcer called for Group 2 to begin their warm-up.

"I'm ready," he replied, and the two took off like racehorses out of the gate.

They sped around the stadium floor, feeling out the surface and the space. They kept up a steady pace with the Spanish pair, but the Italians were faster than ever. Ainslie was just grateful they only had to contend with *one* of the Italian teams in their warm-up group.

Ainslie always found official practice at Worlds to be more nerve racking than the actual competition. At least in the competition they had the floor to themselves. In official practice, they were sharing, and sharing with the best in the world. In Australia, they were big fish in a small pond. But Worlds was cut-throat. The Italian team was fast and strong and refused to give way to anybody. Ainslie had perfected the art of faking the confidence that was needed to go head to head with them, but it was still a struggle.

They marked out their routine, laying it out on the unfamiliar floor and getting their bearings in the large, open space. Then they executed each element in program order. By the time they were finishing their final element, the announcer was calling for them to be ready for their music.

As they skated to their first position and the opening chords of the music began to play, everything that'd happened to Ainslie in the last year flashed through her mind at lightning speed.

Her engagement. Her retirement plans. The fights with Aidan. The dreams of James. The guilt. The suspicion. The explosive break-up. Nationals. The Dinner. James kissing her for the first time. His hands on her skin as they finally crossed the line. The first night they spent together. Then the second and the third. The night he told her he loved her. The accident. The pain, the emptiness, and the heart-wrenching grief. The baulked jumps. The fight to get her nerve back and the feeling of exhilaration when she did.

And now she was here, standing with James at the precipice of the year's crescendo, poised and ready to leap off.

And like with everything else they did, they'd do it together.

CHAPTER 58

When Ainslie and James came off the floor from their official practice, smiles on their faces, sweat on their brows, Sandra's and Paula's feedback was nothing but positive. Sandra looked as proud as ever. Even Paula was looking quietly confident.

Ainslie was feeling good, too, except for the twinge in her hip. It was back. It wasn't quite bad enough to sideline her yet, but she was much more aware of it. And it may not have looked like it from afar, but it was definitely affecting her out on the floor. With every landing, she felt a dull ache there, particularly on the throw triple Salchow, and she'd been working doubly hard to push through it and not let it show on her face. The last thing she needed was James worrying about her out there.

Sandra gave them orders to head back to the hotel and rest, and Ainslie was more than happy to oblige.

Lucy had gone on a daytrip with some of the other dancers, and Jaz was leaving for her own official practice as Ainslie and James arrived back at the hotel, so the girls' room had transformed into a den of tranquillity. Paula was preoccupied with organising the Senior freeskaters, so Ainslie and James holed up in the girls' room together and took a nap.

*   *   *

They were startled awake just after midday by Jaz closing the door rather loudly.

"Oop! Sorry!" she said, shielding her eyes.

"Would you relax?" Ainslie said, grumbling. "We're just taking a nap."

"Thank God," Jaz said, swanning into the room and dumping her bag down.

James sat up. "How did official go?"

"It was bloody brilliant." Jaz looked as if she were about to burst with excitement. "It was such a buzz! How was your practice? You ready to get on that podium?"

Ainslie glanced at James, and he shrugged.

"We're keeping it realistic," Ainslie said. "All we can do is our best."

"I reckon you'll do it," Jaz said.

Ainslie had to admire her optimism.

"So, it's safe to say you're enjoying your first Worlds, then?" James asked.

"I honestly cannot believe I'm here," Jaz replied, shrugging off her tracksuit jacket. "If you told me six years ago that I'd get to do this, I would've laughed you out of the building."

"You've grown up a lot in six years. I remember when we met you, you were so unsure of yourself. So *quiet* and *shy*," Ainslie said and smirked. "Talk about a complete one-eighty."

"Well, I owe that to you guys, don't I? And Lucy and Sandra."

"And Cali?" Ainslie said.

Jaz blushed. "What've you heard?

"Nothing!" James said and laughed. "It's what we *saw*. At the New Year's Eve party."

"Fine, yes. And Cali."

"Pretty rich of you," Ainslie said with a laugh. "You can't keep your nose out of *our* relationship, and all the while, *you've* been sneaky as hell."

Jaz shrugged. "She's the first girl I've really been with since I properly came out, so you know … been kinda nervous about it."

"Well," Ainslie said and smiled, "I hope we get to meet her soon."

*　　*　　*

The rest of the day passed by in a blur. The hours ticked away, and before they knew it, it was time to get ready. Jaz disappeared once again to hang out with the quartet skaters, so Ainslie and James stayed in the girls' room. Ainslie did her make-up while she and James quizzed each other on notes and corrections that Sandra had given them. Eventually, James left to get changed and collect everything he needed for the evening's competition while Ainslie got changed herself. He met her back at her room ten minutes later.

When she opened the door, he cast his gaze appreciatively up and down her body.

"You look so beautiful," he said, his eyes meeting hers.

"I look the same as I always do."

"Yeah, exactly."

She rolled her eyes a little, but she couldn't help but smile.

*　　*　　*

That evening, Ainslie and James sat towards the back of the bus. It was fully loaded with skaters, some competing that night, others simply supporting. Ainslie looked around at the latter group and envied how relaxed they all were. But, of course, their time would come. Eventually, they'd sit in her position, all made up and ready, adrenaline and nerves pumping through their veins.

She folded her hands in her lap and — without even realising she was doing it — began bouncing her leg, causing the whole seat to quake. James reached across, laced his fingers between hers, and rubbed the back of her hand with his thumb. The familiar touch released her tension somewhat, and her leg stilled.

They didn't say much to each other on the ten-minute drive to the venue. Ainslie was too caught up inside her own head, recalling the corrections Sandra had given her and mentally moving through the footwork sequence. She figured James probably was, too, so they just quietly held hands and focused on what they needed to.

When the bus pulled up outside the stadium, Ainslie's stomach lurched. She'd done this so many times before, but it never got any easier. She just got better at handling it.

*   *   *

The atmosphere inside the stadium was incredible. The stands were almost at capacity, and the expectant crowd was buzzing.

The first group of perfectly made-up Senior Pairs teams was circling around in the corner of the skating floor like vultures, waiting for the announcer to let them loose. The second and third groups were mostly still in their shoes, bouncing on their toes and keeping warm.

Ainslie's heart was racing more than normal, and her stomach was a flurry of adrenaline. She heard the crowd erupt into cheers as the announcer called Group 1 to the floor for their warm-up. Sandra was pacing in the marshalling area with her arms folded. Ainslie spotted Jaz and Lucy high up in the stands. Jaz was waving so frantically it looked as if she were about to pop her shoulder out. Ainslie grinned and waved back.

The performances of the first group seemed to fly by with each new song and round of applause, and before she knew it, Ainslie was standing on the edge of the competition floor with her heart pounding in her ears. The thrum of the crowd was nothing but white noise as she fixed her attention solely on herself and the man standing beside her. Her teammate. Her best friend. The love of her life.

Ainslie faintly heard the sound of the announcer calling them forth for their warm-up. Sandra had a hand on each of their backs. She said something about having fun before tossing them out of the nest and onto the skating floor. Somewhere in the distance, Ainslie could hear a voice (presumably Jaz's) screaming their names. She blocked it out. She blocked everything out. The only people who existed in the entire world were her and James.

They paced their way through their routine, warming up each item and doubling back if needed. All the while, the huge clock on the screen that loomed from the roof of the stadium counted down the minutes.

An intense tune began playing over the speakers, indicating they only had one minute remaining. They skated their footwork sequence and repeated their spin pancake lift one last time. Then the music ceased, and the announcer called them off the floor.

Ainslie's palms began to perspire. She vigorously wiped them on the legs of her bodysuit as they returned to the marshalling area. They were the last pair in Group 2 to compete.

*   *   *

James made fists with his hands and drummed them up and down his quads. Ainslie kicked her heels to her backside, one by one, before shaking out her legs and wishing she could shake out her nerves, too. She rolled her head back and forth and focused on taking slow, calculated breaths. With all the excitement of the warm-up, she'd almost forgotten about her sore hip. It'd still been twinging, but she'd been too hyperfocused to really give it a second thought. But now, with the cold starting to settle in, it was beginning to ache a little more. She pushed it out of her mind as they rolled up to join Sandra at the entrance to the floor.

Ainslie's heart felt as if it were too big for her chest. She was pretty sure that at any moment, it would beat so hard she'd crack a rib. James found her hand and squeezed it in his, bringing it up to his lips and planting a kiss on her knuckles.

"You ready, Goose?"

She took one big, deep breath and fixed her eyes on the centre of the stadium. "I'm ready."

"On the floor," the voice over the speakers said in a thick Spanish accent, "Ainslie Wynter and James Sunderland, Australia."

CHAPTER 59

Ainslie and James exploded onto the floor as if they owned it. Cutting through the sound of the crowd was Jaz's voice leading a chorus of "Aussie! Aussie! Aussie! Oi! Oi! Oi!"

They rolled to their positions. Their striking, black costumes popped against the sparse, white floor, making them seem like a beautiful oasis in the middle of the desert. Their gazes locked for a moment. A silent exchange passed between them, and Ainslie knew they were ready, and she knew that no matter what happened, she was so very loved. Then they turned away from each other and hit their starting poses.

A hush fell over the crowd, and the cheers were replaced with the sound of strings as their music began to play — "Never Tear Us Apart". It felt like their song now. Perhaps in choosing it, Sandra had been some sort of prophet.

Michael Hutchence's voice began to flood the stadium. Ainslie took another deep breath, and the magic began.

*   *   *

It'd felt like an out-of-body experience. Ainslie knew she'd skated, but it was as though she'd been floating high above the stadium, watching somebody else. But when the crowd roared with applause, she snapped back to reality.

It was definitely her standing in the middle of the floor.

It was definitely her and James the crowd was screaming for.

She couldn't recall any of the finer details of their performance. All she knew was they'd skated clean.

James pulled her to his chest and enveloped her in his arms. She heard his heart thumping under her head, mixed with the sound of her own heavy breathing.

It was done. The short program was over. And it'd been phenomenal.

James released her, and they took their bows. Ainslie glanced around the stadium, a little dazed, before she felt James take her hand and lead her over to the kiss and cry lounge. Sandra was already waiting there, grinning and clapping ferociously with the rest of the crowd. She swallowed them up in an embrace, and Ainslie was pretty certain she had seen tears welling in her eyes.

The three of them collapsed down onto the lounge, with James in the middle. He pulled Ainslie close to his side as they anxiously awaited their scores. The weight of his arm around her and the scent of his aftershave was comforting, and Ainslie started to feel a bit more grounded.

He kissed her on the side of her head and whispered, "Good job, Goose."

Ainslie's body tingled when his lips brushed her ear. She placed her hand on his leg and squeezed nervously, silently willing the screen that would display their marks to come to life.

When the numbers finally appeared, it took Ainslie a moment to process them. They looked like a jumble of meaningless symbols at first. But the crowd was screaming. And Sandra was smacking her hands together with such vigour. And James had both of his arms around her now, nearly squeezing the air right out of her lungs.

Ainslie blinked at the screen. They were definitely personal best scores. And that all-important little number at the bottom.

Place 1.

She couldn't breathe. Her entire body was shaking. They were in first place. And one of the Italian teams that beat them last year had already skated.

There was still one more group to go, and the *other* Italian pair was in that group. The pair that had won in 2019. They'd probably knock her and James off the top, but even if they did, it would still leave them in second place heading into the long program.

Ainslie's brain finally switched back into gear. She squeezed James and let out a long-withheld shriek of joy.

*　　*　　*

Sandra led them back to the marshalling area. Ainslie felt as if she were floating on a cloud, and she had to keep holding onto James's arm so she didn't fly away.

"You two looked so amazing out there," Sandra said, a smile still plastered across her face. "I can't believe it. My little babies, all grown up and so bloody talented."

Sandra released them so they could head back to sit with the rest of the team. There were still a couple more events before the end of the evening's program, but the last thing on Ainslie's mind was sitting still in the stands for another hour or two. She was absolutely buzzing. She felt better than she'd felt in weeks. Her entire body was a ball of energy, and she needed an outlet. She wanted to go outside and run laps around the field nearby. Or steal away to the gym upstairs and beat the life out of a punching bag. Or grab James, pull him into the nearest bathroom, and let him have his way with her.

They threw their tracksuits on over the top of their costumes and headed back to the stands. As they walked along the corridor that ran behind the seating, Ainslie glanced around to make sure they were alone. When she was satisfied, she grabbed James by the front of his tracksuit jacket and dragged him down a dark tunnel jutting off from the main corridor. She pressed her back against the concrete wall and pulled him against her, kissing him with more hunger and fervour than she'd managed in weeks. His lips were soft and warm against hers, and even though he'd initially been taken by surprise, he was kissing her desperately. His fingers dug into her backside, and she ran her hands through his hair. She rolled her hips against his, and he withdrew, his eyes wide and his cheeks flushed.

"Um, we'd wanna be careful with Paula around," he said, breathing heavily.

"Sorry," Ainslie said and bit her lip. "Skating well really gets me going."

"I can see that — and I love it — but there's not much we can do about it here." He lowered his voice into a sort of growl and put his lips close to her ear. "But when I get you back to Sydney …"

"I don't know if I can wait that long," Ainslie said, groaning into his shoulder.

"Me either. Well … when Tony disappears with some random Italian guy …"

*   *   *

When Ainslie and James arrived in the stands, the team welcomed them back with smiles and hushed congratulations as the final pair (the other Italian pair) were coming to the end of their routine. They slipped into the row beside Jaz and Lucy, and Jaz nearly strangled Ainslie with a hug.

"Oh, my God, you looked so amazing!" Lucy said as loudly as she could while still maintaining a whisper.

"So amazing!" Jaz added. "Also, James, you've got a little something …," she said, pointing at her own lips and smirking, "right here."

James blushed and wiped his mouth with the back of his hand.

Down on the floor, the Italians had finished their program and were heading over to the kiss and cry. Ainslie hadn't paid attention to their performance, but from the sound of the crowd, she got the impression that it'd been pretty good.

There was another tense moment as they waited for the scores to come up, and James grabbed Ainslie's hand again.

The Italian team's scores appeared. They were huge.

Place 1.

Jameslie had been knocked down to second. Ainslie wasn't too disheartened. It hadn't exactly been unexpected. She applauded humbly and waited for the final standings to appear on the screen.

And there they were, Ainslie and James in second place, sandwiched between the two Italian teams. The Spanish pair were fourth, and Tessa and Antony were currently seventh. It wasn't over yet, but they were sitting in a pretty good position. The day after next would be the final showdown.

Ainslie could barely focus on the following events. All she could think about was how they were currently in second place, perfectly primed for the long program, and all she wanted to do was go back to the hotel and have some amazing celebratory sex. She silently cursed the team protocol, knowing full well there was no way that *that* would happen.

Instead, she just rested her head on James's shoulder and watched the skating, her fingers still entwined with his, just enjoying the moment.

CHAPTER 60

The bottom ten Senior Pairs teams were scheduled to compete the following evening, but because of their high ranking, Ainslie and James would compete the evening after that, with the rest of the top five.

They spent their day off with Lucy and Amanda, wandering around and exploring Barcelona while Jaz prepared for her event. The sightseeing had been enough to take Ainslie's mind off the stress of the competition for a while, but before she knew it, she was back in the stands. This time, she was just another face in the sea of green and gold, but for some reason, she felt more nervous for Jaz's short program than she'd been for her own.

Lucy was sitting to her right, drumming her fingers anxiously on her seat. James was to Ainslie's left, and apparently, it was *his* turn to bounce his knee nervously. Down in the marshalling area, Jaz was rolling around with her earbuds in, looking very focused but also a little bit stressed. That was to be expected at her first World Championships. Sandra was pacing again, and all around her, other skaters were flying back and forth, using what little space they had to warm up their jumps and spins.

"Do you think she'll be okay?" Ainslie asked, her knuckles turning white as she squeezed her own knees.

"I thought Lucy was the mum friend," James said, smirking, and Lucy shot him a look.

"I feel responsible. I introduced her to this sport," Ainslie said. "I just want to see her succeed."

"She's going to be fine," Lucy said. "Look at her. She looks focused."

"I think she looks nervous. What if she gets stage fright?"

"When have you ever known Jaz to get stage fright?" Lucy raised an eyebrow.

Ainslie cocked her head. "Uh, the warm-up at States."

"Okay, sure. But she came back from that like a champion. And she's got absolutely no pressure on her. She's already made it to Worlds, and I'm sure she knows she's not going to win. All she needs to do is her best."

Ainslie still felt a little uneasy as the announcer called Group 1 to the floor. She screamed out her encouragement and clawed her left hand away from her knee, only for it to find James's hand and commence cutting off the circulation to his fingers.

Jaz was speeding around the floor, but she was nowhere near as fast as most of the others in her group. There was one skater from New Zealand who looked more in Jaz's league, but the rest of the group was made up of an Italian girl, two Spanish girls and an Argentinian girl. They were strong and powerful and fast. In comparison, Jaz looked like a child.

Ainslie's suspicions were slowly being confirmed. Jaz *did* look nervous. She was skating through the elements, but they all looked slightly off. She also fell a couple of times, which Ainslie knew wouldn't have been good for her confidence.

"Come on, Jaz!" Ainslie screamed as loudly as she could.

She knew Jaz probably couldn't hear her, but it was more for herself than anyone else. She could barely make out Jaz's face, but from a distance, it looked a little stormy, and her countenance definitely wasn't oozing with her usual confidence.

The announcer called the group off the floor, and Ainslie's palms began to sweat. Jaz had the unfortunate luck of being drawn first to skate. It wasn't ideal, but Ainslie was selfishly relieved that it would be over sooner rather than later.

"On the floor, Jayne Bannister, Australia."

Ainslie let go of James's hand only long enough to applaud as loudly as she could.

"Aussie! Aussie! Aussie!" she and James screamed.

"Oi! Oi! Oi!" the rest of the Australian team yelled back.

A hush fell over the stadium. All eyes were on the tall, blonde English girl standing in the middle of the floor, who ironically was the most stereotypically Aussie-looking one out of the entire Australian team.

The opening beats of her music echoed through the building, and Ainslie took a deep breath and held it tightly in her throat as she squinted at her friend. She looked a little wobbly as she began the first movements of the program. They were familiar, but there was something not quite right about them.

"Oh, God, she's rushing," Ainslie said, gnawing at the thumbnail of her free hand.

Jaz was moving, seemingly without purpose, around the floor. It was as if she wasn't even listening to the music.

"Come on, Jaz, relax," James muttered.

Lucy's face had dropped. "She looks about the furthest thing from relaxed."

Ainslie, James and Lucy seemed to hold a collective breath as Jaz headed into her first element, the double Axel. Ainslie's body tensed as her friend launched into the jump. It was off kilter and hesitant, and she crashed to the ground, sliding across the floor on her backside. Ainslie groaned and prayed that Jaz would be able to come back from it, but it soon became apparent that things were only going to go downhill from there. Jaz was out of control, and although she was completing the movements of her routine, they looked stiff and awkward. She stumbled over basic steps and nearly tripped doing a simple transition.

Next element, combination spin. Her heel camel was okay, but she didn't hold her sit spin long enough, and by the time she got up for the inverted camel, she had hardly any power left.

She looked weak and shaky through the footwork sequence, but she made no major errors. Still, the sequence only came up on the screen as a base level, which would award her the lowest score possible above zero.

Next came the triple Salchow. Jaz launched into the jump. One, two, three revolutions … and she went sprawling across the floor.

"C'mon, Jaz!" Lucy cheered as Jaz climbed to her feet, looking sullen.

Ainslie found herself trying to hide behind James as she watched the train wreck unfold in front of her.

Jaz only had two more items to go. She landed the first jump of the combination but followed it up with a feeble, single toe loop instead of the intended triple. That would cost her.

Her last item was meant to be another heel camel, but she lost her footing in the travel and careened into the floor before she even made it to the spin. The Australian team let out a chorus of sympathetic groans, and Ainslie's shoulders dropped in defeat.

The music ended, and Jaz finally came to a stop. It was blatantly obvious, even from a distance, that she was devastated.

Ainslie clapped as loudly as she could.

"On ya, Jazzy," she said softly.

She watched as Jaz skated over to the kiss and cry lounge, head down, arms behind her back, looking morose. Sandra gave her an encouraging pat on the arm, and they sat side by side in relative silence while they awaited the scores.

Ainslie shifted anxiously in her seat. She knew they weren't going to be good. Jaz's technical score was low, thanks to her falls and unconfirmed spins. Her component score wasn't great, either. The screen said she was in first place, but she'd been the only one to skate so far.

After Jaz, skater after skater took to the floor, all giving mostly strong, clean performances. With each new competitor, Jaz's rank was pushed further and further down.

Ainslie had expected her to be back in the stands by the time the second group started warming up, but she was still nowhere in sight.

"I'm gonna go see if I can find Jaz," Ainslie said to whoever happened to be listening.

"Are you sure we shouldn't just give her some space?" Lucy said.

"Maybe," Ainslie said and pursed her lips. "But I'm worried about her."

She squeezed her way out of the row and traversed the corridors. She stuck her head inside every bathroom she passed, calling out Jaz's name to no avail. She finally reached the last bathroom, the one closest to the marshalling area. She pushed the door open and recognised the blue skate bag that was propped up beside the sinks. She rounded the corner into the changing area and saw Jaz sitting on the floor, hugging her knees to her chest, her head buried in her arms and her shoulders heaving.

"Oh, Jazzy."

Ainslie crouched down in front of her and put her hands on her knees.

"Jaz?"

She refused to look up.

"Jaz, look at me, please," Ainslie said, giving her friend's arm a squeeze.

Jaz reluctantly raised her head. Her mascara was streaking down her cheeks, and her eyes were red and puffy. Ainslie shook her head and stood up.

"Get up, darl," she said and offered Jaz a hand. "We're going outside."

Jaz didn't say anything, but she took Ainslie's hand and allowed her to pull her to her feet.

Ainslie reached up and brushed one of Jaz's tears away with her thumb. "Never, ever, let them see you cry."

* * *

Jaz didn't say anything as Ainslie led her out of the stadium and into the cool night air. She just shuffled along, dragging her skate bag behind her. She'd stopped sobbing, but she was sniffing incessantly. They sat side by side on a low wall at the edge of the car park. Ainslie didn't say anything, either. She just sat there, swinging her legs, waiting for Jaz to speak first. She was starting to think Jaz wouldn't say anything at all.

"I cannot believe I just did that," Jaz finally muttered, wiping her nose on her jacket sleeve.

Ainslie kept quiet, giving her space to let it out.

"I just ...," Jaz said and sniffed again. "I got out there, and all of a sudden I just thought ... *Flippin' 'eck, I'm at Worlds!* Like it hadn't occurred to me until then. And there were all these eyes on me, and television cameras around the place, and I just ... I panicked."

"It's your first Worlds *ever,* Jaz. It's totally understandable to get nervous."

"Yes, but I didn't just get nervous, though, did I? I completely lost it. That was the fucking worst skate of my life. I just made a complete twat of myself."

The last few words were muffled as she dropped her head back into her hands and began crying again. Ainslie scooted closer and put an arm around her shoulders.

"Jaz, you didn't make a twat of yourself. We *all* have shit skates. It happens. Sure, it sucks more when it happens at Worlds, but it's not unheard of. You're certainly not going to be the only person this week to have a shit skate."

"Sandra must be so embarrassed by me," Jaz said, sobbing into her hands.

"Hey!" Ainslie hopped off the wall and stood in front of Jaz, resting her elbows on her friend's knees and forcing her to look up. "Sandra is *never* going to be embarrassed by you. She took a chance on you, and look how far you've come! When I met you six years ago, you were like a lost little puppy. You were a former ice dancer who'd never even *heard* of artistic roller skating. You told me once that you learned to jump and spin on a frozen pond with your friend. And now look at you! You've skated at the *World Championships!*"

"But Sandra has a reputation," Jaz said through her tears. "Look at you and James. She's the coach to some of the *best in the world*. And then there's me. She probably regrets ever taking me on."

"That's bullshit, Jaz," Ainslie said firmly. "I've known Sandra almost my whole life, and I can tell you right now, she might feel disappointed *for* you, but she's never going to be disappointed *in* you. *Especially* considering how hard you've worked to be here."

Jaz blinked back her remaining tears, and Ainslie was relieved to see they were subsiding a bit.

"How am I supposed to go out there again tomorrow?"

"You will," Ainslie said, squeezing her arm. "You just will. It's not over. And it won't be over until after you've skated your long. Even then, your career is only just taking off, Jaz. I know you, and I know it's not like you to give up this easily. So you better dig deep, girl, and find the heart to pull yourself back from this. Tomorrow night, you skate with all you've got. And then you can enjoy the rest of your time here. Remember, just being here in the first place is a massive achievement. And it's a privilege."

"I might as well pack it in right now. They'll never select me again after that performance," Jaz muttered.

"Bullshit, they won't," Ainslie said, taking her by the hand and helping her down off the wall. "Do you think every time me and James have been to Worlds, it's been a cakewalk? Our first year in Junior, I got so nervous that I threw up right before we skated, and James had to spend the entire routine pretending I didn't stink like puke. Then in the long program, while we were doing the death spiral, he slipped off his toe stop, fell on his knees, and as a result, I ended up flat on my arse."

Jaz smiled weakly.

"It's okay," Ainslie said. "You can laugh. It *happens*. But it's over now. Just like your short program is over. You can't change it; you can't go back in time. All you can do is accept it, go back inside, and enjoy the rest of the evening."

Jaz threw her arms around Ainslie's neck and hugged her.

"Thank you, Ains. Thank you for introducing me to this stupid sport. It's times like these I hate its guts, but I wouldn't trade this" — she gestured back and forth between herself and Ainslie — "for the world."

CHAPTER 61

Wednesday morning felt like déjà vu.

Ainslie's alarm shrieked at her to get out of bed, and she smacked it to the floor, just as she'd done two days earlier. She showered, dressed, did her hair and applied her make-up, just as she'd done two days earlier. She went through the motions as if she was on autopilot. But there was one major difference between this morning and the morning two days earlier.

Two days ago, she and James had been ranked fourth in the world.

Now, they were second.

But Ainslie was acutely aware that it wasn't over yet. And despite the constant reminders she'd been giving to Jaz not to put too much pressure on herself for the long program, Ainslie was beginning to feel a bit of pressure of her own. It was all building up in her head, and as much as she tried to suppress it, she was struggling to ignore the fact that they were, potentially, one good skate away from the podium finish they'd been working so hard for.

If they managed it, it would be the happy ending they deserved, and it certainly wasn't beyond the realm of possibility now. In fact, it was so close, Ainslie could almost feel the weight of the medal hanging around her neck. And it was stoking a fire in her belly that hadn't been this well fed since Nationals.

That was the first thing James noticed when they nearly collided as he was coming out of his room that morning.

"Oop!" He jumped back as she almost careened straight into him. "Morning, Goose."

She grabbed him by his tracksuit jacket and planted a big, enthusiastic kiss on his lips. "Good morning!"

He smiled, looking a little taken aback.

"This is the happiest I think I've ever seen you before 6 am."

"Today's the day!" Ainslie replied, her face threatening to split in half.

*   *   *

Walking into the marshalling area for their long program official practice was far less intimidating now that they knew where to go and what to expect. Also, thanks to their ranking, now *they* were the intimidating ones. The knowledge that they were a threat was empowering, and Ainslie walked into the building feeling like a million dollars.

Tessa and Antony were currently in fourth place after skating their long program the night before, but the final results would be decided tonight after the top five teams competed.

Ainslie and James set their bags down and began running warm-up laps, chatting and jogging and keeping in the right headspace. But something kept dragging Ainslie's mind away from where she wanted it to be. With every stride she took, her hip twinged, and it was slowly turning into a constant dull ache. Perhaps spending her entire day off wandering around the Gothic Quarter yesterday hadn't been the smartest move. The ache wasn't enough to completely sideline her, but it was enough to remind her it was still there, and every time her foot thumped into the ground, it got worse.

The pair came to a stop and performed their lifts. That was fine. The dismounts were a little uncomfortable, but James was supporting her, so she wasn't taking the full brunt of the impact.

"Jumps?" James asked.

Ainslie chewed her lower lip and nodded, backing up a little to give herself space to throw a double Axel. She galloped up to the entry and launched herself into the air, rotating two and a half times. When she landed, a sharp pain shot through her hip and reverberated down her entire leg. A cry escaped her lips before she had a chance to swallow it down and pretend it had never happened.

"What's wrong?" James rushed to her side.

Ainslie put one hand on her hip, trying to look inconspicuous as she massaged it, and waved him off.

"Nothing. I'm totally fine."

Her voice came out sounding a little more strangled than she'd hoped, and James frowned, looking unconvinced.

"Are you sure?" He reached out and gingerly touched her hip-massaging hand.

"It's just a little stiff," Ainslie said and shook her head. "I swear. I'm all good. I probably just slept on it funny. I'll take some paracetamol, and it'll be fine."

James pursed his lips. "All right. But if it's causing you too much pain, you need to let me know."

"So we can do what? Withdraw?" She scoffed. "Not a chance. I'll be fine. I promise."

Although she was beginning to wonder if it was a promise she could keep.

* * *

"Senior Pairs top five, your official practice commences now."

The voice boomed through the stadium, and the five pairs shot out from the marshalling area, tracing their own patterns all over the white floor.

James had been feeling confident all morning, and Ainslie had appeared to be in a great mood too. But her hip was obviously hurting her more than she was letting on, and James's stomach was twisting with worry. As they skated their warm-up laps, he caught a glimpse of her face. It was contorted into a grimace and completely betraying her. Some would call her resilient and strong; others would call her stupid and reckless. James was just concerned she would end up back in hospital.

The thought of withdrawing at the final hurdle was a horrible one, but so was the thought of him throwing her into a triple Salchow only to have her injured all over again. But she wasn't showing any signs of backing down, and if James knew anything at all about Ainslie, he knew that she was rarely able to be talked out of something once she had fixed her mind on it.

He gritted his teeth as they lined up for their side-by-side double Axels. He landed his solidly. He caught hers out of the corner of his eye and saw her free leg hit the ground behind her, no doubt to take some of the weight of the impact. It still looked pretty impressive to the untrained eye, but in a showdown between the top five at the World Championships, a mistake like that could cost them everything.

But at that point, James couldn't have cared less about that if he'd tried. All he wanted to do was get Ainslie out the other side of Worlds in one piece.

*　　*　　*

When their official practice was over, James watched as Ainslie slowly and cautiously lowered herself into a chair in the marshalling area. There'd been times in the past when she'd been so wired after an official practice that she'd returned to her skate bag by dropping down into a crouch and sliding across the floor on her backside. Now she looked like a wounded soldier.

The practice had been all right, but Ainslie, clearly in pain, had two-footed most of her jump landings. The throw jumps concerned James the most — they were the only jumps where he could see her face when she landed, and he'd seen an unmistakable look of agony flash across her face on the throw triple Salchow.

He crouched down in front of her chair, placing one hand on her hip and the other on her cheek.

"Hey," he said, trying to get her to look at him, "you're really hurting, aren't you?"

Ainslie raised her head. "I'm fine."

She was doing her absolute best to blink back the tears, but to little avail.

"What's going on?" Sandra strode up beside them, arms folded, brow furrowed.

"Ainslie's hurt," James replied, not taking his eyes off hers.

Ainslie glared back at him like a child who'd just been told on.

Sandra crouched down beside James and looked up at Ainslie. "Is that true?"

"I'm fine. It's just a little twinge. It's nothing."

Sandra pursed her lips. "That explains the two-foot landings."

"I swear, I'm going to be all right. I just need a little ice and some painkillers. Maybe a massage."

Sandra frowned and stood up.

"All right." She folded her arms again. "When we get back to the hotel, you're going straight in for a massage, and then you're on strict bed rest and ice until this evening."

Ainslie nodded, and Sandra pulled out her phone, walking off to book an appointment with the hotel massage therapist.

*　　*　　*

Walking back to the bus, James noticed Ainslie was limping slightly. He put his arm around her shoulders, and she leaned on him for support, wrapping her arm around his waist.

"I'm so sorry," she muttered.

"You have nothing to be sorry for. I'm just worried about you. I'm going to be launching you into the air tonight, and I really don't want to be launching you right into the emergency room. Again."

Ainslie sniffled. "Honestly, I want this year to be over now. I want it to be 2021 already. I've had it with 2020. I just want a fresh start."

"Well, there's not much longer now. After tonight, it'll be all over. Then we can look ahead to 2021. Together."

Ainslie sniffled again. "So much for this year, our year, huh?"

James looked down at her and realised she was quietly crying. He stopped walking and took her by the shoulders. The sight of her crying never failed to break his heart.

"It's still been our year, Ainslie." He held her face between his hands and kissed away a few stray tears. "Plus, we'll always have next year. And the year after. And as many years as we want."

Ainslie smiled through her tears. "I do like the sound of that."

"Whatever happens tonight," James said as he brushed another tear away with his thumb, "remember, I am so proud of you. No matter the result, the sun is still gonna rise, and we're still gonna wake up tomorrow."

"I can handle one more skate," she said, nodding. "Even if it kills me."

James chuckled and pulled her into a hug. "Well, I'd really prefer if it didn't *kill* you."

CHAPTER 62

The air inside the stadium was electric. To Ainslie, it felt as if the entire city of Barcelona had come out to witness her and James's final performance for 2020.

In the change room, she stared at herself in the bathroom mirror. Her copper hair was slicked back in a tight, neat bun, and her competition make-up was heavy and dramatic on her eyes and lips. Her costume was hidden safely beneath her Australian tracksuit, and her stomach was churning. She cocked her head and studied her own face in the reflection. She felt old, she needed a holiday, and her hip was still sore. Despite all the icepacks and paracetamol.

It'd been a long and unforgiving year, but in spite of everything, as soon as she'd slid that crimson bodysuit over her skin, she'd felt the familiar ripples of competition adrenaline begin lapping at her feet.

Tonight, there was nothing on earth that could stop her from landing her jumps cleanly, regardless of the pain. Admittedly, the thought made her feel a little ill, but there was no way she was going to do anything less than her absolute best.

And maybe they'd be the underdogs, the kids from Campbellmead who rose through the ranks to become Australia's greatest pride and joy. The country's first world medallists in thirty-five years. Or maybe they'd crash and burn. Maybe Ainslie would leave the arena on crutches.

She looked her reflection square in the eye, steeling her gaze. It was a risk she was willing to take.

*   *   *

Ainslie settled back into the stands between James and Lucy.

"How was your official this morning?" Lucy asked.

"It was okay," Ainslie replied.

Lucy raised an eyebrow. "Just okay?"

"Ainslie's injured," James said.

"No, I'm not!" Ainslie smacked his leg with the back of her hand.

She was a little worried that he'd speak it into existence.

"It's your hip, isn't it?" Lucy's voice was laden with concern. "What are you going to do?"

"I'm going to skate my long program," Ainslie stated flatly.

Lucy glanced at James, and he shrugged.

As fired up as Ainslie was to compete, the Senior Pairs event wasn't until the end of the evening. First, she had to cheer for her friend.

Jaz was rolling around in the marshalling area, looking focused but anxious. Unfortunately, she'd ended up dead last after the short program, but on the bright side, she hadn't been drawn first to skate for the long.

"Did anyone speak to Jaz today?" Ainslie asked as Jaz took the floor for her warm-up. "I didn't see her all day."

"She had her official just before mine," Lucy said. "And I thought she looked a little stressed."

Ainslie nervously chewed her thumbnail as the clock ticked down to zero and the skaters were called off the floor.

The first skater was the girl from New Zealand. She skated a fairly clean program, but most of her jumps were underrotated.

Ainslie could see Jaz with her earbuds in, rolling around the marshalling area. She kept shaking out her legs, then fiddling with the tongues of her boots, as if it was some sort of good luck ritual. At one point, she looked up into the crowd, and Ainslie frantically waved at her. Jaz smiled back, a little half-heartedly.

By the time it was Jaz's turn to skate, Ainslie could feel her own heartbeat reverberating throughout her whole body. She grabbed James's hand with one of hers and took Lucy's hand in the other.

"On the floor, Jayne Bannister, Australia."

Ainslie, James and even Lucy all bellowed, "Aussie! Aussie! Aussie!"

The rest of the Australian team replied, "Oi! Oi! Oi!"

The music began, and Jaz took off.

*   *   *

Jaz's long wasn't as bad as her short. Not by any means. But it wasn't great, either.

She hadn't fallen this time, which was an improvement. She'd tapped the floor with her hand on the landing of the triple Salchow, and it'd been a little underrotated. She'd held *most* of her spins long enough, but not all of them, so her sit spin and one of her heel camels hadn't been confirmed. In general, she seemed a little more relaxed, but she still looked as if she was rushing in places. Ainslie could actually see the tension leave Jaz's body as she skated over to the kiss and cry lounge, looking a little less defeated than she had after the short. Sandra greeted her with a hug, and they sat to await the scores.

Place 1 came up on the screen, and Ainslie let out a yelp.

Jaz had been the fourth skater. She'd done it; she'd pulled her way up from the bottom. There were other skaters still left to compete, but she'd beaten three people, at least. That was going to feel a whole lot better than coming last.

Ainslie stood. "I'm going to go see her."

"Shouldn't you be resting your hip?" James raised an eyebrow.

She squinted at him. "How am I supposed to get myself into the marshalling area if I don't walk? Are you planning on carrying me?"

"If I have to."

"I'll be fine," she said, patting his shoulder. "I'll be back in a minute."

She slipped out of the row, up the stairs and out of the main stadium.

As she neared the tunnel that led to the marshalling area, Jaz rounded the corner. She didn't look thrilled, but at least she wasn't crying. Ainslie half ran, half limped to her, doing her best to favour her good side. She threw her arms around Jaz and pulled her into a hug.

"Jazzy, I'm so proud of you," she said, squeezing her around the middle.

"I'm just glad it's over," Jaz said and sighed. "I don't know if I ever want to do that again."

Ainslie pulled back and frowned. "Do what? Skate?"

"Skate at *Worlds*. That was *way* more petrifying than I ever thought it would be."

"Don't say that. It was your first time! Trust me, it's only upwards from here."

Jaz pouted. "We'll see. We'll see if I ever get selected again."

"You will. I have no doubt you will. You're so strong and determined. And you never, ever quit. There's no way you can let this one skate ruin everything for you. You've got so much more to give."

"I'm sure I'll feel a lot better after I've had a long sleep. And maybe a few drinks at the afterparty." Jaz smirked.

"What are you up to now, Ms I Can't Find My Pass?"

Jaz squinted as she did the mental math. "Um, eleven."

"Flippin' 'eck," Ainslie said in an attempt at Jaz's accent that sounded more Irish than anything else.

Jaz laughed. "But I may have been hiding my pass on purpose."

Ainslie cackled and slapped her friend on the back. "You really *do* take after your Aunty Ainslie, don't you?"

CHAPTER 63

The air in the marshalling area felt completely different from how it had felt before their short program. It was tense, and exhilarating, and thick with anticipation.

This was it.

All of 2020 had culminated to this moment.

Ten skaters. Five pairs. Three places on the podium.

Only one at the top.

From Italy, Letizia Lastra and Lorenzo Conti, and Paola Ricci and Alessandro Blanco, reigning world champions and runners-up, respectively.

From Chile, Chiara Veloso and Luis Aviles, fresh faced and brand new to Senior, but they'd been Junior world champions for the last three years.

From Spain, Sara De Leon and Francisco Romero, the pair who'd come up from behind in 2019 and snatched the bronze.

And from Australia, Ainslie Wynter and James Sunderland, current world number four, lifelong teammates, best friends and the apples of their country's (and each other's) eyes.

In 2019, when they'd headed into the long program in third place, Ainslie hadn't let herself get too carried away. She'd known that being in third after the short was a tenuous position, so easy to let slip through their fingers. But this time, she felt a little more secure in second place. There was a slightly larger buffer between them and the dreaded fourth. And as far as she knew, they hadn't placed second because another team had skated poorly. They'd just been *that* good. There weren't that many points separating them all, and every pair in there knew that it was now or never.

Ironically, the only thing keeping Ainslie grounded was the dull ache in her hip. Without that unrelenting reminder, she might've let her mind run away from her, and the last thing she needed was that kind of pressure. As it was, she was determined to land all her elements on one foot if it killed her. Even if she had to be carried off the floor and straight into an ambulance, she wouldn't let James and Sandra down.

Hell, she wouldn't let Australia down.

* * *

Ainslie and James went about their off-skate warm-up. Sandra had instructed Ainslie to take it easy so she could save her energy for the competition. It was killing her, watching James run laps without her while she threw some air punches, doing her best to get her heart rate up without straining the lower half of her body.

They worked on their lifts off skates, James lowering her down as carefully as possible and punctuating each one with, "Are you okay?"

"Yes! I'm fine!" she snapped eventually before immediately apologising and pecking him on the cheek as a token of her appreciation for his concern.

Ainslie tried to ignore the other teams, but it wasn't easy. Especially seeing them all condensed in that small area. With so many powerful skaters crammed into such a tiny space, it was a wonder the roof didn't blow off the stadium.

We're here too, she reminded herself. *And we belong here.*

*   *   *

The official warm-up was absolute chaos.

Before it officially began, the five teams circled around in the corner of the floor next to the marshalling area, whipping up a hurricane of pure power. The tension between them all was palpable. Nobody acknowledged anyone who wasn't their partner. Even each of the two Italian teams pretended the other didn't exist.

When the announcer called them onto the floor, it was as if he'd let a mechanical rabbit out of its box. The teams shot out like five pairs of greyhounds, ready to rip it to shreds. Each team was unapologetic in their use of the floor, careening wherever they pleased with as much speed as they required, never moving out of the way for anyone. It was a complete bloodbath.

Ainslie couldn't imagine what was going through the officials' minds as they watched. They must've been wondering why the Australian team wasn't doing a whole lot. There were some jumps that Ainslie felt confident enough to skip, but there were a few she wanted to give one last try before performance time. She was starting to wonder if perhaps she'd gone too hard when the announcer called everyone back off the floor.

"You feeling good?" Sandra asked, standing between them and patting them on the back.

Ainslie and James nodded in unison. Ainslie breathed deeply, trying to settle her racing heartbeat.

"We've done all the work we could," Sandra added. "We know what we're doing. Now we just have to go out there and do it one last time."

"One last time for *this season*," Ainslie said.

Sandra smiled at her and squeezed her shoulder. "Of course. One last time for *this season.*"

CHAPTER 64

"On the floor, Ainslie Wynter and James Sunderland, Australia."

Their names sounded strangely foreign. Ainslie feared she would float right out of her body, like she'd done during the short. She felt James's hand capture hers, and he brought her back to earth. Her pulse was fluttering a mile a minute. Her mouth was dry, her hands were sweaty, and in the distance, she could make out the familiar battle cry of the Australian team. She felt all their eyes fixed on Team Jameslie, waiting to see if they'd make history.

It was the last hurrah for the "Bolero" routine, and what a routine it'd been. After Nationals, Rosa Charis had written that watching it was like watching two people fall in love out on the floor.

Ainslie smiled to herself. *If only she'd known.*

James pulled her to his side, and she took her position in his arms, their noses practically touching.

"I love you, Ainslie," he whispered.

"I love you, James."

The sound of the crowd faded, giving way to the slow and steady drumbeat of their music. A melody of flutes and clarinets began to flood the stadium, leaving no space for anything else. Everyone's attention was turned to the pair from Australia, clad in red, with fire in their eyes, as they began to dance together. Every movement, every touch, was fuelled by the energy of their deep and profound love for one another, and it'd never been plainer to see. It'd never felt clearer to Ainslie, either. They were more than teammates. More than friends. More than lovers. They were a melody and a harmony, floating on air and making the sweetest and most beautiful music together.

As the song built, they moved from their opening choreography and into their first transition. Somewhere in the periphery, Ainslie's sore hip was whispering for her attention, but the rhythmic beating of the drum was drowning it out. Her focus was on herself, and James, and the impending throw triple Salchow.

They lined up for the throw, James behind her, hands on her hips. She set herself up and, with his assistance, launched herself through the air. Three rotations and a stuck landing. She refused to let her free leg touch the ground, but the impact took her breath away, and she swerved slightly. Her stomach lurched. It was only the first element, and she was already in excruciating pain. She prayed that James wouldn't see it written all over her face.

They moved through to the next element, a side-by-side combination spin. Most of it was on her left leg, and for that, Ainslie was grateful. Their spins were synchronised and fast, and she felt a surge of joy. But as soon as she focused her attention on the next element, a combination jump, her joy was quickly replaced with worry. She braced herself and took a deep breath. She held onto the landing of the triple Lutz and the double loop, but by the time she got to the triple toe loop, she wanted to cry. She landed on one foot, but as she threw her free leg back to present it, it touched the floor. A minuscule error, but if the other teams had all skated without fault, it could mean the difference between a podium finish and fourth.

The lifts and spins were a pleasant respite from the jumps, which only made her pain worse with every landing.

The second-last element was the side-by-side double Axel. They lined themselves up, setting the jump into position, and leaped into the air.

James stuck his landing perfectly.

Ainslie felt her wheels hit the floor. Then she felt her hip, too weak to support her body weight anymore, give out underneath her. She crashed to the ground. Without missing a beat, she sprung back to her feet as if the floor were made of rubber. Ignoring the pain, ignoring the tears that were beginning to prick at her eyes, she kept going. She had to.

They moved into their final element. The spin pancake lift. *The* lift. She locked eyes with James as they set it up, and she saw his facial expression change.

"Are you okay?" he asked.

All she managed was a nod.

The next thing she knew, she was high above his head, mostly thankful not to be bearing any weight on her hip for a moment. She flew through the air, spinning around and around, and watched the stadium turn before her eyes, knowing full well that after that lift, it was finally all over.

And after her fall, it was unlikely they would've held onto their ranking.

*　　*　　*

The music peaked, and James and Ainslie fell dramatically into their final position. The stadium exploded into cheers, the crowd clearly unperturbed by their imperfect performance.

James looked into Ainslie's eyes as they held their final pose, but instead of seeing the desire he'd gotten so used to finding there, he saw tears. And he knew Ainslie well enough to know she wouldn't have been crying over a fall unless she was hurt.

"Are you all right?" he asked, pulling her up and setting her on her feet.

She let out a little squeak of pain and nodded.

"I'm okay," she said, but her strangled voice gave her away.

He hooked his arm around her back, and she collapsed against him. He supported her weight as she rolled on her left foot over to the kiss and cry lounge.

Sandra greeted them with open arms and pulled them into a group hug, eliciting another cry from Ainslie.

"Sweetheart, it's all right," Sandra said. "I'm so proud of you."

"She's hurt." James hardly recognised his own voice.

It sounded the way it had the day of the accident.

"I'll be okay," Ainslie said, dropping down onto the lounge. "I'm sitting here, and I'm hearing our score."

Sandra sat to her left and put a hand on her knee. James sat to her right and put his arm around her shoulders.

She turned and looked at him, her green eyes filled with a sadness that tugged at his spirit.

"I'm sorry," she mumbled.

He cradled her cheek in his hand and kissed her deeply. He'd wanted to show restraint, keep things professional, but it was a kiss and cry, after all. And she was already crying.

"You never need to apologise to me, Goose," he said, brushing his nose against hers. "At least not for anything skating related, anyway."

The scores flashed up on the screen.

They were tough but fair, considering a fall and a couple of wobbly landings. And there it was again.

Place 4.

*　　*　　*

Ainslie wasn't exactly surprised. Not after that fall. Not after their suboptimal lead-up to Worlds. Not after the year she'd had. But it didn't stop her heart from sinking to her feet.

It was all over for another year, and once again, they'd snatched defeat from the jaws of victory.

On her left, Sandra was patting her on the knee. On her right, James was clutching her to his side and rubbing her arm.

The final standings flashed onto the screen. The Spanish pair had done it again — pipped them at the post to take the bronze. The two Italian teams took the gold and silver once more, and Tessa and Antony had ended up in ninth place.

Ainslie couldn't believe it. So much had changed over the course of the last twelve months, and yet here they were again, back at Worlds, in the exact same position as they had been in last year, bested by the exact same teams. It was so surreal that she had to wonder whether 2020 had even happened or if it'd all been a dream. But James's arm around her shoulders was real. The cheers of the crowd were real. And the pain in her hip was definitely real.

The three of them rose from the kiss and cry lounge, and Ainslie winced.

"That's enough," James said, scooping her up.

James rolled through the corridor and back to the marshalling area with Ainslie in his arms, Sandra trotting along beside them.

In any other circumstance, Ainslie might've been embarrassed. But she was feeling sore and sorry for herself, and if she'd learned anything in the last month, it was that when things turned to shit, in James's arms was the only place she wanted to be.

Sandra ordered Ainslie to see the onsite physio as soon as she'd taken off her skates. He insisted that her injury wasn't serious, that she'd just inflamed the joint and pulled a muscle, and he advised her not to skate for a few weeks and to try to rest it as much as possible. His English wasn't great (although it was streets ahead of Ainslie's non-existent Catalan), so the encounter was a little clunky and confusing, but in the end, he was able to convey that she'd be fine. And that was all any of them really cared about.

Ainslie was actually looking forward to having some physio-mandated time off. Maybe she and James could finally spend some quality time together once they got back to Sydney. Time that didn't necessarily involve skating. A weekend getaway was definitely calling her name.

Forget a weekend. Make it a whole week. We deserve it.

*   *   *

That night, back at the hotel, Antony *finally* disappeared with a random Italian, and Ainslie couldn't have been more grateful.

"World number four again, huh?" she said after she'd checked the coast was clear in the hall and slipped into James's room. She hobbled over to his bed and flopped backwards onto it. "Kinda weird how so much has changed this year, and how so much is exactly the same."

"Not *exactly* the same," he replied, crawling up beside her and brushing the hair out of her face. "I couldn't do *this* a year ago."

He dipped down and kissed her. His lips were soft and familiar as they moved with hers, and one hand slipped underneath the hem of her shirt and skated softly across her skin. She wrapped her arms around his neck and kissed him back even more deeply, her tongue moving with his, the desire that'd been suppressed all week rearing its head once again.

"Do you think we put too much pressure on it?" Ainslie asked when they finally came up for air. "With the whole 'this year, our year' thing?"

"Well," he replied, grazing a finger along her collarbone and down her chest until he was halted by the buttons of her polo shirt, "I still happen to think that this year *has* been our year. We just didn't get a chunk of metal to wear around our necks. But personally, I think what we *did* get was much better."

"Fair point," Ainslie said and smiled. "Still, it might've been nice to have this *and* a chunk of metal to wear around our necks."

"I mean, sure," James said and lay down beside her, pulling her to his chest, "that would've been nice too. But need I remind you that the only reason we made that whole 'this year, our year' vow was because you were supposed to be retiring after today? And unless there's something you haven't told me, I don't think that's happening anymore."

"Another fair point," she replied, her fingers playing with the fabric of his shirt. "But how many more years do you think we could keep this up? We're not getting any younger."

"We're not dead yet, Ains," he said and laughed. "I'd be happy to keep it up for as long as it takes. Even if we're still trying to get up on that podium when we're eighty years old."

"You think we'll still be skating together when we're eighty?"

"I don't see why not."

Ainslie sighed contentedly and nuzzled closer to James's side.

"Let's start with 2021, shall we?" she said. "Maybe 2021 will be our year."

"Goose," he said and smiled, "from now on, every year is our year."

EPILOGUE

Ainslie sat on the floor at Gate 17 of Barcelona-El Prat Airport. Her laptop was open and resting on her knees, and James was off somewhere buying coffee.

Lucy was sitting nearby, leaning against a pole, head buried in a book. She'd been the only one of the four to come away from her performances with a smile on her face. She'd spent the early part of the week quite withdrawn from the others, focusing her attention on her own competition and trying not to get too bogged down by her friends' bad moods. It must've worked because while Ainslie and James were reeling from their near miss and Jaz was moping from her less-than-successful debut, Lucy had skated two personal bests and finished in ninth place: an Australian record for solo dance.

Jaz was lying on the floor, phone in hand, her head resting on Lucy's legs. She'd felt the sting of bombing at her first World Championships, but she was never one to dwell on the negative for long. She'd stomped around the venue for a few days, feeling sorry for herself, but by the closing ceremony, she was pretty much back to her normal loud and excitable self. She'd also informed Ainslie that her snap decision to never skate at Worlds again had been an overreaction.

Ainslie and James accepted their defeat as graciously as they could. Ainslie had seen the Spanish pair at the venue every so often and had tried her best not to scowl at them. She was definitely fired up for a new season, but she was also very much looking forward to some respite. James had suggested they take a trip down the coast, spend some time together, breathe in the fresh sea air and get away from the troubles of 2020.

At any moment, Rosa's 2020 Worlds wrap-up was going to air, and this year, Ainslie knew at least a little of what to expect. The notification appeared on her screen, and she clicked through to the video.

A paper cup appeared before her, and she glanced up.

"Whatcha watching?" James asked, handing her a coffee.

He slid down the wall beside her, and she handed him an earbud. "Rosa's Worlds wrap-up video."

He put in the earbud, and she rested her head on his shoulder.

"I'm so excited and honoured to have a special guest on the podcast today," Rosa said, grinning down the barrel of the camera. "None other than the prettier half of the incomparable Team Jameslie, Ms Ainslie Wynter!"

Ainslie elbowed James. "That was for rejecting her in 2014."

James laughed. "And *you've* got *such* a history of being nice to her."

"Don't worry," Ainslie said, squeezing his leg. "I think you're *very* pretty, and that's all that matters."

Back on the screen, the camera had turned to Ainslie, who was looking rather uncomfortable and not at all unlike a rabbit in headlights.

"Ainslie," Rosa said. "Firstly, let me congratulate you on yet another amazing year!"

"Thank you," Ainslie replied, sounding a little wary. "It's definitely been a crazy one."

"Of course," Rosa said. "For a start, breaking news of the year! You and your lovely partner finally made things official!"

"Oh, I'm lovely now, am I?" James said.

"Sh!"

"We did," Ainslie replied on-screen, blushing a little.

She'd seen that one coming a mile off.

Rosa laughed her light and airy laugh. "And literally no-one was the least bit surprised!"

Ainslie had wondered if Rosa was actually planning on ever asking her a real question.

"But it wasn't all sunshine and rainbows, was it?" Rosa's tone shifted, no doubt for dramatic effect. "Only *four weeks* before Worlds, you had a terrible accident. Did you ... want to tell us about that?"

Ainslie had hesitated.

What she'd wanted to say was, "No, Rosa. I can't say I *do* particularly want to relive my trauma so you can get a few more clicks on your video."

She'd wanted to lash out. Tell her she was out of line. Tell her she was an exploitative bitch. But she hadn't said any of that.

"We *did* have quite a fall," Ainslie said finally. "A really stupid fall. I was in an overhead lift, James was travelling at top speed, and there was a tiny little stone on the floor. I'm sure you can piece the rest together. I was lucky I didn't break anything, but I *did* get a massive concussion and ended up in hospital. And I must've done something to my hip because it's been giving me grief ever since, but for the most part, I've been doing okay."

Rosa looked expectantly at Ainslie, her eyes searching her face as if she were begging for her to spill more. Surely Rosa had heard about the Breakfast Incident by now. Maybe she was hoping Ainslie would shine a light on the whole pregnancy thing. But Ainslie didn't mention it.

"Do you think the injury to your hip hindered your skating?"

Ainslie tried not to take offence. She had thought that was obvious.

"Of course. I think I went so hard in the short that by the time the long came around, I was totally knackered."

Rosa gave a sympathetic nod but kept prodding.

"So, Ainslie," she said, folding her hands in her lap, "we've all been thinking about this since the moment it happened. World number four again. So close and yet so far *again*. And this time, after ranking even *higher* in the short than you did in 2019. I can't even *begin* to imagine how disappointing it must've been."

This was clearly Rosa's thinly veiled way of rubbing salt in the wound.

"Could you …," she said, "I don't know, walk us through how that felt?"

Ainslie wasn't sure what her motive was. Maybe she was actually interested, maybe she was exploiting her. Ainslie figured it was probably the latter, but nevertheless, she felt that if she didn't tell her own story in her own words, it was just going to spread around in other ways, with all the embellishments people could come up with.

In the airport, Ainslie took James's hand, knowing what was coming next. She prayed he'd be okay with what her answer had been.

"You know, Rosa," Ainslie said on-screen, "there was a time not that long ago when I thought that having a bad skate, especially at the World Championships, was the worst thing that could possibly happen to me. Last year, we came fourth, and I was gutted. But then I went back home, and I got engaged. And he was toxic, and manipulative, and abusive. He made me feel an inch tall, he disrespected me, he accused me of being unfaithful — which was rich because in the end, I found out he was having an affair. He *hurt* me. So, I left him. And doing that was, quite frankly, terrifying. But then I found my feet again, and I began this beautiful, amazing relationship with the man I love … the man I've always loved … and then we had a miscarriage."

Ainslie felt James squeeze her hand. She glanced at him, and he was listening intently.

On the screen, Rosa's eyes grew wide. Even though she'd clearly been fishing for details, she looked shocked that Ainslie was finally providing them.

"Until that experience with my ex … until my miscarriage … I'd had a *relatively* easy life. Maybe it could've been better, but it was okay. And you know, it's a massive privilege to be able to say the worst thing that ever happened to you was that you bombed at Worlds a couple of times. And it wasn't until I gained a little perspective by having what has been both the best and worst year of my life that I realised … who the *fuck* cares whether or not we place at Worlds?"

James chuckled beside her, and Ainslie smiled.

"Life is about so much more than just *roller skating*," Ainslie said in the video. "I mean, I love it, and I'm not about to deny that. And I owe so much to this sport. It's given me heaps of opportunities to travel, and compete, and represent my country. It's taught me important life skills, like discipline and time management. It's kept me fit, healthy and out of trouble. It's given me my best friends. It's given me the love of my life. But at the end of the day …"

There'd been a moment during the interview when she hadn't been sure just how much to divulge, but she was all in. And Rosa had been eating it up.

She wondered if she should ask for a cut of whatever revenue the video made.

"A few years ago, James lost his father," Ainslie said on-screen. "He was up a ladder hanging Christmas lights. He lost his balance and fell and hit his head. He thought he was fine, but he died that night. When I found out that I'd miscarried, skating was the furthest thing from my mind. Missing out on a medal at Worlds *pales* in comparison to these things. *These* are tragedies. *These* are shitty days. Not falling on your arse and, might I add, *still* managing to be fourth best in the world."

Beside her, James gave her a shoulder bump of approval. Ainslie smiled. She'd been proud of that one. He was smiling too, but she was pretty sure she'd seen a tear roll down his cheek.

"At the end of the day," Ainslie said on-screen, "if you have a shitty skate at a competition — Worlds or otherwise — sure, it *sucks* at the time. And maybe you throw your skates across the floor and have a tantrum in the bathroom after. But the sun still comes up the next morning. The competition ends, and you go back home. You have to go back to work. You have to go back to school or uni. The world doesn't end because you fucked up. The world doesn't *care* that you fucked up.

"So yes, obviously I'm disappointed right now, but when we get back to Sydney — after I've slept off my bloody jet lag — I'll wake up beside my best friend, and all this will be a blip.

"And you'll see us again in 2021. And we'll give it absolutely everything. We'll work our arses off to try to *finally* get up on that podium and make Australia proud. But we'll do it with a little perspective and a little balance. Because skating is great, but *living* is so much more important."

Rosa had looked a little lost for words; she'd clearly gotten more than she'd bargained for. Ainslie had only seen her that dumbfounded once before, when she'd given her a mouthful at Nationals.

On that final note, Rosa had ended the interview.

Ainslie snapped her laptop shut, and James wrapped his arm around her shoulders.

"I couldn't have said it better myself, Goose," he said, planting a kiss on her temple. "Even though I *think* I tried. I'm pretty sure you plagiarised me a little bit there."

Ainslie cocked her head. "When?"

"Oh, with the whole 'life goes on, the sun'll come out tomorrow if we have a bad skate' thing," he replied, a boyish grin playing on his lips.

"Oh well," Ainslie said and shrugged. "What's yours is mine; what's mine is yours."

"Hold up, we're not married yet."

"*Yet*, huh?" She smirked.

He poked her in the ribs. "Cheeky."

Ainslie was pretty certain she saw him blush.

"So, after all that," he said, "are you *sure* you're still up for another season? Think of all the *living* we could do."

"True," she replied. "But wouldn't life be *even better* as world medallists?"

James squinted. "I think that attitude sort of undercuts your entire speech. But I'm so very easily tempted. Especially when it comes to skating. And *especially* when it comes to you, Ainslie Wynter."

"So," Ainslie said and held up a hand, "2021 it is?"

"2021 it is."

James went in for a high five and caught her hand in his. He locked their fingers together and pulled her even closer, brushing his nose against hers before kissing her softly.

"Next year, our year then?"

"Next year, our year."

ACKNOWLEDGEMENTS

I did it! I finally published this book! The labour has been long and brutal, but this baby is finally out there. I *cannot* believe it. Moreover, I cannot believe that it's only the first in a series and now I have to go and write another several! But before I go and do that, there are some people I need to thank.

First, I want to thank my family. I want to thank my mother for bringing me up in an environment in which I could truly thrive and become whomever and whatever I wanted. I want to thank her for always cheering me on, for being a shoulder to cry on, for being a great sounding-board, for always supporting me in everything I've ever done … and she's definitely crying by now, so I'll just finish by saying that none of this would be possible without her.

I also want to thank my sister, Emily, and my sibling-in-law, Sky. Emily, thanks for all those walks where we shot the shit about our various creative projects, and thanks for being the absolute best sister anyone could ask for. Sky, thank you for absolutely loving this book, and for reading it fifty million times, and for hyping the hell out of it. And thank you both for your tag team effort in creating my amazing cover design! You two are such legends and I love ya both to bits.

I want to give the biggest thank you ever to my editor, Amanda, who helped me transform the World's Okay-est Manuscript into the beautiful, finished product it is today. I cannot thank you enough for everything you've done. Thank you so much for joining me on this journey and for loving this project as much as I do! It has made everything so much easier, and I don't have the words to fully express just how appreciative I am.

I want to thank my beta readers, Karen, Sky, Lisa, Demi, Amanda Webster, Kristina Gray, Fiction Vixen, Tammy Tootle, Anne Novek and Sophie J. Your feedback was so invaluable, and I really appreciate you taking the time to help me with this project! I hope you love the finished product!

I want to thank my ARC readers and all the Bookstagrammers who have been encouraging me and holding me accountable along the way.

Finally, I want to take a moment to thank every person over the last twenty-three years who has made my artistic roller skating career a memorable one. Without each and every one of you, I wouldn't have had the career I've had, and I wouldn't have this book. To all the coaches I've had over the years — Alana, Jess, Lisa, David, Nicole, Esther and Gawaine — thank you for your knowledge and endless support! To my skate fam, my mentors, my training/travel buddies and teammates past and present, thank you for the memories and the friendships!

And thank YOU, reader! I hope you enjoyed reading my book as much as I enjoyed writing it. Here's to many more!

ABOUT THE AUTHOR

There have always been two constants in Alex Ravenscroft's life — artistic roller skating and storytelling — and for as long as she can remember, she has dreamed of marrying her two passions to create fiction for the artistic roller skating inclined.

Alex has travelled the world representing Australia in artistic roller skating and is constantly giving back to the sport as both a coach and an official.

Alex has a Bachelor of Arts (English) and is studying a Master of Creative Writing.

Alex lives and writes on Darug and Gundungurra land, in a little cottage in the Blue Mountains of New South Wales, Australia. She lives with her mother and their three cats, Louis, Pandora and Merlin.